SURVIVAL SHOW

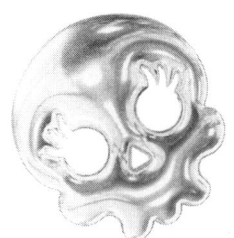

CONTENT WARNING

This is a work of fiction, but deals with many real issues affecting young people. These include themes of mental illness, eating disorders, addiction and suicide.

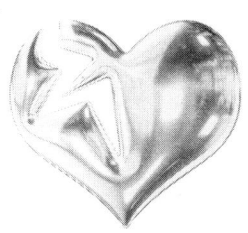

SURVIVAL SHOW

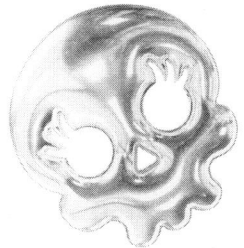

JUNO DAWSON

SIMON & SCHUSTER
London New York Amsterdam/Antwerp Sydney/Melbourne Toronto New Delhi

First published in Great Britain in 2026 by Gallery YA,
an imprint of Simon & Schuster UK Ltd

Text copyright © 2026 Juno Dawson
Illustration copyright for character art and
reverse jacket copyright © 2026 Teja Solar @moonmistix
Cover icon designer © 2026 Aryaman Munish

This book is copyright under the Berne Convention.
No reproduction without permission.
All rights reserved.

The right of Juno Dawson to be identified as the author and Teja Solar and Aryaman Munish as the illustrators of this work has been asserted by them in accordance with sections 77 and 78 of the Copyright, Designs and Patents Act, 1988.

1 3 5 7 9 10 8 6 4 2

Simon & Schuster UK Ltd
1st Floor, 222 Gray's Inn Road
London WC1X 8HB

For more than 100 years, Simon & Schuster has championed authors and the stories they create. By respecting the copyright of an author's intellectual property, you enable Simon & Schuster and the author to continue publishing exceptional books for years to come. We thank you for supporting the author's copyright by purchasing an authorized edition of this book. No amount of this book may be reproduced or stored in any format, nor may it be uploaded to any website, database, language-learning model, or other repository, retrieval, or artificial intelligence system without express permission. All rights reserved. Inquiries may be directed to Simon & Schuster, 222 Gray's Inn Road, London WC1X 8HB or RightsMailbox@simonandschuster.co.uk

www.simonandschuster.co.uk
www.simonandschuster.com.au
www.simonandschuster.co.in

The authorised representative in the EEA is Simon & Schuster Netherlands BV, Herculesplein 96, 3584 AA Utrecht, Netherlands. info@simonandschuster.nl

Simon & Schuster Australia, Sydney
Simon & Schuster India, New Delhi

A CIP catalogue record for this book is available from the British Library.

HB ISBN 978-1-3985-4795-7
HB Special Edition ISBN 978-1-3985-6190-8
Export ISBN 978-1-3985-4794-0
eBook ISBN 978-1-3985-4797-1
eAudio ISBN 978-1-3985-4796-4

This book is a work of fiction. Names, characters, places and incidents are either the product of the author's imagination or are used fictitiously. Any resemblance to actual people living or dead, events or locales is entirely coincidental.

Printed and Bound in the UK using
100% Renewable Electricity at CPI Group (UK) Ltd

*To the ones who know they're
meant for bigger things.*

'To be a fan is to scream alone together.'
Hannah Ewens, *Fangirls*

PHASE ONE:
CASTING

CHAPTER 1

The billboard on Jerrick Street is malfunctioning. It skitters between a FreshElla ad for hair removal cream, and a L'Oréal commercial from last year that features Nico and her UNSTOPPABLE LASHES. The looping images are oddly hypnotic; I fall deep into Nico's pine-tree-green eyes, and wonder who, exactly, is trying to stop lashes?

It takes my mind off what we're about to do. I'm seventeen now. If we're caught, I'll be sent to the rigs.

I sit on a dumpster, waiting. In a baseball cap, baggy jeans and Dad's shapeless sweater, I hope people think I'm a boy. I absentmindedly hum Nico's last single under my breath. So casual, so natural, perched on a stinking bin outside PharmaDoc in Kelso town. Not suspicious at *all*.

Molly says this is a 'victimless crime'.

I don't believe that for a second, but the lie is comforting. I think about Robin Hood: robbing the rich to give to the poor, and he's still one of the good guys. Jenson *needs* this; it's a no-brainer. Medicine should be a right, not a privilege, and decent healthcare shouldn't just be for the rich. But, despite my hoodie, I'm not Robin Hood and, even if you roll it in glitter, he was still a thief.

I stop humming and sit upright as an eggshell-blue van turns the corner. I strain to get a better look. It's him. Same time every other day, like clockwork.

I study his face. The new driver doesn't look much older than us, with a wispy hamster moustache under his beaky nose. We wouldn't try this with a more experienced driver. Lanky, and very bored-looking, he clambers out of his delivery van and slopes to the rear doors. The truck doesn't seem to be locked and he climbs inside to unload his delivery. I cast a sideways glance to the CCTV camera angled over the pharmacy door. We stuck Hubba Bubba bubble-gum on the lens last night. No one has been to fix it since.

So where the hell is Mol? We have the narrowest slit of a window to do what we need to do.

Right on cue, I hear a crash as she steers her rusty old bike into the front of the van, followed by a dramatic pained cry. My big sister lays down, flat on her back, on the tarmac and waits. The bewildered driver hops off the truck and rushes to the front to investigate the commotion. He leaves the doors ajar. Idiot.

Time for action.

The instant he's out of sight, I dart across the street and boost myself into the back of the vehicle. I have only as long as Mol can distract him. She gets to be the decoy because she has bigger boobs than I do.

Boxes, boxes, boxes. There are so many boxes back here. I scan them, looking for the specific manufacturer I need: Healthline G. There are dozens of Healthline G branded boxes, large, medium and small. I curse under my breath.

Outside I dimly hear Molly and the driver dispute her 'injury'.

'I think it might be broken,' she complains.

'It doesn't look bad to me . . .'

'Wait! Don't leave me! It hurts so much!' She's a *bad* actress. Maybe I should have been the flat-chested decoy after all.

Each cardboard box has a printed delivery slip attached, outlining the contents. I know exactly what we need: *Pegagon Pre-Filled Injectable 10mg*. My brother uses this pen monthly; I'm very familiar. *Where is it?* Desperate, I start throwing smaller crates aside.

'Look, should I call an ambulance or not?' the driver says impatiently on the other side of the metal wall.

'No . . . but can you help me up?' Molly whines.

I survey the mess I've made, rubbing my temples. I think I've checked every single Healthline G box. None of the deliveries contain the pen I need. My face is too hot, my chest itches, and I can feel tears pushing at the backs of my eyes. We only get one go at this.

'I think you'll be okay. Can you walk?' The man's voice is much, much closer.

I can't afford to freeze. As his shadow sweeps into the van, I press myself between the two largest plastic crates like a spider. Daylight floods the space and I curl in as small as I can go. I daren't even breathe. I've seen videos on G-Net from inside the prison rigs: the gangs, the initiations, the beatings. I wouldn't last a day.

A box slides out of the truck before the door slams shut. I assume he's taking his delivery inside the pharmacy. I crawl out of my hole and trip over my feet trying to reach the door. With a sinking sensation, as I fumble in the dark, I realize there isn't a door handle on the inside. I'm gonna puke. Now, not only have I failed, I'm gonna be kidnapped too.

I bang on the door, as loudly as I dare. 'Molly? Mol!'

The next township is eight miles away. I have no money for the train or bus. I'm supposed to sing tonight. I start to question if the delivery van is airtight. Can I even breathe in here? Is it refrigerated?

'Taryn?' It's Molly, on the other side of the doors.

'Let me out!' I hiss.

'I can't! He locked it.'

'Are you serious?'

'I'm sorry,' my sister says.

The back of the van is windowless, but it isn't pitch dark. Where is the light coming from? Behind the mountain range of cardboard boxes and crates, pencil grey light filters through a screen connecting to the driver's cab in the front. I push past the upturned stock to get to this inner window. I reach up and realize the hatch can be slid open horizontally. God, I really don't want to do this, but don't see how I have any other choice.

I slide the grille open as far as it can go. Finally, being the flat-chested one is going to pay off. I pull over a larger crate to climb on. It's going to be a tight fit. I slip both arms through the gap first, followed by my head. Nico's new song is playing on the radio. Coincidence.

'What the hell are you doing?' It's Molly again, standing by the passenger-side window.

'What does it look like?'

I furl my shoulders inwards, making myself as small as possible. It hurts, scraping myself through. My shoulder blades grind against the frame, but, from here, I can use my body weight to slide headfirst onto the padded bench of the van's cabin. I wriggle my hips through the window and flop onto my side. Ungainly, but I'm in the front.

'Can I get your number please?' Molly suddenly shouts. 'I might need to sue.'

I duck down. She's talking to the driver. He's back.

I roll over. On the dashboard there's a button with a key symbol. I reach over and press it. I wince at the loud click the van makes as it unlocks. If Molly has intercepted the driver outside the pharmacy, I'll have to use the driver's side. I wriggle over the seat and test the handle. As softly as I can, I tease the door ajar. I'm still headfirst so I'm going out snake-style.

Opening the door only as much as I have to, I slither from the van to the tarmac. I suppress a groan as I land on my hip. From here, I can peer underneath the truck and see two pairs of feet on the other side. I crouch and *very* softly push the door shut, then head to the rear of the van and step onto the pavement where Mol can see me. 'So yeah, watch where you put your stupid van next time.'

'Psycho,' the driver mutters before heading to the side.

Molly pushes her bike towards me without saying a word. The driver eyes me suspiciously as we take the alleyway at the side of the pharmacy, knowing the dead-end fence has a gap we can cut through to get to the Medico-Plus car park. I wait until we're outside the shiny glass frontage of the Rich Hospital before I pull my hood down and shake my hair loose.

My big sister's eyes widen. 'Well? How many did you get?' She stares at me with a look that is somewhere between expectation and desperation. 'Taryn? How many?'

This is every bit as suffocating as being trapped in that van. 'None,' I admit. 'They didn't have any.'

Mol's face turns a nasty shade of grey. 'After all that? Are you sure?'

A flash of irritation. 'Yes, Molly, I am sure. I checked every single box. Twice.'

I lower my voice as a suited older man wheels a poised, white-haired woman into the gleaming entrance of the private hospital. As he passes, he gives us the dirtiest look. We're bringing down the neighbourhood.

'What do we do now?' Molly asks.

I have no clue.

A heist was my very last bright idea.

CHAPTER 2

I can't cook. I can't mend motors. I can't even *steal* so it seems.

I have two talents: I have trained my bladder to hold out for six hours so I never have to pee in the rancid toilets at school, and I can sing.

Only one of these skills will come in handy tonight.

Tonight, it's Merrill Saunders' fiftieth birthday party. The festivities have fallen on what Mum always used to call Fools' Spring; the two or three clear, dry days in March when you can kid yourself that winter is in retreat. Pessimist that I am, I know it won't last, but for this evening, at least, it's warm enough to make a campfire, risk the rations and *sing*. I tune my guitar by ear and wait for my audience to settle.

I hope I never get bored of singing. I hope people never get bored of hearing me sing. I know it's arrogant, but I really am good at this one thing *and* I love doing it. I think that's pretty lucky. I sometimes catch myself thinking about singing, how odd it is. Using your voice to make tunes is mad when you consider it. Did we learn from the birds, or vice versa? If I think about it too long, my head feels weird.

All I know is music is *magic*. I know it makes my heart float up a little higher in my chest; and I know it makes this desolate armpit we call home bearable. For good and bad, music reminds me of Mum. She was a singer too. She used to say that if I wasn't singing, she knew I was ill and not just trying to get out of PE.

I can use this little bit of magic to help the settlement. I sing for them. I sing for Jenson because if I don't, I'll *wail*.

I feel so guilty. We failed him today. As it snaps and crackles, the fire casts ghoulish shadows across my brother's face. He looks puffy, bloated somehow. He sits, sandwiched between Molly and Dad.

'Get on with it, wee Taryn!' Merrill Saunders brays, clutching a cider. 'I'm freezing my arse off out here.'

'Okay, okay!' I wouldn't want to let a bit of crippling anxiety about my brother dying spoil her big day.

Some settlers start calling out requests. The older refugees like the classics: Beyoncé or Adele, while the children like whatever is doing the rounds on Network G. But I know Jenson likes N-TRU5T so I start with an acoustic version of their ballad, 'Me Without You'.

'This is for Jenson. I hope you're feeling better soon,' I say and an expectant hush falls over the camp.

It could be your smile,
or the way that you drive;
it might be your eyes
or the times when you spiral;

it's true.
There won't be a me without you . . .

I don't doubt that the boyband wrote this song for their army of teenage girl fans, but tonight it's about my brother. He was born sick. We have always fought for him. I don't remember a time when I wasn't fighting for him.

I'm a Betweenie, the generation that came between the war and the floods. Jenson is a Waterbaby, born after the sea surges devoured most of the south coast, driving us north of the border.

The long summer nights,
we laugh when we fight;
lazy long Sundays,
together on Mondays so blue.
There won't be a me without you.

I catch his eyes through the bonfire flames, and it's locked in. It's a promise.

I play until after midnight, when my throat is raw and I put my foot down after several rounds of *one more song*. Poor Jenson looks shattered, and we peel away from the now quite merry birthday party in the direction of our unit.

Tobey Faraday falls into step alongside me. His hand-me-down clothes are much too big for him. His skinny neck pokes out of his dad's old coat like a turtle's head emerging from its shell. 'That was really lovely, Taryn.'

'Thanks, Tobey.'

'Would you maybe like to, like, you know, *jam* sometime? I play the keyboard.'

I don't catch the laugh before it pops out. I have heard him sing. Sad-boy-anthems with a lot of emotive hand gestures. 'Sorry, I . . . the word *jam* threw me.' He looks hurt. I know – because my sister is sure to remind me daily – that Tobey has a crush on me. It'll pass. He's only fifteen, a year older than Jenson. 'I think I might be a solo artiste at heart.'

He looks crushed. 'Okay. Got it. Maybe I can play you my stuff sometime?'

The rest of my family has arrived at our unit and I want the night to be over. 'Sure.' I mean it. I take pity on the boy. Enough people had to suffer my early attempts at song-writing. I'll pay it forward. 'Night, Tobey.'

He heads back to his family's unit and I weave my way through the grid system to catch up with Molly and Dad. The QE II camp was supposed to be temporary housing; somewhere for us to wait while the Scottish parliament sorted out permanent addresses for English refugees.

The units are ugly, single-storey trailers, fifty of them, all standing on small stilts to avoid rainwater. When we were little, and it was dry, we would crawl into the space underneath them, hiding from each other or playing commandos. We didn't mind that rats the size of terriers made their home there. These days, I'm astounded at how devil-may-care we were about the disease they spread. What were we thinking? I'm oddly nostalgic for an era when I didn't know what Weil's disease was.

I head inside. The evening is warm enough to save on generator fuel for a night. The solar panels on the roof are worse than useless for nine months of the year. It's *Scotland*.

'Right, you lot,' Dad commands with a clap of his hands. 'Straight to bed. No arguments, I mean it.'

The mere thought of the six a.m. alarm is dreadful. Mol and Dad are up at dawn for the shuttlebus to the construction site, while Jenson and I have school. My grades are *just* good enough that I'm allowed to study until eighteen rather than having to enlist in either the army or Labourforce. I tell Dad that I need a minute to let the performance adrenaline subside, and he permits me to stay up if I make us both a chamomile tea. Deal.

The main room of our unit is a poky kitchen-dining-living room space with a built-in table and benches. As I clatter around at the kitchen end, Dad turns on the little TV screen set into the wall over the dining area. Network G news. I don't know how he can watch that stuff before bed: dengue fever in Central Europa; nuclear bickering between India and Pakistan; the Pure Nation Party winning the Red States election. Enough to give anyone nightmares.

I hand Dad his mug as he frowns at his crappy old phone. In this family, we do hand-me-ups, not hand-me-downs. I gave that handset to Mol before she gave it to Dad. He swears under his breath and slams down the phone.

'What's up?' I slip under the table to sit opposite him.

He rubs his stubbled jaw and lowers his voice. 'Nothing.' I glare because he's lying. 'There's more issues with Pharmaid.'

Oh, I know, but I play along. Molly and I vowed that Dad would never find out what we were planning with the delivery van. 'What now?'

'Something about the floods in Europa meaning delivery is being prioritized over there.'

'They're not sending *anything*?' I ask, incredulous.

'They're saying *delays*, whatever that means.'

When the UK voted to be independent from Europa, is *this* what they had in mind? 'Do we have enough to get by?'

We both know what I mean. 'We might need to halve his dosage.'

Nope. Not an option. Any lingering joy from the campfire is rinsed in a second. Without his meds, my brother runs the risk of needing a liver transplant. He's been on the waiting list since he was *eight*, so the odds of one miraculously being available in the next fortnight seem slim. 'What about the charity application?'

'Nothing. I guess there's the Doctor Lottery.'

Since I turned sixteen, I've joined my sister and dad in entering the weekly prize draw. If you get all six numbers, you get a private operation in a fancy hospital. Any surgeon, any surgery. 'I read somewhere that there's a greater probability of being attacked by a shark than there is of winning the lottery.'

'Is the shark medically trained?' Dad asks and I manage a wry smile. 'Anyway, we can't afford to enter any more times than we already do.' I hear the guilt in his voice at having to include his daughters in this ongoing struggle. With Mum gone, Molly and I had to grow up pretty fast. It has never felt like duty and I have zero regrets. Jenson needs us, simple as that. It is what it is.

My father rests his head in his hands on the canary-yellow Formica table. 'What about Project Population?'

I blink and lean forward in case I've heard incorrectly. 'Excuse me?'

He looks at me, eyes pink-rimmed and bloodshot. 'It's a lot of money, Taryn.'

'Oh shut up . . .'

He goes on. 'No, you shut up. I am Dad, you are daughter. The payout would cover private healthcare and then some. Set you guys up until — '

'No!' I slap my hand on the table and Molly emerges from our bedroom.

'What's the drama?' Mol scowls, toothpaste on her spots.

'Dad wants to go to Project Population.'

'NO.' My big sister is even more no-nonsense than I am. 'If anyone's going to the project, it's me.'

I swear very loudly.

Dad rolls his eyes. 'What are you talking about? I'll get more than you will.'

True. It's a very simple system. Five hundred English dollars for every year you've been alive. The reasoning is that the elderly put a greater strain on the system, so they're incentivized to *retire*. It's quick; it's painless; it's lucrative. And it's so popular that the programme has been adopted around the world. It's cheaper for the government to kill you than it is to care for you.

I was young, but I remember the prime minister standing

outside New Downing Street to make the announcement. With carefully choreographed 'caring' hand gestures, he explained that desperate measures were needed once the supply chains began to crumble. We were told there simply wasn't enough food to go around, not enough hospital beds to care for the sick.

See, I find that doubtful, now, given how well-fed the Prime Minister looked at that podium. I'm not convinced he and *his* family are living off ration boxes, whatever the news-reels say.

'It's not what Jenson would want,' I say, keeping my voice low. The last thing he needs is this on his plate. 'Or us. Dad, we can't do this without you. We already lost . . .' I don't need to say the last word.

Molly gets herself a glass of water. 'I'll speak to Trent Davis,' she mutters, not looking us in the eye.

I swear again. 'Are you insane?'

'Better ideas?'

I glare at her across the unit. 'He's scum. He's a drug dealer, Mol.'

She looks at me like I'm dense. 'We need drugs.'

'No!' We all turn to see Jenson lingering in the threshold to his box room. 'No one is talking to Trent, and no one is applying for Project Population. Not yet, anyway. I will. When I turn eighteen.'

A sentence so ghastly we're all frozen for a second. Then I go to him, but he holds out a hand to bar me. 'I decided ages ago. I'm a burden.'

To hear him say those words makes me want to punch a

hole in these flimsy walls. 'Don't say that. Don't *ever* say that. It is not your fault you're ill. It's not your fault the free hospitals are falling to pieces. *Nothing* is your fault.'

'It'd be easier for everyone,' he says, holding his chin high. 'I shouldn't even be here anyway.' It's true. Just eighteen months after he was born, the two-child cap was introduced.

Dad pulls him into a hug. 'I don't want to live in a world without you, son.'

I wrap my arms around them both and, in turn, feel Mol's body press against my back. If nothing else, we are a unit in our unit.

I can't sleep. Eventually I give up and tiptoe from our bedroom to the living area. I don't turn on any lights. I tuck my bare legs under me and plug my phone in to charge. It only really functions if it's attached to power but I hate using the generator more than I have to.

I'm about to open the Network G app to watch some brainless reality drivel until I get sleepy, but I see that I have a little red number 1 in my inbox. Probably from one of my teachers reminding me about an assignment due date.

I'm tired so I have to read the subject header a couple of times before I can process it. I hold the phone closer to my face to check that I'm not imagining things.

I have one unread email and it's from *Starmaker*.

It's so long since I applied, I forgot I ever submitted my audition. It was what? Four months ago? At least.

Congratulations TARYN BECK

Thank you for submitting your audition video. We're pleased to say your application was successful and we'd love to learn more about you!

Click <u>HERE</u> to arrange a video call with one of Team *Starmaker*.

Your life changes right here, TARYN!

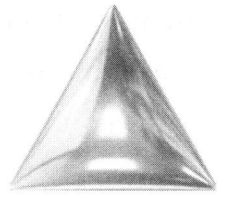

CHAPTER 3

'Come on,' I say to Jenson as we walk the dirt track known as Pilgrim's Way. This path connects the camp to the main road and eventually school. 'Let's cut class.'

'We can't,' he argues, and I remind him that we're working towards algebra exams on a dying planet. There's no comeback to that.

Instead, we take a detour into Kelso Town. Fool's Spring persists; it's much too nice to be stuck indoors. While we were forced over the border, I can't deny we're in a very beautiful part of the world. On higher ground, we're protected from the worst of the weather, and the infinite rolling hills are as plush as green velvet. The little town nestled in the valley is pretty too. Alongside the River Tweed, it's a reminder of what my hometown was like once upon a time. I like the higgledy-piggledy cobbled streets and the imposing turret of the old Christian church, even if the latter is now scrawled in red spray-paint: *GOD GHOSTED US.*

It's market day. Tarp-covered stalls line both sides of what constitutes the high street. It's bustling, noisy, vendors shouting offers over each other. *Five carrots for a dollar! Only oranges in Scotland!* Wealthier townsfolk can bulk out their ration box with extra protein at the butcher's van, or greens from the farm stall. Jen and I head directly for the cookie tent, obviously.

Derrick greets us. 'Here's trouble. School closed today, eh?'

Derrick is Mol's boyfriend's dad. He's really nice, and won't rat us out to Dad. He drops a white chocolate and cranberry cookie into a brown paper bag. Given how scarce sugar is, he may as well have slid us a gold bar. 'Are you sure?' I ask, knowing he'd never take our money.

He smiles, a gap in his teeth from a fight many years ago – or so he says. 'I always say no one deserves anything in this life, but I think *you two* are owed a bit of luck, don't you?'

My stomach twists, giddy, remembering last night's events. Getting the email and selecting an appointment slot could have all been a fever dream if I hadn't woken to a confirmation this morning. It's *real*. I'm talking to someone from the show later today. Suddenly my appetite is all gone, replaced with a horrid stomach swill of excitement and fear.

We take the cookie to the riverbank and lay under a turquoise sky dotted with woolly clouds. We take turns to describe the shapes of them: bunny rabbit; ice-cream van; saggy nappy. Some very cute mallard ducklings come to see us. Can you feed ducks cookie? I can't bear the thought of poisoning them, so keep my half to myself.

'What are you gonna do next year?' Jenson asks, demolishing his half of the biscuit in two humongous bites.

'Don't harsh my bliss.' I scowl at him.

'Taryn . . .' he complains.

'Oh I don't know!' I relent, physically unable to be mad at his cherub face. 'There's no money for university. I don't care enough anyway.'

Only the top ten per cent nationally get to go to higher education and, of that cohort, only a handful of places are funded so *really* only the top ten per cent of the richest families have the chance to qualify for soft-hand professions. 'I guess I'll apply to Labourforce. Hopefully I get something warm and dry.' I shrug. With our misfortune, I'll get sewage duty.

'What about your singing?'

I almost puke the cookie up. It's like he's reading my mind. 'What about it?'

He has a lot of sass for a very sick fourteen-year-old. I think he *might* be gay. I certainly *hope* he is. Most straight guys are unbearable. 'You're too good to stop. Taryn, when you sing it's like you don't even have to try. It just flows out of your mouth like water. Dad says you're even better than Mum was. When I sing it's like my face is wrestling the music.'

I laugh aloud. I've heard him sing and that's a fair assessment. 'I'll never stop singing. Ever. But we need money. I don't think busking, or doing Friday nights at the Acorn Inn is gonna cover it.'

'You should send a video to one of the networks. You're better than . . . Nico.'

'Oh shut up!' I playfully slap his arm. 'Nico is so good she doesn't need a surname.' The true sign of icon status in my eyes. I grew up on Nico's music. Her first album became my entire identity for a year or so. I was a full-fledged Niccie. When she had public beef with Alleyman, I rode for her, posting dozens of poop emojis on every G-Net post he made. I look back at this time with a mixture of pride and mortification.

I consider telling him that I have *already* sent a video to one of the networks, *and* it was an old Nico song I performed. It did the trick, evidently. The secret is like a hummingbird in my throat, dying to break out, but I swallow it back. I can't burden Jenson with this.

The stakes are too high. IF I am selected and IF I make the final ten and IF I'm eliminated, there's an almighty catch. I know it, and he knows it too. We watch *Starmaker* every year.

The clouds above us are becoming less woolly and more steely. It's going to rain, and soon. 'You should get to school,' I say with a sad sigh. 'At least you swerved PE.'

'What?' he protests. 'What about you?'

'Never you mind about me.'

He eyeballs me warily. 'Are you going to meet a boy?'

'What makes you think it's a boy not a girl?' I fire back.

'You've got makeup on. And you did your hair.'

'Don't I normally?'

'No,' he says with a snort and I can't argue with that. 'Tell me, who is it?'

'Just some guy from the private school. Don't tell Dad.' Better for him to think it's a random crush than the truth.

Sometimes people are good. The people of Kelso stopped the old library from being demolished, donated their unwanted books, and volunteered to run it on a rota system. I get it. If we don't have music, and books, and plays and art, we're not even human any more. We wouldn't be living; we'd be surviving.

Their Wi-Fi is better than the woeful service out at the camp, so I reserve one of the antique telephone boxes they've converted into private meeting booths. It's cramped but it means no one will hear what I'm doing (or tell Dad). I make sure to charge my phone to full while I'm here too.

It's 1:58. I check that I'm presentable in my phone camera. I have stolen some makeup from Mol. I'm also wearing her XXL N-TRU5T hoodie and hope that's not too much like I'm brown-nosing. I forced some hoop earrings into my old piercings, trying to create some semblance of the girls I see in the MVs or on socials. I tousle my hair in an attempt to make it more voluminous. It's the colour of milky tea and I wish I'd bleached some stripes in the front. If only I'd had time to prepare.

At two p.m. on the dot, I hit the meeting link.

Your host knows you've arrived. Please wait.

I realize I'm holding my breath. This is a *Network G* meeting room. The *G* is for Global. This person could be calling from anywhere in the New Peace Alliance.

The room pops open to fill my screen and I see a pretty, young woman with perfect teeth smiling out at me. 'Hi Taryn. I'm Willa; thanks for taking time out to talk with me.'

I think she's American, or maybe Canadian I guess. 'Oh my god, no, thank *you*,' I gush. I've seen *Starmaker*, I know they want PERSONALITY over all else. I plaster a grin on my face. 'This is, like, just mind-blowing. Sorry if I seem unhinged!'

I should reel it in a bit. They want charisma, not certifiable.

'Relax, your audition was just perfect. You have a killer voice. This is just an informal chat to get to know you better. Is it okay if we record this meeting?'

They sometimes use this footage. If I refuse, I might as well just quit here and now. I consent. Willa whips through some fairly basic questions, taking notes as I reply. Where did I learn to sing? Have I taken dance lessons? Who are my musical inspirations?

'My mum was a singer; she sang with me every day,' I tell her. Call me cynical but I add, 'She died, five years ago.'

'Oh, sweetheart, I'm sorry to hear that.' Willa doesn't look sorry; I can see dollar signs in her eyes. A sob story is diamond dust on *Starmaker*. 'Five years? French flu?'

I nod. The UK didn't get the vaccine quickly enough. With it, who can say if she'd have pulled through.

'So tell me,' Willa goes on, 'you're living in a refugee camp?'

'My hometown is underwater now.'

'So awful. What's it like, living in one of the camps?'

I can see the backstory film in my mind even now. IF you make the final ten, they send a crew to film your life before you enter the Dreamhouse. Of course I told them about the QEII on my application form. Those shows are always about the narrative. Always. 'It's tough,' I say, 'but we're like a big family.' This is not an exaggeration. 'We all came up from the south and, when things are hard, it bonds you. You have to work together. In a way, it's friendlier than how we lived before. We didn't even know our neighbours back then.'

'Aw, that's lovely.'

I go in for the kill. 'That's why I think I could bring a lot to the Dreamhouse. That's a family too. Sisters.'

I see it. I see the slight smile curve her lips. She knows I know, and I know she knows. She's caught a live one. A little fishy who knows how to play the game. 'Okay, so let me run you through the process, Taryn. We hold national auditions all over the world. Only the very best are shown to Chairman Slade and *he* decides the final ten trainees that'll enter the Dreamhouse.'

If you look online, you can find oblique references to Chairman Slade, the CEO of Elysium Entertainment. He's legendary, the most powerful man in music, but he keeps his face out of the press. If an idol group flops, the fandom lays the blame at his door. All I know is he's been involved with *Starmaker* since the beginning. He *is* literally the *Starmaker*. He shaped Nico, and N-TRU5T, and Cassette Marquez, and The Whiplashes and about fifty per cent of the popstars I grew up with.

'Taryn, I'm legally obliged to ask this next question. Are you aware of the consequences of participating in *Starmaker*?'

'I am,' I say.

'Again, this is a legal requirement. Can you please confirm you accept the following terms and conditions.' She delivers the rest precisely, like she's reading from a document. 'Once participants enter the survival show stage of *Starmaker*, they submit to an elimination process in partnership with Project Population. A winning contestant or contestants receive the prize package which, this year, includes a two-album minimum recording contract with Elysium Entertainment, luxury accommodation for life, and a cash prize of ten million US dollars.'

'Understood.'

She delivers her next line with the same breeziness. 'Eliminated contestants forfeit their life to Project Population.'

'Yes.'

'And, for the avoidance of doubt, you understand that this means death?'

My throat is sandpaper as I say, 'I do.'

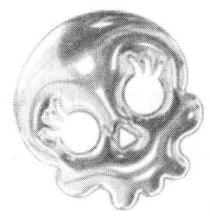

CHAPTER 4

The next day I awake to an email from Team *Starmaker* inviting me to an audition in the Northern Powerhouse.

It's Saturday, and everyone will sleep late, but – as I made the mistake of checking my phone – I'm electrified. I slip a chunky jumper on over my pyjamas, and quietly make a cup of black tea so as not to wake anyone. The ration box comes on Mondays so we have no milk until then.

I take my mug to the front step outside the unit. The ground glitters with frost, but I think it's going to be a pretty spring day. A hazy peach sun peeps over the hills and the birds chirp and chatter. The units are like Monopoly houses and the tracks between them are muddy and pitted, but this hillside has become home. I hear Mrs Jennings's chickens cluck in their coop. Sue Ransome has left her crisp white bedding drying on the line overnight and a bird has kindly pooped on it.

Seven years since we came here. I was ten. Mum was alive. For better or worse, this is all I've known since.

This is all audition anxiety talking. Fear that my life will change. Because, let's be real, this place is a *dump*. We were literally dumped here, and then forgotten. This bitter thinking turns my jitters to iron. Like Derrick said, we deserve better than this. *Anyone* would. It isn't fair that just ten minutes away people live in four, five-bedroom houses, with bathtubs, not a dribbling shower over the toilet. They have gardens and *spare rooms*. What a concept! Imagine having so much space that you have a room that sits empty for most of the year. It is not fair. Did we ask the sea to swallow Exeter?

Starmaker is offering me something *more*.

If I get through the audition.

If I win.

If I don't . . .

Change is scary. Even the thought. I remember how scared I was to leave home, how scared I was when Mum got sick, and now I'm scared again. I wonder if there will be a day in my life when I'm not a bag of knots. My fears start small, but snowball, until I'm fearful of the fear itself.

I cling to one fact. My singing voice got me noticed. I *knew* I had a good voice. Can't wait to rub Mol's face in it.

The door to the unit opens with a whine, and Dad steps outside. 'Did I wake you up?' I ask.

'Nah, love, I've been staring at the ceiling since dawn. Busy head.' He scratches my crown.

Now is as good a time as any. 'Dad, I need to talk to you.'

He sits alongside me on the step. There's a lot of grey in his beard these days. 'Are you pregnant?'

'Ew! No!' I punch his arm quite hard.

'Reassuring.'

My voice is a girlish mumble, my throat tight. 'I've been asked to go to an audition for *Starmaker*.'

I see the tiles in his head sliding together. Dad is hardly a fan, but he's been home enough when we watch. 'But . . . no. No way, Taryn.'

'It's just an audition.' I shrug my shoulders up to my ears.

'I said no.'

'The survival show doesn't start until the Final Ten. The odds of getting that far are miniscule. What do I have to lose?'

His eyes bulge. 'Your life!' He lowers his voice so as not to wake the others. 'That show is . . . ghoulish. I appreciate you trying to support your family but . . .'

I squeeze his hand. 'Dad, can I sing?'

'What kind of a question is that? You got your mum's voice.'

I look him deep in the eyes, hoping I sound more confident than I feel. 'What if I win?'

'What if you don't?'

I shake my head. I have thought of little else all night. I even dreamed that I kept missing the train to my audition. 'Let's say by some miracle I make it through to the live shows. I would be famous. Like *really* famous. I can use the platform to raise awareness. You could start a fundraiser. Dad, it's the most watched programme in the entire world. Win . . . or *lose*, I can help Jenson.'

He doesn't say anything for a long time, but I can almost hear his brain whirring. 'What if I did it?'

'Dad . . . you're not a teenage girl.'

He rolls his eyes. 'I meant one of the others! *Endurance Island* or the wedding one . . . *Bride or Die?*'

The thought of my dad as one of the bachelors on *Bride or Die* is amusing, but he's not exactly the Ken-doll type they go for. 'I searched last night how many people apply for *Starmaker*,' I tell him. 'It's about a quarter of a million people globally. They offer call-backs to a thousand or so.'

He looks at me like, *So what?*

'I did the sums and that's point four percent. I am in the top point four percent in *all the world*.' He doesn't look thrilled, but I sense him coming around to my reasoning. 'It's just an audition. They even said they'd pay for my train to the NP. If I flop, we've lost nothing and I get a day out in the dome.'

He tucks my hair behind my ear. 'I *hate* this, Taryn.'

I shrug. 'I'm only good at one thing. This is how I can help.'

He offers the most imperceptible of nods, and my fate is sealed.

I thought it'd be like a cool movie training montage. It is not.

Every day, after school, I meet Molly and Jenson in the rec centre. The roof leaks and there's a weird eggy smell, so no one really uses the community unit. We push the torn pool tables and the air hockey to the walls. The air hockey table hasn't worked for as long as any of us can remember anyway; it's primarily the surface where a lot of my class lost their virginity.

We start small, with dance-craze videos on G-Net. They're only about ten seconds long, and easy enough to pick up, but Molly quickly evolves into an army sergeant. 'You look possessed,' she barks. 'What are you doing with your face?'

After the first couple of sessions, we find a cracked

floor-length mirror next to the bins outside a shuttered clothes shop, and carry it into the centre. Molly makes me perform the short routines in front of my reflection, and she's right: I look like the village idiot, my tongue poking out of my mouth as I concentrate.

Both Molly *and* Jenson are better at absorbing choreography into their muscles than I am. Mortifying. That said, I'm not as hopeless as Molly tells me. I am on the beat if nothing else. Still, I feel like my limbs are too long; I'm that inflatable tube man, flailing outside the second-hand car garage.

'Get it together!' Molly snaps in our second week of intense training. 'God, you're useless!'

'Will you shut up!' I snarl back. 'I'm trying, Molly!'

She storms out and slams the door so hard the pigeons flee from the rafters. I run the routine alone until my big sister skulks back into the rec room exactly three minutes later and hugs me. 'I don't want you to die because you dance like a potato.'

I manage a laugh and hug her back.

Molly and Jenson took the news surprisingly well. We've watched *Starmaker* since we were kids – we've always talked about what songs we'd choose, what we'd wear, the makeovers. It was only in the last six or seven seasons that the show teamed up with Project Population. When the ratings dipped, they found a way to up the stakes.

We blithely ignore that part, and focus on the winning. One evening, I overhear Jenson asking Dad if, when I make the band, we'd move to America, or the NP, or even New London. Dad said we shouldn't get too carried away.

I keep dancing. I'm not worried about my singing. It's the dancing that scares me.

A week until my audition and I start to . . . not suck. It's amazing what tossing your hair around can do; it diverts attention from my feet.

I squeeze my feet into a pair of Mum's old heeled boots, and Molly plays a dance tutorial video, drilling me, yanking my arms and legs into position, until I get it right. It's well after midnight on the night before my audition when I finally get through the routine without stopping.

When the music stops, I fold at the waist, out of breath. 'How was that?' I pant, noodles of hair plastered to my wet forehead.

Molly nods, curling her lips. 'I've seen worse.' She gives me a wink. From her, that's high praise.

I'm as ready as I'll ever be.

CHAPTER 5

From the train, I can see the wind turbines miles out to sea. I think they're pretty. They've been painted red and yellow and orange, rainbow colours. I can't understand why people used to fight against them. They are no eyesore. They remind me of the plastic windmills I used to stick in the terracotta plant pots of our old garden back in Exeter.

If only they'd built them sooner. Why did they let it get so bad? It's not like they weren't warned.

It's only nine a.m. and I feel like I've lived a whole day. I had to be up at five for my ride to Berwick. The shuttle bus driver, Roger Tweedy, agreed to drive me on his day off which I thought was kind; you need a special license to own a petrol engine and, mysteriously, only very well-off people seem to get them.

I've never caught a train by myself. I feel like an infant, too small in the padded chair. Dad made me a little packed lunch – which I've almost finished already – and Molly did my makeup before I left. It's more makeup than I've ever worn in my entire life. I look like a porcelain doll with my red cheeks, but Molly assures me it'll look much less on camera.

My sister and I also cobbled together my audition look. The tightrope walk is in showing just the right amount of skin. 'You want to look sexy,' Mol explained, 'but never slutty.' There wasn't time for me to unpack that contradiction. In the end, we cut the bottom off a tight t-shirt to show my belly button and paired it with some of her baggy, hard-wearing canvas work pants. The last time they did girl groups on *Starmaker*, B*TRU3 was formed, so we modelled my look on them. They're still making comebacks, three years on.

I know this is a fool's errand. I'll be up against girls who've been to stage school in the NP or New London; girls who've been dancing since they could walk; girls with pushy mothers; girls with mothers, period.

Ah well, I can say I took the train to the Northern Powerhouse. I'll chalk it up to experience.

We cross the border into England, and the conductor stamps my passport. I think we pass Newcastle. I'm so intently focused on the view from the window – more industrial than anything I've seen in a long time – that I don't realize there's a man talking to me.

There are two of them, about my dad's age, on the other side of the aisle. Both are wearing stripy ties and blazers as if they belong to some sports team. 'I'm sorry?' I pull my earbuds out of my ears.

'I was just saying to my friend that you're a bonnie lass, that's all.'

I guess they like the doll makeup and tousled hair. I nod a thank you.

'You travelling alone, sweetheart?' the second man says.

I really can't be bothered to talk to anyone, but I can smell the beer drifting over the aisle. A little early for that. I nod again.

'Ah, we'll look after youse,' the first man, the red-faced one, says with a wink.

'Is your tummy not cold?' the second guy says. He's shorter, bald, a tattoo over his eyebrow.

'No,' I reply meekly, though I draw my hand over the exposed skin.

'You do speak English then?' Redface laughs. I look down the aisle, wondering if I could pretend to get off at the next station and move into the next carriage. Would they follow?

'What's your name, pet?'

I don't know what it is about these men that's making me so awkward, but I feel like I'm shrivelling up, a prune. I just want to listen to my music. Why are they forcing this?

'Don't be shy; he doesn't bite.' Tattoo winks. 'But I do if you ask nicely.'

'Oh just leave her alone,' a new voice interrupts. I twizzle around, and there's a woman, perhaps in her thirties, balancing a little girl on her knee.

At once, Redface becomes even more red-faced. 'Who asked you? Nosy bitch.'

My stomach drops. That went south *fast*.

'Don't you want to talk to us, darlin'?' Tattoo asks me.

I am so grateful for the woman's intervention, but I don't want them to get even more aggressive – not with the little girl right there. 'I . . . I need to listen to my music. For an audition.'

'Oooh, don't she talk posh, like? Lady Muck over there.'

A second woman, this one much older, scowls at the drunk men. 'Oi, give over, the pair of youse. Should be ashamed of yourselves. She's nothing but a bairn. Here, darlin'. You come sit with me.'

I collect my satchel and slide it onto her table as she makes space for me.

'Now behave yourselves, or I'll get the conductor. Lager louts.'

Both men mutter obscenities about what a 'dried-up old hag' my saviour is, before moving into the next carriage, presumably to torment some other poor woman. 'Thanks,' I say to the older woman. She's dressed smartly in a wool coat and hat, but I don't think she's a rich woman, just someone who takes pride in herself on a spring day out.

She offers me a toffee caramel which I gratefully accept. 'Us girlies have to stick together, don't we?'

I don't mention I'm about to fight a thousand girlies to the bitter end.

It's a little after eleven when the train passes through the concrete blastwall to NP1. I haven't been since I was little and I've certainly never been alone. I am dwarfed by the glass giants and flyovers. I think NP1 used to be called Leeds? Honestly can't remember. They all merge into one another now anyway.

My fellow passengers gather their cases and bags and disembark the train like it's no big deal, but I feel childlike, a Little Orphan Annie alone in the big city. *Fake it until you make it*, I think. I copy these sophisticated city dwellers and join the impatient procession through the ticket barriers, and don't even flinch at the police dogs or armed officers.

First impression: the Northern Powerhouse stinks. Literally, not figuratively. I leave the station and there's a distinct difference in the recycled atmosphere under the missile shield. Even outside, the air tastes somehow pre-breathed, mouthy and moist. That and all the car fumes. I don't see *how* there are still so many petrol vehicles when they were phased out before I was born, but it's choking. I can already smell the chalkiness in my hair. I worry this might affect my vocal chords. I fish a filter mask out of my bag and secure it around my ears. Everyone wears them in the city it seems, so I don't stand out.

I log into my map app and start following the arrow towards Maximum Studios. I needn't have bothered. I only walk about five minutes from the train station when I see a line of skinny girls snaking around a corner past a twenty-four-hour private clinic and vit-drip bar. It's a *long* line.

I'm not sure whether to laugh or cry. I knew, obviously, that I wasn't the only girl auditioning, but, looking at this parade of beautiful girls, it really hits home that my odds are . . . dire. And this is just England. All over the Peace Alliance there are girls in identical queues.

I join the back of the line. The girls sip water or stretch their limbs ahead of the dance audition. I see a *lot* of exposed midriffs. We all got the same memo about stomachs. I watch one stunning Black girl lift her spandex-clad leg up against the wall of the clinic and perform the splits. Yeah, I can't do that.

I arrive at the back of the queue, and the girl in front of me looks a little younger than I am. She's with a chaperone,

I guess her mum. 'Hey,' I say. We're gonna be here a while, might as well be friendly.

The girl is wearing a filter too but her eyes smile. 'Hello!'

Her mother eyes me with suspicion. I'm *seventeen*. Is it that concerning that I'm here alone? Or maybe it's disgust, because her daughter is wearing a cute Gucci t-shirt. I know *nothing* about fashion, but even I know what *they* cost. I'm wearing a second-hand t-shirt with a frayed hem. 'I'm Taryn,' I say.

She pops off her mask. 'I'm Emmy! This is my mum. Are you nervous?'

'Very,' I say.

'God me too.' She has braces on her teeth and a smattering of freckles across her nose. Her golden hair has been curled into perfect ringlets and set rock hard with hairspray.

'Do you do a lot of dancing?' I ask out of politeness. I'm glad fate has put us next to each other.

'Emmy is freestyle regional champion,' her mother informs me.

'Wow,' I say, and Emmy rolls her eyes.

'Do you compete?' Emmy asks.

'Nope,' I say, oddly proud of this fact. 'I sing. My mum was a singer in the National Opera before it shut.' If we're bragging, I can play that game too.

The queue moves a few paltry metres, and a ripple of nervous excitement passes down the line like a Mexican wave. I ask Emmy if she knows what to expect. The emails from the Network G recruiters were vague.

We were told to prepare one of two songs to sing. Both

chart hits from the last couple of years, but one, 'Young and Stupid', offers more opportunities to show off runs so I've prepared that one. In terms of the dance audition, we were simply told to bring flat training shoes.

Emmy is as much in the dark but this isn't her first rodeo. 'At most auditions they just see how quickly you can pick up a routine. Don't sweat it.'

But I do. I have plenty of time to worry about it. The line moves forwards at a snail's pace. I see a pair of women wearing Network G t-shirts but they're close to the studio entrance and I don't want to lose my place in the queue if I go ask them what to expect. Girls go in, girls go out. I wish I'd brought a book to read.

Whispers and speculation start to spread down the line, fuelled, no doubt, by nervousness. Someone says they're only looking for girls under five-five. Someone else says they want redheads. Someone says tattoos are forbidden.

By the time I'm in sight of the doors, I feel slightly numb. I can hear a pounding beat and the occasional squeak of rubber soles but I'm not scared, or excited, I'm more embarrassed. The fact that I truly thought, even for a moment, this was my golden ticket is shameful. I'm nothing special; I'm just another girl with a nice singing voice.

The door to the studio opens and every girl's spine straightens. This is it. My turn. A woman with an e-tablet checks my name and citizen ID card. 'Great, thanks. Here's your number.'

I'm not even a human. I'm ENG267. I attach the sticky label to my top. She counts out twenty of us. 'Right!' she announces breezily. 'Next group!'

Okay, *now* I'm nervous. I follow Emmy into the belly of the beast.

'Up the stairs, Studio A please, ladies!' an officious man in chunky red glasses shouts from a mezzanine. 'Right this way.'

I focus on putting one foot in front of the other. All of a sudden, the tedium of the queue is forgotten. This is real. I am here.

I think of Jenson. This is all for a reason. Failure is a luxury I can't afford.

Studio A is huge, each of the walls carpeted for soundproofing. It smells strongly of fresh coffee, a smell I'd all but forgotten; it's so hard to come by. The aroma drifts from a trestle table positioned before a single lonely microphone in the centre of the room.

Red Glasses claps his hands. 'Girls, dump your stuff and line up against the back wall please!'

Emmy's mum licks her thumb and fixes a minute smudge in her daughter's eyeliner before sending her before the firing squad. I throw my bag aside and take my place between two other girls.

The judging panel consists of a man and a woman, both in Network G t-shirts. 'Come along, girls, we've got a lot to get through,' the woman says tetchily. 'I'm Hana, one of the producers at *Starmaker* and this is Evan from the record label, Elysium. First things first, can I get you all to give us a big, friendly smile?'

Red Glasses moves down the line, taking instant-photos of us. He gets to me and I smile as sweetly as I can without looking unhinged. I aim for casual-slash-cool. He says 'fab' and moves on to my neighbour.

Back at their table, Hana and Evan pore over the images, sliding them around like tiles. They mutter, casting the occasional glance our way. 'Okay, can you step forward if we call your name please?' Evan says. I have never listened so hard in my life. 'Carmine, Sera, Flora . . .'

He calls forth seven girls, but he doesn't say my name.

Hana chews on her pen as she delivers the killer blow. 'Thank you. I'm afraid it's not good news, girls. If we called your name, you're not for us.'

There's a moment of stunned silence before it breaks into disbelief. I exhale, relieved. One of the eliminated girls bursts into tears. 'We don't even get to sing?' another asks with disbelief.

Hana holds up a hand. 'Remember we have heard and scored your audition tapes. Appreciate you've done exceptionally well to make it this far. Thank you. The rest of you, get ready to sing.'

I blink, reeling. I almost wish they'd say the quiet part aloud. The girls they singled out aren't pretty enough. That's all it can be. One of the eliminated girls has acne, hidden under thick makeup. Two of them are a bit curvier than the rest of us – but only marginally. If I'm honest, their worst crime is that they are *average*, not faces you'd remember. Not exceptional. Not *idols*. I remember Nico's face on that L'Oréal billboard outside the pharmacy.

I guess that's the reality of the world. Brutal though. If *I* got sent home after travelling four hours to stand in a line for ninety minutes, I'd riot. I *suppose* I should be pleased that my face and butt are deemed *adequate* but it feels like a hollow victory. If I was a good person, I'd follow these girls out in protest. But, come on, I knew what I signed up for. Every single season, some trainee says the immortal *I'm not here to make friends* creed. I'll have to step over a lot more roadkill if I'm gonna take home the bacon for Jen.

I remember what's at stake, and regret thinking of roadkill. Girls, eventually, will *die*. I push it out of my mind. The survival show is a *long* way off.

Hana explains we'll each sing a verse and chorus of the song we chose. Of the twenty girls in my group, thirteen remain. I wait my turn, cross-legged on the floor. We clap and cheer for each girl, which feels nice after the savage cut. Emmy goes before me. Her voice is baby-high, too saccharine and nasal for my taste. She doesn't quite have control of her lower register and tries to cover it up with ad-libs. Still, the judges seem to like her.

'267, Taryn Beck?' Evan calls and I take to the mic. There's a video camera directed at me and I know I'm not *just* singing for the people in the room. I take a deep breath and try to imagine I'm back at the QE II campfire.

I adjust my posture to straighten my diaphragm. I close my eyes and think of Mum standing just over my shoulder, the scent of her sandalwood perfume. *Singing is easy, Taryn. You only have to remember five things: breath, pitch, rhythm, diction and voice.* I have all the tools in my kit, I just have to use them.

'Introduce yourself to the camera, tell us where you came

from and what you'll be singing today.' Hana could not look less interested, her bejewelled nail tapping away on an e-tablet.

I've seen enough *Starmaker* to know that everything is judged. I look coquettishly down the camera as if I am flirting with it. I wonder if this footage goes all the way to the top; to Chairman Slade. 'Hello, I'm Taryn Beck and I live in the Scottish Border Camps. Today I'll be singing "Young and Stupid" by Cassette Marquez.' I smile like I'm full of honey.

'Great. Take it away,' Evan says.

Breath. Pitch. Rhythm. Diction. Voice.

Gonna get drunk tonight
Wanna forget your face
Take myself to the place
When I was young
When I was young and stupid.
Baby I miss your laugh
Who ma gonna call
When I think I'm gonna fall?
Wanna be young
Want to be young and stupid.
Woah, ooh, woah
If this is growing pains
Can't go through this again
Woah, ooh, woah
If it hurts so much
How can this be love?
I'm going back
To being young and stupid . . . now.

Now bloody Hana is looking. I did the first chorus as though it were the last so I could hit the big note. The other girls applaud, some cheer. Like, I can't hear myself how they heard me, but I'm guessing I'm the most impressive of my group so far.

'Very nice tone,' Hana says. Everyone always comments on my 'husky' singing voice. 'Take a seat.'

That's all I'm getting for my efforts. The pair scribble down some notes.

When everyone has sung, another two girls are asked to leave. They cry. I'd cry too. Criticize my face if you must, but I'd be crushed if someone came for my voice.

We're told to take a break while the previous group finishes in the dance studio.

'What a lovely voice you have, dear,' Emmy's mother tells me as I collect my things. 'Your mother must be very proud.'

I just smile and nod.

Eventually, Red Glasses shepherds us upstairs to Studio C. This room is mercifully airier, with high ceilings and huge skylights. It's pristine and white, mirrors on one side. The floor feels springy underfoot.

A tall, thin woman flits about the studio like a wasp trapped under a pint glass. 'Come on in, girls!' She looks exactly how I'd imagine a dance teacher to look, right down to the greased bun and leg-warmers. She moves like she has rubber bands instead of bones.

There are only eleven of us left, and I wish there were more bodies to hide behind. We are told to stretch. I copy what Emmy does, albeit with less flexibility. Now I'm *really* nervous.

In the sort of plummy accent I thought had died out with the royals, the dance teacher introduces herself as Deenie Maskell. There's an implicit suggestion that we ought to know who she is already, and be suitably impressed. 'Very simple, girls,' she says. 'I'm going to teach you a basic routine. You just have to copy.'

I think that this puts us at an equal disadvantage until we begin. Deenie's assistant plays N-TRU5T's 'Cosmic Baby'. It begins easily enough; I just have to bend over and run my hand up my leg and torso. That's where easy ends.

'Then body roll, three, four, pas de bourrée, five, six, hip, hip, shimmy, seven, eight, turn and headroll.'

Why is she going so fast? Why is everyone else able to copy her? The very first time Deenie shows us, Emmy imitates her flawlessly, like she's committing it to muscle memory.

I refuse to ask her to repeat the demonstration, so I instead sidle to the rear of the pack.

'Okay, everyone – your turn!'

The music begins again. I remember the leg stroke and then try to follow the group. I manage to hit some of the poses but transitioning from one to the next is harder; it feels like I'm scampering from pose to pose. I more or less manage to keep time, and end with a big hair flick. I can only pray flipping my hair around disguises my total lack of finesse.

'One more time!' Deenie decrees.

This time I try to arch my back and point my feet. But focusing on these fine details pushes the routine out of my head and I forget where I'm supposed to be. I almost collide with the girl next to me. If looks could kill, she'd kill me.

I finish in the right place and try to look cute. I've messed up. Maybe Deenie and her sidekick didn't notice.

'Thanks, ladies!' Deenie says. 'Head down to Studio B and grab a drink. We'll be right with you.'

The third studio is some sort of holding pen, lined with trestle tables piled with cartons of water and energy bars. There's so much nervous energy in the room, it's almost visible, a shimmer in the air. A miasma of vanilla body spray, chewing gum and Red Bull. There are maybe twenty other girls waiting by the time we're sent down.

I help myself to a water and stow a couple of cereal bars into my bag for later. You don't turn down free food. I think about finding Emmy while we wait, but I see she's buddied up with the other insanely good dancer from our group. In fact, they seem to be looking right at me and talking under their breath.

I've bitched enough times in my life to know they're bitching about me. Okay, whatever, it's par for the course. Girls bitch in the way monkeys pick lice off each other; you pick a few, you get picked on, and female society functions. I'm not so naïve as to think a survival show is going to be summer camp where we feministly girl-boss all the way to the finale. Never gonna happen. Girls are mean.

And in the spirit of meanness, they can dance better than I do, but they sang like geese. So there.

I'm finishing this mean (if honest) thought when a Network G person wearing a headset enters with an e-tablet. 'Okay, girls! Listen up! If I call your number please step forward.'

ENG267. I will her to call it out. Even knowing everything it would mean.

She rattles off numbers. Emmy steps forward. So does her bitchy pal.

She summons only seven people out of the thirty in the room.

She doesn't call ENG267.

'And that's all for now. If I didn't say your number, thank you very much for coming along. Don't be too disappointed. The girls I called, head up to the dance studio.'

So that's that. I'm finished.

Some girls try to argue with the producer, they beg, they reason, but she wisely makes a swift exit. Some girls cry. I don't. I feel numb. I steal another cereal bar. That way I have *something* to offer Jenson on my return.

CHAPTER 6

Worst adrenaline crash *ever*. I pretty much pass out on the train, after setting an alarm so I don't miss my station.

One side of my brain insists it's no bad thing that I won't have to literally sing for my life, but the other, more delusional hemisphere, mourns the death of a very brief dream. For a minute there, part of me *believed*. My own room; big bed; hot water every day. I couldn't help it.

It's almost midnight when I roll into Berwick. It's a bitterly cold night, and I pull my hoodie over my naked tummy. Across a deserted car park, I see my sister standing next to the minibus. Roger Tweedy waits in the driver's seat, keeping warm.

I'm not expecting a welcome home parade. I already sent a simple 'it was a no' message from the NP. Still, it's nice Mol's come to greet me. After all the dance practice, we were in it together. As I get closer, I read her face better. Her expression is more than just disappointed. 'What's up?'

She explains on the way to the free hospital. Apparently Jenson had awoken that morning feeling deeply unwell;

distant and listless. They didn't tell me because they didn't want to screw up my audition. I'm annoyed but would have likely done the same if it had been Molly instead of me.

A Saturday night at the free hospital is no laughing matter. The mood in reception is spiky, blood-splattered. It's noisy, and smelly, and sweaty. People queue anxiously at the front desk, waiting to have their IDs assessed. An old man, his clothes filthy and reeking of cider, sleeps across four plastic seats.

'This way,' Molly says, steering me through a crowd of bleeding drunks and crying, feverish children. Three children a day are dying of measles according to the news.

We have a ward pass, and an armed guard bleeps us out of the lobby and into a corridor that's no less hectic. Here, the walls are lined, both sides, with patients on trolleys. An elderly woman is crying that she needs help getting to the toilet. A purple-faced man staggers, blind drunk, his trousers around his ankles. A nurse, not much older than Molly, tries to corral him into a bay.

Meanwhile, a clean-cut young man with a slick fade and a shiny grey suit goes from stretcher to stretcher. He's handing out Project Population pamphlets.

Molly clamps her hand around my wrist and pulls me through the chaos. Jenson is on the children's ward on the first floor. Visiting hours are long over, but we need to collect Dad. There isn't room enough for him to stay overnight. The ward is divided with cloth partitions, and they do nothing to soundproof the sniffles and quiet sobs.

Molly goes in search of a restroom, and I find Dad resting his head on the edge of Jenson's hospital bed. My brother is sleeping peacefully, his heart monitor beeping out a steady rhythm. I shake Dad awake and he comes to with a jolt. 'Taryn love, you're back.'

'Is he OK?' I whisper.

'He'll be fine. They should release him in the morning . . . if they can get him his meds.'

That sounds like a pretty big *if*. I nod.

'How did the audition go?'

I shake my head. 'I'm going to drop out of school and join Labourforce.' He starts to argue but I shush him and point at Jen. 'With three wages coming in maybe we can get a private prescription or something. We don't have a choice.'

Dad's head hangs heavy between his knees. 'I've let you down. You shouldn't have to live like this.'

I crouch down and embrace him. Once my father was a very proud man. He used to have a pretty good job in advertising, but slowly AI replaced the need for copywriters and designers entirely. He found himself, like so many others, working on construction sites; AI doesn't do bricklaying. Yet. 'No! You do so much. I couldn't even pass a simple dance audition. I blew it, Dad. I'm so sorry.'

He hugs me tighter and I feel his warm breath on my scalp. 'Hey. You have nothing to be sorry about. Listen to us. I'm sure *they'd* love little people like us to take the blame for the state of the world, but none of this is our fault, Taryn. None of this was up to us.'

They. The people who run the world. I think about them all the time. The trouble is, they don't think about us at all.

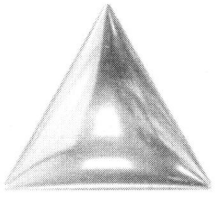

CHAPTER 7

At school that Monday, the metal detectors are down again, so it takes like an hour to get into the building. It's *always* Mondays. And it's drizzling. The slate sky has my mood right. At least Jen is home, tucked up in bed. That's something.

I don't even go to my tutor group; I head directly to Ms Everard's office on the third floor. The Head of College is eating her lunch, an egg and cress roll, at nine-twenty, which I think suggests her day isn't going too well either.

I tell her I'm quitting. 'That's a shame,' she says, wiping a glob of egg mayonnaise off her chin. 'You were doing quite well, Taryn.'

Beyond that, she makes no attempt to change my mind. People drop out for the same reasons every single day; I don't see why I'd be special.

So as everyone else hurries for first period, I aimlessly drift towards the exit. I don't try to find my friends; I'll see most of them at the site or in the town. I take in a final glance at the entrance hall, the papier mâché diplodocus, the 'edgy' artwork

Year 13 made a few years back with melted waste plastics, and breathe in one last whiff of weird cabbage smell wafting from the canteen. I'll never graduate this place; I will only leave.

Maybe I'm a little psychic, because I check my phone at the exact same time it rings. An unknown number. It's probably a telephone scam. I wouldn't normally bother even answering but I'm down for a fight this morning. 'Hello?'

'Oh, hi. Is that Taryn Beck?'

'Depends, who is this?'

'This is Hana Gupta. We met at the audition on Saturday. I'm a producer at *Starmaker*.'

I look around the school lobby. I'm alone. 'Oh, okay,' I say, embarrassed for my sass. She asks if I'm good to talk and I assure her I have absolutely nowhere to be.

'Listen. I showed your audition to my boss.'

'Chairman Slade?'

'You've heard of him?'

'Who hasn't?'

'Well, needless to say, he was really impressed with your voice.' The fact that Mr Starmaker has heard me sing is mind-blowing, but then Hana bursts the bubble. 'Your dancing let you down a bit, Taryn.'

No kidding. 'Yeah, I figured.'

'Looking at the girls we've put through, we have more dancers than singers. Sometimes, on shows like *Starmaker*, we develop some contestants behind the scenes. We're making a TV show after all and we want it to be good.'

I'm not quite sure where she's going with this. 'Okay . . .?'

'We're inviting a few girls, like yourself, to spend some time with our choreographer Deenie Maskell in London. A dance camp if you like.'

I am holding my breath, making myself lightheaded. 'How long for?'

There's a delay and I get the sense she's eating something. 'It'll be intensive because we begin the survival show in late May. Maybe a month or so? Do you think you'd be able to join us? It'll be hard work – training every single day.'

My mouth hangs open wordlessly. It feels like there's a bubble trapped under my skull, squishing my brain. 'I . . . I just joined Labourforce,' I say, trying to mentally tap dance. 'My brother needs medication so I have to work.'

'I read about your situation in your notes. I'm sorry to hear he's unwell.'

I don't say anything because I can't quite bring myself to say no, even knowing that I'll have to. Jenson needs help *now*, not *if* I win some singing contest.

She continues to chew at the other end. 'Why don't you email us the details of what he needs? I'm quite sure we can sort something out.'

'What?' I say much too loudly, attracting a glare from one of the reception team. 'Just like that?'

'We're *Network G*, Taryn! We get the job done!' I hear her chuckle. 'We won't let anything get in the way of talent. It ought to be a level playing field, don't you think?'

I'm speechless. In the space of a three-minute phone call, I've helped my brother. Dad is right; with money, anything is possible.

'So what do you say? Are you interested in coming down to London?'

'I . . . um . . . yes?' If they can find Jenson his medicine without breaking a sweat, what else can they do?

'Oh wonderful! I should say, however, this development phase is no guarantee that you'll make it to the Dreamhouse. That decision is up to Chairman Slade. If there's no improvement . . .'

'Okay. I understand.'

'Taryn, the rest is up to you.'

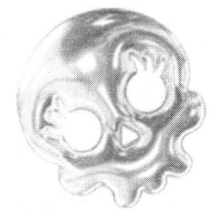

CHAPTER 8

The night before I leave for Old London Town, the residents of the QE II throw a going away shindig. I suspect this is because they enjoy any excuse for a party, but also there's a weird pride at one of their own making it this far. It doesn't matter how many times I explain I'm only going to audition further; my neighbours already have stars in their eyes.

As the bonfire starts to dwindle, Tobey pulls me off the dancefloor. 'Taryn,' he says. 'If you're leaving tomorrow, I need to tell you how I feel.'

Oh god. I'd hoped to avoid this. We continue to a quiet spot away from the speakers. 'Oh, Tobey. I'm going away . . .' I want to let him down as gently as possible. 'And let's be honest . . . we don't know if I'll ever come back.'

He blinks with uncommonly long lashes. 'Taryn . . . does Jenson ever talk about me?'

'What?'

His hands are shaking. 'Oh god. I . . . I think I like him. Like that.'

Huh. It's a good thing I can sing, because I'm totally

clueless about everything else.

'Do you think he likes me back?'

'I . . . don't know.'

'Oh.' The poor boy looks heartbroken.

'I can find out!' I vow that I'll do some love detective work before the night is over. I'm glad of the distraction.

I walk through the site, looking for my brother. My last night in the unit for . . . who knows how long.

A gruff voice barks at me across the night. 'I don't know why you'd want to go on that tripe.' It's Merrill Saunders, sitting in a deckchair outside her unit. She's drunk; her eyes are unfocused, like they're floating in gin.

'I'm sorry?'

'*Starmaker*. It's a sausage factory. Every year they drop in fresh meat and churn out more sausages. And who wins? Darlin', it's not the sausage. That just gets fried and eaten.'

I half-smile. 'Are you calling me a sausage, Merrill?'

But she continues to look at me gravely. 'Och, wee Taryn, I thought you was smarter than this. Even pigs know not to enter the slaughterhouse.' She slurs her words. 'Human sacrifices used to trot up the steps of the Aztec temple willingly too. To appease the gods, they said. Nah, it was to keep the little people in line, nothing more. Gods aren't gods without men to fear 'em.'

I shift uncomfortably, desperate to return to the frivolity in the town square. 'I need to find Jenson.'

But the older woman grips my wrist. 'Just sing down the pub, doll. Sing anywhere you want. Don't give your voice to the gods.'

'You're hurting me.'

'Don't do it.'

I see my reflection in her desperate blue eyes. She *pities* me. 'I know what I'm doing.'

'No you don't.' She releases my arm.

Dazed, I hug myself as I walk away, suddenly chilled in my bones. A horrid greenish feeling floods my guts. For a moment I think I'll puke, but as I slip down the side of the community centre, I hear voices. I find Jenson and some of his school friends hiding behind the block. Jen cannot illicitly drink booze because of his condition, but that doesn't stop his friends.

I'm still shaking from the encounter with Merrill. My buzz is all but gone. Somehow she's made tomorrow feel real. For a second, I forget my task.

'What's up?' he asks. 'You look awful.'

'I'm looking for you,' I tell my brother, forcing the nausea down. 'Can we talk?'

We find a spot next to a bonfire in an old trash can. 'You're not saying goodbye are you?' he asks once we're settled.

'No. I actually came to tell you something . . . Tobey Faraday has a crush on you.'

He blinks. 'On me? I thought he had a crush on you?'

'Turns out my gaydar was faulty.'

'Oh.'

I try to read his expression. 'Well?'

'Well I don't know.' He lowers his voice to little more than a shy whisper. 'I, um, I don't even know if I like girls or boys yet.'

'Oh I've been there,' I say without a hint of exaggeration.

He curls his shoulders inwards like an armadillo. 'It's like, what's the point? Grown up things are for people who are gonna grow up, right?'

I tell him to shut up in the strongest possible language. 'You're gonna be *fine*. *Starmaker* sent a private prescription, right?'

He nods.

'That'll cover us for the next couple of months. I'm gonna get on that show, Jen. For you.'

'Even if it means . . . ?'

I grip his hands tight. 'You are going to grow up and kiss a million boys or girls or both or neither. Got that?'

'That's a lot of kisses.'

I start him off by giving him one on the forehead, but I'm still rattled.

Even pigs know not to enter the slaughterhouse.

N-TRU5T ARE N-MORE
Fan devastation as chart-topping boyband calls it quits.
EXCLUSIVE by Showbiz Editor Dean Sutton

After weeks of speculation, Elysium Entertainment put out a statement today confirming Trusties' worst fears. Five years after they were formed on *Starmaker*, members Sonny Feldman, Cade Kekoa, Yun Ye-joon, Rico Lopez and Erik Rasmussen will end group activities and focus on solo endeavours.

The writing was on the wall following leader Sonny's decision last month to go on indefinite hiatus from the band to complete his academic studies.

So far, only bandmate Cade has broken his silence on socials, posting a photo of him and Sonny at their final concert in Media City, MI, with the following caption:

'Brother, I love, respect and miss you. Trust is for ever.'

However, the post was swiftly deleted and replaced with the official statement from Elysium Entertainment announcing a new album, *TRU5T GOLD: Greatest Hits.*

PHASE TWO:
TRAINING & DEVELOPMENT

CHAPTER 9

This can't be right.

Little bag in one hand, and Mum's old guitar case in the other, I check the house name again – Grenville Abbott – and look back to the taxi driver. 'This is the place, love,' he says, rubbing his rough chin.

But it's derelict. The mansion, not far from Hampstead Heath, is in ruins. The pillars outside the front door are covered in graffiti: *EAT THE RICH* is scrawled in red across the palatial double doors. Some of the many windows are smashed, some are boarded over.

At school, we learned that much of Old London Town was bombed during the war. People left and never came back. So why am I here now?

Only then the front doors open with a creak and Deenie Maskell fills the gap, exactly as I remember her from the audition; lean and limby, like a mug tree wearing bangles. 'Taryn, darling! Come on in!'

She gives the black-cab driver a nod and the taxi crunches back down the long driveway. I approach the haunted house.

'I wasn't sure this was right . . .'

'Oh I know, darling, it's a dump, but I got it for a song right after the war. Bought it off a sheikh in Oman, can you believe it?' She beckons me inside.

The grand entrance hall is only marginally less dilapidated. Chunks of exposed brick peek out from cracked plaster and the chessboard tiles have gaps. Still, once, this place must have been a palace. Double sweeping staircases hug the hallway. I'm in a fairy-tale castle. The rot and decay only make it more *Sleeping Beauty*. 'It's beautiful,' I say and mean it.

'Be thankful you're not here at the height of winter.' Deenie instructs me to leave my little suitcase at the foot of the stairs and insists I join her for tea and scones.

The kitchen is rather more homely, full of mismatched chairs and tables. I suspect she lives out of this room. I was so intimidated by Deenie in the NP, but seeing how she lives makes her human. She isn't a being of pure dance after all.

'Have a seat, sweetie,' she says as she lifts a whistling kettle off the hob.

'Am I the only student here?'

'For now. There's to be five of you in total. A nice little group. We have a lot of work to do, don't we?' she says ominously, before adding, 'It'll be fun, I promise.' Only four others? That's interesting; I imagined a fleet of us. Such a small cohort suggests they're watching us very closely.

Scones demolished, Deenie gives me a guided tour of Grenville Abbott. I try my best to ignore the damp patches and missing floorboards as we roam endless draughty corridors. Beyond the windows, the grounds are just as wild as the house, ivy swallowing up statues. A fountain is bone dry.

'I'm old enough to have seen Madonna's last tour,' she says as we explore the library. 'Right there and then, my friends and I decided to run away to London and become dancers. Needless to say, we didn't live in digs like this back then! There were four of us in a one bed flat in Stratford, darling!'

She looks wistful, her eyes glazed over. 'And then came the war. The West End isn't there any more. I miss Pineapple Studios. I miss the Phoenix Club. I miss Shaftesbury Avenue.'

I don't know what any of those things are. 'People didn't want dancers any more?'

'Goodness no, darling! They wanted us more than ever! They wanted stories to make sense of the madness. Stories keep us human, however we choose to tell them.' She waggles a cherry red nail under my nose. 'Remember that. Songs are stories. Dancers tell stories too.'

At that, we arrive in front of gilded double doors. 'The ballroom,' she says. 'And now, my home.'

She opens the doors with a magician's flourish. Heavenly light floods the corridor and I inhale sharply. *This* room, she's looked after. There's a domed skylight, ivy creeping over the frosted glass like veins. She's installed mirrors and a ballet barre, and the floor is sprung.

'C'est magnifique, isn't it?'

'It's gorgeous.'

'I'm glad you think so; you'll be in here a lot.' Deenie positions me in front of the gleaming mirror. 'Let's get a look at you.' She scans me up and down. 'Good height. Nice long legs. Pretty little face. Awful posture.' She tugs my shoulders back and down, tilts my head upwards and then thrusts my hips forward. 'We'll make a dancer of you yet.' She gives me a wink. 'Come on, darling. You get first dibs on bedrooms.'

There are private bedrooms but there are clearly leaks in the pipes: ominous black mould running from the cornice. I opt for a twin room that doesn't let in the elements. I think this is a smart choice.

Once I'm in bed with a hot water bottle, I finally open Dad's letter. I was given very strict instructions to save it until I arrived.

Dearest Taryn,

This is my final plea: come home now. I don't want you on that show.

There, I said it, knowing that you'll ignore me. You always have since you were old enough to crawl.

You are every inch your mother's daughter, and I want you to take that with you on this voyage. Think to yourself, what would Mum do? I believe that moral compass will steer you right.

Nevertheless, you better win this thing. Stay honest and sing, sweetheart, sing for your life.

Jenson, Molly and I need you back here. This isn't a family without you.

Love always,
Dad xxx

Inside the envelope, there's a photo I don't remember seeing before. It's of me and Mum. I must only be about two years old but I have a tiny pink microphone in my hand – maybe a karaoke toy? Mum and I are singing together. Tears prick my eyes, and I *never* cry.

I press the photo to my heart and save it there for later.

CHAPTER 10

I get my first glimpse of Leela in the arrivals lounge at Terminal 5. I have never seen anyone cooler in my whole life. I'm in Dad's sweater and leggings, looking like human trash. Deenie dragged me out of bed at six a.m. and I seized what was closest on the bedroom floor.

Even in a crowd, I know it's her as soon as she steps through sliding doors to customs with a little pink cabin case. Leela Weber is tall and skinny, lanky almost. Her bleach-blonde hair is in messy space buns and she wears cut-off dungarees over a tie-dye t-shirt. Her platform trainers are highlighter yellow and I've never wanted to be someone else more than I have her.

'Leela!' Deenie waves a card with her name on it. 'Over here, dear!'

Leela's face lights up and she wheels her case in our direction. 'Hallo,' she says shyly.

'Lovely to see you again. How was your flight?' I understand from the drive to the airport that Deenie also ran some of the audition sessions across Europa. 'Leela, this is Taryn, another hopeful.'

'Hey.' My mum had a simple philosophy: never keep a compliment to yourself. 'I need those shoes,' I say.

Knowing a little of Berlin's reputation, I was briefly worried that Leela-from-Germany would be one of those miserable art school types who think smiling is for losers, but she blushes and covers her mouth with her hand like she's shy of her teeth. She needn't; she's exceptionally striking, like eighty per cent cheekbone. 'Oh, thank you! You are kind. My, um, how you say – *room friend* – let me have them in case I am on television.' Her accent is super-cute. I'm impressed with her English. I know about four words in German and they're all curse words.

'Come along, girls,' Deenie shoos us towards the exit. 'Let's grapple with the M25.'

Leela and I ride together in the back of Deenie's ancient Mini Cooper. I guess Network G staff get gasoline. Much of Old London Town still resembles a warzone. It was never truly rebuilt and now nature has reclaimed what was once the capital. Deenie points out the rusted, skeletal arches of something called Wembley Stadium. Apparently it was once where all the biggest popstars in the world performed. Now it's a conservation centre, she says, home to bats, warthogs, adders. She promises to take us.

Leela and I compare notes on the drive. Leela auditioned in Berlin and also made it through on the caveat that she take extra dance training. I get this. If she walked into *my* audition looking like she does today, I wouldn't let her go either. She exudes cool. She already *looks* like an idol.

'I am studying acting?' she says, gesticulating hands with

acrylic nails. Each coffin-shaped nail has a different tiny Sanrio character glued to it. 'But I make music with my brother. He is producer and I sing.'

I wonder what she has to gain from going on *Starmaker*. I feel like Leela would make it without a helping hand from Network G. Dare I say it, she's too cool for *Starmaker*.

'What do you do?' she asks.

'I sing a little.' I squirm slightly as I admit it. So English.

'Ah so I am guessing we are the voices?'

I shrug. 'Someone has to be.' Online, everyone drags B*TRU3 because not one of them can sing live. They're pretty much a joke. They *look* great when they lip-sync though. I remember what Hana said about there being a lack of vocal talent. I file that away for later. However these dance classes go, I have my voice.

'We can sing together,' Leela says. 'Write some lyrics maybe?'

'There's a piano in the ballroom,' Deenie chips in, slowing to avoid a herd of deer crossing the motorway.

'I'd love that.' I say, and mean it. I haven't written song lyrics since Mum died and I had a lot of feelings.

It's been noted (by Molly) that I don't have too many female friends at school. When we got to Scotland, a lot of the girls were settled into their cliques and seemed wary of the refugee girls in particular. They thought we were cuckoos, there to poach their crushes. My friends tend to be guys from the camp. It never occurred to me when I sent my audition clip to *Starmaker* that I could make a very cool German pal.

Only then a second voice slithers into my head, and the

silken tongue says: *Can I sing better than Leela?* and then, *don't get too attached Taryn; you might have to watch her die.*

We call ourselves 2LEFTFEET. Maura, Lieke and Anjali, the rest of our Remedial Dance girl group, arrive over the course of the following twenty-four hours. Suddenly Deenie's crumbling mansion feels a lot smaller. Discarded trainers fill the hallway and now phones, chargers, flavoured lip balms, and hair ties litter every flat surface in every room.

With us all here, and with introductions done, we can't put it off a second longer. It's time to dance.

We gather in the ballroom and run through some comprehensive stretching. From discussions over breakfast – I don't even wanna know how Deenie got hold of bacon and eggs but I'll take it – I've established that *none* of us are dancers. We're all in the same boat and that's comforting.

Because Leela and I are sharing the twin room, I know her a little better than the others. Anjali is a tiny thing and looks younger than her fifteen years. She has Disney princess eyes, and her hair shimmers like a black waterfall down her back. Maura is a freckled redhead and I can see why they'd cast her; she exemplifies Irish stereotypes, and they *love* a stereotype on *Starmaker*. Lieke, from the Netherlands, is more of an enigma thus far – androgynous with her bowl cut hair and tank top, and she doesn't talk much. A part of me thinks she'll need to conjure a personality if she's gonna make the cut. The other part hopes she doesn't because that's another one down.

Stretching done, Deenie approaches the laptop she's hooked

up to the speakers. 'Okay, ladies! Are we warmed up and ready to go?'

'No!' I call out, and everyone laughs. I needed to pop the nervous bubble.

'Oh we're starting with a very challenging number from yesteryear . . .' Deenie hits play. I don't recognize it.

'Ladies, may I introduce the "Macarena". Follow me.'

Arm, arm, arm, arm. Chest, chest, head, head. Waist, waist, hip, hip . . . and jump. She repeats this routine. Surely it can't be so easy. All facing the mirror, we copy Deenie. We're on the third rotation – now facing the back of the ballroom – when Leela starts to laugh. It's infectious. What the hell do we look like?

'This time make the hips work, dip a little lower. That's right, girls, now you look very sexy!' We all laugh at that.

We scroll through the simple routine until the song ends and I feel honestly a bit dizzy. 'Is that as hard as it gets?' Lieke says, taking a sip of water.

'You wish, my dear,' Deenie says. 'The point of that was to teach you the most important lesson of all: Dancing is meant to be *fun*. Dancing *together* even more so. Once upon a time, young women who sang and danced together were called witches. Why? Because there is a power in it, a female unity. Yes, the dance steps will get much harder, but it's always about finding that unity.'

I've never thought of it that way. It's a team sport, not a race. If someone is trying to outdance me, they're actually ruining the dance.

'Right! If you enjoyed the "Macarena", you'll lose your

mind for "Saturday Night". Follow me!'

I laugh so much my face aches by the end of the day. When it hits three p.m. Anjali and Maura have to go to a tutor to do school work so we wrap it up then. Deenie, I think, might be a genius. By the time we finished, we were doing "Saturday Night" in double speed, and turning in different directions to one another, to make it more complicated. She filmed us on her phone and we looked . . . okay? I'm definitely not the worst.

Rehearsal done, we pile down to the kitchen. There is more food in Deenie's home than I can remember seeing in my life. The fridge and pantry are stuffed to overflowing.

'I guess it's all from Network G,' I say, helping myself to some crisps and cola.

'This is what life will be like for the winners. We'll never be hungry again,' Lieke says.

We gather at the kitchen table. Leela dips a carrot in hummus which I think is the height of sophistication. My cheese and onion crisps seem a bit childish now. 'What if we are the band?' Leela ponders. 'This is all pretend and they're filming us right now?'

No survival show, no rankings, no savage competition . . . just a series about some friendly girls training to be idols. 'That's a nice thought, but would anyone watch that?'

'I would,' Leela says.

'Me too actually. I hate the bit when . . .' The rest doesn't need saying. The bit where they die.

Lieke shrugs. 'Sacrifice is vital for the survival of the human race. We will be remembered as heroes. I am glad to die for my country.'

Leela and I share a subtle look. Like, is she okay?

That night, after a carb-loaded dinner of pasta Bolognese with cheese, we realize – with abject horror – that Deenie doesn't own a television. 'There's nothing worth watching,' she insists and I wonder if she knows that's a damning indictment of her employer.

With our only other options being reading or chess, Leela petitions us to return to the ballroom piano. There, she performs a dainty tune in her acrylics. Impressive. Damn; that's something she has on me. She writes songs *and* plays piano *and* studies acting. A double threat, if not triple. 'What song do we all know?' Leela asks.

'What about something by Nico?' I suggest to much agreement from the others. We all grew up on the Nico diet.

'I can play "Lovers' Lament"?'

We all know that one; it's maybe her biggest ballad. Lieke asks who is a soprano or an alto, and neither Anjali or I have a clue. It's been ten years since I last heard Mum use those terms.

'Taryn, you go first,' Leela says as she plays the intro.

I dig into my internal catalogue and pull the lyrics from memory.

A black hole where you used to be
Lately I'm stranded at sea
Drowning alone
There's nobody home
Please pick up your phone.

Leela takes over for the second part of the verse.

All of those things that we said
Getting so cold in our bed
Dreaming again
Can we still be friends?
Is this where we end?

Leela's voice is breathy, sensual and unique. Damn. If you heard her on the radio, you'd know it was her in a second. Do I have such a distinctive voice?

Maura takes the bridge, and then Lieke jumps in for the chorus, with Anjali throwing in some insane harmonies that I didn't see coming. By the second chorus, we sing as a group and it sounds beautiful. Deenie admires us from the threshold of the ballroom, seemingly summoned by our chorus. She was right. Singing as one does feel like witchcraft; we exist together in a moment.

At the end of the song, I tackle some of the more ambitious ad-libs (*will I ever feel normal agaaaaaain?*) and I briefly see Leela glance up at me, impressed. Good. I hope the others hear too.

As Deenie applauds, I feel a little snuggle of pride in my chest.

It doesn't last. For the first time, I'm *scared*. And that's like a sliver of ice in my ribcage.

Having a good voice isn't going to be enough. We *all* have nice voices. I need something else or I'm going to die on television.

It doesn't take me long to pack my meagre things into my holdall. I work in silence. Leela's rhythmic breaths tell me she's deep in sleep. I slip out of our room unnoticed.

It's after one-thirty in the middle of the night and Grenville Abbott is quiet aside from the steady dripping of rain hitting the tin bucket at the foot of the stairs.

I don't have much of a strategy beyond getting to the coach station at Victoria and waiting for the first bus north. I have *some* money. I hope it's enough. I lift my suitcase off the hallway tiles so I don't make any noise. I tiptoe towards the front doors.

'Are you leaving?'

I don't scream, but I inhale so sharply my back arches. 'Holy crap, I didn't know you were there.' Little Anjali is in the drawing room off the hallway, sitting in the dark. 'What are you doing?'

'Couldn't sleep. I miss my mum and brothers. I made some hot chocolate. You want some?'

Even in the gloom, her doe eyes glimmer hopefully. 'Anjali, I . . . yeah. I'm leaving.'

'What? Why?'

I take a seat on the musty chaise longue opposite her. I sigh deeply. 'Because tonight it hit me: if we get picked for the survival show there's only a fifty-fifty chance we . . . *survive.*'

Ten girls enter the Dreamhouse, only five girls make the cut.

'But we sounded so good.'

'You're *fifteen*.' She says nothing but she knows what I mean. She is a child. 'Don't get me wrong, I've watched *Starmaker* for years, but they were just faces on a screen. They weren't real people. I had favourites, and I hated some of them. They were heroes and villains, but it was all fake. They were just like us. And they *died.*'

Anjali sits up straight. 'My sister died of measles when she was a baby. My grandma died of the French flu. The guy next door fell down the stairs and died because the ambulance didn't get to him for two hours. What makes you think you won't die anyway? At least this way there's a chance.'

I am speechless. How can this cute little thing be so jaded? I wish I could argue, and say all the best things in life are free, but she's right. Medicine, sun screen, fresh food, air purifiers, and water filters all cost money. The best things in life are reserved for the rich.

If I go home now, it might be Jenson. It might be Dad. It might be me or Mol. This whole wretched world is a survival show.

'Go on then,' I whisper. 'I'll have some hot chocolate.'

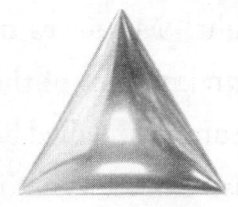

CHAPTER 11

Deenie promised it would get harder, and she wasn't lying. On the second day, she started teaching us some proper girl group choreo. I don't know if she's trying to be funny, but we learn the routine to another of her childhood favourites: 'Survivor' by Destiny's Child.

It is not like the 'Macarena'.

I don't think I've truly appreciated how physically demanding dance is. Thank god for lugging gas tanks across the camp or I don't know if I'd have the stamina.

On the morning of Day Three, I awake to legs so stiff, and a butt so sore from squatting, that I can scarcely walk downstairs to breakfast.

Day Four is 'Survivor' again. Stomping, a lot of stomping. 'Girls!' Deenie hollers over the music. 'You're meant to be fighters. Think about your faces!'

In the mirror, the only thing I look like is clammy and milky white. My arms are fine. My legs are fine. Making my arms and legs move at the same time proves impossible. My brain can't process it all.

The only saving grace is that I'm not the worst. That honour goes to either Leela, whose longs limbs aren't ideal for street dance, or Anjali, who seems to forget routines seconds after Deenie has shown us what to do. She gets flappy and frustrated when she stumbles.

We are expected in the studio at nine a.m. for stretching and warm-up. Deenie then runs us through some basic terminology: locking; popping; isolation; plié; whacking; canon versus unison. I like the new vocabulary more than I like doing it. It turns out I have muscles I never knew I possessed.

Lesson over, we put what we learned into practice: watching music videos and studying Deenie. We walk through each section before we try it to music. Somehow, this munches up time and, before we know it, we break for lunch. The afternoons are spent perfecting what we've learned in the morning. Anjali and Maura go for school lessons at three, so Leela, Lieke and I remain to practice singing at the same time as dancing.

By the time night falls, I ache all over. I stink. Every day brings a weird new blister. I'm collapsing into bed before nine, utterly spent.

Day Six and we graduate to 'Gnarly' by Katseye. I remember this from when I was little. This routine is even more complex than 'Survivor'. It's faster and involves formation changes – or switching our positions on the floor to get into the centre. Deenie sticks little spots on the ballroom floor, each a different colour, so that we can learn the sequence by colour: red to yellow to blue to red again to purple, then green.

Predictably, our first attempts involve a lot of collisions and hurried *sorrys*. Deenie films us. We watch the video back, and we look like a dropped trifle.

'Girls,' Deenie says, despairingly. 'Do you understand there are going to be finalists who've been learning these skills since they were four or five years old? This simply isn't good enough!'

When everyone else has left the ballroom, I remain, trying to weld the steps to memory. Why can't I get my feet to move at the same time as my hands? It's akin to rubbing my stomach and patting my head simultaneously. I just can't.

I'm so hot-faced with frustration, I don't even realize that Deenie is in the ballroom. 'Come downstairs for dinner, Taryn.'

'In a minute,' I say.

'I don't think a minute is going to transform you into Ginger Rogers, dear.'

Who? 'I have to nail this.' I fold to the floor like a puppet with cut strings, and rest my head in my hands. 'Otherwise, all this was pointless. I could have been working by now. That's a month's wages I gave up to be here.'

'You're getting better every day.'

I look up at the older woman. 'You don't think I'm a hopeless case?'

The dance teacher crouches at my side, with the springy knees of someone far younger. 'Don't say that, sweet girl. Your generation is this planet's only shot. If *you* lose hope now, we're all doomed, I fear.'

I make a wry huff out of my nostrils.

'Taryn, I know you think of yourself as a born singer, but no one is. I don't think talent is some innate genetic trait. I'm sure you sang along to the radio from a young age, and *that* was your training. You've just come to dance later. It's a muscle. The more you work it, the bigger it gets.' She plucks a stray hair off my face and lowers her voice. 'Sweetheart, there's something inside you. I see it, and I'm seldom wrong. An inner strength, a core of steel. You can be whatever you want to be.'

'But what if I don't know what I want to be?'

Deenie smiles. 'That's the actual hard part.' She offers me a hand. 'Come along. It's shepherd's pie for supper.'

As I eat dinner with the others, I wonder how it is that Deenie can see something in me, because I'm pretty sure I'm just a hollow shell filled with tangled anxieties where organs should be. I run an inventory of my feelings while I eat. I know I want to win this thing for Jenson, so we can be the little pigs who build their house out of bricks. I know I love to sing. Maybe being certain of those two things is enough.

But I would be a fool to think I want this any more than these other girls. I wonder what their reasons are. Or do they really think they're that good? I wish I had their confidence.

It gnaws away at me well into the night. Sleep feels miles away. I hear Leela tossing and turning in the other bed. 'Lee?'

'Ja?'

'Are you awake?'

'Nein.'

I prop myself up on an elbow. 'Can I ask a question?'

Leela faces me in the silvery moonlight creeping in at the edges of the curtains. 'You may.'

'Why are you here?'

She considers me a moment. 'I could ask you the same question.'

'My brother,' I reply without hesitation. 'He's very sick.'

She nods, almost imperceptibly. She sits up and wraps her quilt over her shoulders like a cape and crosses the bedroom to perch on my bed. 'If I tell you, you cannot tell anyone. *Starmaker* do not know.'

Her icy blue eyes bore into me. She's earnest, but she always is. I think she's insane to tell me anything I could use against her. I'm not evil, but she doesn't know that. 'Leela, is this going to get me in trouble?'

'No.' I nod, signalling for her to go on. 'Okay. I am telling you my truth. When I was born, they are saying I am a boy.'

'Oh. You're trans?'

She nods. 'In Germany is not illegal.'

She's referring to the Deviancy Act. When I was little, the British government brought in new laws to *protect family values*. If anyone – doctors or teachers – help children transition, they face jail for *grooming*. And it's not just trans people. The first time I kissed a girl (Kristen Miller, down by the river), I was terrified someone would report me for "public obscenity" under the same laws.

Leela goes on. 'But my mother and father are, how do you say? Assholes?'

'That is what we say.' I smile meekly.

'So I am living with my grandmother in Berlin until she

died last year. Now I have nothing. I work two jobs to pay my college fees and for my hormones.'

'But this show . . .'

Leela shrugs. 'I would rather be dead than live as a boy.'

'Don't say that.'

She doesn't flinch. 'But it is my truth.'

I take a deep breath. Leela *really* shouldn't have told me that. In the Blue States of America, it's perfectly legal to be trans, but I have no idea what *Starmaker*'s rules are regarding transgender competitors. Wasn't there a trans man on one of the boyband seasons? I think there was but he didn't make it far. Might have even been a first out. 'Are you going to tell *Starmaker*?'

'I don't know. Maybe if I am selected for the survival show.'

'It's a good story.' The cynic in me can't deny that.

She sighs sadly. 'I am not sure that the assholes online will agree.'

She has a point there. I'm certainly not planning on telling anyone I'm queer for the same reason. 'Look, I promise I won't say anything. I'm not that girl.'

'I know,' she says. 'This is why I tell you.'

It is a madness to get attached to anyone here, but nonetheless I open my arms wide and offer her a hug. She hooks her chin over my shoulder. 'Thank you for trusting me.'

The next morning, Leela and I eat cereal in friendly quiet. It's like we've psychically agreed that what we spoke of at midnight will never be spoken of again. We finish breakfast and head to the ballroom. It's finally spring, and golden columns pour from the skylight to the dancefloor.

Only Lieke and Maura are warming up with Deenie when we arrive. She throws us an impatient glare. 'Let's get going, girls. You're late.'

'Where is Anjali?' Leela asks, peeling off her hoodie.

Deenie pauses, and the silence chills the studio. Something's the matter. Deenie doesn't look us in the eyes as she says, 'It wasn't working out. She wasn't making progress. We agreed she should go home last night.'

It feels like there's a cactus wedged in my throat. I never got her number. There's no way to say a farewell. Maura is avoiding my gaze, but she has pink-rimmed eyes. They were roommates.

I can't believe they just sent Anjali away. So cold.

But, on the other hand, they haven't sent me home yet.

Hope after all.

STARMAKER: YOU DECIDE!

This Military Heroes Day, **YOU** decide your ***STARMAKER*** finalists!

Step 1: Download the official Starmaker app.
Step 2: Register your face ID, iris and fingerprint.
Step 3: Watch all hundred contenders perform.
Step 4: LOVE or SHOVE each performer!

It's THAT easy!

Only ten performers with the most fandom love will proceed to the Dreamhouse for a chance to join a new idol girl group.

STARMAKER — coming this summer only on Network G.

Sponsored by FreshElla: The Ultimate Feminine Protection

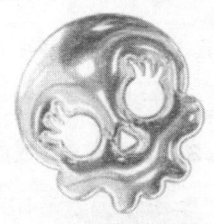

CHAPTER 12

They take us in blacked-out solar SUVs to a studio compound in somewhere called Watford. It's a spiteful, drizzly day, like the sky doesn't want me looking my best for the online portion of the contest.

On this drab day, Hana hustles us into an even drabber cube of a building. If I thought this was going to be glamorous, I was wrong. I'm briskly separated from the others and dropped at an individual dressing room where I'm greeted by a busty woman with lilac hair. She chews on a wad of gum the size of a golf ball. 'You awight doll?' She gestures that I should sit in her salon chair. 'I'm Lavinia. I'm your glam for the day.'

'My glam?'

'Well.' She rolls eyes framed with spiky blue lashes. 'We call this Girl Next Door. They want you looking natural so your makeovers are more dramatic if you get into the Dreamhouse.' She pronounces it *Dreamarse* and I stifle a giggle. She sounds like how London people used to sound. I can imagine her pumping a beer tap in an old East End tavern.

We are here to create the content for *if* we make it to the online eliminations. Every year, to build hype for *Starmaker*, they whittle it down from a hundred to ten using an online vote. They need to do these pictures today with the British girls they've already selected, but we have also been warned that the producers have not yet decided on the final hundred. We *also* don't know how many other girls are at the studios today. Being kept in the dark isn't helping the reptilian voices in my head telling me to despair.

I'm not the only one. On the drive up, Maura and Lieke bickered the whole way about a granola bar Maura had allegedly stolen. I wonder if the producers want us frayed; makes for great TV down the line.

Lavinia cleanses my skin and applies some light makeup. It's not the swipe of mascara I do if I'm trying to impress someone; in the space of twenty fast minutes, she transforms me into a young *woman*. No spots or blackheads; my wonky eyebrows are suddenly even. She blow-dries my mousy hair in such a way that it looks thick, bouncy and healthy. I look like I should belong on one of the Network G teen dramas: *Cadets of Courage* or something.

With annoyance, she realizes her hairspray has run out. 'Hold on here a sec, doll; I'll get some from next door. You sit tight though; you ain't meant to meet each other.'

I don't ask why. I play on my phone for a moment, sending a selfie to Molly. She won't believe how good I look. She'll think some private school pony-girl has nicked my phone. I can't believe how much I miss her and Jenson.

In the mirror, I see a familiar woman swoop down the corridor beyond my dressing room. At first I think she's one of the production team, only then I place her: it's Emmy's mum – from the NP audition. That must mean Emmy made it to the final cut too. She was kind of catty, but I do want to see her and tell her I got this far. Of all the girls who queued across England, two girls randomly next to each other in line made it through. What are the odds of that?

Ignoring Lavinia's warning, I slide off my seat and follow Emmy's mother to the dressing room three down from mine. My hand hovers before it can knock, halted by angry voices on the other side. 'Mum, I feel really sick! I can feel the chunks coming up!'

'Oh shut up, Emmy! Just shut up! I'm sick of hearing it.'

'Please, I can't do it.'

'Are you going to tell Daddy you wimped out at the last minute? Are you? After everything he's spent on your lessons? On your nose?'

Emmy goes quiet. I back away from their door. Now is clearly not the time for a reunion. It's weird: Emmy's mum being a psycho only makes me miss *my* mum even more. She never made me sing; she would have been quite happy for me to listen. I remember her singing us to sleep in our old Exeter home. The memory is so gauzy it might not even be real; it might be a lovely lie I've painted on my brain in watercolours. I recall her stroking my hair as I fell asleep. She would sing 'Moon River'. It was from some ancient movie. *My hukka berry friend.* I never did find out what a hukka berry is.

'Oi!' It's Lavinia, FreshElla hairspray in hand. 'What did I say 'bout wandering off?'

'Sorry,' I say.

Before I leave, I turn back to Emmy's changing room and bang on the door. I want her mum to know someone is listening and she shouldn't speak to her daughter that way. 'Five minutes!' I call, hurrying away before I'm sighted.

Deenie's Remedial Dance girls *are* allowed to mingle in a cramped kitchen area because we already know each other, so where's the harm. Each of us has been given a very simple black, skin-tight, *Starmaker* t-shirt to wear. At this stage, we're supposed to be judged on our talent alone, not the visual. That said, we all look very pretty with our Girl Next Door glam. Leela really could be a model. She's effortlessly chic. I think fans will be obsessed with her.

After what feels like hours of waiting, Hana enters our little holding area. 'Okay! Taryn, we're ready for you.'

I'd anticipated something fancier from the studios. One anonymous corridor pivots into another; a beige labyrinth, marked only with ON AIR light boxes above the doors. With every step, a nervousness seizes up my muscles, like I'm being filled with liquid cement. Oh god, I thought I was fine. I am *not* fine.

As if sensing this, Hana stops me outside one of the studios. 'Okay, this is us,' she says. 'Do you need anything? Your guitar and some water are already inside.'

I tell her I'll be fine. I attempt a smile, even though I think I'm now physically shaking and struggling to blink.

The soundproofed studio doors open with a strange sucking noise and I enter. The room is dark, aside from a bubble of bright spotlight in front of the *Starmaker* logo. Each of us had a choice: sing, dance or both. I guess this influences which studio we're assigned. I just wanted to sing, obviously, so my room is compact. I can make out padded walls on all sides. A single camera is posed before a stool against which a guitar is propped.

This could not be more strange. Sometimes I sing to myself, but – let's face it – any performer is a needy li'l junkie who thrives on the drug of attention. Now I'm singing to an unmanned camera lens. It stares at me, unblinking, like a cold, black eye.

I step into the spotlight. I clear my throat and take up the guitar.

'Hi, Taryn!' A disembodied voice is piped into the studio. 'My name is Sven; I'm recording today. Whenever you're ready, you can begin. Don't worry if you make a mistake; we're gonna do three takes.'

Oh yeah? 'You use the best take right?'

There's an *almost* imperceptible pause. But I perceive it. 'Oh, of course!' he replies. 'Off you go! Good luck!'

I exhale. In my mind, the charcoal foam walls fall back and I'm around the campfire at the QE II. I have done this a squillion times.

Here I only need to pull it out three times. How hard can it be?

I've chosen to sing 'Bridge Over Troubled Water'. Yes, it's a huge risk to perform a song that's almost, like, a hundred years old but it recently went viral on G-Net so I thought it was quite a canny choice. Plus, Dad loves this one. Plus, plus it's notoriously hard to sing so I'm showing off.

All I can do is sing the ruddy song. On the second time I

fluff a couple of chords but I doubt you'd notice. By the end of the third take, I've half zoned out, thinking about what they'll give us for lunch. I couldn't say which my *best take* was.

'Thank you, Taryn. That was lovely.' This is a new voice, not Sven's. It's deep and rich, curling around the studio like cigar smoke.

'Hello?'

There's a long silence. I watch flecks of dust swirl under the blinding spotlights pointed right at my face.

'Am I done? Do I go now?'

'Taryn, this is *Chairman Slade*.'

I sit upright on the stool.

The idea that he just heard me sing (three times over) is insane.

'Are you here?' I ask, awed.

'I'm watching online from our offices in New Japan.' His accent is placeless; sort of British, or maybe Dutch? 'So you already know who I am?'

'Who doesn't?'

'I'm flattered. That was very polished.'

'Thank you.'

'How badly do you want this, Taryn?'

My mouth hangs open, a surprised O. 'I . . . I'm really passionate about music . . . and . . .'

'Tell the truth,' he snaps. He sounds impatient. 'Say what you mean, not what you think I want to hear.'

Oh sod it. 'Okay. My family has nothing. My brother is sick. This could change our lives.'

'Are you prepared to die for this?'

I get it. This is the Bad Cop Final Warning. I guess to scare off potential last minute dropouts.

I slump on the stool, like my spine has given up on gravity. 'Do you know what the average life expectancy is for someone living on ration boxes in a settlement camp? Fifty-nine. My dad is forty-seven. I want more than twelve years with him.'

There's another long pause. 'You are excused. Thank you, Taryn. Good luck with your final evaluation.'

CHAPTER 13

Five weeks of dancing and singing. We are joined by Justyna and Eva, a couple of girls from Poland; their English isn't great and they keep to themselves after hours.

We are mostly too exhausted to do anything except train, eat and sleep, but chronically online Leela has some friends in Old London Town. Eventually, even the sprawling mansion starts to feel too small, and I agree to go out-out with her.

Artists can afford to live in the former capital again now that it's a ruin, and a couple of times we go to parties in disused churches or hangar-sized old factory buildings that have been converted into communes. Leela, who can make anything she wears look like a fashion statement, blends in effortlessly while I feel like her dowdy sidekick.

She asks that I don't tell her friends – who are all performance artists or indie musicians – that she's in training for *Starmaker*. She tells me they wouldn't approve. Turns out she's right.

One Friday night, we're in one such squat. There are maybe seventy or eighty bodies pressed into the loft. A DJ plays grinding, dirty, industrial techno. This is how I imagine music to be in Berlin. It's loud enough to block out most of my thoughts about the competition and maybe that's the point. It's nice to dance how I used to dance, just throwing my limbs around without caring if I am synchronized.

Sweat running down our backs, Leela and I grab water bottles and retreat to a sofa covered in cigarette burns and questionable stains. We're joined by Jamila, who is wearing sunglasses at night, and Tommy, a white man with dreadlocks. He vapes constantly, puffing foul faux-blueberry gas into our faces.

'Who was it who said television was the opiate of the masses?' he asks.

'It was Karl Marx,' Leela says. 'But he is saying it about religion.'

He doesn't look thrilled that she corrected him in front of Jamila. 'Whatever. It's true though. They're sheep.'

'Who?' Jamila asks.

'All those basics in the towns and villages. While the planet is literally dying, they just turn on their TVs and rot their brains.'

'Opium is a painkiller, right?' I say. 'I think we know we're doomed, and it hurts because we can't do anything to stop it. So we take the painkiller to . . . get through it. It's too scary to think about what's gonna happen to us.' The students look at me as though I am an alien, or, worse, a child. 'Or something.'

'I think you're right,' Jamila says. 'But we have to resist. You guys coming to the march tomorrow?'

'What march?' I ask.

'The demo,' Tommy says. 'There's a massive protest outside the new Network G station.'

'What are you protesting?' Leela asks.

Tommy makes a face as if she is simple. 'Um . . . Chairman Slade is scum? Network G is trash. Killing kids on TV. And they're introducing new rules on G-Net where the police can arrest you for posting "treasonous sentiment". Like, what does that even mean?'

Leela frowns. 'How will marching stop them?'

'Make our voices heard.'

You can make your voice *loud*; it doesn't mean it's being heard. It's so naïve I almost feel sorry for him. If the public are eating popcorn while kids are dying on TV, does he really think a placard is going to shift the moral needle? I remember what Deenie said all those weeks ago about hope and despair, but hope is on a losing streak.

Back in the day, Mum and Dad marched against the relocation scheme and, for a while, that satisfied them that they'd done their civic duty. We were still relocated, but they said then that it was better than doing nothing. Doing nothing is complicity. 'We'll go,' I say suddenly and Leela frowns.

'Taryn,' Leela says. 'We can't.'

'Why not?' It may well be futile, but – as annoying as I find him – Tommy is right. We can't do *nothing*.

Groggy after getting in so late, I very nearly change my mind to stay in bed. Leela, however, has had a change of heart. 'My brother, Felix, says we should go.' Leela talks a lot, and always with great admiration, about her older brother back in

Germany. 'He says we must cover our faces.'

No problem. We take air filtration masks and wear hoodies to Piccadilly Circus. Once, this was all shops and restaurants. Now, the stores are mostly boarded up, but Network G has rebuilt all the vast electronic billboards and installed a new TV studio overlooking the junction. They broadcast local news from here I think. One of the massive screens changes from a Coca-Cola ad to one that reads: *Starmaker: Coming Soon*. It's like they know we're here.

The intersection is closed to traffic, and already crammed with masked protesters. They're mostly our age, but not exclusively. The handmade placards carry slogans like NETWORK G FOR GENOCIDE; FREE SPEECH IS FOR EVERYONE NOT JUST FASCISTS; KILLING KIDS FOR ENTERTAINMENT; FIVE FAMILIES RULE THE WORLD. I don't know what they all mean. The Five Families conspiracy is an online thing Molly goes on about sometimes.

The perimeter of Piccadilly Circus is encircled by armoured, and armed, riot police with visors and shields. There seems to be almost as many police as there are protesters, which is excessive given that the mood feels more like a festival than a disturbance. Like Tommy said last night, I think the people here just want to be seen and heard. Maybe someone at home will see us all on TV and realize they're not the only ones who think the system is unjust.

We locate Tommy, Jamila and some other art students in the throng. 'Do your phones work?' he demands as soon as we arrive.

I check, and I have no reception at all.

'They're blocking the signal,' Jamila says. 'Can you believe it? So we can't stream footage.' So much for inspiring the folks at home.

A middle-aged woman with a shaved head clambers all the way up the statue of Eros. She has a loudspeaker in her hand. There's a banshee howl of static before her voice booms across the junction. 'Network G is owned by a corrupt billionaire.' Yep, that's what Molly says too. I find conspiracy stuff a bit tin-foil hat. 'Kerwin Groenveld decides who we vote for; he doesn't pay taxes; he pushes propaganda and drives millions into poverty. His grip on the media has normalized the suffering of ninety-nine per cent of the world's population. Network G is lying to you. Film this! Film this and flood G-Net. They can't arrest us all! LIAR! LIAR! LIAR!'

The crowd takes up her call. I pull my hood further over my face. There are TV vans outside the Network G building. I'm terrified we'll be caught on camera and disqualified. This was a bad idea. 'Come on,' I tell Leela. 'I think we've made our point.'

She nods, also wary of the cameras. 'Okay.'

We weave our way through the crowd, attempting to get back down Regent Street, only to find our exit blocked by the riot squad. I try to squeeze through, but a police officer shoves a shield towards me. 'Stay on the square!' he barks.

'There must be another way out,' Leela says. We push through the throng, this time leaving via one of the other arteries off the circus. I'm not sure if it's my imagination, but the crowd seems to be getting more tightly packed. I find my face pressed into someone's armpit: a mixture of deodorant and BO. I try to back up but there's nowhere to back up to.

As we make our way towards Coventry Street, the mass of bodies starts to sway. Pushing and shoving causes a ripple through the human tide. An undercurrent. I feel my heartbeat quicken. My blood feels fizzy. 'I don't like this,' I mutter to Leela.

'Me either.'

Everyone seems taller than me. I can't see the sky. I try to gulp in some air.

Suddenly the entire demonstration lurches forwards. Someone behind us is pushing towards the line of riot shields. 'GET BACK!' an officer yells.

'We're not doing anything!' someone screams in reply.

I see it on faces. Worry. Everyone, all as one, turns for the way out. The crowd surges and I'm once more moved without moving. 'Stop!' I bleat, but no one listens. My body moves independently of my feet, carried on the wave. Leela grips my wrist. 'Don't let go!' I cry.

I'm pressed against Leela to one side and a wiry man to the other. Someone close by cries out in pain. Someone screams *let her stand up*. I hear a police horse whinny.

'GET BACK!'

We're so compressed, I don't know which way is out any more.

'Tear gas!' someone shrieks.

Are they serious?

'Cover your eyes!' Leela gasps.

What is happening? This went south so fast. I cling to Leela. I feel like I'm at the bottom of a human pile. I'm drowning. Now the protest swings in the opposite direction, trying to avoid the gas. People start to scream.

A shot is fired, a whipcrack. My stomach drops. They're shooting at us. Or is it warning shots to the sky? I look up and see a mounted horse steer into the crowd. The horseback officers carry what look like electro batons, they lash them down on heads below. A woman covers her head with her hands as a female officer cracks her baton onto her skull.

'This way!' It's Leela. She's found an opening. I gulp as much air into my lungs as I can. She drags me towards Shaftesbury Avenue. I almost trip, but she yanks me along. Demonstrators have broken through the police line and are sprinting towards Leicester Square. 'Follow them!'

The riot police flourish their electro batons, but there are too many of us stampeding past them to be effective. All around me I hear the *clak-clak-clak* of volts discharging. I brace for a pain that doesn't arrive.

To my right, a spooked horse rears up with an anxious whinny, before stamping down on a young protester. She screams as she goes under the hooves. Leela drags me away.

With the boundary broken, we manage to put some distance between us and the crowd. We find a place to rest by something called the Windmill Club. It looks like it's been derelict for years. Leela rubs her eyes. 'Are you okay?' I ask.

'I got some gas I think.' Her eyes look pink and watery.

'We need to rinse them. Let's find water.'

We head towards the shabby sex shops and tattoo parlours of Soho. Gay bars are legal as long as they have no windows and a bartender in the Duke of Wellington takes pity on us and lets us use their bathroom. It's only there that my heartrate returns to normal. We are safe. I help Leela rinse her eyes at the sink, repeating *we're okay, we're okay* like some sort of mantra.

I'm not sure who I'm trying to convince, her or me.

That night, once we're back at Deenie's mansion, we watch Network G news on Leela's laptop.

'Further updates on today's civil unrest in Old London Town,' the plastic blonde newsreader says sombrely. Behind her, still images are displayed of what looks to be sinister, masked rioters - all hulking men - attacking the police. 'Violence erupted after armed extremists attempted to force entry to a Network G building. Police horses were attacked, and two insurgents were killed as authorities tried to maintain the peace . . .'

A simpering politician comes on to condemn the protesters. She looks half-human, half-mole. We can't say anything with the other girls present, but I look to Leela and I know we're thinking the same thing. *Network G lies.*

CHAPTER 14

We're kept in the dark about the timeline of the auditions – none of us are sure why. All I can think is that *Starmaker* wants to keep us on our toes. After Anjali left, we never knew if any given day would be our last. No one from Production comes to Grenville Abbott. Deenie sometimes refers to them as *the Powers That Be*.

Somewhere around the fourth week, she introduces the concept of Final Evaluation. Because we've been so routinely filmed, I always assumed *someone* was watching the footage, but now we are to be directly compared to the other finalists. This is the last chance to impress our way out of Remedial Dance 101.

'Next week, we start Final Evaluation,' Deenie explains one afternoon in the ballroom. 'You'll perform 'Gnarly' as a group and then 'Survivor' solo. The footage will then go all the way to Chairman Slade so he can make the final decision about whether any of you will proceed to the online vote.'

Justyna rapidly translates for Eva. Lieke mutters something to Leela.

'You will also sing a song of your choice to show off your vocals. This is the last audition, girls. Last chance.'

'Have you met Chairman Slade?' Leela asks.

Deenie, unconsciously I think, looks over her shoulder. 'Of course.'

I'm a little surprised. The man is a recluse. 'Really? What's he like?'

'He's a very clever man,' she replies cautiously. 'He knows exactly what fans want. He respects precision and perfection. That means you girls need to be precise and perfect. There's no room for mistakes. A mistake could cost you your life.'

When the day comes, I'm so nervous my insides feel pretzel-twisted. The anxiety curls my bones. For the first time, some Network G people, including Hana, come down to Old London Town and invade Grenville Abbott. Cameras and blinding white lights are set up in the ballroom. It's strange how quickly this ramshackle manor has come to feel like home and I don't like these intruders stomping about in their utility shorts and *Starmaker* hoodies.

Leela does my makeup. Stage makeup is not the same as makeup-makeup and she piles it on. Justyna is a natural leader, and suggests we pool our clothes to come up with some notion of a group 'look'. Between us we have enough combat pants and tank tops to form a vague khaki desert trooper concept.

We take it in turns to do the solo bits. We go alphabetically, so I have to wait until last. I sit outside the ballroom, upstairs on the marble landing, dangling my legs over the regal entrance hall, forced to listen to the other five sing in turn. If I never hear 'Survivor' again after today, I'm fine with that. We're too nervous to talk to each other. I think there's a risk that if we open our mouths to speak, we'll puke. I don't know where the others are.

Deenie comes up the staircase, cupping a hot lemon and ginger in her thin hands. The worry must read on my face. 'You have nothing to worry about, Taryn.'

I look up at her. 'Do you know how many girls we're up against?'

'There are about three hundred girls still in the running I believe.'

I almost drop off the landing. 'Oh my god.'

'Don't even think about them!'

'But I'm not the best—' I start.

Deenie cuts me off. 'Piffle. The *best* one never wins. The *favourite* one does.' She squeezes my hand. 'They saw *something* in you, or they wouldn't have brought you here. So sell it.'

'I don't know how,' I confess.

'Act. Just fake it. Who's your character?'

'What do you mean?'

'I've been doing this a long time and idol groups are all the same. Are you the cute one? Are you the sexy one? Are you the bubbly, fun one? The leader?'

I think a moment. 'I'm the fighter. The scrappy, gobby one.'

She smiles. 'Then get in that room and *fight*.'

* * *

'Hi, Taryn,' Hana says. She's positioned alongside the cameraman. 'Whenever you're ready, introduce yourself to the camera.'

'Hello. I'm Taryn Beck. I'm seventeen and I'm a refugee from Scotland.'

The music starts.

As I perform 'Survivor', I think about the words. A rebuttal to a bitter rival, or an ex who thought I'd never achieve anything. I'm a refugee from a camp. The world gave up on us as soon as our homes were flooded. We became a problem to be swept under a rug. We were unwanted.

I glare down the barrel of the camera and I am fury. I don't even have to fake it. I stamp, I punch, I kick. *I fight.*

I *am* a survivor.

And . . .

We get sent home.

Anti-climax barely begins to cover it.

We are told nothing except that someone from the production team will be in touch.

Saying goodbye to Deenie is unexpectedly tough. I should have seen it coming, but losing even a strict, bendy version of a surrogate mother figure feels like a kick in the ribs. She drops me at Kings Cross train station on my last day.

'Will you be there?' I ask as rain pitter patters on the windscreen of her car. 'In the Dreamhouse?'

She barks a bitter laugh. 'Oh, darling, they don't want my withered old face on the television. You'll get some shiny young thing who's never taught a day in their life.'

I shrug. '*If* I get in.'

Deenie cups my cheek with bejewelled fingers. 'Given all that's at stake, I can't decide if I'm rooting for you or not, sweet thing. You're my favourite. Don't tell anyone I said that.'

I smile. 'Did you say that to all of us?'

'Yes.' She winks, and steps out of the Mini to fetch my guitar from the boot.

In the meantime, Leela and I message every day asking if the other has heard anything. It's a fun game.

I return to a smaller version of the QE II. It hasn't physically shrunk, but after six weeks in Old London Town, the camp is an ant farm. Everything looks rusty and dog-eared. Compared to Grenville Abbott, our unit is a shoebox; much too small for four grown bodies. I had a glimpse of something bigger. And now it's gone. The thought that this is all there will be for the rest of my life is suddenly quite sickening. Whatever happens with *Starmaker*, I'm not sure my future is in this little town.

Still, Dad has barely left my side since I got back. I hurt my shoulder during rehearsals for Final Evaluation so, in the evening, he ices the injury and we watch whatever movies I want to watch. Jenson goes out most nights. He doesn't say where he's going, but I suspect he's seeing Tobey from round the corner. I hope he's being smart. No holding hands or anything in public. Since the law changed, some thugs have taken it upon themselves to 'enforce' the Deviancy Act. Homophobic pricks.

We're watching *Dig for Victory* on Network G when my phone pings.

It's a text message, a *text message*, from Hana confirming that I have made it to the elimination round. I passed the Final Evaluation and am in the last hundred girls. I feel jubilant for about two seconds before I realize, with a sour feeling, I've technically just been promoted to worst of the best. There's no guarantee *any* of us will progress to the Dreamhouse.

Hana doesn't say I can't tell anyone, and as soon as the voting window opens, I'll know anyway so I instantly go to message Leela. She's one step ahead of me; three dots are already typing.

'I DID IT,' she says.

'ME TOO.'

She sends a heart emoji and I know exactly what she means. How else do you express *Yay, we might die on TV.*

The voting portal goes live on the G-Net app two weeks before the survival show is due to commence. Jenson, Molly and I are poised at the little dining table, anxiously refreshing our phones as we wait for midday.

'It's up!' Mol cries and I almost hit my head on the ceiling.

'Just one phone!' I demand. I can't have three girls caterwauling over each other at the same time; I'll lose my grip on sanity. We squash together to watch Mol's phone.

The hundred finalists are shuffled randomly, and we don't know who is from what country to curb blind nationalistic voting. For the same reason, each girl is made to introduce herself in English only. Nor can the videos be shared across socials to prevent anyone with thousands of followers getting a free ticket to the Dreamhouse. It's really simple. If you watch enough of a performance you can score it out of ten, though you can swipe her into oblivion at any point.

'Let's just swipe all the others,' Jenson suggests, but I grab his wrist.

'No! I want to see the competition.' I frown. 'But we'll give them all one star.' I'm not *that* sporting.

There really are a lot of dancers in the mix. Emmy pops up eighth in rotation. She introduces herself, wide-eyed. She looks like a deer in the headlights. 'Hello, I'm Emmy and I want to be a star.' She smiles, but what's left of tears glisten in her eyes.

She performs a Nico track, 'Ghetto Baby', but she comes across as a very prim white girl trying to be 'street'. I actually wince a bit. It reminds me of the time my dad tried to rap.

After a while the girls blend into one. A lot of hair flicks; ill-advised attempts at whistle tone; winks. I get really sick of girls biting their tongues. Ick.

I leap out of my seat at the next girl. *I'm Leela, and I want to be a star.* 'That's my friend!' I cry, and I give her ten stars.

I appear on screen right after her. A weird coincidence. I recoil. Seeing myself onscreen is like seeing a doppelganger. I don't recognize this girl with her raccoon-dark eyes, overdrawn lips. My siblings shriek in each ear. I shush them. We listen, none of us breathing. If nothing else, my stripped-back performance is a tone shift. This is the first ballad we've heard.

Okay. 'Bridge Over Troubled Water'. I exhale. I'm on key. I make *some* eye contact with the camera, though not enough. I guess better to come over as shy than cocky. Everyone hates a confident woman on reality TV. The final *ease your mind* soars, and I'm quietly impressed with my own voice. I blush. I never normally hear myself outside my head.

'Babe, you smashed it.' Molly grips my arm.

'You don't think people will think I'm a joyless emo bedwetter?'

My brother and sister don't emphatically deny that, which plants a new worry to fester in my mind. I refocus and concentrate on the competition. Of the remaining girls there's only one singer – Flora – who I think rivals my voice. She's a bit *theatre* and sings 'Golden' from *K-Pop Demon Hunters*. I let her play twice. On the second viewing, I linger on her prominent teeth and too-close-together eyes. Flora is not pretty. Idols are pretty. It's as if Molly can read my mind.

She says, 'if she gets through, they are gonna give her so much plastic surgery, it's not even funny.'

Irish Maura from the mansion made it through Final Evaluation too. She *is* pretty, but she chose a song partly in Gaelic. I wonder if that will count against her. I certainly hope so.

As soon as these hateful thoughts bleed into my mind, I scold myself. The hell is wrong with me? I'm not even in the competition yet and already there's poison in my blood. *That's the game*, I tell myself; these girls will fight to kill me. Unless I kill them first.

I have to exploit every weakness; every physical flaw; every bum note. It's Starmaker, not Friendmaker. I need to cut out my heart and leave it right here with my brother and sister.

No.

That's not me.

Perhaps it's best my journey ends right here at home, where I belong.

Of course, the call comes the very next day.

I've agreed to walk our neighbour's dog, Gremlin, and I'm high in the hills when my phone rings. I hear, 'Hello, Taryn, this is Hana . . .' before I lose signal and the line goes dead. Just my luck.

Feeling sick and sweaty, I race down the hillside, dragging the bewildered Staffie behind me. As Hana's call came from an unknown number, I have no way of calling her again. I get back to the camp and wait in the unit. Twenty minutes go by but they feel like twenty hours. I'm going to be sick.

I message Leela: *Hana just called but it cut out. Did you hear?*

Another ten minutes crawls by. I put Nico on, loud. My lucky song.

My phone lights up again and I jump on it. It's just a text from Leela: *No I have not heard.*

I don't know if that means something or not. I'm about to reply when the phone rings in my hand. I almost drop it like it bit me. I answer and put it on speaker. 'Hello?'

'Oh, Taryn, hi it's Hana. I called earlier but lost you.'

Really? Hadn't noticed. 'Sorry.'

'No worries! Okay, I'll put you out of your misery. Taryn?' A long pause. I'm lightheaded and I realize I'm not breathing. I hear her smile. 'Chairman Slade has personally selected you for the Dreamhouse. Congratulations!'

I freeze. I don't know how to react. I can't even blink. My life just changed in a single second. Every book I read as a kid was about the Chosen One but, as I grew up, the fairytale that I'd be plucked from my crappy life and magically transported to a world of sexy fairies, or wizards or superheroes turned to mulch. In real life, people are not chosen, they *choose*.

Only I am now, literally, the Chosen One. One of ten.

'Taryn?'

'I'm here. I . . . I don't know what to say.'

'Well, we're all very much hoping you'll say yes . . .?'

So there *is* a choice to be made. I say no and stay here, scraping together enough for Jenson to survive. Or I take a gamble. I spin the wheel. I step off the ledge. High reward . . . high risk.

'Yes,' I tell her.

This contract is made on _____
between TARYN FAE BECK and ELYSIUM ENTERTAINMENT / NETWORK G.

1 IT IS HEREBY AGREED as follows:

1.1 TARYN FAE BECK (the 'contestant') consents to being filmed for *STARMAKER* S13 (the 'show') and for all footage to be used for transmission or online by ELYSIUM ENTERTAINMENT / NETWORK G (the 'producer'). The contestant asserts no ownership of their likeness on the basis of promotion, merchandise and marketing.

1.2 The contestant agrees to reside in the Dreamhouse, Media City, Michigan, USA for the duration of the show.

1.3 The contestant agrees to abide by the rules as set out below:

- The contestant will participate in all challenges as defined by the show. If they are unable to participate on health grounds, they must report immediately to a member of the production team so provision can be made.

- The contestant consents to an image 'makeover' as determined by the producer.

- The contestant agrees to uphold the stringent moral values of the show and the producer in their conduct, both online and in real life. The definition of 'values' is determined by the producer and can change over time.

- The contestant must not sabotage another contestant during the show. To do so will result in disqualification, with further consequences at the discretion of the producer.

- The contestant will sign a non-disclosure agreement (NDA), and must not post any content from the Dreamhouse on social media without consent from a member of the production team.

1.4 Contestants can be eliminated from the show at any stage.

1.5 Contestants will be judged on their performance and ranked through a public vote and producer assessment.

1.6 Eliminated contestants consent to forfeit their life to Project Population (see separate contract).

2 PRIZE PACKAGE.

2.1 The winning contestant(s) will receive the following prize package.

- US$1,000,000 cash prize.

- Real estate to the value of US$2,000,000.

- Recording contract (separate) incorporates one winner's single and one debut album TBD by the producer. Subsequent releases are provisional on the success of the debut.

2.2 The producer asserts the right to any future recordings created by the contestant in the ten (10) years following the show.

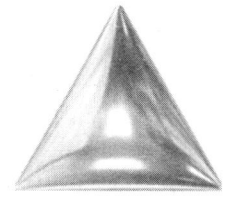

CHAPTER 15

'Here's the vision!' says Zara.

Zara is the show director. A woman made of eighty per cent Red Bull. She spirals around the camp, arms wide.

'Taryn comes out of the unit carrying her laundry basket to the launderette. As she passes, you kids kick the football to each other, okay? Can you do that?'

Ally and Rabbie, the twins from next door, nod their agreement, excited to possibly be on TV.

Zara looks me over. 'Can we lose the makeup, Taryn? Remember this is the *before* section. We want you natural. Is that all right?'

I head back inside the unit to wash my face. They don't want me natural; they want me *poor*. In the extensive chats with Hana and Scottie – her American counterpart – I have been asked so many questions about my life as a refugee that I *fully* understand my character. I am a tragic urchin; Tiny Tina; Olivia Twist; raggedy Cinderella before the fairy godmother's arrival. I'm surprised they haven't asked me to wear rags and soot.

It's ironic, because today Hana is wearing a Balenciaga sweater that's been artfully distressed to look like it's torn. I wonder what it cost.

There is a lot of interest in what we're doing here in the camp. Officially, the camera crew is here for a documentary about the modern life of teenagers. This lie might have worked if the entire camp hadn't known I auditioned for *Starmaker* in March. How was I supposed to know it was meant to be kept secret? Thankfully, our neighbours play along.

I just wish I could tell Leela the truth. It was the first question I asked when Hana called, and I was told if I spill to *anyone*, I risk being disqualified before I even got in the house. I just sent her a simple message: *It's a no* ☹. From her, I received a *Same*. I'm gutted she won't be there. It would be cool if I could trust at least one trainee.

We film the strange, silent laundry run before gathering some residents around an unlikely daytime campfire. I sing the N-TRU5T song I did for Jenson. Aware they're being filmed, everyone watches with a forced intensity: nodding and clapping as though they're in a bad school play. Only Merrill Saunders hangs back, observing sourly from the porch of her unit.

Then it's back to our own trailer to be asked a gazillion questions for my intro film. With the lights and cameraman all crammed into the trailer, I feel surrounded, pinned against the sofa.

Hana and Zara sit off camera. Hana is doing the talking.

'What I need you to do, Taryn, is answer my question and also include my question in your answer. So if I say, "how long have you been singing for?" you say, "I've been singing for however many years". Does that make sense?'

I tell her it does.

'Okay, sweetheart. What was it like when you lost your home?'

Wow, starting with the light stuff. I remember what Deenie said about my character. *The Fighter.* 'When I lost my home, it was really tough. A lot of bad things have happened to my family. It's sad but it makes you strong. You either break down or keep going. The river started to burst its banks when I was about three. I knew we might have to flee and when we had to leave Exeter, I was ready. My whole life I've been trained to survive. And now I'm ready for *Starmaker.*'

She asks about my mum, about Jenson, about how I discovered my voice, my favourite artists, what sort of artist I'd like to be. It goes on and on and on.

'And finally,' she says after what feels like hours, 'did you have a chance to read through your contract?'

Dad has been hovering in the next room, keeping an eye on proceedings. He enters the cramped living space. 'Before she signs anything, I have a few questions.'

'Of course,' Hana replies.

Dad wriggles past the lights and joins me on the dented settee. 'What if she gets there and hates it?'

Hana inhales through her nostrils. 'Well, Mr Beck, that is covered in the section on elimination. We refer to quitting as *self-elimination* and the contract dictates that in such circumstances . . .'

'She'd still go to Project Population?'

'Yes, Mr Beck. You see, without that measure in place, if a contestant felt they'd had a bad week, they'd simply drop out to avoid . . . the consequences.'

'I see.' Dad now looks to me. The plum circles under his eyes speak of sleepless nights. 'I *hate* this, Taryn.'

I say nothing, but Hana reaches over and pats his hand. 'I shouldn't be telling you this, but – as it stands – the plan is to form a five-piece group. Taryn has a fifty per cent chance of winning!'

'Or dying,' Dad says, voice strained.

They face off for a moment.

'Give me a pen,' I say. Hana retrieves a gold-plated fountain pen from her Prada purse. I flip the brick of a contract to the final sheet.

'Taryn . . .'

I silence him with a stony glare. I have come this far. There's no turning back now. I have been selected from hundreds of thousands of girls. Only nine girls left to fight. I'm a fighter. Mum would do it in a heartbeat.

I scribble my signature onto the page.

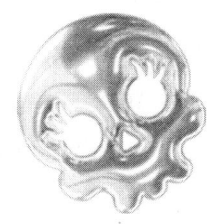

CHAPTER 16

Things I watch on the eleven-hour flight to Media City:

Toy Story (Live Action Remake)
Bride or Die USA Season 3
Terrifier IX
Two episodes of *The New Adventures of Supergirl*

I eat chicken in sauce and then a croissant before we land. In the rigid economy class seat, I don't sleep a wink.

This is so unnatural. I am assured I was taken on an aeroplane when I was a baby. Mum and Dad took us to Lanzarote. It was still safe to sunbathe and there was a pool. I know because there are pictures of me in a rubber ring.

Apparently people used to fly all the time; like normal, not millionaire, people. Fuel used to be so cheap, folks could just fly places willy-nilly. As it is, for the first time I am able to recall, I am inside a floating metal tube, forty-thousand feet above the Atlantic Ocean. I don't understand how we're staying in the air and it's freaking me out.

'Miss? Are you okay?' asks a pretty American air hostess, leaning over me.

I nod, but I am not okay.

At least the terror of plummeting into the sea takes the edge off the terror of being on television. That's something.

The plane bumps down in Media City. I look out of the porthole window and see only grey: grey skies, grey tarmac, grey airport. It's weird. I thought America would have a peachy, movie-like gloss to it. It looks like home, but greyer.

I have never felt so childlike in my life. As I leave the jet, I feel like I should be escorted by one of the crew. I clutch my passport in my hand so I don't lose it before border security. *If* I'd been under sixteen, I'd have been sent with a chaperone, but as it is, I've come alone.

I follow some passengers I recognize from my flight through passport check, where ginormous armed guards loom over me. I had to get a special visa to be allowed into the States; they even scoured my G-Net usage to make sure I wasn't watching any content deemed radical. A miserable-looking man gives me only a fleeting glance and stamps my passport. I hurry through to baggage reclaim.

'Welcome to Media City, Michigan!' a jaunty voice blasts from speakers around the arrivals terminal. Billboard screens show vistas of turquoise skies, gleaming glass towers and Lake Michigan sparkling like diamonds. 'Home of the movies you love, the shows you binge, and the music that soundtracks your life!'

After Hollywood burned and New York was submerged,

they moved the entertainment industry to somewhere cooler and drier. I think it used to be called Great Rapids or something?

My suitcase appears on the carousel and I manage to haul it off. Now what?

I don't have to wait long for an answer. As soon as I wheel it out of the baggage reclaim area, I see a grim-faced old man waiting with a MISS HAGGIS sign. I was told that would be my codename in case any sneaky reporters got hold of my identity and leaked it to the press.

Mercifully, my driver isn't chatty. I message Dad to tell him I've arrived in one piece, and, before I know it, we pull up outside my hotel. I glance up at the twenty-eight-storey building in awe. While the flight over didn't feel very fancy at all, this does. I haven't stayed in a hotel since I was a toddler.

The lobby is as impressive as the exterior. The lilac-scented air is cooled to perfection. The floors and columns are smoky marble and bellboys in pristine uniforms with shiny gold buttons scoop my case out of my hands. I check in and take the elevator to the fifteenth floor. I almost skip down the corridor to my suite, I can't help it; the carpet is so soft and springy.

I enter room 1509 and gasp. While the room is lovely, the view is *breathtaking*. I run over to the floor-to-ceiling window in awe. I can see out over the whole city, and the lake far in the distance. The Network G building dominates – the tallest downtown – and you can't miss the chrome G at the pinnacle of the skyscraper. I wonder if that's where we shoot the studio parts.

I press my hands to the cool glass and try to reconcile the

excitement with the dread. These conflicting feelings clash against each other like mighty waves in my stomach. They don't make sense together. I know what's at stake, but I'm also... keen to get going?

On the desk, underneath a TV only slightly smaller than our entire unit, there's an A4 envelope with my name – well *Miss Haggis* – on it. I rip it open.

Welcome to Media City!

Get comfy in the Hotel G! While you are NOT permitted to leave your room (except in the case of emergency), you may order room service and TV-on-demand. Your expenses are covered by *Starmaker*. Do NOT use the restaurants, gymnasium or swimming pool. This is to ensure you do not meet with other trainees until launch. We have members of the team at the hotel and we are monitoring trainee rooms.

Tomorrow you will meet with your showrunner, **Clancy Sinclair,** and creative director **Lars**. You will also be assessed by our team psychologist.

Until then, have a lovely stay and get an early night! It's a big week!

The letter isn't signed. There's a number to dial if I need anything. I look around the room, at the plush bed and big bathtub in the en-suite. I guess there are worse places I could be held prisoner. *You may order room service.* I start to hunt for the menu; I don't need to be asked twice.

The next morning, I eat breakfast on the doughy white expanse of my bed. Croissants and ham and cheese and yoghurt and granola and fruit; some mysterious green fruit with little black seeds. It's nice. I'm watching Cartoon Network, and wearing the fluffy hotel dressing gown when I get a knock at the door. Worried it's a rebel trainee, I call through the wood. 'Hello?'

'Taryn? It's Clancy and Lars here, can we come in?'

I don't have time to shower or get dressed. I'm glad I'm awake at least. I open the door to a frumpy woman who looks, like, Mum-aged? Somewhere around forty I guess. Her hair is messy, a little greasy even, and she wears a shapeless *Starmaker* hoodie. Behind her is a man so cool I can hardly look at him. He has platinum silver hair and a matching beard. He has more piercings in his face than I can count. He's dressed in a denim jumpsuit that looks like it's gone through a shredder.

'I'm sorry I'm not dressed,' I say, blushing.

'God, we've seen worse,' Clancy says, stealing a tiny pain au chocolat off my breakfast tray. 'Do you mind? I haven't eaten since . . . well I don't know when.'

'Are you the British one?' Lars removes his aviator shades and looks me over.

'Yes?' I say tentatively, clocking that means there are no other Brit girls. Emmy didn't make it.

He makes a *hmm* noise. I think he's mentally measuring me.

'How was the flight? Is the hotel okay? Do you need anything?' Clancy speaks so fast I feel a little dizzy.

'Good. Good. No.' I stand in my robe, unsure of what to do with my arms.

'Greatfabulouswonderful.' I'm not she'd have cared if there *had* been a problem. I get the sense she has ten girls to get through. 'So! Big day tomorrow! Launch day! Are you so excited?'

'Um . . . yeah.'

'So fun, right? Super straightforward. Hair and makeup here, and then a runner will collect you from your room and take you to your car. We drive you to the Dreamhouse and you go inside to meet the other girls. Easy!'

'That's it?'

'That is it! Your Starmentor will be there to explain the first challenge.'

'Are you allowed to tell me who the Starmentor is this year?' Each year an alum of seasons past returns to steer trainees through the process. They have, like, fifteen years' worth of winners to pick from.

Clancy taps her nose. 'Wait and see! Tomorrow!'

Lars reaches into his pocket. 'Hold still.' He takes hold of my chin and, in a flash, a pair of tweezers attacks my face.

'Ow!'

'Babygirl, I couldn't let you go on TV with a monobrow! There! All better! We'll get the rest at makeovers. If you get that far.' He turns to Clancy. '*Please* tell me we're doing the teeth?'

She nods. 'This afternoon.'

'What?'

Clancy smiles with *very* white teeth. 'A hygienist is coming here at three to whiten your teeth. High-definition television! What can I say? You don't want your teeth to look like tofu!'

Lars adds, 'Don't worry; we can use the really strong bleach here that's illegal in Europa.'

Is that a good thing? 'Great.'

He hands me a garment bag. Memory unlocked: my dad used to keep his suits in these, back when he had need of suits. 'What's this?'

'Your uniform,' Lars explains. 'Schoolgirl concept. Try it on please!'

I shuffle towards the bathroom. 'You'll have to get used to changing in front of people, Taryn!' Clancy calls after me. 'No privacy backstage at the Superbowl!'

Well, until that day, I'll change in private.

I lock the door and unzip the garment bag. Inside is a royal blue blazer with a red sleeveless sweater and pencil grey kilt. The crest on the blazer is a Union Jack. Oh I get it; each uniform is in national flag colours. Do I tell them the United Kingdom hasn't been *united* in nine years? Why I have to dress up like a schoolgirl is a mystery. I haven't worn a school uniform my entire life. With a sigh, I slip out of my robe and hurriedly change.

Back in my room, Lars scans me over. 'What's with the uniform?' I ask.

'You have to match,' Lars says with a mouthful of pins. 'You wear this to enter the house and when you're off duty.'

'It's all about branding,' Clancy explains. 'If you win, your twelve-inch fashion doll will wear it.'

'I get a doll?' I ask, incredulous.

Lars ignores me and explains I have a second kit of vest, gym shorts and tube socks in the same national colours for dance training waiting for me at the Dreamhouse. He fusses over me, adjusting the fit of the uniform. 'I pushed really hard for a *Sailor Moon* Japanese thing, but they said it was cultural appropriation. And there are no Japanese girls this year.'

'Lars!' Clancy snaps. Another spoiler.

'Whoops! My bad.'

He turns up the skirt to make it shorter.

'Oh, one more thing,' Clancy says as she turns to leave. 'I'll need your cell phone.'

I'd rather give her a kidney. 'What? Why?'

'Oh don't worry; you'll have a phone – a Network G C-Shell Flipfone. They're a key sponsor this season. But here's the thing: you can't actually use them to call home. We need to record those on the house phone. Those emotional moments make for great scenes, so we can't have you having private conversations.' She holds out her palm expectantly. 'We don't have all day.'

With a sigh, I hand my battered, cracked old iPhone over. My connection to the real world, gone.

As promised, that afternoon a woman comes to whiten my teeth. It burns my gums and all I can do is dab away at my watering eyes with toilet tissue while I lie flat on the bed. I can't talk for ninety minutes while the thick plastic gumshields are in my mouth. Longest hour-and-a-half of my life.

When the nurse finally pulls them out and lets me rinse, she gives me a hand mirror. My teeth are now inhumanly white.

As she is leaving with her little wheely case, she collides with a bearded, handsome man on his way in. 'Knock, knock,' he says brightly, standing in the open door. 'May I come in?' His accent is American-tinged, but I don't think he's from there originally. He could be from anywhere.

'Sure,' I say, my teeth now sensitive to the air-con.

He fully enters my hotel room. 'I'm Dr Malachi Anders. Did the team tell you I was coming?'

'They did.'

He gestures that I should take a seat, and I perch on the bed while he sits on the one armchair. He wears tortoiseshell glasses and an argyle cardigan, and maybe it's the woollens, but he gives off a warmth. I like him.

'So, I'm the shrink I'm afraid. I'm here to make sure you're psychologically ready for the show.'

My mum always taught me to respect my elders, so I don't bite back that only a mad person would enter *Starmaker*. Mad, or desperate. 'Okay,' I say instead.

'I know, I know.' Maybe he reads minds, or faces. 'I'm here as a box-ticking exercise. Network G paying lip service to your mental health. But, putting that aside, I like to think I've helped trainees in the past.'

'How?'

'Well, the Dreamhouse is tough, Taryn. Being filmed

twenty-four/seven is intense. I'm on hand to talk day or night. Our sessions are always off camera too, so you can say just what's on your mind without worrying about fan voting.'

I file that away for later. It might be good just to have ten minutes not being scrutinized by the world.

'Your job is to focus on winning, not losing,' Dr Anders says. 'But remember that thousands of people turn to Project Population every day, all over the world. It's not such a bad thing – for the planet, for society. Try to see it as doing your duty.'

I can't stop a wry snort from bursting out. I don't think there are many seventeen-year-olds handing over their remaining years. 'I'm not going to Project Population,' I tell him. 'I need to believe I can win this thing, or I'll go insane. I'll run out the door right now and never look back.'

He nods, looking satisfied with my answer. 'That's the right attitude going in.'

I don't know if I believe it, but I repeat it like a mantra: I *can* win this. That much is fact. Only five girls stand between me and the prize.

'This last question is the hardest, Taryn,' Dr Anders says, very solemn. He leans in, elbows balanced on his knees. 'If you enter the Dreamhouse, you either win or you die. This is your absolute last chance to bow out. What's it to be?'

PHASE THREE:
SURVIVAL SHOW

CHAPTER 17

The car windows are blacked out. I have no idea where we're going. The partition is up so I can't see my driver. I might even be in a self-driving car. A runner, Jacey, sits beside me in silence. They explained back at the hotel that they used they/them pronouns but I could have guessed because they have a messy bleached mullet haircut, a nose ring and a neon pink *Starmaker* hoodie. I suspect their only job is to make sure I don't escape.

We've been on the move for about forty minutes when the car slows and I hear tyres crunch over gravel.

'Good luck,' Jacey says simply. 'I'll see you on the other side.'

The rear door opens automatically. My entire body freezes. I sit.

'Taryn, go on,' the runner prompts.

I feel like I'm on a conveyer belt. It's moving so fast, I'm not sure I could step off even if I wanted to.

A well-worn memory comes to me. Chlorine smell. Standing on the diving board at the local pool, with Mum watching from far below. 'You can do it, Taryn!'

I stepped off then, shooting like a skinny dart into the turquoise water.

I can step off now too.

I step out of the car.

My mouth opens but no sound comes out. Framed by a neon-blue sky, the Dreamhouse is real. I've seen it a hundred times on TV, but it was no more real than Sleeping Beauty's castle. Here it is in front of me, solid. The sun beats down on my face and crickets chirrup in the scrublands around the house. The mansion looks more like an Aztec temple than a home; palm-flanked stairs lead up to a sand-coloured monument with slit windows, and a vast façade of blocks and one enormous central window. Somehow, these blocky columns remind me of teeth. It's almost like staring into the mouth of a great white.

My luggage has been sent ahead of me, so I focus on putting one foot in front of the other as I climb the stairs in my knee socks and Mary-Janes. It's blisteringly hot and the white sun sears my eyes. I can't swallow; my throat is too tight.

The front doors swing outwards, again on autopilot.

From within I hear a booming computer voice announce my arrival: 'TARYN! REPUBLIC OF SCOTLAND!'

I'm sure I catch a quiet shriek. I head inside the house.

The first thing that hits is a wave of crisp air conditioning. Much welcomed. The next thing is a tall blonde girl racing towards me. She's such a blur that it takes me a second to realize it's Leela. She throws her arms around me. 'I cannot believe you are here!'

'Leela! Oh my god!' Can I say *God*? I wish I'd asked.

'I'm so sorry that I am lying to you!'

'Same!' At once my heart feels ten times lighter. I squeeze her hard. 'I'm so happy to see you!'

She releases me and I take in the grand foyer of the Dreamhouse. The marble floors swirl under the light of an ultramarine-blue stained-glass ceiling. The main window over the entrance is a video screen also, and now displays an image from my photoshoot this morning in my uniform. I got my hair and makeup done by a makeup artist, and I scarcely recognize myself.

'Are you the first one here?' I ask Leela.

'Ja!' She hugs me again.

Two down, eight to go. We don't have to wait long for another housemate. About four minutes after I enter, enough time to run the pre-recorded at home segment, the doors open again.

'DOMINO! BRAZIL!'

The first newcomer is a petite, biracial girl with a mane of black curls. As she hugs me, I can feel that her body is lithe and muscular and I know at once she's a dancer. As the booming voice-of-God announces each trainee, their photo appears on the giant window screen.

'ASHANTI! THE GOLDEN SAND NATIONS!'

With great poise, regal Ashanti enters the house, a waterfall of ebony hair down her back. She looks a little older than me, and certainly carries herself like a leader. I glance up at the screen and see she's twenty-one: right at the cut-off. She greets each of us politely with air kisses.

'SUKI! AUSTRALIA!'

So keen is Suki that she almost tumbles through the door with a scream. She's cute, cherub-faced, explaining at a million words a minute that she was born in South Korea, but has lived in Australia – and acquired the accent – since she was four. She's adorable, her smile infectious, and I like her at once. She's only fifteen, I see.

'LUNE! SWEDEN!'

Okay, we're all screwed. Lune is so blonde and so pretty in her yellow and blue blazer. She looks like Princess Elsa if she somehow became real. If I were making a girl group, I'd want her in it. The palatial lobby is filling up, not so much with bodies as with excited squeals and giggles.

'BRIAR! BLUE STATES OF AMERICA!'

Briar enters with an affable, 'hey, hey, hey!' The Black girl sports natural curls and wears very cool retro sunglasses. She walks with studied confidence, but I see her hands shaking. She's pretending; we all are. She says she's from the East Coast. I see her eye Domino warily.

'MINNIE! SOUTH KOREA!'

As Minnie enters, Suki screams. She explains that they too know each other from auditions in Seoul. 'You got your nose done! I love it!' Suki gushes, and I hope, for Minnie's sake, they edit that out. Minnie's English isn't that good and Suki translates bits and pieces into Korean for her friend. Concerning: the South Koreans do not come to *Starmaker* to play.

I do a headcount. Eight girls. Two to go. There's a delay of a few minutes, and I wonder why. Finally, the doors open again and *two* girls enter at the same time.

'MADISON AND SHAYNA! RED STATES OF AMERICA!'

Their uniform colours are like mine, but reversed: red blazer with blue sweater vest. The brunette enters first, the blonde close behind. They are both beautiful, expensive-looking, with deep tans and thick, lustrous hair. And that's *before* the makeover episode. In a thick Southern accent, the brunette announces, 'Hi y'all! I'm Madison and this is my little sister, Shayna.'

Madison is familiar somehow, and I wonder if they're already big on G-Net. Sisters, though, good angle. Wish I'd thought of that; could have brought Mol.

The sisters work the crowd, greeting us in turn. Madison air kisses both cheeks and I get a lungful of her heady jasmine fragrance. 'You're so pretty!' I tell her.

'Bless your heart.' She smiles, but her blue eyes remain as cold as an iceberg. She looks vaguely disgusted, as if I'm a plague peasant.

There's a knock at the door and we all freeze as if we've been caught somewhere we aren't meant to be. With the exception of the sisters, none of us quite look like we belong in this mansion.

The doors swing open, and a familiar figure bounds into the Dreamhouse. DJ Mojo Frenzy has hosted all but one season of *Starmaker* since the very beginning. He sat out season nine (*Starmaker: Rock Stars*) after a DUI arrest, but fans petitioned for his return and got their way the next year. He looks taller on TV.

'Let's! Get! Psycho! Welcome to the Dreamhouse, ladies!'

We were told to scream, and we all scream. Personally, I find

Mojo – and his catchphrases – super annoying, but I scream. It's a weird reflex. He's famous – of course I should scream.

'We got some psycho talent up in here, am I right?'

We scream again.

'Just think, just think. In this room right now, I am looking at the newest, baddest, most flavoursome girl group on the whole planet. That's right. Five of you will be . . .' He gestures at the screen. 'DOLLHOU5E!'

The silhouettes of five anonymous AI-generated girls appear on the screen with the name of the group. Capitalized, with a '5' for an 'S'. The numbers-for-letters thing is kind of a trademark: N-TRU5T, B*TRU3, CRE8TOR.

DOLLHOU5E though? I hate it.

Mojo goes on. 'All around the world, a new fanbase of Dolls is ready to choose their final band as you undertake five challenges in singing, dancing, teamwork and charm. Each week, the two trainees with the lowest fan scores will face the judges, who will decide who enters the dreaded Elimination Chamber. Only the final five lucky girls will debut in DOLLHOU5E.' The words *Elimination Chamber* cast a long shadow, but he sails past that part. 'Guiding you ladies through all this will be your Starmentors. Are you ready to meet your lead mentor and head judge?'

'YES,' we all scream. I really do want to know. I hold Leela's hand.

Mojo holds up a finger to silence us. 'Girls, please welcome someone who needs no introduction.'

The doors open once more. The hall fills with celestial midday sun. A tiny golden woman enters, a goddess stepping off clouds from heaven. This time I gasp for real. I clamp a hand on Leela's forearm to steady myself.

I always assumed she must be ten-feet-tall, an amazon, but even at five-two she somehow dominates the grand hallway.

'Hello, girls,' she says with a radiant smile. 'I'm Nico.'

We *scream*.

The blood rushes to my head. Nico is here. NICO IS HERE. My feet stamp around on the spot like I'm on hot coals. Briar flops to her knees. Suki starts to cry.

Nico smiles a perfect smile. Her hair cascades to her waist like platinum sand dunes. Much has been said on G-Net about her rumoured 'work' (boob job, chin implant, brow lift, buccal fat removal, upper bleph and rhinoplasty) but I think she is *flawlessly* beautiful. If it's ten years since she won, now she'll be almost thirty.

As a group we are beyond hysterical. Domino starts to cry. Minnie bows to her. Nico was the soundtrack to our childhoods and now she is right here – flesh and bone – in front of us. I could reach out and touch her. How can this be real? How is this my life?

Only then, just as I'm about to faint, Clancy scurries in behind Nico, hand pressed to her production headset. Somehow she looks even more exhausted. 'Okay, girls, thanks. Let's do another take. You screamed over Nico's line. Same energy, just a beat later.'

CHAPTER 18

I am still shaking, physically, when we reset in the den. I sit on my trembling hands so I don't look insane. There's a retro sunken conversation pit upholstered in pink suede with fluffy alpaca cushions. On a branded glass coffee table is a platter of sweets from candyshop.com, as if we're gathered for the ultimate sleepover.

Now that the weepers have stopped crying and had their makeup redone, we can begin. Mojo has departed, leaving Nico in charge, although Clancy lurks, ever-present, out of shot.

There are no camera operators, but cameras are everywhere. They are cleverly disguised, hidden, so we don't perform for them. I look around the den and wonder if they're embedded in the eyes of the past winners whose portraits decorate this lounge area.

With one perfect leg crossed over the over, Nico begins. 'So girls, are we ready?' She is *radiant*, a goddess gracing us with her presence on Earth. We all chant that we are. 'I remember being where you are. It's ten years exactly since I won *Starmaker*. Can you believe it?'

We cannot. Time flies when you're the biggest star in the world. I remember when her Nicommotion Tour came to the Northern Powerhouse. Some rich girls at school got tickets and it broke my heart. Why did they get to see Nico when they could never love her as much as I did? They came to school the next day in tour t-shirts and I've never been so jealous.

'Girls, I won't lie. This is going to be really tough, but I hope it'll be fun too. I had a great time on my season.'

Yes, but that was before they started killing the losers. Nico's presence is almost enough to push Project Population out of my mind. She was born in Mexico, but grew up in Florida. She was a refugee too, and look at her now. I wonder if she knows we have similar back stories.

'I'm sure you have loads of questions?' We do because Clancy gave us each a question in advance.

I am picked first. 'What's the one piece of advice you wish you'd been given before you entered a survival show?'

'Great question, Taryn.' *Oh my god, Nico knows my name. This may honestly kill Jenson.* 'I guess remember that fans don't vote for the *best* trainee, they vote for their *favourite* trainee. It's important to bring your A-game, but it's about more than that. Be yourself and you can't lose.'

I smile broadly, haunted by Molly's warning that I am in possession of a 'resting bitch face' that could get me eliminated. 'Thank you,' I say.

'This year,' Nico says, 'for the first time, *you* will get a say in who makes the final band.'

I look to Leela. That's new.

'As well as the judge and fan vote, you will also secretly

rank who you'd most want to make the final five. Girl groups are about sisterhood, after all.' She smiles. 'So play nice, ladies.'

A nervous titter travels around the doughnut sofa. Under the eye of the cameras, we couldn't be *openly* cutthroat anyway, but now we can't even risk being bitchy off-camera either. I have to appeal to fans online *and* the other trainees. This adds a new level of brain-strain to my already strained brain.

The other trainees ask their pre-planned questions: which idols does she like; what's her career highlight; most embarrassing moment. I strongly doubt they'll all make the final cut. This will all become 'flashback' footage for the first live show on Saturday night.

Q&A over, Nico gets to business. 'We have five days until the first live show. Are you ready to hear your first challenge?'

We all scream approval again, and it's already getting old. I feel like I'm at a child's birthday party interacting with a magician.

Nico takes out a hot-pink envelope with a gold *one* embossed on it. 'Challenge One: Vocals.'

My heart soars. Thank god.

'This week, you will split into two groups to perform a vocal harmony number. The theme is . . . in honour of Taryn . . .' *What?* 'Great British Girl Groups!'

Everyone claps and cheers. I'm thrilled because they can't edit that out and I got a mention.

On the ginormous TV screen mounted on the wall a spinning wheel appears.

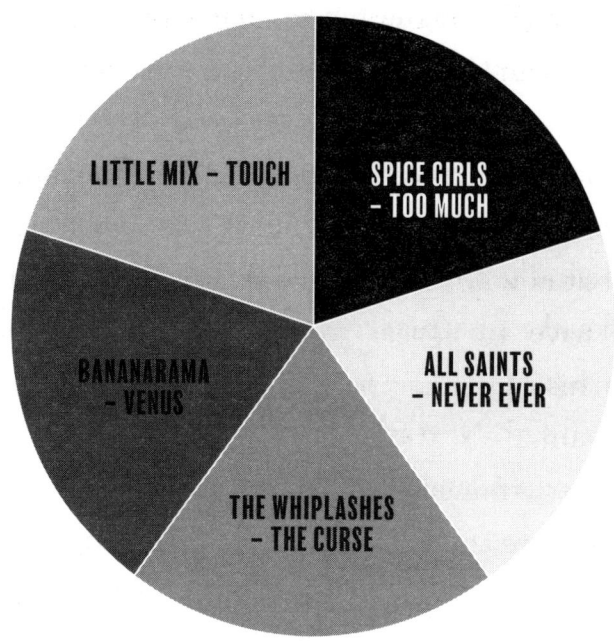

God, those songs are ancient. Only 'The Curse' is from this decade.

'I can't believe The Whiplashes are up there,' Suki says.

'It's such a shame when one girl ruins it for everyone,' adds Madison. They're referring to lead singer Frankie Doyle and her drug problem. She had to quit the group in shame. She still sometimes pops up in magazines, falling out of a bar somewhere. It's sad, really. She looks like a zombie.

'Girls, settle down!' Nico tries to rein us in. 'I'm going to give you two minutes to get into two groups of five . . . GO!'

Instantly Madison takes charge without anyone asking. 'Okay, who are the big voices?'

I'm saying nothing until I've heard everyone sing.

'Stick together, okay?' Leela breathes into my ear and I nod.

Ashanti proclaims she's a 'lead vocalist', whatever that means, and Madison grasps her and Minnie, hauling them to her side of the doughnut. She too must be fully aware that Korean contestants always do well.

'Can I join you guys?' Suki asks Leela, who agrees.

Domino jumps towards Madison's team, leaving Lune and Briar to join us. I can't help but notice that Madison's group is all the flawlessly pretty girls and we are . . . the quirky ones. Lune looks like an actual china doll with her saucer eyes and porcelain skin.

'Okay, all set?' Nico asks. She points to my team first. 'You guys are Group A, and you'll be Group B. Let's see what songs you'll be learning . . .'

The wheel spins. I pray for The Whiplashes and I get my wish.

'Amazing,' I say to my team. We all know it, and there are some big notes. Group B get the All Saints, which I confess I am not familiar with.

'On top of your vocal harmony performance, you'll all take part in a group dance number that will *not* be assessed by the judges, but may influence voters at home.' *Oh, damn.* 'Sleep tight, girls, because tomorrow the hard work really begins.' Nico smiles and gives me, I think, a friendly wink.

'Cut it there!' Clancy cries, entering the room with a young man who I guess is Nico's assistant.

At once Nico's grin fades. 'Is my car ready?'

The assistant nods. 'Right outside.'

'Can we get a pick-up on that last part, Nico?'

'Not now, Clancy. I have oxygen therapy. Just dub it from behind.' She turns to her PA. 'Okay, let's go.' She doesn't even look over her shoulder as she sweeps out with her minion.

* * *

I think we're off duty now, although Clancy stresses that the cameras are always running. We are always being watched. The producer runs us through the house rules as we tour the rest of the mansion from bottom to top.

The gym and pool in the basement: 'Stay fit, ladies, but don't injure yourself whatever you do.'

Upstairs, there are five bedrooms and we pretty naturally divide. I will share with Leela, next door to Lune and Ashanti. 'The bedrooms are filmed, remember, girls.'

'What about the bathrooms?' Briar asks. 'That's . . . not cool.'

'The bathrooms are not filmed for obvious reasons,' Clancy explains. 'Do not go to the bathroom together. Conversations must not take place in secret.'

Well there goes my first rule-breaking suggestion.

We conclude the tour in the enormous kitchen – the most modern room in the house. It's overflowing with food. They have *bananas*. I haven't seen a banana in years. From nowhere, I remember making banana bread with brown, overripe ones with Mum. The thought alone brings a tear to my eye. 'You okay?' Suki asks.

I nod, not daring to talk.

There are hundreds of plastic bottles of H2Eau brand vitamin water; they must be a sponsor. The food all comes from EasyMart; their logo decorates the walls. The produce stocked in the kitchen could feed the entire QE II camp for a week. There are only ten of us.

'Okay, let's talk food planning,' Clancy says, brandishing

a folder full of menu cards. 'Each of these recipes has been designed by our team of nutritionists to ensure you stick to your calorie goals.'

'Calorie goals?' I ask.

She explains that we shouldn't be eating over a set number of calories a day. Everything I know about calories comes from our ration boxes and I know what she's suggesting is considerably less than our recommended intake.

'Girls, I'm serious,' she says. 'We need you fit and healthy. You need to think of yourselves as athletes. You are idols now. A billion little girls are looking to you to be the best of the best.'

If Clancy is on screen, I know this won't get used on TV, and so I say, 'Do we have to be *thin* to be the best of the best?'

Briar snorts and covers a smile with her hand. 'Truth,' she mutters.

Madison's eyes widen. 'Okay, this one has a death wish,' she says, plenty loud enough for me to overhear.

Everyone now looks to Clancy to return my serve. 'These recipes are delicious and nutritious, okay? And let's be real, if we send you on TV looking like a hog, you know what people will say online, right? They're *brutal*. We're just looking out for you. Something to think about, Suki.'

We are all silent. I can't believe she singled Suki out. I suddenly *hate* Clancy so much my face prickles. Suki lowers her head, nodding ever so slightly. Suki is nowhere near 'hog', and even if she was, who cares? Her talent should be all that matters.

When Clancy starts lecturing us on where everything

goes in the cupboards, I give Suki's hand a squeeze. 'Ignore her, okay?'

'I've been stress-eating,' she hurriedly explains, although she has no need to. She shrugs like it's no big deal. 'They already told me to lose weight back in Melbourne; it's fine.'

I give her a supportive smile. I've been so naïve. Maybe I thought everyone would be as nice as Deenie was back home. In a world where seventy per cent of the population is starving, we're being told to lose weight.

CHALLENGE ONE:
VOCAL HARMONY – 'BEST OF BRITISH'

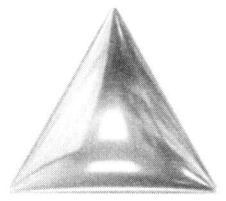

CHAPTER 19

From upstairs, I can hear Ashanti whistle toning like she's trying to summon dogs to the mansion. Madison gathered Group B right after dinner to start learning the All Saints song.

Alone in the kitchen, Leela and I load the dishwasher together and compare notes. 'I cannot believe we lied to each other,' she says. 'So stupid.'

'I was scared they'd eliminate me!'

'Me too.'

'Lee, I am *so* glad you're here.'

'Me too. It would not be feeling real if you weren't here.' She scrapes some leftover tofu stir-fry into the waste disposal. Ten girls, but only Briar had the first clue how to find her way around the kitchen, so she made a surprisingly tasty dinner for us all. I didn't volunteer the information that most of our food comes in little sachets you just tip into a pan. 'I want to tell you something,' Leela says.

I stop loading plates. 'What?'

'I tell the producers that I am transgender,' she admits. 'Like you said, it is my story. It is who I am. I am not being ashamed.'

'What did they say?'

'You are right. They love it. They want me to find a time to tell everyone.'

Yeah, sounds about right. Milk that moment for all it's worth. Imagine if she dared to do it off camera. 'Okay. But only if you want to. Don't let them pressure you into doing something you don't want to do.'

Leela gives me a puzzled look. 'Are you saying this so I do not get a big story?'

I'm shocked. 'No! No way! Leela, that's not how I'm playing the game. I just mean . . . look at what they said to Suki about her weight. I think . . . I think they only care about making a TV show, they don't care about you . . . or what people online will say about you.'

Leela comes close to me and lowers her voice. 'Taryn, please be careful. I know what people will say about me, but if you keep . . . critiquing?'

'Criticizing?'

'Yes. If you keep criticizing the show you will be punished.'

'I know,' I sigh. So far none of us has dared utter the phrase *villain edit*, but I've seen enough trash TV to know that, if they want to, the producers can make me look like a heartless scheming bitch. 'But she called Suki fat.'

'Clancy will hear this conversation.'

I nod. She's got me there. I need to play a smarter game. I glance around the kitchen. Cameras could be everywhere. 'Come on, let's get this show on the road.'

Suki, Briar and Lune are in the den, watching the looping

footage of *Starmaker* alumni on the big screen. After dinner, they've changed into the branded EasyMart pyjamas that were left on our beds. 'Who was your favourite in N-TRU5T?' Suki says. Both she and Lune are wearing gloopy sheet masks on their faces and look like ghosts.

'Sonny!' I say without hesitation. The tan, the golden curls.

'Girl, same! I was such a Sonny stan. I used to write fan fic.'

'You did not?' Briar shrieks. She's wearing a very cool faux fur hat over her curls in a way that I could never pull off.

'I did!' Suki insists. 'Really horny stuff too. Like filthy. I was thirteen. If my mum read it, she'd have sent me to a convent.'

We laugh, and I'm glad that she doesn't seem too badly scathed by Clancy's thorns. 'Come on, Group A . . . let's get to work,' I say with a sigh.

'You're right. We should make a start.' Briar closes her book – a copy of *1984* that cannot be a coincidence. She was the quietest over dinner, but there are a lot of big personalities sucking up air. It was hard for any of us to slide a word in sideways between Madison and Ashanti. 'Group B are on it, and I wanna whoop those skinny bitches on their skinny butts.'

'I second that,' I say and we gather in the conversation pit around the glass table.

We've been given matching phones pre-loaded with all the songs and copies of the lyrics to learn. We were told to name the brand as much as possible. Leela does the honours. 'Guys, we should listen to the song on our new Network G C-Shell Flipfones.'

We burst out laughing again. 'So natural!' I cackle.

'Effortless,' Briar agrees.

We listen to The Whiplashes' ballad. It's a rocky, bittersweet song of a relationship ending, but knowing it was bad for you all along.

> *I don't want to let go*
> *But staying is worse*
> *If love is a blessing*
> *Then why are we cursed?*

The songwriter credits include *Francesca Doyle* and I wonder if this song was personal to her. If it was about a partner, or about her relationship with drugs and alcohol.

> *Every time I leave*
> *I find myself here*
> *Supposed to be laughing*
> *Can't see for these tears.*

Maybe. We listen through the song twice. 'I think we got the better song,' I whisper.

'Totally,' Briar agrees. 'Okay, here's the first potential drama llama tripping in . . . how do we decide parts?'

'Please no fighting,' Lune says, peeling off the facial mask with French tip nails. 'Reminds me of my parents' divorce.' We laugh kindly and she explains that her mum is a pretty famous actress in Sweden and her dad is a painter. The arts are in her blood, I guess.

Mercifully there's no squabbling, which makes for a nice evening but probably poor television. Feeling confident, I'll start us off, and Lune wants to do the middle eight, which has a showy high note. I'd have preferred that but I can't have it all. We agree we can all do some fancy ad-libs over the choruses so we each get a chance to shine.

'That was easy!' Suki says. 'You just know Ashanti's up there taking all the best lines . . .'

'Against Madison? Good luck to her,' I add quietly.

'Group A rocks!' Lune says, indicating that we should all put our hands in the middle.

There's an instrumental backing track on the phone so we sing it through. It's . . . dare I say it . . . really good? I've never sung with skilled singers before. I think, with Mum's old opera training instilled in me, I'm technically the best, but Leela has her breathy thing and Lune sings higher than I do. That's not to say that Suki and Briar are tone deaf, but they come from dance backgrounds.

'I was doing ballet when I was two!' Suki says. Her enthusiasm is constant and infectious. She's like a puppy, a little Pomeranian. 'Then tap, and jazz, and contemporary. But I saw *Starmaker* when I was, like, six, and it's all I've wanted since. I wannabe an idol. No second choices.'

'What about you?' I ask Briar. She definitely has the toned, sinewy physique of a dancer.

'Okay, don't make fun of me?'

'I swear.'

'I got a cheerleading scholarship to college.' Far from mocking her, we all think that's amazing. What could be more

American than a cheerleader? I'm obsessed instantly. We force her to teach us a simple routine right there in the lounge. It's harder than it looks.

Briar explains, 'I was kinda torn between sticking with cheering or applying for this . . . but, well, here we are!'

'What do you think of the other girls?' Lune whispers.

'Keep an eye on Min-jee,' Suki says.

'Who?' I ask.

'Oh, *Minnie*. They made her change her name to make it easier.' Suki rolls her eyes. Easier for who? If people can learn how to pronounce *Timothée Chalamet*, they can manage a Korean name too. 'She's been a trainee at one of the big K-Pop companies in Seoul since she was eleven.'

'Eleven!' Leela gasps. 'Is child labour.'

'Clearly Madison thinks she's in charge,' Lune says sourly.

I've learned my lesson in the kitchen. 'We shouldn't bitch,' I tell her sternly, and then nod at Briar's novel. 'Big Brother's watching.'

We rehearse for an hour or so, but everyone is on an adrenaline dive. We've been in the Dreamhouse for less than twelve hours, but it feels like forever. The day finally catches up with us all, I think.

Leela hits the shower room, while I unload my allocated wheely suitcase. I carefully unpack the photoprints I have brought from home – safely shipped inside my notebook – and tape them over my bed. I want them here as a reminder of why I'm putting myself through this. I have one of Mum and me with the pink microphone, and a second one of Dad, Mol and

Jen taken a couple of years back at the camp.

'Is that your family?' I look up, and Briar stands on the threshold of my room. She's sharing on the next floor up with Domino. She's in flannel pyjamas and smells sweetly of shea butter.

'Uh-huh.'

She enters the bedroom and comes to take a look. 'Brother and sister?'

'Yeah.'

'Cute.'

'Thanks,' I reply. I tap Jenson. 'He's the reason I'm doing all this.'

'Your momma's so pretty.'

'Isn't she? She, um, she died a long time ago.'

Briar's face falls. 'Oh, girl, I'm sorry.'

'No, it's okay. When your parent dies, no one talks about it in case you burst into tears and make everything awkward. But I like talking about her. She was the best. She's where I got my voice from.'

Briar gazes at them a moment longer, almost hazy-eyed.

'What about you?' I ask. 'Who's cheering on the cheerleader?'

'I don't have a family,' she says sharply.

'Oh. Do you wanna talk about it?'

'Nothing to say. I've looked after myself for a long time.' I can see I'm not getting blood out of that stone. 'Good to meet you, Taryn.'

'You too.' Unwise to like her, but I like her. I feel safe with Briar, like there's a grown-up in the playpen.

'Sleep tight, we got a big day tomorrow, baby.'

I nod agreement as she leaves. I guess we all have our sob stories. I wonder what hers is.

Alarms went off at six-thirty. The meal plan says breakfast is porridge or fruit. I have both.

The meal plan says Briar and I sit at the dining table, bleary-eyed in our skimpy dance kit. Our names are written across the chest in a letterman-style font so people at home know who is who. We have to wear black spandex 'safety shorts' *under* the gym shorts to keep our butt cheeks from showing. Modesty is key. So why not just give us longer shorts in the first place?

Shayna bounds downstairs with bouncing blonde curls and false lashes on.

'Girl, what time did you get up?' Briar asks.

'Five,' she replies sweetly. 'If I learned one thing from the pageants back home it's that if you stay ready, you don't gotta get ready.'

I pluck a yellow square out of the fruit salad. 'What's this?' I ask, taking a sniff. 'Is it melon?'

Briar frowns. 'It's mango?'

I nibble the corner off. Nothing like melon, but delicious.

'You ain't never had mango?' Shayna asks, incredulous.

'No.' I shrug.

Madison descends into the kitchen, as glam as her little sister. 'Madi, you'll never guess; Taryn never had mango before!'

'Shayna!' she snaps. 'It ain't Christian to make fun of poor folks.'

'God bless you,' I tell her through gritted teeth. Briar chuckles under her breath.

Getting ten of us ready in the morning is like herding sleepy kittens. 'Girls! Come ON!' Clancy now screams as the clock strikes eight.

The hot water doesn't work in one of the bathrooms so we all had to share. Suki spilled coffee down her training top. Leela dropped my only mascara down the toilet. Minnie is crying because she has lost her phone somewhere in the mansion. Domino requested a size four shoe but they've given her a five. Ashanti's endless whistle tone has given her a sore throat and she wants some specific medicine.

This is chaos. No wonder Clancy looks so ragged.

We don't know where we're going, only that we were told to wear the dance kit and gather in the den. I wonder if *Starmaker* wants us in a state of confusion. If this constant cloud of anxiety will make us more likely to break down and act out for TV. They want glistening teardrops on perfect cheekbones.

Once we're all ready, we're frog-marched through the garden by runners to a neighbouring one-storey structure just down the rugged hillside. It looks, and smells, brand new, erected especially for us. We have our own state-of-the-art dance studio to one side of the building and a recording studio to the other. The walls are once more dotted with roaming cameras. Heat-seeking, they swivel to find us as we make our way into the dance studio. We're hustled into a large, sleek room, newer than Deenie's and much more sterile. Pink neon strip lights glow around vast mirrors.

Clancy instructs us to start warming up, and at once the nerves kick in. I don't want to be singled out as the sickly dance runt in the pack. If the group gets wind of a weakness, they'll gang up to pick me off.

After all, it's what I would do. If I were smart.

I'm half-heartedly stretching out my hamstrings on the floor next to Leela when I hear a soft male voice. 'Hey, girls.'

We all look up and there's an almost comical second of silence while our brains process the new arrival.

The dimples are unmistakeable.

The smile.

The *arms*.

Cade Kekoa.

Cade Kekoa from N-TRU5T is in the room.

The screaming starts. A different kind of scream from the one we gave Nico. This one is tinged with a sweaty, hysterical desire. I was twelve when N-TRU5T was formed and they were the core of my very first fantasies.

Imagine holding hands with Sonny. Imagine walking together in a leaf-strewn, autumnal park drinking pumpkin spice lattes.

Imagine Sonny telling you that he loved you.

Imagine kissing Sonny.

Imagine if Sonny . . .

And so on.

Yes, Sonny was always my bias, but Cade, standing right here in the flesh, is *gorgeous*. The teeth, the eyes, the hair, again, the *dimples*. He's somehow even more stunning IRL; he was always the rogue of the group, with a knowing, cockeyed smile that suggested he was fully aware that he was about to ruin your life. Oh my god. He's wearing a tight running vest to show off his biceps. The way it grips his chest. His short shorts. His thighs. His butt.

Get a grip, Taryn.

He's more than a tight body, he is *proof*. Proof that you can survive this, and go on to be successful beyond anyone's wildest dreams. Their last world tour, now a farewell tour I guess, was over a hundred sold-out dates all around the Peace Alliance.

I'm not okay. I feel dizzy. Leela grips me so hard it hurts. Suki bursts into tears.

'Girls, it's okay!' He grins, no doubt used to this reaction. 'We're cool, we're cool. Calm down!'

'I can't!' Madison gasps, fanning herself, and we all laugh because we're right there with her. 'I love you so much.'

'Well, you're gonna need to take a big breath, girls, because I'm gonna be your dance mentor this season.'

More screaming. This isn't a hit-and-run; we're actually going to be working with Cade Kekoa. A LOT. I know all about him from the N-TRU5T annual I got one Christmas: Cade Jayson Kekoa was raised in Hawaii until it was evacuated, and then moved to Houston. His father is Filipino-American and his mother is half-Norwegian. They travelled a lot because his dad was in the navy. He is the youngest member of N-TRU5T. He is five foot nine. His favourite animals are dolphins and his favourite possession is his skateboard.

'Gather round, gather round.'

He summons us to sit before him in a horseshoe. This close,

I can smell his powdery deodorant. This is surreal. He's solid, not just pixels on a phone.

'I don't know if you remember my season . . .'

'We definitely do,' I say with a smile. The other girls chime agreement. It's rude to interrupt, but I have to think about getting camera time, or I'm dead. He smiles back.

'So you'll know I was *not* the best dancer. Never had any training. I had to work so hard to win my place in the band. I think that's why *Starmaker* asked me to be your mentor this year. I know what it's like to be in your shoes. So if I get real tough on you, just know it's from a place of love.' He places a hand over his heart. 'This Saturday, on the launch show, you'll do a group routine to "Spice Up Your Life" by the Spice Girls. Remember them?' He makes peace signs with his fingers. 'Girl Power!'

There's some excited *oohing* from the trainees who know it, and a little confusion from the girls who don't. It's, like, a classic, but then I'm British.

'This is the top of the show before the challenge, so this will be the first impression you give to the folks at home . . . and the judges.' I swear he looks me right in the eye. 'No time like the present. Shall we get started?'

He promises us the first number 'won't be too tricky' but he is lying. Ten girls weaving in and out of one another to create a lattice sounds good in theory, but in practice is mostly us bumping into one another and saying sorry a lot. Right away it's clear who the dancers are: Domino; Suki; the sisters; Briar and Minnie. They only have to see Cade once to copy him. As for the man himself, he makes it look so easy; each movement is fluid, precise, but never less than masculine. I'm transfixed.

We take a break and Cade singles out Madison. I eavesdrop. 'Good job, Madison! I know your sister, don't I?'

Madison smiles and blushes slightly, like she's been caught out. 'Yes, sir . . .'

'Did you girls know this?' Cade is naturally mischievous, a naughty glint in his hazel eyes. The rest of us fall quiet, intrigued.

'We didn't tell them yet,' Madison adds, coy. Tell us what?

'Ladies! We're in the presence of greatness,' Cade teases.

Shayna joins her sister. We all look on expectantly. 'We haven't been entirely honest with you, girls,' Madison says.

'We didn't want you to treat us special,' Shayna puts in. From the way they strut around the Dreamhouse, I'm not sure that's true.

Madison's smile is catlike, smug almost. 'You guys already know our big sister . . .' The penny drops in my mind seconds before she says it. 'Peyton Silver from B*TRU3.'

That's why she's so familiar. Strong family resemblance. The last girl group was on the show two years ago. Peyton, like her sisters, was an all-American sweetheart. *Apple pie, yes ma'am.*

The other girls bombard the sisters with giddy questions, closing in on them.

'Did they ask you to audition?' Suki asks. Madison says no, they auditioned like everyone else.

I hang back from the scrum with Cade. 'You good?' he asks.

'Yeah.' I blink. I can't lie fast enough, and I think Cade knows I'm reeling.

'What is Peyton thinking?' Leela wants to know.

'She's so proud of her little sisters,' Madison beams. 'I truly hope that someday DOLLHOU5E and B*TRU3 can tour together. Can you imagine? How fun?'

My heart drops. They're *legacies*. The rest of us can't hope to compete with that; an army of B*truthers will be voting for them. Two out of five places in the band are essentially locked down. The rest of us are now fighting for just three positions.

Eight girls, *three* spots.

Liked by **nico, cade.n.tru5t** and **others**

starmaker

Here they are! Your finalists! An all-new season of Starmaker: DOLLHOU5E begins this Saturday 1900 ET/1800 CT only on @NetworkGlobal!

Comments

peytonsprincess 23s
OMG MADI AND SHAYNA I CANNOT BREATHE

iheartpeyton 35s
no way is that pey's sisters???

popgirly 1m
only 1 plus size girl DO BETTER STARMAKER

beetrue333 1m
I stan Madison and Shay Shay so hard they better debut or I will die

musicwatcher18 1m
always so many americans the favouritism is real

starffaker 1m
MINNIE DEBUT DOMINO DEBUT MADISON DEBUT SHAYNA DEBUT LUNE DEBUT

adam4peyton 2m
madi facecard never declined

sososostacy 2m
scottish girl is pretty german girl is cool could be model

queenshit21 2m
how is it fair that peytons sisters are producer picks??? nepo babies not cool starmaker

fiercelyreel 3m
I do not want to see any discussion of Suki's body or we ride at dawn

willagreen 3m
Briar repping for the dark-skinned girlies I fear we stan

opalbaby222 3m
Ashanti Habibi debut x

libertyboiii 4m
faces like pigs ugly sluts

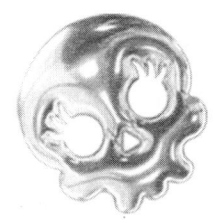

CHAPTER 20

That night, I dream awful dreams.

I dream I can't find a toilet ahead of the live show and pee myself during the dance number.

I dream I open my mouth to sing and I have an eel where my tongue should be.

I dream the bus takes me to the wrong studio.

It gets light at about five and I wander the gardens in the pool area with a cup of coffee. While I'm in a house with coffee, I'm making the most of it. It's still blissfully cool and the grass is dewy under my feet. The dawn sky is pear drops pink and yellow. I feel time move a little slower. I'm grateful for it. The week is slicing along way too fast.

I roll up my pyjama bottoms and dangle my feet in the swimming pool. What if this is my last week? Some little birds flit down from the lemon trees to drink from the pool. I'm oddly jealous of the simplicity of their lives.

Even at this hour, Ashanti, Madison and Shayna are on treadmills in the gym. I distantly hear the slap of their sneakers and the whir of the machinery. Honestly, it'd never be me.

Suki goes to join them. They revealed us on socials last night. I only looked once, and that was enough. Never again will I read the comments. Most of the noise, predictably, is about Madison and Shayna, but Suki's body is mentioned a lot. Some of the comments are cruel, others celebrate her figure, but either way, her body is up for discussion. The reverse is true also: I am deemed *too thin*; Leela's legs are *bony*. People speculate about which of us have eating disorders. All this before we've even been on TV for a single second.

I make my way to the telephone room. If we want to make a call home it has to be in here so the conversation can be recorded for TV. The booth is supposed to be soundproof, but it very much isn't. I calculate it'll be late morning back home.

He answers at once. 'Hey, Jen?'

'Taryn! Are you okay?'

'Yeah, I'm good!' I fill him in on Nico and Cade, ensuring that I remain upbeat and peppy. This conversation could be transmitted. 'How are you feeling?'

'Taryn, I'm fine. Stop worrying about me. We're all so excited for Saturday night!'

Because of the time difference, *Starmaker* goes out on Sunday teatime in the UK, but you can watch it live online. My family will have to stay up until eleven p.m. to see how I fare.

'Me too.' I don't even convince myself.

'Are you nervous?'

'Yes,' I admit.

'Taryn,' he says seriously. 'This is your chance for everyone to hear your voice. Just *sing*.'

I nod, forgetting he can't see me.

* * *

Once we're all ready for the day in our uniforms, we trundle down the garden path to the studio annex next to the dance hall. I enter first, and Nico is already here. She's wearing a baggy pinstripe suit that, on anyone else, would look insane. She, however, looks like the most powerful woman on earth. Her makeup artist fusses over her face. 'I don't want to look like a drag queen,' Nico snaps. 'It's too much. Stop!'

Only then does she realize we've arrived. That was a mean thing to say. Couldn't she have just said *not too much, please*?

Nico snaps into pro-mode. 'Oh hey, girls, come on in! Gather round!'

Standing alongside Nico is a tall Black man with a neat beard and a single pearl earring. He has an open, friendly face, although I'm grown enough to know they sometimes come attached to liars.

Clancy snaps, telling us to shut up.

'Girls.' Nico smiles. 'I want to introduce you to a very good friend of mine. He produced my first album ten years ago and I asked him especially to be your vocal coach this year. Please give a warm welcome to our new Starmentor Andre Brookes III.'

'You guys just call me Dre, how about that?'

We clap and cheer, and then Clancy makes us do it again because apparently we looked tired.

Dre explains our morning. 'Today I'm going to help you arrange your vocal harmonies ahead of this week's challenge. I wanna take your singing to the next level. It's gonna be fun! Are we ready to warm up?'

It actually is sort of fun. We do some vocal exercises in the dance studio and, to my amazement, Nico gamely joins in. We make faces; we pretend to be monkeys and helicopters. A distance remains however; she's here, but she's not *here*. It's almost like there's a mysterious actress playing the role of Nico, pop idol. She plays her very well.

Dre summons Group A into the recording studio first while Madison's group goes with Cade to learn some mic-ography. I feel instantly at home in the windowless, padded studio. The room is divided into a lounge of sorts, with carpeted walls, and a studio booth on the other side of a glass screen. Dre tells us to take a seat on the mismatched bamboo sofas. Everything in here looks like it came from a flea market; eclectic vintage. I love it.

Nico remains with us, sitting alongside Dre.

'I started singing as soon as I could talk,' Dre tells us and we nod along. 'You too? I was *such* an attention seeker.'

'Same!' Nico laughs.

'In church I was straight up that aisle, taking on the solos. I am so blessed that I do what I love every single day. That's what this is about, right?'

I nod, because I *wish* that were true. I wish this were just my way of doing what I love. Instead, I'm fighting for my life *and* my brother's. It feels like none of this is exactly on my terms.

'Okay, let's hear what you ladies have come up with . . .'

We file into the recording booth and position ourselves behind the five microphones. I think we look amazing. What if *we* were the winning band. Fat chance. Based only on the one social media picture *Starmaker* released, I'm not sure we're the hot favourites. Lune maybe? I was scarcely mentioned at all in the comments.

'The Curse' begins and off we go. Last night we must have done this fifty times, but I'm suddenly nervous. On the other side of the glass, actual Nico is listening to me sing.

My first verse is fine. No disasters. Dre told us to keep going even if we messed up. Briar is a little shaky. Lune is out of key on the big note. She hits it about a third of the time, which is a worry.

We go out on a high. As the song ends, the tension bursts like a bubble and we all collapse into a messy group hug. I see the coaches have a conflab, but we can't hear what they say on this side of the glass. Dre's voice fills the booth. 'Great job, girls! Sounding sweet today! Can I hear Taryn sing the middle eight please?'

Oh clever; creating drama where there was none. Lune's doll eyes dip, but I don't see how I have a choice. 'Sure.'

At the desk, he cues up the track. I haven't rehearsed this part, but know the song off by heart: *Can't see you with her / it's making it worse / better alone / breaking the curse.* The same lyrics twice over, the second time an octave higher. It's a difficult note, but I think I reach it.

Briar nods her approval. 'Okay, she understood the assignment.'

'Girl, you nailed that,' Dre says. 'Let's switch up those parts. Lune, you take verse one.'

I wish I didn't feel bad for Lune – this *is* the name of the game – but I do. 'Sorry,' I tell her.

'No, it's a team effort,' she says, not quite masking her

disappointment, and gives my hand a squeeze.

In the lounge, Nico gives me a warm smile and two manicured thumbs up through the window and, for the first time, I don't think she's acting.

It's after ten when I finally get the dance studio to myself. Group B has hogged it all evening. I'm trying hard to embrace the message of Girl Power and female unity, but they're really starting to get on my tits.

Lights on low, I warm up and turn the music on. Like Deenie taught me, I place some little stickers on the floor so when I change positions I'll know where to land. The Spice Girls dance itself isn't *too* hard, but we constantly formation-switch to get a turn in the centre. This dance is supposed to introduce us after all.

I go over the routine two, three, four times. Every time I mess up, I force myself to return to the start.

I'm so lost in watching my reflection, that I don't realize I'm not alone. 'Working late?' a voice says.

Cade stands in the shadows. How long has he been watching? I couldn't feel more exposed if I was naked. I try to style it out. 'Do they make you sleep in here?'

He smirks. 'They might as well.' He wiggles a phone charger at me. 'I left this behind.'

'You don't have a spare?' You'd think Cade Kekoa would have an assistant to run around after him.

'I'm living downtown in a hotel during filming.'

'You don't live in Media City?'

'God no, I hate it here.' He fully enters the studio. He's

dressed-down in a hoodie and parachute jeans. 'Technically I don't live anywhere.'

'What?'

'All my junk is at my folks' place in Boulder. I'm never in one place long enough to get an apartment. I haven't stopped since . . . well, since I applied to *Starmaker*.'

I don't know what to say. I'm on the very edge of saying something utterly cringe, I can feel it. But, for whatever reason, I don't want the conversation to end. 'Do you think you'll move to Boulder?'

'Nah. Colorado was never home.'

'Hawaii?'

'Yeah.' He looks to the floor. 'No going back there though.'

'I . . . I had to leave my home too. It went underwater like ten years ago.'

'I saw in your notes. You're the plucky refugee? That was my arc too.'

I look at the cameras, not sure if they're getting all this, or if he should be speaking so candidly. 'I like to think my arc is good singer, awful dancer.' I attempt what I hope is a wry chuckle.

'Okay, well that was also my arc. You can't be worse than I was.'

'Oh I don't know . . .'

He drops his Vuitton satchel to the studio floor and pulls off the hoodie. 'Let's run it.'

'Now?'

'You got somewhere better to be?'

I raise a brow. 'No, but don't you? You're *Cade Kekoa*.' Oh god, I just told him his own name; I want to die.

He smiles lopsidedly, half-tired, half-wired. 'Taryn, once you've been in as many hotel rooms as I have you'll understand. There are only so many club sandwiches you can stand.'

He hits play on 'Spice Up Your Life' and joins me at the back of the room, where I start. 'Five, six, seven, eight!'

We parade towards the mirror in time to the beat. As I try to be beguiling, even sexy, he effortlessly makes the same moves masculine – I think it's all in the wrists and fists. He watches me, and I can't take my eyes off him; the way he sways his hips, how he flexes his hairless, muscular arms.

He turns to mirror me and lifts my limp arm to precise shoulder height, where it ought to be. 'There. You're getting it now,' he says.

In the mirror, we look good together, he and I.

CHAPTER 21

I read somewhere that a bunch of girls in Portugal once came down with a weird sickness at the same time. The twist was that the illness itself was fictional; they'd seen it in a soap opera on TV. A similar mass hysteria seems to have gripped the Dreamhouse. As Saturday's live show careens closer, we all – to varying degrees – break out in acne and dry, itchy patches of eczema for no discernible reason.

No discernible reason except fear.

This Saturday, ten of us will enter the studio. Nine will leave. It's too much to contemplate.

Friday is studio rehearsal day. A luxury minibus ferries us to the obelisk skyscraper that is the Network G building. The glass tower, it transpires, is the executive offices. The studios are the hangar-like warehouses in the lot beyond the high-rise. They're beige brick, anonymous blocks. This isn't nearly as glamorous as I expected.

Once inside, we take in the vast soundstage, and I think it hits all of us. For the first time in a week, everyone falls silent;

even Suki, who literally never stops talking. 'It looks smaller on TV,' she says eventually, breaking the tension.

'It'll feel smaller when the audience is in,' Clancy says. She has also fallen foul of the phantom ailment; her left eye is pink and swollen with a nasty-looking stye.

'Where's . . .?' Briar starts. 'Where is . . .?'

Clancy understands. 'Eliminations are filmed next door. No studio audience.'

I think back to my history lessons at school. The way people used to gather in cobbled town squares for public hangings or floggings. Now they just gather in front of the TV with snacks. There is something in us, as a species, that is fascinated by death. He is our greatest fear, but we love to flirt with him.

The day is exhausting. Over and over, we run both the group dance routine and our vocal numbers so the camera operators can practice. Even Cade seems nervous, pacing and pounding ginger shots as he finetunes 'Spice Up Your Life'. I sense he is being judged alongside us.

This gives me my first opportunity to hear Group B. Annoyingly, they're pretty good. Ashanti is doing a lot of the heavy lifting, even if I find her tone a little nasal. Vocally, Domino isn't as good as she *thinks* she is. She *barks*. All belt, no light and shade. I bet she's the first up at karaoke night every time.

We don't get back to the Dreamhouse until after midnight. I haven't eaten, and I stink, but I'm too tired to even contemplate cooking or bathing. I collapse into bed and try not to think about how this could well be my final sleep.

* * *

Saturday. Live show number one.

I feel like cargo. There's *almost* no time to think, and I wonder if that's deliberate. Not that any of my thoughts would be happy ones.

An army of *Starmaker* hoodies and headsets descends on the Dreamhouse for hair, makeup and costume. I am assigned Jacey as my personal runner for the day. I have to ask them for permission when I need to pee. 'You can pee after your costume fittings,' they tell me, checking in with Clancy via their walkie-talkie.

Lars approves my (frankly hideous) dance outfit. We're all in neon bralettes and parachute pants that glow under UV lights mid-routine. Domino and I got searing lime green, coincidentally the colour of my stomach acid right now. At least that's how it feels. 'Should I take out my nose stud?' I ask the stylist.

'No,' he replies. 'I like it. It's on brand.'

His brand, or my brand? I can't worry about that now.

In the upstairs get ready room, I sit on a high stool at a vanity unit, and wait for my makeup artist to finish on Lune and get to me. A manicurist files away at my fingers.

Suki and Leela, both in Barbie pink, come over. They are finished, buried under foundation, blush, false lashes and hairspray. We all have matching nude nails. 'How you going, limey?' Suki says. 'What's with the sad face?'

'We might die tonight?' Saying it aloud takes some of the weight out of the demon on my back. 'What are we doing? Seriously?' My eyes feel heavy, full of glue.

'Surviving,' Leela says matter-of-factly.

From behind, Suki drapes her arms around my chest and rests her head on my shoulders. 'I don't know how I know this,' she says, looking my reflection in the eye. 'But I'm special. I'm a star. I've always known I was different from those other girls in Wagga Wagga. I'm supposed to be someone. And you know what?'

'What?' I say.

'I think you're special too, Taryn.'

I feign a smile. 'You think?'

'I know. And I'm never wrong. It's a gift. We're not gonna die because we're not there yet.'

'Not where?' Leela asks.

Suki scrunches her button nose. 'I don't know where we're going. But we're going *somewhere* big. I feel it. Don't you feel it?'

In that moment, I believe her. I swizzle in my stool and give her a kiss before folding her and Leela into a tight hug. 'You have no idea how much I needed to hear that,' I tell her.

'Hey, can I get some of that action?' It's Briar – in zingy orange – fresh out of hair and with two Bantu knots on her head like little horns. I'm a little surprised; Briar is normally so aloof.

'Get in here,' Suki says, and Briar wraps us all together and squeezes hard.

I breathe in a lungful of hairspray, deodorant and perfume, sucking a little strength from them all. I was mad to think I could get through this all alone. I really, really *need* friends right now.

Clancy sweeps across the get ready room. 'T-minus one hour to buses.'

I jump off the stool. I need to puke. I get to the bathroom just in time. I see from suspect yellow splatters around the porcelain bowl that I'm not the first one to lose my lunch. Better here than on TV, I guess.

We deal with the nerves differently.

Ashanti and Domino are complainers.

Briar, Lune and Leela are anxious-bladder girlies, making constant trips to the studio restrooms.

Minnie, Shayna and Suki are last-minute rehearsers, staring at the wall whilst running the routine like they're possessed. Girls, if you don't know it now . . .

Only Madison and I are silent warriors. We sit on opposite sides of the green room, our backs against the walls. We mirror each other, ignoring the buzzing hive around us. I can only focus on breathing, on not screaming.

I plan an escape.

I could say I need the toilet and leave through a window. I could fake a medical emergency and throw myself out of the back of the ambulance. I wonder if Madison is thinking the same.

'Taryn? You good?' Dre comes between us. We just did vocal warm-ups with him. I can only nod, incapable of doing anything except the task at hand. Cade is similarly silent. He catches my eye and offers a secret smile. I'm sure it's all in my mind, but I feel like he's singled me out. Maybe I just need the most help.

In my silent forcefield, as the other girls flit around, I see everything in slow-motion. It's clear now. I am not scared of dying. Either I won't know anything about it, or my mother awaits. What scares me is failure. If I gave up everything only to fail Dad, Jenson and Molly . . . Without me, I don't know how they'll cope. Sure, they'll get my meagre Project Population payout, but that won't last long. Then I'll be a ghost to haunt them; the guilt will kill them if the hunger doesn't.

'Girls!' Clancy claps. 'Up! Up! Up! This is being filmed for socials! On your feet!'

We gather and Mojo Frenzy and Nico enter. He is in a sequinned tuxedo; she is in a lilac gown, glimmering with a million Swarovski gems in powder pink. Her hair cascades over one shoulder like a waterfall. How is she real?

'Ladies!' Mojo says. 'This is it. It's Saturday night! Psycho! Smile, have fun, sell it!'

Easy for him to say. He's definitely going home tonight.

Nico adds, 'We'll see you out there on stage. Break a leg, ladies.'

The hosts turn to leave.

'Nico?' Suki raises a hand nervously.

The idol turns back to us. 'Yes, Minnie?'

'I'm Suki.'

'Oh, sorry.' Nico's amber eyes are a little glazed. Is she drunk?

'Do you have any advice before we go out?'

'Yeah,' she says. 'Just don't mess it up. One bad week, and . . . you're fucked.'

Oddly, that's the best advice any of the mentors have offered thus far.

Clancy hurls herself in front of the camera like an SAS bodyguard. 'Aaaand we'll cut there. We go live in ten.'

Like many women my age, I'm starting to worry about becoming a burden on my son and his young family. I'm becoming forgetful and always have aches and pains.

That's why I reached out to

PROJECT POPULATION

Not only is it kinder to the planet, it's easing pressure on the health service. I sleep better knowing that if my grandchildren get sick, they won't have lengthy waits at the ER. What's more, my son will receive a life-changing cash pay-out on the day of my departure.

GIVE YOUR FAMILY THE GIFT OF DEATH TODAY.

PROJECT POPULATION sponsors *Starmaker*.

CHAPTER 22

'Ladies and gentlemen, boys and girls, eithers and neithers, welcome to a brand-new season of *Starmaker*! Welcome to the stage, NICO!'

From the darkened wings, I hear Mojo's booming voice and the loudest scream I've ever heard as Nico struts on stage.

She performs 'Even These Dreams (Leave Me Lonely)' which lasts precisely three minutes and thirty-three seconds. Her vocals are pre-recorded. I wonder if it's as obvious on TV as it is here.

Her song done, she launches into scripted chat with Mojo.

'Girls, gather around,' Madison commands. Who put her in charge? I roll my eyes at Leela, but we form a circle in the shadows, hands joined. The Texan bows her head and closes her eyes. 'Whether you believe in our one true lord and saviour Jesus Christ or not, listen up. There's a plan for us. We're supposed to be here in this moment and he's watching over us. This is exactly where we're meant to be. Don't you listen to your inner saboteur telling you that you don't got this. That right there is the devil's tongue tryna steer you from the Lord's path. Go forward in the knowledge that this is what's meant for us. Amen.'

Shayna loudly concurs. Briar mumbles a low *amen* under her breath.

We get into our starting positions.

I do not believe in God. I don't claim to know whether he is *real*, but I don't believe he's got our best interests at heart if he is. Nonetheless, I find a weird comfort in Madison's words.

I *am* here.

I am.

Be here now.

A stage manager with a bright red beard stands in the shadows, counting us in. 'Ten seconds, girls, nine . . .'

I face the back of the LCD screens. From this side it's just wires and sticky tape.

Eight, seven, six.

There's no going back now. This is for Jenson. If I die, he dies.

Five, four, three.

Like Nico, I will play the role of a wannabe idol.

Two . . .

I force a broad smile onto my lips.

'Performing for the first time ever, it's the DOLLHOU5E trainees!'

The music starts. Hidden, burly men push the LCD screens apart down the middle, revealing our colosseum beyond. That growling carnival rumble in the intro of the track. And then go; the train leaves the station. I find, in the moment, my feet know what to do.

La la la . . . In formation we prowl through the partition like we're being birthed from the ginormous screen. The spotlights hit my eyes. Screams fill my ears, deafening.

By now, my feet have the steps on autopilot. SELL IT. I repeat the mantra in my head over and over. I smile. I find the camera and make eye contact. I'm only marginally aware of limbs and hair whisking past my nose as I turn and step, switching positions with each of the girls. They pass as a blur. First verse, bridge, chorus.

My turn as centre: *Arctic ice to Timbuktu / power for both me and you.* The camera is only metres away. On *me and you*, I decide to pump fake a punch to the camera, making a fist. I give a wink – just kidding!

Only the move throws me out by about a second and, as we switch, I clash shoulders with someone. A toss of chestnut hair tells me it's Madison. Damn. *Of course* it's her.

Don't lose time. Where are we? I fix myself and pray no one notices.

They will absolutely notice.

But I can't worry now.

I just have to finish this dance. *One dance at a time, Taryn, one at a time.* Cade is on the judges' panel, eyes on me.

By the end I'm back in formation and we finish in a hero pose. *Hai! Si! Ja! Hold tight!* I'm squatting, left leg outstretched like Black Widow. Something twinges in my hamstring. I'll feel that tomorrow.

Cade trained us to control our breathing so we don't look like panting dogs just in from the meadow. I smile and try to flick the hair off my face.

Did it. Minor collision aside, the hard part is done.

And the cheers. They love us. Mojo and Nico return to the stage and we stand. As we head to our marks, I see a little girl in the crowd holding a Union Jack flag. She's painted TARYN across the middle with splodgy, messy lettering.

She sees me seeing her, and screams, grabbing at her dad.

I can't lie. It's exhilarating. Even with everything I know, this is a rush.

Only then, as we stand in line, Madison smiles sweetly as she leans in to my ear. 'Darlin'? If your two left feet land me in the bottom, I'll kill you myself.'

The following sixty minutes are a conveyer belt, every second accounted for. Only during the commercial breaks are we truly free, but even then, the ads are streamed into the soundstage. *Starmaker: brought to you by FreshElla – the ultimate feminine protection.*

During the second interval, Clancy gathers us all. We're back in our schoolgirl looks. 'Group B, change of plans. You're up first.'

I don't especially question this until Clancy has exited the green room and Madison punches the wall. 'This is bull hockey!' she snaps. 'Everyone knows they put the best song on last – the voters remember it better. Why are they doing this to us?'

'Okay, you need to chill,' Suki says.

'Our song is poppier or whatever,' Briar says. 'It figures you'd put the slower one between the two faster ones.'

'All the best girls are in our group,' Madison snarls. 'This isn't fair!'

'Oh shut up,' I say. I'm nervous enough without her getting in our heads.

'Excuse me?' Madison blinks.

'You want subtitles? I said, *shut up*. You're doing my nut.'

'Okay, what does that even mean? Is that like British trailer park slang?'

If I punch her in the face, I'll be disqualified. I dig my nails into my palms. 'You go sing your song, and we'll sing ours. May the best singers win. Why do you even care, Madison? You're a nepo baby, you're safe whatever.'

She glowers at me. 'You have no idea where we come from.'

Madi squares up into my face and I think, for a second, she might actually hit me. That's one way to get rid of her. Only then her sister intervenes. 'Forget her,' Shayna says, scowling at me through thick lashes. She pulls her sister away from the confrontation.

Briar pulls me into a hug and squeezes tight. 'Taryn, you're a boss. I've been dying to tell that bitch to shut her goddamn mouth all week.'

'Well now I'm *really* fired up.' I look to Suki, Lune and Leela. 'Let's show them how it's done.'

Search: #Starmaker

@crispybaybi that English girl can SING! #Starmaker

@bendywendy544 blonde girl can't sing for shit lol #Starmaker

@manunitedqueen Taryn's voice is fire. Like vintage Amy or Adele vibes. #Starmaker

@starfakergurl Tops: Taryn, Leela, Domino, Madison. Bottoms: sorry Lune and Shayna. #Starmaker

@freddiebooger lol at that Swedish girl. god luvs a try-er. #Starmaker #backtoIkea

@tomtombakerboi someone meme that bum note at once ooooof #Starmaker

@dinahcarrew21 I swear I thought Taryn would be first out and then she drops that vocal. Iconic tbh. #Starmaker

@ntrustbiggistfan CADE FOLLOW ME #Starmaker **@CadeKekoa**

@starmakermemes222 Briar and Domino are like a plastic surgery before and after photo hahahaha #Starmaker

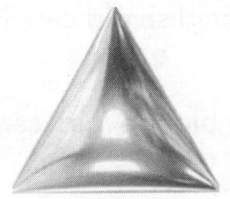

CHAPTER 23

Live segment done, Lune is still sobbing when it's time to record the results show. We gather around her chair in the hair and makeup station, trying to console her. We've had a chance to watch the footage back.

'I was pitchy too,' Briar says.

'And me,' Suki adds. 'But our group was definitely better overall.'

That's probably true. While they were certainly competent, Madison's group didn't have the highs that we had. They were . . . fine? Forgettable even. I see why they put us on last.

But Lune really did sing a very off note during her ad-lib at the end. Like a bag of cats hitting a wall.

Regardless, during the segment where we each went into the Ranking Pod to 'secretly' cast our votes before the entire planet, I naturally ranked my team in the first four positions. I placed Madison and Shayna last because I don't feel it's fair that they already have a huge online following, and I said so. Not that it *really* matters; our votes count less than both the judges and the viewers at home. I suspect it's mostly to cause tension. I just know our 'private' rankings will be made public at some point.

'Taryn? Tell me the truth. Was it bad?' Lune asks, big eyes watery.

'Look, it was one note,' I reply honestly. 'Your verse was spot on.' Also true.

Jacey, my runner, approaches, holding their earpiece. In a sea of similar-looking young runners, Jacey stands out with their mullet, so I at least remember one name. 'Guys, we're on in two, but take time if you need it.' Then they add, 'You can relax now; the results show isn't live.'

Relax is a bit rich, but I turn to them. 'Jacey, why isn't this bit live?'

They look me squarely in the eye. 'In case of irregularities with the result.'

'What does that mean?'

They shrug, aiming for nonchalant but failing. 'Just . . . sometimes there are delays or whatever so they might need to edit things out.'

Something isn't right, but I can't quite name it.

'GIRLS!' Clancy shrieks, clapping her hands like a performing seal. 'On set now!'

The studio audience has been sent home so spoilers can't leak online. We file down an endless, draughty connecting corridor between Studio Four and Five. Runners stick to the edges, allowing us to pass. Behind us follows a trio of security guards, built like brick walls. Guess they don't want anyone trying to leave.

It feels funereal. This is a death march for one of us.

We have changed into our farewell looks: all white, all of us, head-to-toe. I have a leather mini kilt, a torn t-shirt and white Doc Martens boots. I hold Leela's hand all the way down the hallway.

Jacey opens the door to Studio Five and I see it for the first time: the pyramid.

Every year the Elimination Chamber is different.

One year it was a water tank. One year it was an incinerator. This year, we have a glass pyramid. Sleek, pristine, standing about seven-feet tall. It's like a shark's fin, and inspires the same fear in me. There's something cold and deadly about its hard edges.

The studio is dark, the only light the cold white illumination around the tomb. Dry ice rolls over the floor.

'What is it?' Briar mutters on my left.

I stall on the threshold. 'You're fine,' Jacey breathes in my ear and I wonder if they know something I don't. Either way, I'm hustled onto the soundstage.

'On your marks, girls!' calls the same bearded stage manager.

Nico, Cade and Dre are already seated at the judging panel, receiving last-minute touch-ups from the MUAs.

We are to stand on steps before them and await our fate. Five security guards are positioned off camera. They're from a company called Securiforce and they're dressed in iridescent mother-of-pearl bomber jackets and wear baseball caps low over their faces. They'd *almost* blend in if it weren't for the guns they carried. At first I thought the security detail was here to protect us from overzealous fans, but now I'm not so sure.

I wonder if this is why the results show is pre-recorded.

I don't recall any trainee being dragged to the Elimination Chamber; they always just *go*. The military rifles the guards are holding tell me *why* they always just go. It was Edgar Allan Poe, I think, who said there's nothing more poetic than the death of a beautiful woman. The people at home want to see us die *prettily*. Only the grand final features a death live on stage.

'Girls, how are we all doing?' It's Dr Anders – Mal – the therapist guy. He's wearing an argyle sweater and khaki slacks. I'm not sure he's going to make any of us feel better about this. 'There's nothing I can say to make this any less nerve-wracking, I'm afraid. Just know that I'm here and I'll meet with you later. I wish you all the very best of luck.'

The makeup artists scurry away to the side-lines and Mojo Frenzy hits his position. He rabbits away; something about how well we all did and we should be so proud, blah, blah, blah, but all I see is the glass pyramid. It's silent, watching me somehow, with great malice.

'Aaaaaand we're rolling!' the stage manager calls, snapping me out of it. 'Action!'

'Girls, the votes have been counted and verified and it's time to find out who will be leaving DOLLHOU5E tonight.'

The lights dim. The foreboding overture, which I'd always assumed was added in post production, is actually played into the studio. It's not helping.

'As ever, the top eight idols with the most public votes will progress to next week, while the bottom two will face our panel of judges. I will now reveal the ranking as decided by Starmakers at home all over the world,' Mojo says sombrely. 'In first position is . . .'

I repeat *Taryn* in my mind over and over, willing him to say it.

'Domino!' I feel her sigh of relief on the back of my neck. 'Go to your podium.'

Individual white podiums flank the incline leading to the pyramid door. Domino pushes past me and heads to the #1 plinth right next to the glass tank.

'The next girl safely through is . . .' The pauses are torture. 'Madison!'

There's a scream down the line. She hugs her sister and heads for the second podium opposite Domino.

'Ranking third is . . .' *Say it, say it, say it.* 'Taryn!'

Did he say it, or did I imagine it? He said it! He actually said my name. My spine almost gives way. I flop forward at the waist. I feel hands rub my back. 'You did it!' Leela says alongside me.

'Taryn, head to your position.'

Almost floating across the fog on the floor, I find my way to the third podium. I'm dizzy, vision glittery. I did it. I survived. Third, behind only the hottest one and a nepo baby.

Fourth place is Shayna, fifth Ashanti, sixth Leela.

Thank god. I wish I could run to Leela, but I can't. We were told to stay on our podiums.

'Four girls remain,' Mojo states. 'Two are safe, two will be judged. The girl in seventh place is . . . Minnie.'

Her eyes close. She exhales before taking her plinth in her usual serene, swanlike manner.

I look to the last three girls: Briar, Lune and Suki. All part of my team. What did we do wrong? Or is it really just that we aren't the prettiest? If this is a beauty pageant, I may as well get in the Elimination Chamber now.

'The last girl safe this week is . . .' The longest pause yet. 'Suki.'

Suki bursts into noisy, ugly tears. She manages a few steps to her position but she can hardly breathe. You know what, screw it. I step down from my plinth and go to comfort her. I see Clancy frantically waving at me, emphatically signalling that I should get back on my mark. Screw her, too. I hold Suki tight and steer her onto the eighth plinth.

'You're okay now,' I tell her, wiping her tears away with my thumb. 'You're okay.'

I give Clancy and Dr Anders a steely look before I go back to my podium.

'Lune and Briar, I'm afraid you're our final two.'

Lune weeps. Briar is grimly stoic. I eye the security guards. Their weapons are poised.

'Judges. What do you think went wrong for these girls tonight? Nico, I'll come to you first.'

Nico waves a manicured hand at thin air. 'I mean . . . I don't know what to say. I guess other girls were better.'

Is that the best she can do? I'm oddly furious. After all these years worshipping that woman . . . is she a bit thick?

'Cade Kekoa, what say you?'

Cade shakes his head. 'This just sucks. You both worked so hard. Lune, you know you had some vocal issues. Briar, I have no idea why you're standing here right now.'

'I do,' Dre adds, under his breath, but doesn't elaborate. 'This is awful. No one wants to be the first to go. I feel like we don't know you yet.'

Clancy crosses the floor and mutters amongst the judges. I can't hear what's being said. I do, distantly, hear her say *Chairman Slade*. Oh, I see. I understand with perfect clarity. The final choice doesn't come from the judges at all. It comes from Slade.

Clancy slithers back into the darkness and Mojo takes his mark once more. 'Nico, as Head Judge, what decision have you reached?'

'Mojo, this is awful. Cade and I remember what this was like, and . . . we wish there was another way. But this is the game. Girls, you knew the rules when you signed up.' She exhales. Her tone is flat. 'This week, we voted to save Briar.'

It's as though the room cracks in two. The relief from Briar is palpable. She drops into a squat, head in hands. Lune is frozen. With her big eyes, she looks like a rabbit before a huntsman.

The Securiforce guards take one step forwards in a pincer movement.

'What?' Lune says. 'No, please.'

'I'm so sorry, sweetie,' Mojo says. 'You did great.'

The tiny young woman approaches him, palms open, almost begging. 'Please, I can't go. I need to talk to my mom.'

The judges are ushered out to spare them any unpleasantness. As he goes, Cade turns back and looks me in the eye. I acutely feel his sorrow. He shakes his head in shame. He's powerless to stop this. Clancy and Dr Anders prise Lune out of Mojo's arms and he too exits.

'Just stay where you are girls,' Clancy shouts at us.

Briar is left on the stairs. I beckon her over, and wrap her in a tight embrace. 'You're okay,' I breathe into her hair. Are we though?

'Lune, my dear,' Dr Anders says. 'Would you like a sedative? It'll make this all easier.'

'Please!' Lune weeps. 'Please let me go. I won't tell anyone. Just let me go home. I want my mama.'

I cover my eyes. I cannot watch.

'There's the easy way or the hard way,' Clancy says, getting impatient. 'This goes for all of you. This is *Starmaker*; you all knew what you were getting into.'

'Please . . .' Lune says again and again.

'The pyramid is painless,' Dr Anders says, his voice steady. 'It'll be just like falling asleep.' He takes her arm and administers some sort of injecto-pen. Within seconds, Lune's hysteria subsides, her eyes glazing over. She sways slightly on her feet.

'Right!' Clancy barks. 'Ready to sing, girls. Let's get this done in one take and then we can all get fried chicken.'

This is surreal. The most dreadful nightmare. The music begins. We've been learning the song all week. I see now why we laid down backing vocals earlier in the week, because, right now, I can't form words.

Goodbye, sweet friend
'Til we meet again
You are in my heart
End to start.

A camera tracking her every move, Lune, her cheeks wet with tears, walks the ramp to the glass pyramid. The side closest to us lifts skywards to grant her access to the chamber.

> *Goodbye, sweet child*
> *Run free and wild*
> *A sacrifice*
> *To paradise.*

She passes my podium as if she's in a trance. Whatever Dr Anders gave her has turned her into a zombie. I will her to turn and run. When it's my turn, I think I'd rather have those guards shoot me in the back than step into this human bell jar.

Lune climbs into the pyramid and the fourth wall lowers. It makes a suction noise as it seals shut.

> *No matter where you are*
> *Goodbye, my star.*

And *hiss*. All at once, the pyramid fills with a billowing pink cloud, the sugared pink of bubble-gum and strawberry milkshake. Lune is swallowed in the plume.

'Gas!' Suki exclaims. Next to her Leela's eyes are screwed shut. A reflex, my hand shoots out as if to pull her free.

'Girls! Stand still!' Clancy barks. 'Stay right there. Do. Not. Move.'

The candyfloss gas disperses and, when the cloud clears, the pyramid is empty.

LOVE LUNE?
GET THE GHOST JUKEBOX!

DON'T FORGET THAT YOU CAN LISTEN TO ALL YOUR FAVOURITE SONGS RECREATED WITH LUNE'S VOCALS USING THE VERY LATEST AI VOICE CAPTURE TECHNOLOGY.

DOWNLOAD THE *STARMAKER APP* RIGHT NOW FOR ACCESS TO MILLIONS OF SONGS IN THE GHOST JUKEBOX FEATURING LUNE AND ALL THIS SEASON'S ELIMINATED TRAINEES.

DOLLHOU5E OR BRAWL-HOU5E?
Bitter backstage catfights threaten new *Starmaker* series.

Inclusion of so-called 'nepo babies' causes arguments in and out of the Dreamhouse.

EXCLUSIVE by TV Editor Dean Sutton

Insiders at the most-watched television event in the world, *Starmaker*, have revealed exclusively to *The Globe* that the young trainees have turned against sister hopefuls Madison and Shayna Silver.

At Saturday's first live show, which saw 18-year-old Lune Karlsson of Sweden eliminated, tensions were running high backstage. One source said, 'Some girls aren't happy that Madison and Shayna already have a huge social media presence. They feel it's giving them an unfair advantage.'

The Silver sisters, Madison (18) and Shayna (15), are the younger sisters of B*TRU3 idol Peyton Silver, who was part of the winning group on Season 10 of the hit Network G series. Some fans have taken to G-Net declaring they believe their participation is 'a fix'. Sources say that bosses are in 'crisis talks' to stop in-fighting getting out of hand with rumours that some trainees threatened to quit following Karlsson's exit.

Madison and Shayna were ranked in second and fourth place respectively on Saturday's results show. Pretty Brit hopeful Taryn Beck, 17, <u>a flood refugee from Kelso</u>, placed third in the vocal challenge.

The Globe: always the first with *Starmaker* exclusives!

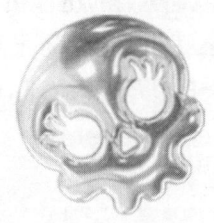

CHAPTER 24

Leela yanks the duvet off my body. 'You need to get up,' she says.

'You're so German.'

'That is a stereotype. But GET UP.' She sits on the edge of my bed. 'We're going to go downtown. There is a doughnut place, Briar says.'

'I don't want a doughnut. Are we even *allowed* doughnuts?' Sunday is our one day off. No cameras, no Clancy. 'What's the point?'

'Because the only other choice is to be sad.' Leela's eyes are pink-rimmed.

Lune's death fills my veins like quick-setting cement. I'm not sure I could leave this mattress even if I wanted to. I'm haunted by how little I knew about Lune. I know she was from Stockholm. She lived on a diet of gummy sweets and Diet Coke. She loved Hello Kitty socks and fluffy leg warmers. I don't even know if she had brothers or sisters.

I stare at the ceiling. I'm not sure I'll ever feel joy again, as if that part of my brain went into the pyramid with her. 'What are we doing, Lee?' My voice is hollow.

'Long-term, I do not know. Today, we get doughnuts.'

Put like that, it makes sense. Lune was not expecting to be the first out. None of us were. I think, with hindsight, I *must* have held a belief that I *could* make the band, or I'd have never entered the house. But, applying that logic, all ten of us must have felt that way. Five of us are in for a nasty surprise.

I can't erase Lune's stunned face from my mind. Her pleas. I don't think she really believed she was going to die even as she stepped into the Elimination Chamber.

God, if I stay here in bed, all I'll see is her face on the ceiling. 'Okay,' I concede. 'Give me ten minutes to shower.'

I've never seen anywhere quite like Media City Plaza before. It's brand new. Everything is shiny and clean and glass and steel. Children play in the jets of water that shoot out of the central square outside the mall. My first experience of an American mall might be fun if we weren't all so morose.

Even worse, the first thing we see when we we step out of the (frankly unnerving) driverless cab is *us*. A ginormous LED billboard sits above the main entrance, and we are on it; our individual publicity photos somewhat crudely superimposed side-by-side as if we were in a line-up. We're all in colour, except Lune, who is now in black-and-white.

'Is that supposed to be tasteful?' I say, before swearing loudly.

'We need to be careful,' Briar says. I don't know what she means until I realize that a group of teenage girls are staring at us from across the fountain. They're trying to work out if it's really us or not. Maybe this trip wasn't such a good idea.

'Were we meant to leave the house?' I ask, a little wary now.

'Not *strictly*,' Suki says. Great. Now she tells me.

'Come on, girls; I've got an idea,' Briar says, and confidently sets off in the direction of the Disney Store.

'What is she doing?' Leela asks, but we follow.

Once inside the store, Briar hands each of us a baseball cap. I get Minnie Mouse. 'Here,' she says. 'Your first celebrity baseball hat. Should we get sunglasses too?'

I put the hat on. 'Happy?'

'Not really,' Briar concedes as she puts a Lion King cap on. 'But at least they won't see we've all been crying.'

Suki sighs. 'Look, guys, I know this really, really sucks big time, but we need to dig deep if we're gonna kick butt. We can't back out, and if we let last night get in our heads, we might as well hand the win to the Group B girls.'

I look to Briar who sort of nods. I exhale, almost ridding my lungs of fear and fury. 'The only way out is through,' I admit. 'Come on, let's go spite Clancy with calories.'

In a store called Cake Station, I get a red velvet cupcake and a blueberry matcha latte. The show gives us a 'per diem': an envelope of dollars for things we might need during our stay. I was planning to save mine up and send it home, but I think I'm allowed a treat.

The restaurant is a candy fantasy of pinks and purples, and I think they're pumping a sugary smell into the environment. We squish into a lilac vinyl booth and make sure we've all tried everyone's choices, like carbohydrate tapas. Suki's bubble-gum milkshake is a shade of Smurf blue that can't be good for her. I swerve that.

'If Clancy saw this, she would be having a stroke,' Leela says, shoving some apple pie cheesecake in her mouth.

I'm suggesting she needs something a little stronger than a stroke when a cherubic little girl tentatively approaches the table. She stares at me, eyes wide, mouth gaping like a goldfish. 'Hey,' I say. 'Are you okay?'

'Are you DOLLHOU5E?' she says sweetly.

A woman, her mum, I guess, looms over her, nudging her forward. 'I'm sorry to disturb you, but could we get a picture? We love the show.'

Did they enjoy the bit where Lune died? My first thought is to hide all the food in case Clancy sees it on G-Net, but the girl looks so hopeful. She's maybe six or seven. 'Sure thing,' I tell her. 'Come sit with us!'

Briar scooches up and the grinning girl slides alongside her. 'What's your name, sweetie?' Briar asks.

'Willow.'

'Oh that's super cute!' Suki smiles.

'Who's your favourite trainee?' I ask.

The little girl blushes. 'I like Leela.'

'Aw! Really? Thank you!' Leela beams.

When I was her age, playing Who Is Your Favourite? was one of my top games to play at primary school. Choosing your bias is half the fun of being a fan.

'Everyone smile!' the girl's mother says and we all pose for a picture.

Of course, this kerfuffle has attracted the attention of a thirteenth birthday party happening at the far end of the counter. 'Oh my god! It IS them!' one girl cries.

Now that young Willow has broken the seal, it's open season on photos. Birthday girl Kennedy and her friends swarm us, shoving camera phones in our faces. One little fan wasn't too scary, but nine teenagers is . . . a lot. They lean into me, pressing their faces against mine. I don't know what to do with my face so I just grin like an idiot and make a peace sign. Is this what fame is like? Sort of flattering, but also . . . smothering? I remind myself that only five of us will ever truly find out. This acute attention could be very temporary.

The questions come thick and fast.

'What's Cade like?'

'Is Madison coming?' one girl asks.

'I love Domino so much!' another says.

It's stifling. One of the baristas comes over to ask for an autograph. I do not *have* an autograph so I just write Taryn and a little heart which feels utterly inadequate.

I catch Leela's eye. She smiles politely but it's like she's sending me a psychic message: *this is a bit weird*. These people are strangers. We are just girls who have been on TV one time. Is it okay for them to come over and start taking pictures? Suki is only fifteen.

One thing is clear: we can't stay here. Word has spread, and now girls are pressed against the window to see if it's true.

'What say we bounce?' Briar says, sounding a little nervous.

We leave our half-finished cakes and drinks in the booth and tell the crowd that our car is waiting for us. A lie. Arms linked for security, we exit to a wall of phones making videos. If we don't smile and wave, we'll be flamed on socials for being rude. We don't have a choice as I see it. The mall forecourt starts to congest with mostly teenage girls, but plenty of curious grown-ups too. *Everyone* watches *Starmaker*.

'Guys! We really have to go!' Suki is good at this. 'Peace out, everyone! Don't forget to vote this weekend!'

Suki drags us through the forming crowd. I clamp my teeth together and focus on my smile. Female idols are accused of the cardinal sin of Misery much more than male ones. Boys get to be brooding or aloof; girls are called bitchy.

'Taryn!' Someone screams my name. They know my name. After one week. I wave gormlessly.

As a four-piece hybrid we tumble out of the mall and into fresh air and daylight. But now we have a small army of teenage girls following us, armed with phones, only drawing yet more attention. *And* we're back under the bloody billboard. This is where our lie crumbles; there is no car waiting at the rim of the plaza.

Only there *is*. It takes me a second to realize that a horn is honking repeatedly. 'Taryn!' The voice is coming from inside the car.

'Guys . . .' I summon the others.

I peer inside the onyx BMW solar SUV. Cade leans over the passenger seat. 'Get in!'

I don't even care why he's there, I'm just glad he is. 'Quickly,' I tell the others before our new following realize who's driving.

I fold myself into the passenger side while Suki, Leela and Briar crush onto the backseat. The doors aren't even shut when Cade pulls away from the crowded plaza. 'What are you doing here?'

'I went to the house and Madi told me you were here. You should have come with a Securiforce guard. What were you thinking?'

'Are we in trouble?' I ask.

'If Clancy finds out, yes. Every year someone tries to . . . well, escape,' Cade says. I hadn't thought of that.

'*That* was freaking crazy.' Briar looks shellshocked.

'Are we famous?' Suki looks out of the rear windscreen as the *Starmaker* fans shrink into the distance.

'Famous is just another word for *watched*,' Cade says gravely.

'Why were you looking for us?' I ask.

'I was looking for *you*, Taryn.' He keeps his eyes on the road. We drive out of the downtown zone and hit the freeway. Without traffic, it'd be a five minute drive max, but we'll sit in gridlock for half an hour at least. It's like America didn't get the memo about restricting car use.

'You were looking for me?'

'To talk off camera.'

The girls in the back of the SUV fall silent. 'Okay . . .' I say.

'There was a meeting this morning. Chairman Slade dialled in. The producers decide the plotlines for the week ahead . . . and you're it.'

'Me? Why?'

'They didn't like you running over to comfort Suki during elimination.'

'But . . .'

'That's not fair!' Suki pipes up. 'I was a hot mess; she was just helping.'

'I know, I know. They think you're a troublemaker. This week is a dance challenge. The narrative is about how you're the weakest dancer.' He speaks dispassionately, telling me exactly how it is. 'Here's what you're going to do. You're going to fake an injury in rehearsals. That way, if you even hold it together, you'll look like a hero and get through the vote.'

Briar leans forward. 'Are you saying they pretty much choose who's eliminated?'

Cade's silence says it all. 'It's all in the edit,' he eventually admits.

'Are you allowed to be telling me this?' I ask.

'God no.'

'Then why are you?'

Another long pause. The expanse of the Dreamhouse complex is now visible on the arid hillside. 'Because I've been through all this. I think it should be fair. It should be about talent and nothing else. Listen; you guys have got to stick together. They are going to try *everything* to break you up. They don't want alliances; they want you to be out for yourself. If you work together, you're dangerous.'

'Dangerous to whom?' Leela asks.

Cade shakes his head. 'To *what*. To their control.'

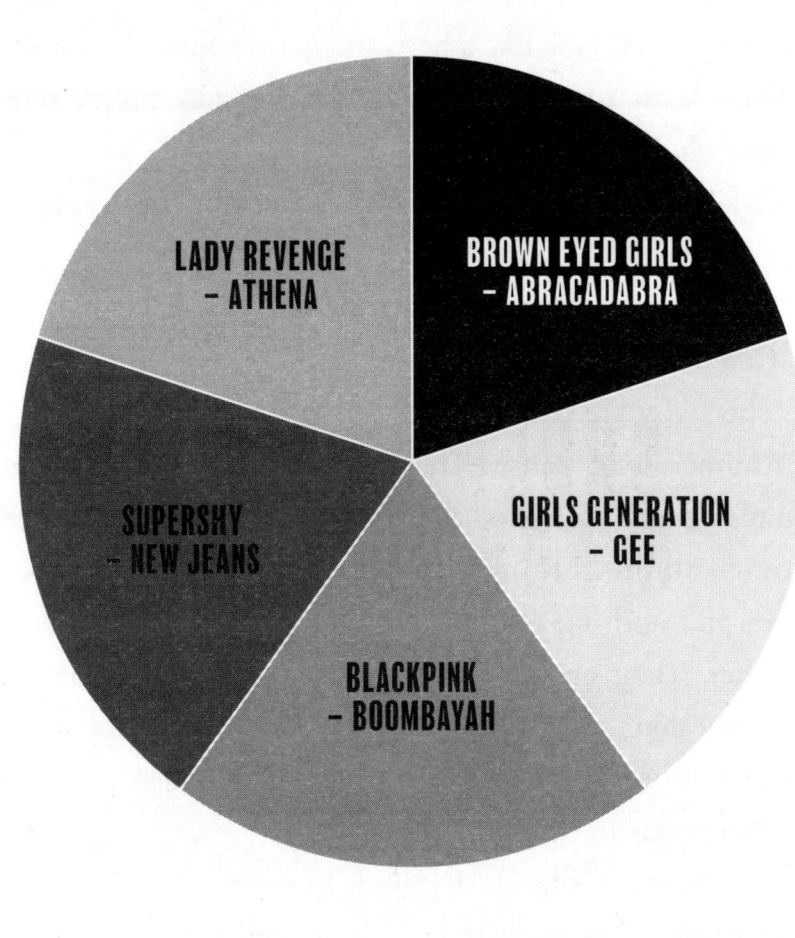

CHALLENGE TWO:
GROUP DANCE – 'K-POP CLASSICS'

CHAPTER 25

A very different version of Cade – all business, all smiles – stands before us in the dance studio to introduce Challenge Two. We await our mission in our groups from last week.

'Okay, Madison,' he begins, 'switch teams with Leela.'

Oh god, not this. The producers have got wind of our green room argument, so *of course* they are forcing us to work together. I don't miss Madison rolling her eyes at Shayna or giving me a poisonous side-eye as she joins our team. I ignore her; I'm not giving the producers the drama they so badly need for ratings.

'We ranked you based on vocals and dance skill ahead of the Dreamhouse and now each team is balanced.'

My team is now four-strong: me, Suki, Briar and Madison. On the other side of the studio, Leela looks bereft. I offer what I hope is a solidarity smile.

'This week, in honour of Minnie's home nation, each group will be assigned a classic K-Pop routine. In a change to the rules, fans will vote this time and the member from each team with the fewest votes will face the judges' verdict.'

We're asked to react, and make an ominous *oooh*. I can't help but note our odds are worse than the other team's because there are fewer of us.

'Let's see what routines you'll be tackling . . .'

The wheel spins on the studio TV. Group B gets 'Boombayah'. We get 'Abracadabra'.

Cade shows us the original music videos for both songs. Okay. It's clear – both on the screen and in the room – that 'Boombayah' is the more difficult routine. However, my initial smugness lasts about half a minute. The Brown Eyed Girls number is all about attitude and, well, *sex*. While Group B look panicked, I almost envy them the simple challenge of non-stop arm windmilling and hair-flips, while I have to muster slinky hips and what old people would call *Come Hither Eyes*.

'And of course,' Cade goes on, 'any idol group has to dance alongside professionals . . .'

He gestures to the door and five male dancers file into the studio. Some of the girls giggle and whisper as though they've never seen a boy before. Honestly, dignity costs nothing.

'That's right, girls. This week you'll be joined by our *Starmaker* dance squad: Eli, Joaquin, Trent, Paulo and Kenji.'

'Hey, ladies,' they chant on cue. They are all very cute, but the only thing I see are five walking traps: they've been airdropped in to cause more drama. The powers-that-be are hoping one of us will be stupid enough to enter into a romantic subplot. Death on shows like this: I'd be slut-shamed all the way to the Elimination Chamber.

The dancers and Cade walk us through each routine,

starting with Group A. I'm assigned dancer Eli and it's immediately cringe. To make matters worse, *our* dance will be in three-inch heels to mimic the original. I'm handed a pair of ankle boots.

'Legend has it, when this song came out, it caused a huge stir,' Cade explains. 'It pushed the boundaries of what was acceptable for a girl group in Korea.'

As I paw and stroke poor Eli, I've never felt more like a 'tomboy' in my life. 'I'm gay, just go for it,' he says, but it's only marginally helpful. I attempt my sexiest prowl-walk, but I imagine I look like a toddler walking in her mum's stompy shoes. Eyes on me, Ashanti whispers something in Shayna's ear and the younger girl giggles cruelly.

Joke's on her. The heels will only make my forthcoming injury more believable. I think I'll save my tumble for closer to the live show, for more impact.

'Let's run it with music,' Cade announces. 'Just see how it feels, take it easy.'

The music starts. Cade is looking at me. Am I meant to feign an accident now? I'm pondering this timing, when, in a flash of hair, Madison goes down.

'Keep going,' calls Cade over the beat.

'I can't!' Madison cries. 'I rolled my ankle! It really hurts.'

'Stop the music!' Cade shouts and runs to her aid. 'Can you get up?'

She shakes her head, cradling her left foot.

Cade signals to Jacey, the runner. 'Can we get an ice pack, please?' He turns his attention back to Madison. 'Okay, take a break. Let's do Blackpink.'

Cade and I briefly lock eyes. It doesn't need saying. As Jacey escorts a limping Madison off the floor, followed intently by the camera crew, I silently retreat to the wall, grabbing my water bottle. I don't want the cameras to see my face. Purposefully or not, Madison just stole my safe passage to Challenge Three.

All I can do is train.
And train.
And train.
But by Wednesday, I'm still struggling. The move, *the* move, in our routine is the hip-sway-turn. I am assured it's iconic. I have to turn, sexily, while rolling my head backwards and swinging my hips side-to-side like a pendulum.

'Again!' Cade snaps. I sense his frustration. It's late afternoon. Group B are out in the garden running their routine while we hog the studio. 'Back to ones. Full out, Suki.'

Little Suki pants, red-faced. 'I'm sorry. I'm tired, and Clancy says I can't have lunch any more so I feel really weird!'

'We aren't stopping until Taryn gets it.'

I sigh. There are blisters on my little toes, my lower back hurts from arching my butt and stress ulcers line my cheeks. Being a trainee idol *looks* glamorous. It is not. Clancy is back to monitoring our meals so I too feel faint much of the day. The woman has positioned some weighing scales in front of the fridge as a 'reminder' to stick to our meal plans.

The music begins again and off we go. I'm so busy worrying about the hip-sway-turn I mess up even getting into position.

'Again!' barks Cade.

'She's useless!' Madison lets rip. Her ankle is still bandaged but she seems to be managing which makes me think she *has* faked an injury to stay prominent in the edit.

'Oh leave her alone,' Briar snaps back, though I can tell she's frustrated too.

'I'm trying!'

Just then someone grabs my wrist and yanks me around. It's Cade. 'You're not trying hard enough! Don't you get it? If you don't do this right, you will die.' He's so close I feel his breath on my cheek.

I tug my arm free. 'Let go of me,' I snarl, pushing him back on both shoulders. I wouldn't let a man put hands on me back home, and I won't here either, even if he is an idol. The other girls tense up, falling silent.

'I'm sorry.' He cools himself. 'Just . . . you need to believe you can do this. I can't do it for you, Taryn. You're in your head.'

Madison scowls at us as she sips some water. 'Why do you care so much about her?'

Cade looks to the floor, embarrassed. 'I care about all of you. I remember what it was like to be the underdog.'

Underdog. Clever Cade. This is all being filmed. If I can convince the people watching that this is all a part of my *journey*, I might just survive the week. That's *if* they use this footage. Neither of us control that.

It's getting dark outside. I want to shower and find something to eat that isn't *one cup of salad and protein.*

Cade squats on his haunches, forehead glistening with sweat. His jersey is stuck to his chest. 'Taryn, let's run it solo. The rest of you can call it a day. Get some beauty sleep; tomorrow is a photoshoot.'

I tie my hair up and towel off my chest as the others pack up their stuff and head back to the house to shower.

'Are you happy to go again?' Cade says once we're alone. He sounds apologetic after his fiery outburst.

'Yes,' I say. 'Like you said, I don't especially want to die.'

He beckons me over and positions me in front of the mirror. 'You dance like a confused robot.'

I have to laugh or I'll weep. 'What?'

'It's true! I think you're overconcentrating.'

'I doubt that.'

He hovers his hands either side of me. 'May I?' I nod and he gently places his palms on my hips. 'You have to *feel* it. Sink lower. *Sway*.'

Him behind me, together we rock side-to-side. His hips pressed against my waist.

'Fluid, gentle, like calm ocean waves.'

I get it – like a cat's tail, not a clock pendulum.

'Better. The song is about casting a spell on your ex to win him back. Hypnotize me with your hips.' He takes my jaw in his palm and tips my chin up. In the mirror I meet his eyes. 'Hypnotize me with your eyes. Don't look so scared.'

I try for a seductive expression.

'Better. Shall we try the turn? Pivot on the right foot using the left, roll head clockwise. I've got you.' He wraps an arm across my chest to keep me upright and we turn together. Leaning on him, I don't need to worry about balance; I roll my neck and complete the steady orbit. 'There you go. You did it.'

For a moment, he holds me. His front is pressed against my back. I feel his warmth. The air between us is somehow too thick.

Then he lets go, and I realize I'm not breathing. I try to make a joke . 'Great. Just the other three minutes to perfect.'

'Just keep that level of focus. That sensuality.'

I muffle laughter. 'Well that's the problem,' I say. 'I'm not exactly *sensual* am I?'

'Who told you that?' Cade says, almost carelessly, and he turns the music on.

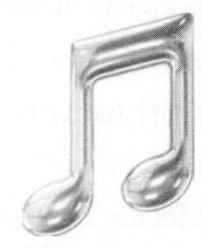

CHAPTER 26

'What's on your mind?' Briar asks in the makeup chair next to me.

'Nothing,' I lie, mumbling as the makeup artist overdraws my lips.

Cade is on my mind. It's absurd. I am eye-to-eye with the actual Grim Reaper, but my heart feels like one of those melt-in-the-middle puddings over some guy. Almost embarrassing, really. It's the same *feeling* I rehearsed with Sonny from N-TRU5T, but this is solid, and all the more dangerous for it. My imagination is addicted to scenarios I've invented for the next time I see him at dance practice. I've even started planning witty little things I could say to him.

You'd think I'd be more focused on the whole staying alive part. I need to sober up.

But he said he thought I was cute.

Even though he didn't use those *exact words*, it's where my head has landed.

I have *got* to focus. I should be running dance moves, not flirting.

A red-faced Clancy sweeps into the makeup gazebo. 'Can I get a time check please?'

The makeup artist says that about half of us are ready to go, and so Clancy collects me, Ashanti, Shayna and Briar and leads us to the set.

We're shooting a digital cover for the new issue of *Feminasti* magazine at a car wash in downtown Media City. This is surreal. I grew up on *Feminasti*, an online magazine started by Dionne Malik – a super-smart girl not much older than I am. It's gritty, and funny, and knows how wild it is to be a teenage girl in a world that detests both girls and teenagers.

I'm not entirely sold on the photoshoot concept, however. It's a wet t-shirt contest scenario, but apparently car wash fundraisers are a *thing* over here so it'll all make sense to the intended audience. As one of the under-18s, I'm in a cropped Union Jack t-shirt and red short shorts. The over-18s are in skimpier bikini tops. It's such a weird double standard. We're *all* dressed like jailbait, but the younger girls get two more inches of polyester to protect our purity. Kinda gross all round.

The car wash forecourt is warped under the boot of the midday sun. The sky is the sort of luxe azure we rarely witness in Scotland. I'm going to burn. I doubt anyone cares.

'Okay, girls!' Damon, a very hip photographer with a navy-blue beard, calls over. 'Let's get you on the car.'

The car in question is a filthy 1967 red-and-white Chevy truck. His assistant hands us our props – buckets and sponges – and, with the help of a little ladder, we're artfully positioned over the vehicle. As you do.

We've been split into two different groups for this set-up.

Briar and I are with Shayna and Ash. Ashanti makes sure she's front and centre, obviously. That girl was born ready. One of the over-18s, she arches her back over the bonnet in a metallic-gold bikini, throwing a sizzling stare over her shoulder. Damon, however, looks up from his camera. She parts her lips and licks her teeth. 'Okay, Ashanti, a little less Playboy and a little more playful?'

To her credit, she laughs throatily. 'Spoil-sport! I was serving!'

Briar, in a miniscule stars-and-stripes bikini, laughs along. 'Sure, these outfits are so Disney channel!'

Ash rolls her eyes. 'Truly wild.'

'Ready for the foam?' Damon asks.

'What?' I reply, but it's too late. The hapless assistant aims a cannon at us, and we're showered with thick, white, bubbly foam . . . or 'soap suds' as they're meant to be.

None of us prepared, we all scream, flinching from the torrent. Shayna slides from the top of truck, down the windscreen and into Ashanti.

'Girls!' the photographer shouts. 'Stay pretty!'

It's very hard to stay cute while being bombarded by freezing cold foam, even on a sweltering July afternoon. I try to pose, hands on hips, in the back of the pick-up. Only when Briar looks at me, soaking wet and with a false lash hanging off her cheekbone, do I break character.

Soon, none of us can breathe from laughing. Two hours in a makeup chair to look like drowned rats. I toss my sopping hair around my face, aiming for some sort of sassy. I clamber on top of the truck, pretending to scrub it down. The four of us switch positions around the car, for the first time feeling like a team. My shoulders creep down my back as I get into the rhythm of it. Under the baking sun, the foam is cool and . . . wait . . . is this *fun*?

Lune would have loved this.

Her face pops into my head and it feels like a blade twisting in my guts.

Ashanti and I sit side by side on the bonnet. She rests her head on my shoulder. I know what she's doing; the audience will buy into the whole wholesome Besties Girl Squad thing. 'That looks sick!' Damon calls. 'Smile, Taryn!'

I do as I'm told.

'Perrrrfect!'

Ashanti beams at me. 'That'll look gorgeous,' she says, quite genuinely. She offers a high-five on a job well done. Maybe I got her wrong and she's simply a *professional*. She knows what the producers want and she's giving it to them in abundance. Maybe there's something I can learn from her.

An electric ripple passes over the forecourt of the carwash. I sense him before I see him. Cade Kekoa is on set.

Here I am, soaked to the skin on top of a pick-up truck, and he looks flawless in sweatpants and a form-hugging vest, a Lakers cap pulled low over his eyes. Somehow I know he's looking my way and I feel winded, like his gaze alone is a physical extension of his being.

'That's a wrap on this set-up,' Damon says.

Cade offers a hand to help me off the truck. My butt gives a mortifying squeak as I slip off. 'Let's get you a towel,' he says, smiling.

From a place of insanity, I decide it would be cute to dollop a fistful of foam onto his head. I don't know what possesses me.

With ninja agility, he ducks out of the way. 'Oh like that is it?' He grabs a rogue bucket of soapy water and dumps it over my head.

'Oh my god!' I splutter and wipe water from my eyes. He backs away, eyes full of mischief. 'You're dead, mate. Girls . . .'

My teammates circle him.

'Don't . . .' he warns.

'Get him!' I sound the battle cry, and the rest of the trainees move in for the kill, hurling foam at our mentor.

Madison takes hold of a hosepipe and sprays him right in the face. 'That's for making us dance for twelve hours' straight!'

For five minutes of bliss, we're just nine girls having a water-fight. I am just a girl, a girl from a different time. I've read about girls like this; girls from before the floods, before the war. We were born with all the planet's strife in our DNA. What if we could live like this every day?

Clancy, looking on in despair, throws her hands in the air. 'Oh, I give up.'

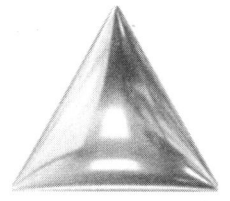

CHAPTER 27

Friday. Studio rehearsal day.

There's so much waiting around for lights and cameras to be set up that it's *almost* a relief to be summoned to my weekly session with Dr Anders. Our session is in an unused dressing room. It smells musty, a little damp. I can't decide if the odour is coming from the threadbare carpet, the shower cubicle, or the beaten sofa he instructed me to take a seat on. I suspect Nico's dressing room is a lot fancier.

'You don't seem very happy today,' he observes. This week, from his extensive woollens collection, he's selected a chunky mustard-colour knit.

I think about telling him I'm fine, but, as these sessions are my only opportunity to speak off camera, I plump for honesty. 'How can I trust you? You put Lune in that pyramid.'

He nods sadly. 'I gave her a powerful sedative. She sleepwalked into the chamber. She won't have felt fear, or sadness, or anything, I promise. When . . . if . . . your time comes I recommend you accept it too.'

I look him squarely in the eye. 'Keep it. I'm not planning on losing.'

He smiles. 'Has anyone ever told you that you're a little spiky, Taryn?'

I smile back. 'A thick skin is gonna come in handy here.'

He nods agreement. 'To keep feelings in, or keep people out?'

'Little of column A, little of column B.'

'Understandable that you'd want to defend yourself, but I'd warn you against becoming hard. If you don't let people in – the other trainees for example – you won't experience the lows *or* the highs. No friendship, no warmth, no love.'

I stifle a bitter laugh. Bitter is where I'm at. 'This is reality TV right? *I'm not here to make friends.*'

It's a lie and I know *he* knows I'm lying. The psychologist wears a disappointed expression I've seen on my father on the handful of occasions I got drunk with kids from the camp. 'Well I think that's a real shame, Taryn.'

I shrug. 'Let's see if I get through tomorrow night and then I'll worry about friends.'

'Do you want this?' He leans in and takes off his glasses.

'What do you mean?'

'This is my third year on *Starmaker* and you kids are usually so hungry for it. The money, the fame, the fans. My job is usually helping them realize those things often bring more problems than solutions. You're different.'

After all this time, tears finally prick my eyes and I don't fully know why. 'Of course I want to win. For my—'

'No. Be honest, Taryn. Jenson isn't the only reason you're

here. There are easier ways than this to raise funds for his treatment. So what is it *really*? Go deeper.'

I squeeze my eyes shut. 'I want a miracle.' I try to pass it off as a joke, but my voice breaks. A tear rolls.

'It's okay. Go on.'

'I remember a time when we were happy. When Mum was alive; when Jenson wasn't as bad as he is now; when Dad smiled. You know, I can't even remember the last time I heard him laugh. I want to take us all away from this life. To somewhere, anywhere, better. I need this to change my life.'

'What makes you think winning *Starmaker* would change it for the better?'

I laugh bitterly. 'It couldn't be worse.'

Dr Anders considers me and hands me a tissue from a box on the coffee table. 'Winning *Starmaker* won't bring your mother back.'

'I know.' I now cry freely, the dam all but burst. 'But when I sing . . . it's like she's in me. My voice is her voice. We're together again.'

A creak of springs as Dr Anders reclines in his seat. He nods thoughtfully. 'Great work today, Taryn.' And then he adds, 'Say *that*. Say that on air and you might just get through this week.'

I barely sleep a wink Friday night. I dream of the pink pyramid, what it would be like to see the other girls, all blurry, from inside the glass walls. I dream they are singing me to sleep with their deathly lullaby.

Studio rehearsal came and went. After we'd done two

run-throughs of 'Abracadabra', Cade said nothing, but his jaw was clenched tight. That day there was none of the breezy, playful Cade from the photoshoot. I don't understand; I've improved, and it's not like I'm standing on anyone's feet or tripping over things.

Seeing Cade after our private training session feels different. There's a knotted, almost chewy feeling in my middle. I read paragraphs into every minute gesture; if he nudges me with a shoulder or watches me rehearse. My brain fills the silences. At home, we'd ride bikes down a hillside called Devil's Pike, and I feel with Cade the way I'd get at the summit of the pike. A sense of risk that makes me quite high.

This is the difference between Cade and thirteen-year-old me's crush on his bandmate, Sonny. Sonny was a poster on the wall. The feelings were safe; a thought experiment a million miles from reality. Cade Kekoa is right here, with his warm fingers and thick lashes; with his dimples and perfect lips . . . not safe. Not safe at all.

I tried to speak with him before the other team got their turn. 'Well?' I asked.

'Too aggressive,' he muttered. 'Relax. Feel the music. Tell a story.' Then he had moved on.

Both Dr Anders and Cade offering the same message: I'm a problem. Too prickly, too hard-faced. Can they blame me? I can't get Lune's fate out of my head; it's hard to feel *sensual*. I don't think I've *ever* felt sensual. I thought I attracted people with my killer sense of humour if anything. Why does Cade care so much anyway? I wonder if he's put a bet on me. Since they clamped down on legal gambling, there's a lot of dodgy money to be won at the underground casinos.

The mood this morning is dour. I look around the breakfast table. I suspect I'm not the only one to have had nightmares. Every face looks puffy, every eye shadowy. Leela disseminates cooling sheet masks, and we silently poke oatmeal through the mouth slits, looking like ghosts. I don't know who laughs first, but it spreads like wildfire, and soon we're hysterical. Nine girls, dying of laughter. I am bent double on the kitchen floor.

Clancy enters, perplexed. 'What's so funny?' This only makes us laugh harder.

We sober up pretty fast once we're on the bus to the studio. One by one we're taken for *confessionals*: straight to camera discussions with Clancy in the empty audience stalls. She feeds us a line we have to respond to.

I remember Cade's warning – that I'm being set up as the weak link this week. The one who is doomed to go home. I refuse to fit their narrative.

'How do you feel about being the least experienced dancer?'

I'm not admitting to that. 'I love dancing,' I lie outrageously. 'You know, even though some of the other girls have been training since they were little, I'm just going to enjoy it. Dancing should be fun I think?' I smile sweetly.

I see from Clancy's face that this is not what she wants. 'Do you think you're in danger this week?'

'I really want to make it to makeover week! I really hope everyone at home remembers to vote.'

She keeps prodding, trying to get the answer she wants. 'But would you say you're in danger?'

I won't give it to her. 'I think we're *all* in danger every week. It's up to fans to decide who they want in the band. I'm just going to focus on trying my best and enjoying it!' Another saccharine smile.

Does Clancy not realize I've seen every series of *Starmaker*? Well, except the boring folk music one. The *authentic talent* on display was harder to swallow than our sugarless oatmeal.

I remember what Dr Anders said. 'I'm just thinking about my mum, looking down from heaven. As long as I try my hardest, I know she'd be proud of me.'

Clancy sighs, barely bothering to hide her annoyance. 'Fine. We're done. Head to costume.'

The dressing rooms are set up like a conveyer belt. We move down the corridor going from costume to hair to makeup. The glam squad is about twenty people, ever-ready for touch-ups and fixes.

When I arrive in wardrobe, I find Madison in tears. 'I can't!' she wails at Lars.

The stylist looks unimpressed, but then he always does. 'What's wrong?' I ask, ignoring the meltdown. 'Is she okay?'

Madison appeals to me. 'Taryn, will you tell him? I can't wear this costume. It isn't something a Christian lady would wear.' She brandishes the mesh bodysuit that Lars has selected for her. I'm confused. We were fitted yesterday and she didn't have an issue. All our team's costumes are made of black mesh and Lycra – inspired by the original Brown Eyed Girls costumes.

'We can swap I guess?' I suggest. 'I don't mind.'

Lars rolls his eyes. 'Whatever. I cannot adjust them. If it doesn't fit, it doesn't fit.'

Madison changes into my shorts, bralette and mesh overshirt and sweeps out to hair and makeup. Lars helps me into Madison's body suit. It does need a little adjusting, but it looks good. I don't get it. There is perhaps an inch less fabric on this costume; it's no more or less revealing than the other one. It's certainly a lot more modest than our carwash looks. What is she playing at?

I join Madison in hair and makeup. Barbs, the hairdresser, beckons me into the chair. With no cameras here right now, Madison scrolls away on her phone, ignoring me. Her makeup is already done, and she looks quite striking with her black eyes and orange lip. 'What?' she snaps, looking sideways at me in the mirror.

'What was *that* about?'

Her mane has been ironed, pin straight. 'What?'

'The little meltdown in costume?'

She looks at me like I'm the village idiot. 'Haven't you ever seen *Starmaker*?'

'Um, yes?'

'Then you should know they just want six weeks of good TV. Singing and dancing is a bonus. You should be grateful we have beef. The first ones to go are the forgettable ones. Look at Lune. People have to remember you to vote for you. Just don't be boring. *Anything* but boring.' She looks to her MUA. 'Am I done?'

She slips out of the chair. 'Thanks for the advice,' I say caustically.

Madison hovers behind the chair, appraising Barb's work thus far. The stylist is scraping all my hair into a high bun, ready for the fake forty-inch ponytail. 'Hmm. You know, you are actually really pretty when you try.' She pouts thoughtfully and exits.

Gee, thanks, Madi.

Showtime.

Team 'Boombayah' goes first. This is the first time I've seen them do it all the way through. With the male dancers, it's a truly impressive formation. The only question mark is Leela. At five-eight she's a good four inches taller than Ashanti, the next tallest. While her long legs would be an asset if she were a model, they make her look like a giraffe when she dances.

She stands out – I'm not sure in a good way. Only then I remember what Madison said about standing out. Domino is, as I've come to expect, the MVP in their group. She moves like liquid lightning and the smile never once slips. Minnie too dances like a weapon: perfectly precise, with impossibly clean movements. God, I don't want Leela to go. I pray that people simply forget to vote for the three middling dancers.

And with that in mind, I make a decision. A very, very risky one.

Mojo cuts to the commercial break and they reset the stage for our performance. Briar clutches my hand. 'You got this,' she says. 'You *can* dance.'

I nod but my heartrate thunders. If I speak, I might puke.

Madison once more gathers us together for her prayer circle. 'Lord, give us all your grace. Our dance is a reflection of your glory on Earth.' We're on camera, so there's no way of knowing if she really means that.

Suki says, 'Girls, remember to smile and wink. Be sexy, but not slutty.'

We all look *incredible* in our gothic, black mesh ensembles. My fake ponytail falls almost to my butt. Briar's hair is plaited to her scalp in a pair of whip-like braids, while Suki's hair is twisted into two knots. We're slowly, surely, turning into idols. A normal girl could never look like this, and that's what makes an idol.

'Group A, positions!' the floor manager calls.

In the dark, I silently take my spot amongst the male dancers. I balance my elbow on Eli's shoulder. He whispers good luck, but I've filtered everything out. Timing is everything. When do I pull my little stunt?

Mojo reads his link from the autocue. 'Our second performance of the night is "Abracadabra"!'

The music starts. An electronic buzz. I have to *feel it*, the way Cade said. I imagine it's just him and me, alone in the studio, his hands on my waist. I feel that strange warmth at my core, and we begin.

I try my very best, I really do. I swing my hips, I pull off the hip-sway-turn. I smile – as alluringly as I can – at the camera. I wink. I even do the racy butt-lift downward-dog that got the Brown Eyed Girls in trouble decades earlier.

But in the final minute of the song, I stumble. Accidentally-on-purpose. I make it look like my ankle's gone. I go down on one knee, steadying my hands on the floor.

A gasp from the studio audience.

Like Madison said. *Stand out.* Anything but boring.

I quickly recover and get back into position, faking a slight limp. Madison shoots me a glance but is too busy grinning and winking to even judge my 'error'. The song ends and we freeze frame in our final poses.

Mojo and Nico parade over as the audience applauds. Suki and Briar check that I'm okay, forcing Madison to ask after me too. 'What was that?' she breathes, pretending to give me a friendly hug.

'Just standing out, like you said,' I whisper through her hair.

'Lord help you, darl.'

We are back in the silent studio. The pyramid awaits.

'Results have been counted and verified.' Tonight Nico stands before us, dressed in amethyst silk, tiny pink butterflies woven into her caramel locks. I am in a different elimination outfit, but again, we are all in white head-to-toe. For me, white ripped jeans, a tank top and a furry bolero. I feel like a *Bratz* doll.

I don't know why the Elimination Chamber studio has to be so goddamn cold. Is it something to do with the pyramid, or the dry ice, or do they just want to see our nipples on TV?

'The rankings, after Challenge Two, are as follows,' Mojo says.

'In first place,' continues Nico, 'is Domino.' The Brazilian squeals and hurries to the first podium.

Mojo calls Minnie next – she's jumped way up the rankings. In third place is Madison. She's slipped a place; she'll hate that.

Say my name, say my name. TarynTarynTaryn. The mantra worked last time.

'Next up is Ashanti,' Nico says.

'Suki!' Mojo says and I clap my hands together. Thank the stars for her. Suki kisses my cheek and heads for the fifth podium down. The audience is getting to know her, and to know her is to love her.

'Shayna,' Nico calls. I briefly wonder why Shayna isn't as popular as her sister.

No time to think about that now. It's me, Briar and Leela leftover. My gamble has failed. The people at home didn't take pity on me; they voted for the best dancers. Madison was wrong: sometimes standing out doesn't work.

This is BS. Briar is a *way* better dancer than Ashanti or Shayna. This isn't fair. Briar holds my left hand, Leela my right. Cade is at the judging panel with Dre. His jaw is tight. There is nothing he can do. One of us is going to die tonight.

'Only one more girl is safely through to next week,' Nico says. It has to be either Briar or myself: one girl from each team *has* to be in the bottom.

'The final girl with immunity is . . .' Mojo drags it out. I cannot stand it; I stare at my crisp white sneakers. 'Briar! Well done, Briar, go to your plinth.'

'Oh my god!' she erupts. She clings to me. 'I'm so sorry.'

'It's okay.' My tongue is cardboard. I look to Leela. Words aren't necessary. She's paler than snow.

'Leela and Taryn, please step forward,' Nico says. 'Two talented, beautiful girls stand before me, but only one of you will remain in DOLLHOU5E.'

Leela grips my hand so tight it's agony. But I don't let go. I need to feel this.

'The girl to be eliminated this week...' Mojo says sombrely.

A pause.

The longest yet.

'... Will be announced after this short break.'

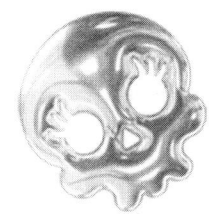

CHAPTER 28

And we're live again in four, three, two . . .

'Welcome back to *Starmaker*.' Nico is grave.

Mojo continues. 'Tonight, either Leela from Germany, or Taryn from the Republic of Scotland will face the Elimination Chamber, bravely sacrificing their life to Project Population.'

We weren't allowed to move during the ad break, even though we're not live. My hand has not left Leela's. Cade quit the set. He had to be forced to return to his seat by Clancy. I wish I could speak with him. Does he know the result ahead of time?

Nico looks between us. Resting between her bejewelled fingers is a dusky pink, iridescent envelope containing my fate.

Only then she looks past Leela and me, towards the pyramid. 'Ashanti, please step forward.'

What? Ashanti, as confused as the rest of us, points to her chest. 'Me?'

'Join Leela and Taryn on the steps please.'

What is happening? All the colour drains from Ashanti's face. She stands next to me. I don't especially like the girl, but I give the back of her hand a supportive brush with my index finger. The cameras are rolling.

'Ashanti,' Mojo begins, 'is there anything you'd like to tell us?'

'No?' she mutters, brow furrowed.

Nico inhales. 'It's come to our attention that you haven't been honest with us, or the *Starmaker* team.'

What the actual . . . I realize I'm lightheaded from not breathing. I feel almost drunk, like the time I stole Merrill Saunder's dusty bottle of sherry.

Mojo continues. 'You told us you were born in June, and that you're a Gemini. But you lied about the *year* you were born, didn't you?'

'What?' she gasps, though, looking at her face, I see utter guilt. 'No! No way!'

'Ashanti,' Nico says. 'Your birth certificate, your *real* birth certificate, shows that you're, in fact, *twenty-six* years old.'

I gasp. I can't help it. That's a big lie.

'She's *old*!' It's Shayna, from her podium.

Too old.

'Starmaker rules clearly state that all trainees must be between fourteen and twenty-one years old . . .' Mojo says.

'I didn't mean to lie,' Ashanti starts to plead. 'I didn't know when I applied.'

'You gave us fake identification,' Nico says.

'I'm sorry! I just wanted a chance—'

'Because you broke the rules,' Mojo cuts in, '*you* will be eliminated tonight and the votes for all trainees will roll over to next week.'

'No! You can't do this!' Ashanti cries. She makes for the

exit, but the Securiforce guards barricade her in. 'Let me go!' She attempts to shove past the beefiest guard, but he pushes her back with his rifle.

A pair of guards – one male, one female – take hold of Ashanti's skinny arms, dragging her up the incline towards the glass pyramid. Instinctively, my feet move towards her. Two huge guards on one petite woman isn't fair. But Leela's fingers grip my forearm and I see why: a third guard has turned his gun on us.

Clancy sweeps in from the wings, waving her arms overhead. 'Cut there! Disarm the pyramid! NOW!' she shouts over the kerfuffle. 'No one move a muscle.' She addresses the guards holding Ashanti. 'Chill okay? Everyone just chill.'

They unhand Ashanti, who looks like some terrified prey. 'What's happening?'

Both Dre and Cade come out from behind the judging panel. 'What the hell is going on?' Cade demands.

Clancy ignores him, instead pulling Mojo and Nico aside for an urgent conflab. I don't hear what they're saying, but Clancy jabs a frenzied finger in Ashanti's direction.

I'm still gripping Leela's hand. 'Are we off the hook?' I breathe.

'For now,' Leela says. Her serene façade cracks. A tear runs down her cheek. I pull her into a fierce hug. I feel arms around us. By now I recognize the lavender tinge of Suki's perfume.

Clancy claps her hands loudly. 'Girls, go get changed. We're gonna wrap there for the night.'

'But . . .' It's Madison, looking for answers. 'We didn't do the ending . . .?'

'Just GO!' Clancy barks.

I don't need telling twice. I haul Leela off the white steps towards the fire exit. Ashanti is surrounded by all six guards, held in place. She is crying, begging us. 'Don't go! Don't leave me here!' She reaches out for us with sparkling cat-eye nails.

There's nothing we can do. More Securiforce whip past us into the studio to assist their colleagues.

I don't take my eyes off Ashanti until I'm pushed into the corridor by Shayna. The door swings shut, and I don't hear her pleas any more.

CHAPTER 29

Laundry room at midnight.

Those were the words he whispered in my ear as we left the studio.

The laundry room is in the Dreamhouse basement next to the gym and steam room. It's perhaps the only solely functional room in the mansion. Until now I haven't even set foot in here – all my dirty laundry has been kicked under my bed. This is as good an excuse as any. I tell Leela I'm too buzzed on adrenaline to sleep and carry an armful of clothes downstairs just before the clock strikes twelve.

I'm half-hypnotised by the spinning drum of the washing machine when I hear someone knock on the high slit window. I climb on top of the tumble dryer and slide the window open. It's *just* large enough for Cade to slither in, feet-first.

'I can't believe they haven't figured this trick out yet,' he says as he hops down from the dryer. 'I was tipped off by someone on the season before ours that you could do whatever you want in here: no cameras. It's where you could come to . . .' He freezes and blushes slightly. 'Do whatever.'

'What are you doing here *now*?'

He looks confused. 'I came to make sure you're okay.'

Now *I'm* confused. 'I'm fine,' I blurt out. He looks at me doubtfully and I tell the truth. 'That's a lie. I'm . . . numb. I almost *died* tonight. It doesn't feel real. None of it felt real. Do you know the result? Was it me or Lee?'

He shakes his head, leaning casually against the tumble dryer. 'I don't know. But that's not the interesting part.'

'It's not? What is?'

'I think production knew about Ashanti for *weeks* – they run background checks. But I didn't know until you did.'

'Okay. So what?'

'Don't you see? There's a reason they chose to expose Ashanti this week. Nothing that happens here is a mistake, remember that. Taryn, they *saved* you. Or Leela.'

I run the numbers in my head. Leela hasn't disclosed her birth gender yet. That's some great TV they wouldn't want to miss out on, so it makes sense they would keep her in for that. Why they'd save *me*, I don't know. Although it occurs to me that, with Ashanti gone, I'm among the most reliable vocalists.

'Did Ash . . . is she dead?'

Cade glances around and beckons me closer. 'She's on a flight back to Dubai.'

'What?'

'Turns out Ashanti's father works for Mohammad Al Kamal.'

He may as well be speaking Arabic. 'Cade, I don't know who that is.'

He sighs impatiently. 'The Five Families?'

What? I crinkle my nose. 'That's a . . . paranoid internet conspiracy thing.'

He huffs. 'I'm sure they'd like you to believe that.'

A sarcastic laugh pops out. 'Said like a true paranoid conspiracy theorist, well done.'

He's gripping my hand, almost too tightly. He's not in the mood for jokes. 'The Kamals; the Groenvelds; the Van Der Vaals; the Volkovs and the Brookmans. Between them they run the whole world.'

I roll my eyes. 'Cade. Come on . . .'

'Taryn, I'm serious. If you own the entire "free" media, you create the culture, the conversation. You decide what's in and what's out. You decide the "truth". Politicians are just chimps, dancing to the beat those Five Families set out because *they* pick the presidents and prime ministers.'

I can't fault his logic there. 'What does this have to do with Ashanti?'

'Her dad is besties with the Al Kamals. Ashanti has friends in very high places.'

'But what about the result show?'

'You didn't watch it on catch-up?'

'Of course not! I don't wanna see that.'

'They cobbled together footage and made a deepfake. Everyone thinks she got in the pyramid. They faked it.'

'But why?' I say.

'They need it to look like there's no way out,' he replies.

I feel dizzy on all this. 'The house always wins,' I say at last.

'Exactly. Don't for a single second think it's a *level playing field* or whatever. Ashanti's father has money. Simple as that.

How do you think Erik got into N-TRU5T?'

I recoil in shock. 'Really?'

'Have you heard him sing? His mother works for the record label.'

'He's a nepo baby?'

Cade nods. 'If you expect them to play fair, you'll die.'

My head whirls. Ashanti is alive; that's a good thing, I guess, but the injustice of it burns in my chest. Lune is very much dead because she couldn't buy her way out of the Elimination Chamber. And neither can I. I curse loudly and sit on the floor next to the tumbling washing machine, crossing my legs.

'What do I do? All the votes roll over to next week. I have to pull something out of the bag, or I'm dead. My dad is a *carpenter*.'

Cade paces the cool tiles, chewing his thumbnail anxiously.

'What?' I can tell he's hiding something.

'Taryn, there's stuff you don't know.'

I gaze up at him. 'What sort of stuff?'

'You can't know. It's dangerous.'

I arch a single brow. 'More dangerous than being a trainee?'

He can't deny that. 'Valid. I *had* to take this gig. I had no choice, you know? If you look at your contract it's tucked away in a subclause on page fifty. I have to fulfil my "mentor duty" or they can claim back some of my prize package.'

'Relaunching your solo career is a bonus though, right?' It's so sour I almost shock myself.

His face goes slack like I've physically slapped him. Suddenly, Cade drops into a squat, hiding his face with his hands. His back shakes as he silently weeps. I feel awful for my sass.

'Cade? I'm sorry, I shouldn't have said that. What's wrong?'

He wipes away the tears with his sleeve. He inhales shakily, steeling himself. 'Applying for *Starmaker* ruined my life. It's the biggest mistake I ever made. If I could go back . . . It's so much worse than you think. I want them to *pay* for what they did.'

I can't *hug* Cade Kekoa, but I place a hand gingerly on his arm. It's firm, warm and muscular. 'What did they do?'

He looks me dead in the eye. 'They killed my best friend.'

'What?'

'Taryn, they killed Sonny Feldman.'

DIAMOND DOLL

RebeL DOLL

SLAMDUNK DOLL

Hoedown Doll

Kitty Doll

Baby Doll

Star Doll

DISCO DOLL

CHAPTER 30

They schedule the makeovers at the midpoint of the series to stop people getting bored. They used to do them before the live shows, but they realized that the makeover episode was a huge ratings winner, so it gets its own dedicated week.

On Monday, Clancy wakes us up at dawn. We come downstairs in our pyjamas to find Nico waiting for us in the hall. 'Morning, girls! I hope you don't mind the wake-up call!'

She looks flawless as ever in a velvet jumpsuit and thigh boots. Yes, it's mortifying to be standing here looking like crap, but that was their intention so I just grin back. Next to me, Briar is still in her silk bonnet.

'I'm here bright and early with a very special guest . . . who some of you know very well . . .'

The front doors open and Madison and Shayna scream before I properly clock our visitor. In walks a tiny sparrow of a woman with waist-length blonde extensions. It's Peyton from B*TRU3. The eldest silver sister.

'Hey, girls!' She gives a coy wave to her sisters.

The first thing I notice is that she does *not* look well. In fact, she looks frail. Ill. She was never 'big' but since winning, she's gone from *thin* to *poorly*.

'I'm Peyton Silver from a little band called B*TRU3, but to Madi and Shay, I'm just big sis Pey! I'm here to help you channel your personalities in a way the public can understand. For instance, in my band, we all bring a unique flavour to the mix. I'm the sweet, fun one; Kaya is the badass rapper; and Sayaka is fresh off the runway.'

Nico explains. 'You are all very special girls, each with your own cultures and personalities. So Peyton and I put our heads together and have come up with some nicknames for each of you too.'

On the huge screen over the door, eight labels materialize, each a different type of doll.

'Is that our makeovers?' Suki yelps.

What else could they be? I don't know how I feel about being a *doll*, but I really *really* hope I don't get Hoedown Doll.

'Maybe . . .' Nico smiles teasingly. 'But who is who? We'll leave you to figure that out!'

'Good luck, girls,' Peyton says. 'Don't forget: *Be true to you, be true to me, and be true to us.*' We all chant the last part. Their group mantra.

By this point we only care about what hair we're getting, but Clancy sweeps in and says she wants us to do the whole scene again.

The van ride to the salon is the giddiest we've been so far. Makeovers is one of those milestones, I guess. No one wants Hoedown Doll. Madison is already upset because she's decided it's her. 'Like, it's almost offensive,' she whines. 'Just because I'm from Texas don't mean I'm, like, some . . . hillbilly.'

'It could be worse.' Briar rolls her eyes. 'Me or Dom are *definitely* getting Slamdunk Doll. They might as well have just said Black Doll right?'

'Or Spice Doll!' Domino laughs. 'Or Fiery Latina Doll. Or Salsa Doll. Empanada Doll.'

'Baby Doll is definitely Shay,' Suki shouts over the racket in the back of the minibus. 'She's our maknae.'

'I can rock Baby Doll,' Shayna agrees.

'Taryn is Rebel Doll,' Leela says.

'No I'm not!'

Everyone screams that I am. Oh god, they're going to shave my head aren't they?

Consensus is that Min is Diamond Doll because she's clearly the chicest, and Suki is Kitty Doll, perhaps because of some vague reference to Hello Kitty. I personally think Lee is Rebel Doll because she's the most alternative in her style, which only leaves Star Doll or Disco Doll, which could mean anything.

I wonder what Lune would have been. Or Ashanti. There's now a bruise on my heart, and every time I think of them it's sore. Or is Cade right, and Lune and Ashanti were never destined to get this far because the whole process is predestined by Chairman Slade?

While the other girls fizz over with excitement, I think only of Cade. I've now had a whole day to process what he told me about Sonny. It's a lot to process.

I believe him. Without question. I saw *TRU5T in Summer*

Love, the N-TRU5T movie, and he's not that good an actor. He's telling the truth.

Sonny Feldman is *not* finishing his studies at an undisclosed university campus. That's a lie. He is dead. Because he took his own life in a lonely hotel room in Tokyo. *That* was what Cade's now-deleted G-Net post was about. It was his *obituary* until Elysium made him delete it. According to Cade, Sonny had been in a bad way for the last couple of years: substance abuse, junk food, touring constantly.

On the one hand, it seems impossible. Sonny, all blonde surfer boy curls, looked like a Botticelli painting come to life. He had a serene, sunrise-on-the-beach aura. To think of him in such turmoil feels like a heel on my heart.

But I'm also learning, rapidly, not to trust my eyes. Just because something *looks* good, doesn't mean a thing.

It's one thing to *imagine* Sonny's strife, but it was quite another to experience Cade's in that laundry room. Something raw and painful pulsed off him – it was almost too much to stand. I once found Dad crying into a pillow after Mum died. He didn't want us to see him like that. I think I learned to keep that banshee inside. To see it escape from Cade was a reminder of something still dormant in my heart.

If they'd just listened to us, Cade told me through the tears. *We all tried to help him. We needed the ride to stop, but they wouldn't let us off, not even for a week. He needed help. We all need help.*

Cade Kekoa isn't a sentinel, an inhuman demi-god. He isn't an *idol*, he's just a guy. He's bone and breath. I held him tight in the laundry room until he almost fell asleep in my arms and my laundry was all but dry.

He departed as the first birds started their morning chorus. His own refrain was darker: *I'm gonna destroy them, Taryn. For Sonny. That's really why I came back to this hellhole.* He didn't specify how. And now I can't breathe a word of this to anyone. I don't know if I'll see Cade before next Saturday at judging.

It's hard to care about a haircut. It'll grow back.

The sliding side door opens and we pile onto the curb outside a Goliath downtown salon. The Remy Laine Salon. The way some of the others gasp makes me think I should definitely recognize the name.

We bundle into the salon in a stampede. Everything inside is gleaming mirrors, frosted glass and chrome, like we're onboard a spaceship. Nico has beaten us here, and is waiting to receive us along with stylist Lars, Cristobel from the makeup squad, and a tiny woman with magenta hair who she introduces as Remy Laine herself.

'Are you dying to know what makeovers you're getting?' Remy says.

'YEEESSSSS!' we duly chant.

Big shocker – Briar is sporty, athletic Slamdunk Doll, Domino is Disco Doll. Briar smiles with gratitude, but I swear I can read her mind.

'Suki!' Nico says. 'You are just so cute, so youthful. You're our Baby Doll!' Is that a little bit . . . ick? I think it's a bit weird but Suki seems pleased. Shayna, I notice, exchanges a terse glance with her sister.

'Madison: you are giving us luxury. You are giving expensive. You are Diamond Doll!' Madison looks pleasantly surprised. 'And Shayna, you are pure American apple pie. We're gonna make you our Hoedown Doll.' Shayna's face can't hide her disappointment. 'Happy with that?' Nico's tone is leading.

'Sure,' Shayna lies. Not very convincingly.

Minnie is Kitty Doll; feline, elegant. Leela is Star Doll: ethereal, space age. And that leaves me to last. 'Taryn, you're our London girl,' Nico says in a dreadful imitation of a cockney accent. Also, I'm not from London. 'Punk rock, Rebel Doll.'

'Please don't shave my head,' I say with a broad smile, and everyone laughs. After twelve seasons, I know that to bitch about your makeover is basically suicide. If they superglue a bird's nest to my head, I will smile gratefully and gush about how it's elevated my style.

Nico takes the opportunity to also introduce our next challenge. 'This week, your challenge is to pick a solo song that reflects your makeover *and* we'll be interviewing each of you live to assess your charm and personality.'

And with that we're ferried to individual salon chairs. Remy Laine herself whips a gown over my shoulders. 'Oh, sweetheart, we've got big plans for you,' she says with a wink. One of her stylists wheels over a metal trolley. I can't help but notice a pile of bright red hair extensions.

'Red?' I say.

'*Very* red,' Remy replies. 'Like a London bus.'

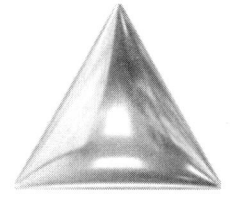

CHAPTER 31

We are now several hours into makeovers. It's weird to think this will all be a three-minute montage come Saturday.

Leela, Suki, Minnie and I are in a row of salon chairs, waiting for bleach to do its thing. My scalp burns. I am told this is to be expected. As we're here for the long haul, we each sip on a low-cal protein shake. Mine is banana.

'I'm not doing it!' The shrill cry alerts us all, and we crane as best we can with cellophane wrapped over our heads.

At the other side of the salon, Madison is comforting Shayna. 'What's up?' I mouth at a wincing Briar who is having her hair painstakingly braided between me and the unfolding drama. Briar shrugs.

Lars appeals to Shayna. 'Sweetheart, you have such a pretty face. All this hair is doing nothing for you.'

'I don't want to look like a boy!'

'You won't! Every girl group needs one with short hair. It's, like, a rule.'

Shayna storms across the salon floor, trailing after any production person she can get to listen, her gown billowing like a cape. 'But Suki is getting short hair.'

'She's getting a bob; you're getting a pixie.' Lars couldn't care less.

I should have seen this coming. Shayna's golden tresses must have twinkled to the magpie eyes of the producers. 'Please don't cut my hair. I've been growing it my whole life.'

'Sweetie, it'll grow back.'

'It'll make you stand out.' Madison intervenes, head covered in foil wraps. She looks around the room, no doubt searching for hidden cameras. Her eyes carve into her sister's. 'Just. Go. With. It.'

'Easy for you to say, Madison! They're barely touching yours.'

'Shay!' Madison snaps more forcefully. 'Quit being a baby.'

'Too right. *I'm* Baby Doll,' Suki says quietly on my right.

I chuckle, but this is more serious than it looks. I don't particularly want bright red, waist-length hair, but I don't want to end up a sobbing meme, or, worse, punished at Saturday's vote. 'Shayna!' I call over the salon. 'You'll look stunning.'

'You got this,' Briar adds, grimacing as the hairdresser tugs on a braid.

But she continues to shake her head. 'No. I'm not doing it. I don't care.'

'Shayna...' Madison gives her a deathly glare, digging her nails into her sister's arm.

Lars looks bored. 'Hon, you need to understand that DOLLHOU5E is a group. Everyone is making sacrifices to the design. Think about the silhouette. Leela is getting long blonde hair, so you need to be different.'

'You can cut mine,' Leela volunteers, scratching her peroxide-covered scalp with the pointy end of a rattail comb. 'I don't care.' This is the big week for her. The transgender *reveal*.

'No,' Lars says quickly. 'Nico and I picked out these makeovers to suit each concept.' He turns back to Shayna. 'Idols don't get to choose who they are, Shayna. So what is it to be?'

I want to go over there and punch him. Every day is a test. *How much do we want the prize?* I swallow my anger down. Tastes bitter. I have to be smarter than they are manipulative. I won't survive otherwise. Shayna knows this too. The Silver sisters have seen this all before during Peyton's season. I guess today they caught her on her period or something. Maybe they finally broke her.

At the sink, as a girl rinses the chemicals from my hair, I can hear Shayna ugly-crying as they cleave off her ponytail.

Stupid girl.

Nine – NINE – hours after we entered the salon, I am dispatched to makeup and costume for my 'After' photoshoot. They've turned a corner of the basement at the hair salon into a makeshift studio.

I look myself over in the mirror.

It has been a very long day, and I'm very tired. Tears prick my eyes. Can't help it.

'You like?' Lars purrs, witnessing how moved I am. I can only nod.

I am a different person. Tousled, ruby red waves tumble

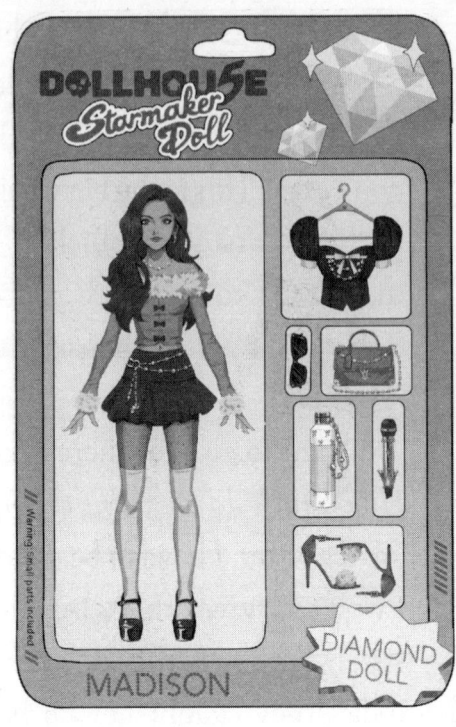

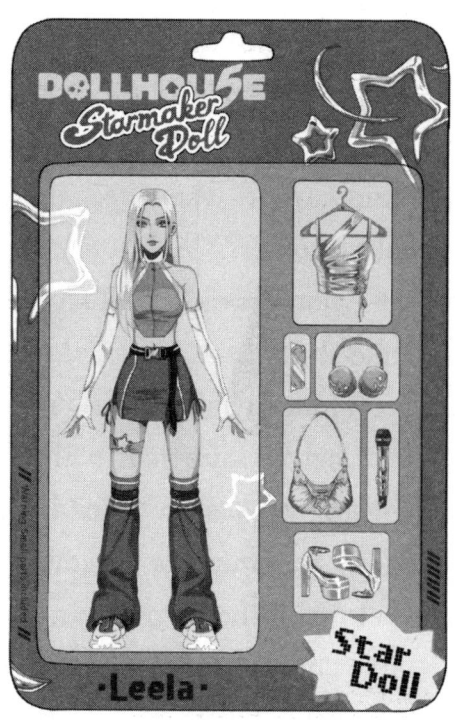

to almost my waist. My nails, now acrylic talons, are as black as my eyeliner. I have a studded dog collar at my throat and biker boots on my feet. 'This is all archival Westwood,' Lars said earlier, when he handed me a tiny kilt, stockings and black corset.

I don't look like Taryn Beck, schoolgirl refugee. I look like an *idol*.

'Honestly,' Lars says, 'my favourite makeover this season.'

I bet he says that to all of us, but I'm too stunned to joke. Seeing what's about to happen, he hands me a tissue so I don't mess up the makeup. 'I've never seen myself like this before.' I know I'm meant to be tougher than this, but I feel like I'm glowing. I hate this, but I love it. Honestly, this whole contest is splitting me in two. Taryn One recognizes that this makeover is stupid, shallow, but, at the same time, Taryn Two can't resist it.

I look *fucking fantastic*.

'Babe, you look like a *winner* to me.'

Snap, snap, snap. Click, click, click. Wind machine. Twenty flashes, and my turn with the photographer is done. My day complete, I am delighted to find we've been rewarded for our trauma with pizza. I chill on a sofa in the salon reception area, waiting for poor Briar and Domino to be finished. Briar's goddess braids and Domino's voluminous new weave are taking forever.

Lounging around the salon in our new outfits, we look both insane and amazing. I chill with Suki and Leela. Suki looks like a sugarplum fairy with her cotton-candy-pink bob, while Leela is channelling Galadriel with her silver-white hair extensions and bleached brows. Truly ethereal.

After all the tears, Shayna actually looks really cute in her elfin pixie – our maknae. The 'hoedown' concept really just translated to a frayed denim top and suede tassel skirt with some cowboy boots. As much as I hate to admit it, Lars knows what he's doing when it comes to our clothes. We each look like a different 'doll' but we're all very clearly from the same set. I suppose that's the whole point. We're a girl gang.

I'm demolishing my second slice of pepperoni when Cade and Dre enter the salon carrying huge, glossy shopping bags. I'm so shocked to see Cade, I almost drop the pizza into my lap.

'Hey, girls,' he says, all smile and dimples. This isn't the same Cade I was with on Saturday night. 'Don't you all look amazing!' I might be imagining it, but I swear his gaze lingers on me as he says it.

The mentors gather us around in the salon foyer. 'I hardly recognize you!' Dre grins. 'Taryn! Shayna! What a transformation. To help you with your new images, our friends at Media City Mall have gifted you all some cherry-picked designer clothes and accessories.'

We don't clap and cheer appreciatively enough so Clancy makes us do another take. Cade and Dre dole out the swag. Dre holds out a bag for me, but Cade intercepts.

'Wrong one. This one's yours.' His eyes drill into mine like he's trying to convey a secret message. What, I don't know.

'Thank you,' I say.

'Don't forget your laundry,' he mumbles and I understand. He wants to see me again tonight.

* * *

Shayna continues to whine about her haircut well into the night. After a shower, she complains that she looks like a baby owl. I'm done. So is Madison. I hear them through their bedroom wall.

'Shayna, you have got to get over it. Do you want to come across as a whiner? Quit it.'

It's excruciating waiting for the others to go to bed. Everyone is high on the adrenaline of Makeover Day, trying on the outfits that have been selected for us. I can live with mine; it's all slashed jeans, band t-shirts and micro kilts. I'd rather that than Suki's pastels or Madison's logo-filled designer gear. Briar lucked out with sportswear; at least she'll be comfortable.

I pretend to fall asleep on the sofa in the den. Leela covers me with a blanket and, one by one, everyone heads for bed. As soon as the Dreamhouse is dark, I tiptoe downstairs to the laundry room. Cade is already waiting outside the basement window and he scrambles inside.

'Have you been out there long?' I ask.

'No. I had to keep my eye out for the security guy but I think he's fallen asleep.'

'God, it's like a prison,' I say.

'You have no idea. It's all a cage, a rhinestone cage.' He stops, like he's seeing me for the very first time. 'You look incredible by the way.'

I've washed off the makeup and the metre of hair extensions have been tied back. My scalp is sore and swollen from the microbands holding them in. I'm now wearing sweats and I'm no good at taking compliments. 'Well . . . Lars did a great job.'

'The hair suits you. Red like fire.'

'Where I come from, it's red like a bus.'

He smiles. 'You're weird.'

'*You* have no idea. What's up? You didn't come here just to talk hair.'

'No. I came to talk gifts. Did you get the Punkcat?'

In my goody-bag there was a furry green Punkcat keychain. They're huge in Japan, Suki informed me. 'I did.'

'That was from me.'

'Um . . . thanks. It's really cute.'

He rolls his eyes. 'Taryn it's a spycam. Her eyes are lenses.'

'What?'

He inhales deeply. 'Can I trust you?'

I bat that one right back at him. 'Can I trust *you*?'

'I'm the same as you, Taryn. A refugee kid who somehow got through this bullshit.'

I can see he's earnest. I don't know if I trust him, but I *believe* him. I believe he doesn't wish me harm, but I don't trust him enough to follow him blindly. 'So what?'

He takes a deep breath. 'Four girls are going to die this year. Five boys died last year. *Seven* girls died the year before that. It just keeps going. We keep dying, even if we win. Look at Sonny.' Hearing his name is like a needle into my heart. 'No one wins, except *them*. Slade gets richer. Elysium gets richer. The family that owns Elysium gets richer. *Starmaker* is a monster, an insatiable beast that feeds on desperate kids, and it will keep gobbling us up unless we stop it.'

I am feeling big feelings, bigger than I can handle. It's like they're boiling over, trying to find a way out through my skin. 'But, Cade, I *am* desperate. I need to win this. It's the only way I can help my brother.'

'Winning won't help,' Cade says, not skipping a beat, and it's like a slap. 'That's how they trap you. They sell you a dream, but the dream is a *nightmare*. Believe me, winning is only the beginning. They'll own you. They'll own your brother too. They own me. I want to break free, Taryn.'

I slide down the wall and sit between the counter and the tumble dryer. 'And how are you going to do that?'

He nods as if giving himself permission to go on. 'I'm working with an undercover journalist from Bastion Press.'

The seriousness of the situation hits. He isn't talking big talk; he's actually *doing something*. 'Who?'

'I can't say who, but it's someone on your team.' My mind runs through everyone I've met. It's definitely not Clancy; she's too awful. Dre? Lars? Nico? Dr Anders?

'How do I know this isn't, like, a weird test?'

'You're right to be paranoid. That'll help you. But, Taryn, I swear you can trust me.' He takes my hand and presses it to his chest. Through muscular pecs, I feel his heart beating fast, like he's trying to prove his soul to me.

'Why would you ask *me* for help?'

'Because you're smart and I can tell you don't believe the lies they're pumping out. You really are doing this for your brother. This isn't about your ego.'

He can flatter me all he wants but I'm immune to it; being smart is a curse. How I wish I could walk around clueless; life would be easier. 'If they catch us . . .'

'They'll kill us. But they might kill you for a bum note, so it's all relative.'

I laugh a harsh, gallows laugh. 'What do you want me to do?'

'Nothing. Just take the Punkcat everywhere you go. My contact is working on a piece that'll expose Elysium and Chairman Slade as an abusive piece of crap. Any evidence you collect will be priceless. Get it all: the diets, the bullying, the schedule, the fat-shaming . . . any queer girls in the house?'

'Maybe,' I say, still cautious even now.

'Rico from my band is gay. He's permanently terrified they'll discover his boyfriend . . . we all had to sign a "morality clause" promising we'd behave "appropriately".'

What does *that* mean? It's like they keep shifting the goalposts; Leela's gender is a good angle for them this week, but Rico dating a guy is inappropriate? How does that work? I know the answer, of course. Rico needs to appear single, and straight, for their female fans. In his case, his sexuality might lose them money. 'It isn't fair.'

Cade shakes his head. He looks exhausted. 'The whole system is like this comic book monster with a hundred heads. *Starmaker* is only one part of it, but if we can chop off one head, it wounds the whole beast. It's a start.'

'I'll do it,' I say. It feels like a reflex. Cade's face lights up; a flicker of hope. It is right, and what they're doing to us is wrong. Also, selfishly, this could be my safety net; I could threaten to expose them myself when the time comes. 'When are they going to run the exposé?'

'As soon as we have enough evidence. I've spoken to the journalist, and so have other survivors, but unless it's something current, *Starmaker* will say it's all historical and that they've improved.'

That makes sense. After all, that's why they've brought Dr Anders in – part of their image rehabilitation. It's all surface though. 'Okay.'

Cade seems quietly relieved. He helps me up off the floor and embraces me. 'Thank you,' he breathes into my hair. 'I know what you're risking, but this could change everything.' He holds me by the shoulders. 'And if they discover the camera, I'll say it came from me and that you had no idea. You're protected. I would never hurt you, I hope you know that, Taryn.'

I nod, absorbing the enormity of what I've agreed to.

'Thank you.' He wraps me in his arms, cradling my head in a big hand. 'Together. We can do this.'

A game within a game. I hope I'm playing for the right side.

CHALLENGE THREE:
BE YOURSELF

DOLLHOU5E LEELA:
I was born a boy.

Transgender shock rocks competition.

EXCLUSIVE by TV Editor Dean Sutton

German *Starmaker* sensation Leela Weber (19) tearfully told *The Globe* about her secret childhood in Baden-Baden as Frank. 'I always knew I was born in the wrong body,' she reveals. 'On the inside, I have always been a girl. I told my mother and father that I was a girl when I was four years old.'

Sadly for brave Leela, her parents were not understanding. 'I was told it was a phase and that I would grow out of it.' At the age of twelve, Leela moved to Berlin to live with her loving grandmother, Ute. 'There, I could be myself and started to live as Leela.'

Germany has more relaxed laws surrounding gender transition for minors. Under the UK's Deviancy Act, gender transition is not legally recognized. Leela hopes to use her platform on the global singing contest to raise awareness of transgender issues. 'Trans people are just people. We are not this big scary thing. That is why I want to be open about who I am.' This weekend, Leela will perform a track by German transgender icon Kim Petras, who was notably forced to flee the United States. Following the civil war, Blue States President Alaina Fox reinstated protections for LGBTQ people meaning Leela is able to perform in Media City.

Related: Ladyboy bride wedding shock!

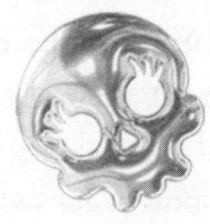

CHAPTER 32

It's probably my imagination, but could it be that, after many hours of dancing, I'm getting better at it?

Hypothesis Two: the makeover has given me an armour to hide behind. With my Rebel Doll glam and costume, I feel indestructible. Either way, the darkly gothic, Latin-inspired opening routine for Live Show Three *feels* easier. We show off our new looks to 'A Palé' by Rosalía while fire blasts from cannons all around us. I feel the flames warm my cheeks and worry about tossing my new hair too close. Maybe I just adore this song. Mum used to listen to it in the car.

I switch positions with Minnie to take centre as we hit the chorus. My little moment. The audience screams and I wink to the camera with a smile. I *am* getting better at something; better at *pretending*. Is this why they assigned us characters? I am Taryn no longer; I am Rebel Doll. They might live to regret that.

This week's challenge is very simple – we will perform a song of our choosing that represents our new character. On lush velvet sofas in the studio, we have a sit-down chat with

Nico and Mojo. Briar is up first, followed by Minnie. Shayna is third.

'Now Miss Shayna,' Mojo starts. 'Is it fair to say you weren't too happy with your shakeover?'

I see her tense up, as I watch on the monitors in the dark backstage area. She smiles her most cutesy smile. 'I've had long hair my whole life. It was a real big shock, Mojo.'

'Let's take a look, shall we?' They roll VT and Shayna's salon wails echo out through the studio. They show the entire meltdown with a dramatic score. This week, she's getting the villain edit. Madison is statue-like next to me, face grim.

I am on last this week. The wait is agonizing. 'It's a good thing,' Cade tells me in the green room during the commercial break. 'It means they think your song is a good finale.'

After the ad break it's Leela's turn. Her big moment. She's hardly spoken all day, lips tight. 'Hey,' I tell her backstage. 'You've been through hell to be who you are. Who's stronger than you? This is nothing.'

A single tear escapes her eye. 'I know. It would be nice to have one easy day. Just one.'

I nod silent understanding. The intro music plays and a runner signals for Leela to head on stage. 'You've got this, Lee.'

She gives a brusque nod and strides out. On the monitor, she takes her seat opposite the hosts. Right away, Mojo's and Nico's tone are softer. Leela's 'news' was leaked to *The Globe* earlier this week, quite deliberately. Tasteless, but – as Clancy explained – without the tabloids on side, the group will have no future beyond *Starmaker*.

If there *is* a group. All week I've carried the fluffy Punkcat, attached to my bag, to rehearsals and briefings. Where I go, it goes. I caught the moment when Clancy told Suki to start using something called Slendajab. Apparently the daily injections will help her lose weight. The fact that she's since had diarrhoea all week doesn't concern Clancy in the slightest.

Also caught on camera was the sound engineer who insists on referring to Leela as 'bro'. As was the moment the team forced Domino to rehearse with crippling period pain. When she complained, Clancy told her she was being 'aggressive'. In the end, Dom danced with tears running down her face. I caught it all.

I don't know where the footage is downloading to. With each morning alarm call, I log straight onto a news app to check if the mystery journalist has launched a nuclear missile at *Starmaker*. Nothing yet. Maybe I haven't caught anything bad enough to bring *Starmaker* down. What will it take? I need this to happen NOW before another girl gets in that pyramid.

'Now, Leela, it's been a massive week for you,' Nico says, more tenderly than I've heard her up to now. 'How are you holding up?'

'I am okay,' Leela begins. Her shoulders sink down. 'I am glad I don't have to keep secrets. I am who I am.'

'Yes you are,' Nico says. 'I've always been so proud of my LGBTQIA fanbase. They mean the world to me.' There's a cheer from the studio audience. She still performs in the Red States though. If she cared that much, she wouldn't.

'We love you for who you are,' Mojo adds.

'Most people have been so kind,' Leela lies. Column inches for

Starmaker have made a pole to crucify Leela on. The comments online have been a bin fire. God knows how, but the internet got hold of some old school photos. Some rabid transphobes have been jamming the complaints hotline at Network G, protesting the fact that a 'biological male' is competing to be in a girl group. I wasn't aware my singing voice came from my ovaries. The notion that *Starmaker* ought to be a 'safe space for women and girls' is laughable. It's a literal slaughterhouse.

'Some people haven't been too nice,' Nico comments. 'What do you say to the haters?'

Leela shrugs. 'They can vote for someone else.' Her abrupt response catches both hosts off guard and they laugh. It's fun to see them unrehearsed.

Leela performs her Kim Petras song, backed by the boy dancers. She throws in some choreo as if to apologize for last week. With her white hair, angel wings and acid green PVC miniskirt, I am obsessed with her. She's who I'd vote for. She's the *cool one* and I hope people vote in.

Finally, my turn. I take my place on the sofa during the ad break. *FreshElla – the ultimate feminine protection.* The MUA performs his checks on Mojo. I've changed into an outfit I suggested to Lars: a vintage corseted ivory wedding dress, ripped to the thigh, with my dog collar and knee-high boots. Something so archetypally feminine reclaimed. Lars loved the suggestion and here we are. Nico offers me the weakest of smiles as we wait. 'You look good,' she mutters.

'Thanks. So do you. You always do,' I babble.

'Well, this is what a lot of Botox and filler looks like, but thanks.'

There's an awkward silence and I find myself filling it. 'Do . . . you . . . still enjoy all of this?'

Nico looks surprised. I don't know if that's because of my audacity in talking to her, or whether no one's considered her enjoyment in a long time. 'This is my job. Free advice, Taryn – everyone is going to think they know you because of what they see on TV. Nico isn't who I am, it's what I do. For now.'

For now. What does that mean? I don't have a chance to ask because the director shouts that we're ready to go live.

'Welcome back!' Mojo announces. 'Just in time to kiki with our final trainee, from London, it's Rebel Doll Taryn!'

I think of Nico's words. *Rebel Doll isn't who I am, it's what I do.* Maybe I can afford to be a little standoffish. I don't answer. I just smirk. 'Your makeover is getting a lot of love online!' Nico says.

'This is what I look like in my head,' I say. 'A manga punk.'

They are smart; I have to be smarter. We chat about my dad, my mum, my brother. I don't think it's very on brand to cry, so instead I fake a moment where I'm *almost* reduced to tears. 'Sorry, can I just have a second?' My voice trembles as I discuss Jenson. 'I'm doing this for him.'

'But look at how you've changed,' Nico says.

'I'm evolving. Every week I get stronger. I'm not taking any bull— any nonsense.' I almost swear. But don't. I'm Rebel Doll, not Stupid Doll.

'Do you think you can win this?' Mojo asks.

The way I win is not by beating the other girls, but by beating Chairman Slade. 'I do.' I look straight down the camera. 'I didn't but now I do. I have the best voice. Fight me.'

'Fighting talk,' Nico says with a sly smile. 'Let's see what you've got . . .'

'The Show Must Go On'. That's my song. It feels right. Who is a bigger rebel than Freddie Mercury? Proof that queer people get a pass when straight people love you. Dad *loves* Queen. I've seen all their performances online. I've seen the old movie.

No dancers, it's just me and a wind machine and a stark white spotlight.

In the front row of the studio audience is a woman with Mum's haircut. With the spotlight in my eyes, it could be her. I remember the way she beamed at me from the front row the year I was the Angel Gabriel in the infant school nativity play. I wore a white bed sheet then, and a piece of silver tinsel on my head.

The lyrics are right too; my heart *is* breaking, but I sing on.

Mum would be so proud. I fall to my knees at the key change. I sing my heart out of my throat. I sing for my life.

Back in white, before the glass pyramid. On the judging panel, Cade sits, grim-faced. Mojo is ready to deliver our fate. This is absurd. How did we wind up here? And by *we*, I mean the world.

'The first doll to advance to the next challenge is . . .' We all wait for Domino's name. 'Taryn!'

I blink doltishly. Did I hear right? Last week, I was Bottom Two.

'Go to podium one, Taryn!'

'Oh my days,' I breathe, and walk, almost in a trance, to the first position. I send a psychic *thank you* to Freddie.

Next up is Madison, *then* Domino. Fourth is Suki; fifth is Leela. Oh thank god for that.

Remaining on the steps are Briar, Shayna and, biggest shock, Minnie. I glance at Suki and she's as surprised as I am. South Korea is so important to pop music, I think we all assumed Minnie was a cert for the final group. Suki describes herself as Australian, but I guess she is Korean too. Her makeover – the pink bob – is getting a lot of love online, even if her bleached hair is literally snapping off.

I hate myself for thinking this way, but I start to inwardly chant Briar's name. She looks to me and shakes her head, almost resigned to her fate.

'The final girl safely through to next week is . . .' Mojo draws it out. 'From Korea, Minnie!'

Min-jee bursts into tears and covers her face with her hands. Head low, she shuffles to her platform. It's oddly surprising to see her so human; she's been flawless every week. Briar looks to me again, as if to say *I know, it's okay.* It's not okay though. She's been in the bottom every week. We both know she's on borrowed time.

'Judges, the girls in danger this week are both American; Briar from the Blue States and Shayna from the Red.'

Shayna sobs, face red and blotchy. Briar is stolid, staring into nothingness. Beside me, on podium two, I hear Madison's breath rattle. 'Lord Jesus in heaven above, protect my baby sister.'

'Who will you save this week?'

Cade's face is sickly green. Dre's head hangs low. Once

more, Clancy swoops in and whispers in their ears. Nico nods and stands to deliver the verdict. 'Mojo, this competition has never been about the best voice or the slickest dancer. It's about finding idols who connect with fans and represent *Starmaker*. It's about having the right attitude. Briar, while we're worried about your consistently low ranking, we think your personality is what will make fans love you. Shayna, I'm afraid you're eliminated.'

Shayna crumples.

'No!' Madison screams. 'Please, God, no! Please! She'll try! She'll do better!'

Mojo holds out a hand. 'Madison, stay where you are.'

The security guards swim in from the periphery, armed and ready.

Nico gestures to the Elimination Chamber. 'Shayna, you know what to do. Trainees, let's sing our goodbyes.'

Shayna looks to the wall of masked security staff and Dr Anders, ready with his injectopen sedative. I see it in her eyes: the moment she reconciles herself to this fate. The baby of the competition looks to her sister and shakes her head. It's an admission of sorts; *I blew it*. Shayna slowly turns towards the pyramid and starts her final walk. The 'farewell song' overture begins.

'Shay!' Madison weeps. 'I'm so sorry. Shay, please, look at me!' Her sister's gaze is fixed on her feet.

Some of the girls sing meekly. I do not. Shayna reaches the exterior of the pyramid. It waits like a jaw, ready to swallow her.

'Wait,' I say, and then more loudly. 'Stop!'

'Stay where you are, Taryn. Sing the song please.' It's the director, calling from across the studio.

'Stop!' I jump off my podium, in the correct position to step in front of Shayna, barring her progress. I can't see another girl die. I can't. There is only one thing I can think of. 'Look, we know that Ashanti didn't die!'

The rest of the girls *don't* know this. There's a moment of silence and someone gasps *what?*

'Cut!' Clancy shrieks. 'For God's sake cut!'

'What do you mean?' Briar asks. 'Ashanti's alive?'

I plough on, ignoring her. I plead with everyone, anyone who'll listen. 'That means we don't *have* to die!' On the panel, Cade can't meet my eye. I have to protect him. 'Just let us go. Do whatever you did with Ashanti. Fake it! We won't tell anyone.'

The guards move in. I push Shayna behind me.

'Get back in line, Taryn!' Clancy cries.

'No! This is insane! You proved you don't have to kill— '

I barely register the butt of the rifle until it's too late. I feel it before I see it. It clonks against the side of my skull just above my ear. The pain comes a second later, both dull and sharp. My brain feels like it's been kicked and I realize my legs have gone. Sparkles dance across my vision as my shoulder hits the studio floor.

I hear gasps and cries. Someone yells *no*, someone else shouts *don't*. It's all very confusing. My head isn't working right. I see shoes running towards me. Woolly arms scoop me up: Dr Anders. 'What are you thinking?' he snaps at the guard.

'Is she damaged?' Clancy, shriller than ever, squeals. 'Did he mark her?'

I am a commodity to them. An object.

I lie back against Anders, too dizzy to get up. Four spinning Cades kneel opposite me. I look him in the eye, even as my field of vision whirls. I hope he can sense my resolve. If I wasn't in before, I'm all in now.

They fucked with the wrong doll.

@d0llh0u5estan

I ship taryn and madi so hard

@taryndolllover

when she spoke up for shayna. i would die for her

@tarynleeladollfan

I AM THE BEST SINGER FIGHT ME!!! I see no lies.

@bootslaycntcnthousedownboots

did not clock leela. putting the doll in dollhou5e!

@dolldollydollhousedolls

Taryn Debut Minnie Debut Domino Debut Suki Debut Madi Debut

@starmakerslilbitch

sucks to be madison tho – watching her sister die 😭

@popculturevultcha

Taryn Beck is rapidly becoming my favourite trainee. Is she too good for Starmaker? See also Leela Weber. They should go solo.

@sickboiiiiiii

maybe madison should have prayed louder lmao

CHAPTER 33

Japanista is designed to look like a futuristic Shinto temple. It's actually a sushi restaurant and club downtown. Hottest spot in Media City according to Clancy. The place to be seen, also according to Clancy. We are made to pose for paparazzi photos on the palace steps, dressed in head-to-toe sponsored products from Adidas, and flanked by electric neon cherry blossom trees. The flashbulbs are staccato lightning. Nico ensures she's in the middle of every photograph.

Taryn! Taryn! Look this way! Over here! Taryn! Give us some teeth!

'Smile, doll,' Nico murmurs through my hair. 'You survived another week, didn't you? It's not a funeral.'

Isn't it? Madison was excused from this press opportunity. She was inconsolable. Dr Anders took her back to the Dreamhouse, sedated. I wish I was sedated too.

Alas, attendance at Japanista for the rest of us wasn't up for discussion. Elysium is throwing us a party to celebrate the halfway point of the contest. Only two more murders to go before the band line-up is finalized.

Inside the Asian 'inspired' restaurant, a bored-looking DJ plays pounding reggaetón beats from her booth, surrounded by cherry trees and pagodas. Everyone wants a slice of our cake. People I've never met descend on us, keen to tell us how *fierce* we are. They want selfies and autographs. I think they're a mixture of staff from Elysium and Network G, and influencers they've handpicked.

It's all too much. I feel sick and dizzy. A waiter swipes a tray of prawn nigiri under my nose and I almost puke right there on his slate serving platter. 'No . . . thank you.' I turn to see Briar moving in, arms wide for a hug. 'Come here.' She folds me into the embrace and strokes my hair. 'What you did was brave. *Crazy*, but brave.'

'It didn't change a thing.' All I have to show for my efforts is a sore lump under my hairline. My intervention was obliquely shown in the results show, cleverly edited naturally.

'Well, it meant something to me.' She sighs. 'I'm glad Ash made it.' She kisses the crown of my head.

'But Shayna. I can't stop seeing her face.'

'I know. She looked so *small* in there.' Her voice wobbles. 'God I can't cry. If I start I'll never stop. Honestly, girl, the hell are we doing?'

Briar is the most mature out of all of us. She can help. I contemplate telling her Cade's secret, 'Bri, there's something . . .'

Suddenly, Nico's arm cuts between us to pluck two flutes of pink champagne from the selection on the bar top. 'Champagne?' she says.

'We're underage,' Briar replies.

Nico frowns as much as her dermatologist allows. 'You're

idols now; you can have what you want. You can shoot up in the middle of the dancefloor if you want so long as there aren't any cameras around.' I *hope* she's kidding but I think of poor Sonny Feldman. 'Believe me, the perks make it all slightly more bearable. Enjoy it while you can.'

'I can drink back home,' Domino says, leaning over me to grab a flute. 'Go crazy, guys. It's a party.'

Leela – also of legal drinking age in Germany – helps herself too, but I refrain. I don't deserve a party.

It's like Nico can read my mind. 'Girl, lighten up. Such a downer, honestly. You knew what you were getting into.'

'I did . . . and I didn't,' I say over the banging music.

The idol shrugs it off, rubbing her nose. She lowers her voice. 'Free advice. You sold your soul for nice hotel rooms and free drinks. Just go with it, less friction that way.' She clinks my glass of sparkling water and sees someone she recognizes. 'Darling! You made it! The new face looks wonderful!' Off she goes.

'What was that about?' Suki asks.

I scowl after the idol as she expertly mingles. 'Nico thinks I should forget about how Shayna was *just gassed* and enjoy myself.' With everything that's going on, being *disappointed* in my former role model is the least of my worries.

Suki nods. 'This sounds so freaking dense, but I didn't really think about the dying part until it was too late.'

'On TV they were just characters,' I say. 'But Shayna was real. She was weird. And kind of mean. But she was real. And now she's gone. Forever.'

'Who'll eat all the Cheerios?' Suki says sadly.

'Right?' That girl always had a hand in a cereal box.

'Like she only ate Cheerios. What was that about?' Suki says, half-laughing.

'Like four times a day.'

'She must have had very odd poops,' Suki says thoughtfully, and I embrace her tightly. I guess *this* is how we get through it.

'Poor Madison,' I say. I have no great affection for the girl, but she's all alone in that big mansion. 'Do you think I should go home and check on her?'

Suki shakes her head. 'Dr Anders gave her a shot, remember. She'll be out of it for hours.'

I know she's right. On the other side of the venue, I see Cade and Dre talking with some grey men in grey suits. 'Is one of them Chairman Slade?' I ask.

Suki frowns. 'I don't know. He doesn't allow photos right?'

'Why?'

'Maybe he's shy?'

Sceptical. 'Yeah, sure.'

I weave through the crowd, fending off more compliments about my makeover and voice. I can't pretend they're not pleasing to hear, but I also can't reconcile the nice stuff with the death; my brain won't allow it. Maybe Nico got a free lobotomy when they did her browlift.

Cade sees me coming and his face brightens. 'Hey, you. First rank.'

'Bottom to the top,' I say flatly.

Cade steers me away from the execs. 'I'm glad. You're no good to me dead.' He blushes. 'Sorry, that came out all wrong.'

'I'll let you off. Are you mad at me? For the Ashanti thing?'

He crinkles his nose. 'No. I can see your logic in the moment. You were desperate to save Shayna. I can't be mad at that.'

That's a weight off. That had been a stone in my shoe. I care what Cade thinks of me more than I'd like. 'Is Chairman Slade here?' I ask, changing the subject.

He scans the party. 'I don't know. I've never met him.'

'What? How?'

He arches a brow. 'I doubt the CEO of McDonald's spends much time with the cows either.'

'Good point.'

'He sends his minions. He has spies everywhere. Be careful what you say about him. God, I sound like a paranoid headcase.'

'I'm getting there myself. I'll prepare a tinfoil hat.'

A new track comes on and I hear a whoop over the music. Domino drags Joaquin, one of the *Starmaker* dancers, onto the dancefloor. Suki, Leela, Briar and Min-jee follow, albeit reluctantly. It's really noticeable that there are fewer of us now.

'This is the best song ever!' Domino decrees. 'Come on! I'll teach you the dance!'

I note she's holding Joaquin's hand and not letting go. He is the most beautiful of the dancers: chiselled cheekbones and amber eyes. Great curls too.

'I'll be right there,' I tell her. I'm absolutely not feeling it.

'You wanna get out of here?' Cade says.

'What? Seriously? *Can* we just go?'

'I'd like to see them try to stop me. We just need to make sure we aren't seen leaving together. Let me make a call.'

He does so and, moments later, as everyone is distracted watching the suits from Network G give a speech, Cade takes my hand and leads me downstairs. We pass the restrooms and head into the thrum of the kitchen. It's hot and noisy and smelly, all clanging stainless steel and swirling steam from the dishwasher. Fat spits from a bubbling fryer.

'Don't mind us!' Cade says, as we hurry past a line of confused chefs towards the fire escape.

We exit into a filthy alleyway where a limo is waiting next to the dumpsters. 'Quick, get in!' He hustles me into the back of the car. 'God, if I stand next to a girl – or a dude for that matter – for more than a minute, the rumours start.'

Being one of a long dynasty of people to be romantically connected to Cade Kekoa puts a weird taste on my tongue and I don't know why. He was most recently linked to some perky Disney actress. 'Do you have a girlfriend?' I ask, as I slip into the pristine backseat of the car. Brand new leather smell.

'No,' he says. 'We weren't allowed while the band was active. We had to sign a contract.'

'The band is over now.'

He looks at me a moment too long. 'I guess so.' I wonder if he hasn't realized that until this moment. He just got his life back. 'I've been so focused on Sonny . . . and working with . . . the undercover journalist . . . I haven't really even . . .' He tails off. 'Like, how do I even date? I don't know how. Everyone wants something from me. It . . . it's hard to trust someone who hasn't been through all this.'

Someone like me? Is *this* a date? No, because that would

mean *I* was dating Cade, which feels like fan fiction I'd have written when I was twelve.

'Where are we going?' I ask, changing the subject to something less punchy.

'A friend's place. You'll love it.'

We drive for about thirty minutes until, out of the window, I see the moon rippling on the sea. 'Lake Michigan,' Cade explains. 'There's a beach bar here. I love getting out of the city whenever I can. I feel like I can breathe out here.'

I don't understand how the borderless expanse before me can be a lake, not an ocean. They really do like to supersize things over here. We turn off the coast road and down a steep, crunchy track to a shed-like structure on stilts overlooking the bay. Even with everything that happened to our home, I still find a certain peace in the sea.

Our driver parks up and we head up the sandy plank stairs to the left of the shack. The tide shivers over the silt; my favourite sound in the world. 'Will they let me in?' I ask.

'I know the owner, you'll be fine.'

As we enter the bar, there's a cheer from a young man in an apron. 'Eh up! There he is!'

I'm so happy to hear a Yorkshire accent, I almost burst into tears on the spot. Homesickness gets you at the weirdest times.

The two men have a back-slapping hug before Cade introduces us. 'Taryn, this is Tabby Macfarlane. Fellow Brit.'

He offers a fist bump. 'Hiya! You off the telly too?'

'For now.'

Tabby ducks under the flap in the bar. 'What can I get you

guys? Oh, by the way, boss, still no European spirits getting past customs.'

'Keep me posted,' Cade says, perching on a bar stool. The bar is how I've always imagined an American bar would be: pool tables, low pendant lighting and a jukebox playing vintage Janet Jackson. The décor is sort of tiki themed; perhaps a nod to Cade's heritage.

'You're the boss?' I ask, intrigued.

'The bar was due to close and I loved it. So I bought it. Probably not the smartest investment, but . . .'

'It's so cool,' I say. The venue is about half full of surfer-looking hipster types. A lot of stick-and-poke tattoos and mullet haircuts. No one seems to pay Cade any mind; I guess he's here all the time and the novelty has worn off.

Tabby brings us canary yellow mocktails in tall glasses with pineapple and umbrellas. The drink is creamy and delicious. 'You gonna sing for us tonight, boss?'

'Ah, I dunno.'

'Not like you to be shy. It must be you, Taryn, love.' The bartender throws a jaunty wink my way.

'You sing here?' I ask.

'I do.' Cade drains his glass in a single gulp. 'For the longest time, *Starmaker* made me hate singing and dancing. When I got this place, I started singing some covers, and then a couple of tracks I wrote. I realized it's *Starmaker* I hate, not music.'

I nod. I wonder if I'll suffer the same fate when singing becomes inextricably linked to death in my mind. What would a DOLLHOU5E album sound like? I think about lyrics in bed at night as I fall asleep; I can't help it. Just the way my brain works.

'It's funny,' Cade goes on. 'I love some N-TRU5T stuff too, but it's hard to be objective, you know? Maybe in time, they'll feel like my songs, not something we were forced to do.'

I look up at the bamboo façade, worried the tears I can feel forming might roll. 'I feel guilty.'

'Why?'

'Because, despite everything I know, everything you've told me . . . a part of me actually wants to win,' I confess. 'I want what you had. I want to record an album, make music videos, go on tour. Does that make me the worst person in the world?'

Cade's hand starts at my knee and then slides up a couple of inches. I hold my breath. 'Oh I remember that one. You're not a bad person for wanting something better for you and your family. That's human nature.'

'People are *dying* and I'm writing song lyrics . . .'

'Because you're an artist. It's like breathing for me too. I have to create or I'll go insane.'

I nod and swallow back a lump of emotion. Truth isn't always black or white, I guess. I can want to burn *Starmaker* to the ground and also want to be an idol. I shake it off. I'm so bored of tears. 'I wanna hear one of your songs,' I tell him.

'Really?'

'Yeah. Is that weird?'

'No. I guess not.' He calls to Tabby. 'Tabs, can you bring the mic up?'

He flashes me a grin and heads for a little stage at the end of the bar. This man has played at stadiums, and now I'm getting serenaded from seven feet away.

'Hey, everyone.' His voice booms from the speakers and the patrons stop what they're doing to look his way. They don't seem fazed and I guess this happens all the time. 'I got a request from a very special person so I thought I'd do a couple of songs if that's okay?'

'Dude! Not again!' a regular heckles.

'Screw you, Toni.' Cade laughs. 'Just for that, I've added "Love Shack" to the set list; I know it's your favourite.' He gives Toni the finger.

Cade tunes an acoustic guitar. He softly clears his throat. There's a moment of hushed anticipation, and he begins.

Seen the pyramids
And Kyoto
The fall of the Kremlin
You're my go-to.
Niagara
Victoria
I'm a lamb to
Your slaughter.
One, two, three, four, five, six, seven
You're the eighth wonder.
Seen past the sky and into heaven
You're the one I want, yeah.

His voice is gossamer, falsetto. He never sang like this in the band. *These lyrics are not about me,* I tell myself. This is what idols do, this is their skill: to make every word, every glance down the lens, about *you*. I feel it. I feel every line at my core, like he's somehow strumming strings within me.

Only this time, he *is* looking at me. I'm not the little girl playing pretend in front of a poster on her bedroom wall any more. He is singing to me. It's more than I can stand. I look to the floor.

He rounds out the set by performing an acoustic version of N-TRU5T's ballad, 'Me Without You'. The song is his as much as it is Elysium's. It's a chicken or egg thing; Elysium might have given the band a song, but without Cade's charm, it would just be words on a page, noises made by some middle-aged Swedish producer.

'That was incredible,' I tell him as he joins me at the bar.

He flushes. 'My guitar was out of tune.'

I take hold of his chin, forcing him to receive the compliment like a man. 'Cade,' I tell him more firmly. 'It was beautiful.'

He says nothing but looks deep into my eyes, searching. *Is he going to . . . ?* I see a question mark hanging and, without saying a word, I grant him permission. I invite him in. He leans forward, cups my cheek with his palm and kisses me tenderly on the lips. Not wanting the moment to end, I return the kiss.

It's as if the world starts to spin a lot faster, the room whirling around us. It's the most blissful, feather-soft feeling. After forever, or a second, he pulls away.

'Wow,' he says, flustered. 'That was really unprofessional.'

'Do I look like I care?'

I kiss him again.

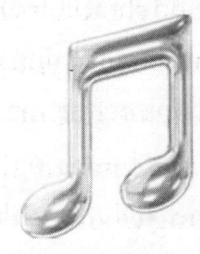

CHAPTER 34

I am still floating the following morning. Sunday is our only lie-in and the Dreamhouse is quiet when I rise to make an illicit (under Clancy's rules) breakfast. Planning a very calorific fry-up, I get out the frying pan and some eggs. Was last night real? Everything that happened after we left the party has the same soft-edges as the most delectable dream.

I'm replaying the kiss in my mind when the kitchen door opens unexpectedly and Domino slips in, makeup smudged and still in her Adidas clothes from the party last night. She raises a finger to her lips and I grin.

'You dirty stop out!'

'Don't tell anyone,' she whispers, pleading for me to lower my voice.

She must know there are like ten hidden cameras in this room alone, not including the Punkcat which is attached to my backpack on the counter. 'I won't! But where did you get to?'

'Giiiiirl,' she says dreamily. 'I went to a rave at some warehouse with Joaquin and the dancers. So much fun!'

'Would you like some breakfast?'

She investigates what I'm about to cook and crinkles her nose. 'Baby, move over.' She shoulders me out of the way. 'I'm hungry, but what is with you and your white food?'

'I'm *English*. Essentially, we live off bread and potatoes.'

Domino dances over the kitchen tiles to the fridge. She never stops. She has a spring where her spine should be. 'Have you had huevos rancheros?'

'What now?'

'Okay, I make you a proper, honest Mexican breakfast.' She digs some tomatoes and avocados out of the giant fridge. 'Where were you last night? We lost you.'

I don't want to get Cade into trouble . . . and nor do I wholly trust Dom. Other than Madison, she's by far the most competitive. 'I just came back here. I felt a migraine coming on.'

She seems to accept this lie and grabs a frying pan. One-by-one, the other girls start filtering down, no doubt lured by the smell of Domino's feast. Eggs sizzle in the pan and she warms flatbreads on the stove.

'Don't worry, I cook for everyone,' Domino says. 'This is how mi avó used to make it back in the favela. Brazilians – not so big on brunch. Mexicans get it.'

She serves up a rainbow dish: sunny yellow eggs, served on a flatbread with salsa and guacamole. I'm suspicious at first, just because I've never eaten anything quite like it, but it's warming, spicy and delicious.

'You grew up with your grandma?' I ask.

Domino continues to flit around the kitchen, sprinkling coriander over our plates. 'I never knew Mama. I know she love me, but she love drugs more,' she delivers this lightly, after years of building up inner walls I suspect. 'So mi avó was my mother and my father. This is all for her.' She points to the heavens, and she doesn't need to expand further.

'Where's Madi?' I ask, changing the subject.

'I think she's in her room,' Briar says, her braids hidden under a silk bonnet.

Minnie shakes her head. 'No. She is in phone room.'

'OK.' Someone *has* to see if she's okay. I decide to use Dom's eggs as a cover to see if she's hungry.

The phone room is a little booth off the den. The soundproofing isn't nearly as good as we were told, and all our calls are recorded anyway so they can use them on TV. I hear right away that Madison is on the phone, and her mother is on speakerphone. I hover back, but can't help but overhear.

'You will not quit, so get that outta your head right now!' a strong Southern voice yells.

'I can't stay, Momma.'

'You got to. If you leave, they'll kill you anyway.'

'I don't care,' Madison sobs. 'How do I go on after what they did to Shay? I'll look like a monster and . . . and I just can't. Momma, you weren't there; you didn't see her face.'

I don't know how I know, but this is the real Madison. I don't think she's performing for the cameras.

'They promised me,' Madison goes on. 'They promised me, Momma.'

Her mother tsks. 'They promised shit in writing and that's all that counts.'

'They said we'd both make the band . . .'

Now *that* is interesting. I tiptoe closer. *Who* promised her that? I knew it; the sisters *were* production plants. They never queued up to audition like the rest of us. I didn't buy that for a second.

'Now you listen here, Madison Jean Silver, you got this. Just go out there and give it one million per cent.'

Madi's strained reply is high, girlish. Under the diva hair and makeup, it's easy to forget Madi is only a year older than me. 'But, Mom, what about Shay?'

'She was weak. She didn't trust in the Lord and she gave up.'

'She didn't, Momma. She said her prayers every night.'

'Yes she did. As soon as she started whinging and moaning about her stupid hair. She knew better than that. You are the most talented Silver girl, Madison, you know that's true. You want it more than either of your sisters.'

'But, Mom . . .'

'No, no more buts. Silvers do not quit. Shayna knew it. I been training you girls since you was old enough to walk. You're my little star. You got this. Go out there and make Momma proud.'

I hear Madison sniff. I'm not expecting the phone room door to open so suddenly. She must have hung up on her mother. I'm caught red-handed, eavesdropping.

'Oh, Madison, hi! I wondered if you wanted breakfast?' She looks vacant, eyes pink. I relent. 'That's a lie. I came to see if you were okay.'

She says nothing, her face drawn.

'Just let me know if you want anything,' I say, turning back towards the stairs to the kitchen.

'Thank you,' Madison says suddenly. 'For speaking up at Elimination. You didn't have to do that.'

I shrug. 'I think I did.' I can't say much more with hidden cameras all over us.

'I'm going to tell Clancy that I quit.'

I glance around, then speak quietly. 'Madison, you can't. We both know there's no quitting.'

She shrugs. 'Either way, I'm cooked. What kind of sister would I be if I went out there and sang a merry little song this week? I'll look like a heartless bitch.'

'Make it a tribute song. They'll *love* that.' *They* being both the producers and the voters.

'I don't know if I can do it.' I didn't realize how tiny Madison is until now. In my head she is a giantess. Today, she's a deflated balloon.

'Madison, you are a precision missile. You were born for this.'

She laughs bitterly. 'You heard my mom then?'

'Sorry. I didn't mean it like that.'

'I did. Us "goddamn babies" ruined her figure so she couldn't be a dancer. She's told us that every day of our lives. We have to do it because she couldn't.'

'Jesus.' I said the wrong thing again. 'Sorry.'

Her blue eyes glint like stainless steel. 'Maybe she shouldn't have gotten herself knocked up at sixteen, huh? You know what, Taryn? I looked for Christ in my heart last night.' Madison's eyes glitter. 'For the first time in my whole life, he wasn't there. It's like he looked away in shame.'

'Guess he's not a *Starmaker* fan.'

Madison throws her head back and laughs, sniffing back the tears. 'Maybe he changed channels.'

Her laughter is contagious. 'Sure. He definitely has Netflix.'

For the first time, Madison and I share a genuine smile, not the pretend sisterhood we fake on stage. 'Come have eggs with us? Domino cooked.'

'Okay.' She hooks a pinky finger around mine and I lead her downstairs.

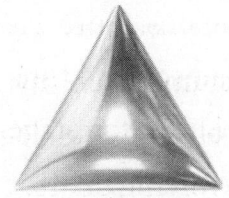

CHAPTER 35

There are so few of us now that Leela and I are alone in the back of the SUV. An early call to the studio at Elysium Entertainment. Dawn is only just breaking as we drive through the Media City hills. I'm half asleep with my head resting against the window when Leela pokes my arm. 'Hey. Where were you?'

'What?'

'After Japanista? You vanished. With Cade.'

'I didn't.' It just pops out. Leela fixes me with a sharpened *bitch please* stare. The furry Punkcat still hangs from my bag, recording all of this. 'It was nothing.'

'Are you and he . . . ?'

Every inch of my body is on alert. Cade has instilled in me an acute paranoia. I can't trust anyone, even my best friend in this hellhole. I lean in, checking that the driver isn't listening. She has Airpods in so I think we're safe. 'I . . . OK, I have a crush. But nothing's gonna happen, is it?'

'So where did you go?'

'He just drove me back to the Dreamhouse. I swear.' I

am lying to her face, and I don't think she believes me for a second. This competition is poisoning our friendship. Maybe that was inevitable.

Our arrival at Elysium saves my skin. The offices are modern, chrome, the blazing sun logo rendered in jagged scrap metal over the revolving doors.

Dre looks as bleary as we do when he greets us in one of the sleek, windowless studios. He wears a vast hoodie and a vintage LA Rams cap. 'Girls,' he explains. 'Big day. Today we record the winners' single.' At the news, we excitedly whisper to one another. 'That's right. The song we lay down today will be the debut for DOLLHOU5E.'

We are all quite giddy about this. Even with everything I know, I am . . . curious to see what they've come up with. Will it be sweet and sugary, or dark and gothic, something urban, or something for the clubs?

'Today all seven of you will do a vocal take, but only the winners' voices will be used in the final mix.'

'Brutal,' Briar comments.

'Right?' Dre agrees. 'Okay, anyone interested to hear your debut single?'

We gather around the mixing desk to listen to a demo sung by AI voices. It's called 'Come Get Your Man'. It starts with throbbing, electric waves before crashing into a rappy first verse:

> *He tries not to stare, caught in a snare*
> *Really not fair, never learned to share.*
> *I'm flexy, I'm sexy*
> *Don't have to try all dressy.*

> *Sorry 'bout me, it's easy to see*
> *I'm about to steal your man*
> *It's never in my plan.*

And into a bridge and chorus.

> *You can call me a bitch*
> *You can call me a ho*
> *But I hit it, I quit it*
> *Get ready and go!*
> *Come get your man; I'm done*
> *Come get your man; so fun*
> *I like it, I try it*
> *Don't buy it, don't cry, bitch*
> *Come get your man*
> *Come get your man, done*
> *Come get your man*
> *Come get your man, son.*

'Okay! What do you think?' Dre beams.

There's a tell-tale moment of silence. 'It's a bop,' Briar says uncertainly at last. 'It goes hard.'

'You can totally dance to it,' Suki adds. I murmur agreement. It's a standard, attitude-heavy Girl Crush concept, and I can picture the video in my mind. But . . .

'What's wrong?' Dre says. 'I sense you're not loving it?' For some reason everyone looks to me. 'Taryn?'

'What?' I squeak.

'Your silence is deafening.'

'Okay.' I inhale. 'Did a man write the lyrics?'

'Yeah, one of our top Elysium writers in Stockholm.'

'I . . . I just think if we start out with a song about how we want to steal everyone's boyfriends . . . girls will *hate* us. That's . . . not ideal.'

'We'll get the slut-shaming,' Leela adds. 'And it reinforces the stereotype that transgender girls are predators.'

'Shit, I didn't think of that,' Dre mutters under his breath.

'Can we write some new lyrics?' I say.

Dre rubs his jaw. 'I don't know, ladies. We have one day to do this . . .'

'Just give us ten minutes,' I say, turning to Leela. 'We did this back at the house in London, didn't we?'

'Yeah. We can do it again.' Leela sounds more confident than I do.

Dre shakes his head. 'Fine. You have the time it takes me to get an iced matcha latte.'

Kneeling around the coffee table, talking over each other at a thousand words per minute, the seven of us quickly thrash out new lyrics with a different angle. None of us want this to be a song about how much we want a boyfriend. Like, what year is this?

'When I go out I just want to dance,' Domino says. 'I don't want hands all over my ass.'

'Right?' Suki agrees. 'And it's always some bogan old enough to be your dad.'

I feign gagging. 'So we write a song about how men are human garbage. I can get on board with that.'

It's very much a team effort, all of us throwing lines

around. 'Throw your hands in the air like you just don't care,' Briar offers. 'It's a classic.'

This is the most we've laughed in weeks. I look to Madison, who's still grey at the gills. 'You okay?' I ask.

She takes a Sharpie and pops the lid off with her teeth. 'Let's do this.'

Minnie asks if she can include a couple of lines of Korean, which we all think is a fantastic idea. Domino offers to add some Portuguese too.

> Here with my girls, no care in the world
> All about dance, keep romance.
> I'm gatinha, I'm segsihan,
> Don't have to try, not stressing man.
> But these boys in the club, are starting to rub
> Get your hand off my back
> Before we attack.
> You can call me a bitch
> You can call me a tease
> Your ego's in need
> I'm telling you please
> Come get your man; I'm done
> Come get your man; he's dumb
> Annoying and cloying
> So over this boy thing
> Come get your man
> Come get your man, son
> Come get your man
> Come get your man, shunned.

The soundproofed door opens with a muffled suck, and Dre finds us cackling around the table like witches around a cauldron. 'How's it going? Having fun?'

'We make it better,' Leela says in classic Leela style. She holds up a piece of paper with our scrawl all over it.

Dre looks doubtful but gestures towards the recording booth. 'We'll see. Who's up first?'

I am shoved into the booth first and do three or four takes of the whole track, increasing in confidence each time. I've never done this before, and I'm very much not a rapper, but I like being alone with just my voice and the microphone. Dre plays back my vocals into the headphones and I get a slightly chilling insight into what I sound like to other people. *No one likes hearing their own voice. Ever.*

All warmed up, I'm doing some ad libs over the end of the song when I see Clancy and Dr Anders enter on the other side of the studio window, alongside some grey men in grey suits who I don't recognize. Something about them says *lawyer*.

'Dre?' I speak into the mic. 'What's going on?'

No one answers.

'Dre?'

I watch as Domino is escorted from the studio.

EXCLUSIVE PICS: DOLLHOU5E DIVA BEDS DANCER

'Disco Doll' Domino caught canoodling with *Starmaker* hottie.

Exclusive by TV Editor Dean Sutton

Hot favourite in this year's *Starmaker* talent search, Domino Augusta (20) put on a sexy display with professional dancer Joaquin Cruz (23).

The pair were snapped in a steamy clinch at an afterparty last Saturday at the trendy Japanista nightclub, mere minutes after the elimination of contestant Shayna Silver. Our sources told us, 'They are clearly besotted; they couldn't keep their hands off each other.' The spicy Brazilian contestant and her Mexican partner were seen leaving the Adidas party together and, according to a source close to the singer, Augusta spent the night with Cruz outside of the *Starmaker* Dreamhouse compound in Media City.

Elysium Entertainment, who sign the winning *Starmaker* acts, has strict rules about idols dating. Idols must not form romantic relationships although many do unofficially. We reached out to Elysium for comment but were told they do not comment on contestants' personal lives.

EXCLUSIVE: 'DOMINO HAS BROKEN MY HEART'

DOLLHOU5E diva already had secret boyfriend.

By TV Editor Dean Sutton

Heartbroken semi-pro footballer Miguel Santos (21) has broken his silence after seeing our scandalous pictures of starlet Domino Augusta in a steamy embrace with *Starmaker* professional dancer Joaquin Cruz.

In an exclusive interview, handsome Santos told me how he and Augusta met in school and have been inseparable ever since. 'Domino's dream is to win *Starmaker*. We knew we had to keep our love secret. I cannot believe she would betray me like this.'

Sultry Disco Doll Augusta had been the hot favourite on the latest season of the global talent search, but this week's revelations may have damaged her chances according to bookmakers. 'Idols are expected to behave in a morally upstanding fashion,' said one. 'Fans will not stand for it.'

Full story on page 2, 3 and 4.

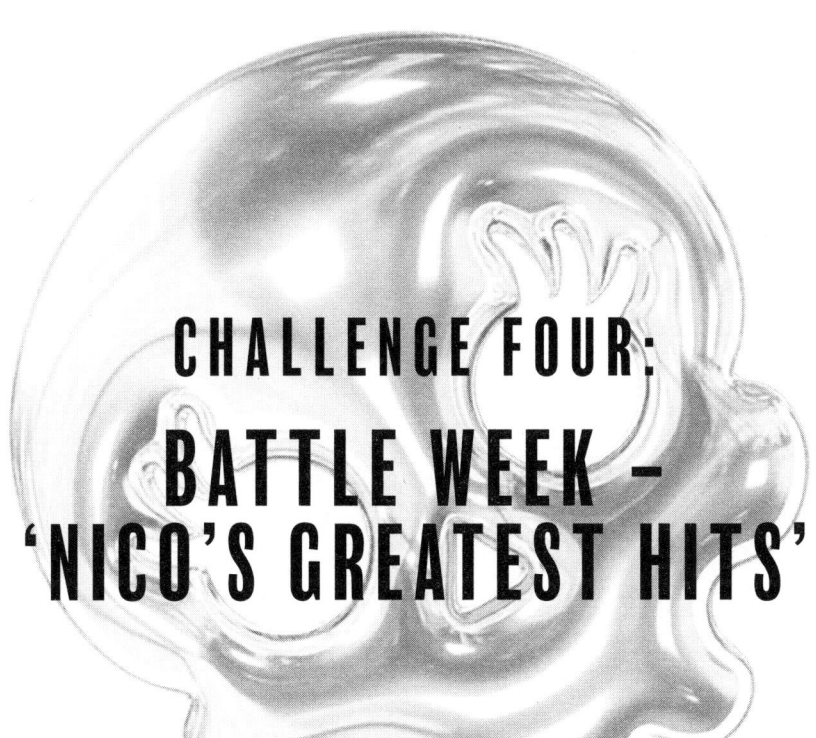

CHALLENGE FOUR:
BATTLE WEEK –
'NICO'S GREATEST HITS'

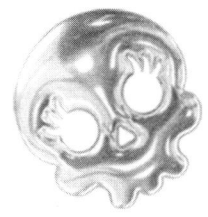

CHAPTER 36

'It's not true,' Domino tells us that night over a meagre dinner of brown rice and vegetables back at the house. 'Miguel and I broke up like two years ago. We dated for five minutes.'

To read the story in *The Globe* you'd think they'd been married for decades.

'This is so unfair,' Suki moans. 'Someone must have told the press about you leaving the party with Cruz. What kind of dag sells stories like this?'

'It could have been anyone at the party,' Leela says.

Someone must have sold the pictures from the party at Japanista. I frown as I add chilli flakes to the flavourless dinner. It's a miracle they didn't get pictures of me leaving with Cade. 'But how did they know she stayed out all night?' I ask.

Domino eyes me warily.

Of course; I saw her sneaking in the next morning. 'Dom, I swear on my brother's life I didn't tell anyone, and you know what that means to me.'

'I believe you,' she admits. 'I am an idiot. I should never have drunk alcohol at the party.'

'Hey,' Madison says. Now Monday, she looks more like herself. She hasn't mentioned quitting again as far as I know. 'Don't be so hard on yourself. It was a party. And Joaquin is cute.'

'I really like him,' confesses Domino. 'And he likes me too, I know it. It's a powerful thing.'

I can't help but think of Cade, our kiss. I know our . . . *thing* is the worst possible idea, a stupid fantasy, and yet – at the same time – I love the feeling of it in my veins. When his face drifts into my thoughts, which it does a lot, it feels like golden syrup has replaced all my blood. I want more. It isn't rational or smart. I guess that's why we need a word for love; it's not the same as logic. Not that I'm in love with him. It was one kiss. God, I need to keep a lid on it. Watching the fallout from Domino's night out has only cemented how serious it would be if it leaked.

Clancy wants Domino to issue a grovelling apology on the *Starmaker* G-Net channels. There are calls for her to quit and forfeit her place. Un-idol-like behaviour apparently. It leaves an acid taste on my tongue; the notion that young people – just because we're performers – can't have boyfriends or girlfriends.

It reminds me of a history report I once did about the Vestal Virgins of Ancient Rome. The handmaids of the goddess Vesta, the Vestals, were treated like princesses unless they 'lost their purity' in which case they were buried alive. I wonder how much has really changed.

Nico-themed Battle Week.

The rules are simple, Mojo explains as we're lined up on

stage. It's Saturday night and we're live to the world. I'm in a gunmetal-grey boiler suit, cinched at the waist with a Chanel belt. Lars explained that I have to wear something children can't afford, or they won't look up to me.

'Our wheel of fortune picks who sings against who *and* which classic Nico hit you'll be performing. After the performance, the judges decide who progresses to the next stage and who is the overall winner. That lucky trainee will have immunity from elimination this week. Then it's over to you, our viewers at home, to vote as normal.'

The wheel spins.

Round One is Suki versus Minnie. The wheel selects one of Nico's early, poppier numbers and it fits Suki to a tee. It's close, but Suki proceeds to Round Two.

Suki versus Domino. We watch from stools at the edge of the stage. We all know Domino *needs* the immunity. This week, she's been in the papers every day. The initial salacious stories gave way to online discourse about idol culture, slut-shaming and double standards. A female columnist at the *Telegraph* in England doesn't want 'improper' Domino being a role model to her daughters. Suffocating.

They draw a track from Nico's club years. Vocally, neither is outstanding, but Domino dances rings around Suki. The judges save her. I think Suki will be safe. Younger fans *love* her.

Round Three: Domino versus Leela. Leela is stronger vocally, but is static on stage. Domino is more alive than I've ever seen her, fighting for her life. She drops into the splits and the audience loses its mind. Nico chooses to save Leela, but Cade and Dre save Domino, and she progresses.

Round Four: Domino versus Briar. The closest battle yet. I can't call it. The judges save Domino. Briar's face is grim as she returns to her stool.

'It's fine,' I mouth her way.

'Is it?' she replies.

Briar, softly spoken and quiet, doesn't seem to be connecting with voters. Her fans on G-Net speculate it's because she's the only dark-skinned Black girl. I wish that weren't true but . . .

The wheel spins. 'Domino will now face . . . Taryn from London.'

It takes me a second to realize that's me. I join her centre stage. After three performances, Domino's top lip gleams with beads of sweat. I give her a stoic nod. We both rank highly – at least we did last week. I *think* I can get through without immunity; I don't know if Dom can. Her week has only got worse. Yesterday *The Globe* dug up some girl accusing Domino of being a high-school bully. The twist: Domino never even attended the high-school in question, yet it was reported as fact. By the time the online article was retracted, the damage was done.

The thought enters my head. Do I *let her win*?

A very, very big risk.

The wheel spins and lands on 'Firefly Nights', one of Nico's sweeping ballads from some movie soundtrack. Damn; if it had been a dance track, no one would have expected me to win.

Grinding my teeth, I go to my mark. I fleetingly catch Cade's eye on the judging panel. I see him give me an almost imperceptible shake of the head; he knows exactly what I'm thinking.

And then I remember Jenson. He needs me to win in order to survive. Sorry, Domino. My loyalty must remain with him.

Mojo introduces us and the backing track begins. A crescendo of violins and we begin, taking alternating sections. My voice crackles and I pull myself together.

> *The clock strikes thirteen*
> *You hold me close*
> *Awake in a dream*
> *Swimming in moonlight*
> *Pull me under*
> *Into firefly nights.*

I look to Cade as Domino sings her part. He doesn't take his eyes off me. I think of our night at his beach bar. My turn again and this time, I sing for *him*. Just for him. I want us to have more of those firefly nights.

The song concludes and Mojo stands between Domino and me for the result. He throws to Nico first.

'That was just beautiful,' she says. 'Both of you did the song justice but, for me, Taryn, you brought something so truthful to that performance. I vote for you.'

Dre goes next. 'Taryn, we know that vocally you're not leaving any crumbs, but I think that was genuinely Domino's best vocal in this entire competition. I choose Domino.'

Domino closes her eyes and exhales deeply. That means the deciding vote is down to Cade.

'Taryn, that was shaky at the start,' Cade tells me. He's mad at me. He thinks I tried to rig it. 'Domino, I agree with Dre that that was your best vocal technically. But I have to go with the singer who put real emotion into it. So I choose to save Taryn.'

It's two against one. I'm through and Domino is out. I look to her, genuinely penitent. Domino's eyes glaze over. We both know what this means. She's in serious danger.

The final round is myself and Madison. During the ad break she warms up, stretching vigorously. God knows what she has planned. We have to perform 'Crazy Loca', Nico's biggest ever hit. 'Hey,' she says, as we head to our positions. 'Don't you dare go easy on me like you did with Domino. And don't think I owe you a thing for last Saturday.'

'Good to see you back,' I tell her.

We take our places. Me and Mol used to sing and dance to this song all the time. I can give Madi a run for her money. Boom! The music begins.

Before we met I was a normal girl
Like Queen B I run the world (girls!)
Never thought that love would get to me
Never thought that I'd fall so easily
But now I'm crazy, crazy, loca, loca
Silly, foolish, stupid, joker
Crazy, crazy, loca, loca
Todas nos volvemos un poco locas

I try to remember the old routine as best I can, ignoring the fact that Madison is holding her left leg in the splits over her head. Fingers crossed she's wearing her safety knickers. All I can do is try not to pant as I sing and hope my vocal gets me through. At the end, I copy Nico's ad libs. I know them well. I let rip, literally. The high note feels like it's tearing at my throat.

In the final chorus, Madison struts towards me with laser focus, puts her hands on my hips and pulls me close. Our bodies press together and I understand; she wants to dance with me. Yes, it's a contest, but Madison does know how to put on a show. We fall into rhythm together, gyrating our hips in sync. Something for the dads at home. Even in the moment, I know this is going to go viral all over G-Net. This provocation lasts only a few counts before we stomp to opposing corners for the big finish.

The song ends, and the studio audience jump to their feet. The judges give us a standing ovation. I look to Madison and we share a smile, begrudgingly. We went ten toes down.

'Girls!' Nico begins. '*That* was the performance of the season. Hands down.' The audience continues to scream. 'But I'm afraid only one of you can win immunity. I've conferred with my fellow judges, and the girl who is safe from the Elimination Chamber is . . .'

CHAPTER 37

They saved Madison, but I don't care. As soon as they yell cut, I run to Cade at the judging panel. 'Can we talk?' I say urgently.

Nico looks at me with distaste, like how dare I come so close. 'Taryn, you know judges can't talk to you mid show. Go back to your pen.'

He gives her serious side-eye. 'It's fine. Let's find somewhere quiet.'

He steers me into the dark backstage, amidst the cables, crates and rigging. 'What are you doing?' he hisses, 'We're still on camera.'

'We have to stop this. They're going to kill Domino for some drunken snog.'

'Drunken what?'

'A *kiss*,' I whisper. 'And if that makes her impure, then I guess we're impure too.'

'I don't know what you want me to do,' Cade says.

'Stop it,' I plead. 'You want to bring this all down – well, do it now. Tell the producers you've got footage of them abusing us and you'll go to the press. They've got Suki on a liquid-only diet right now. She almost fainted after her number. End it tonight.'

Runner Jacey approaches, their mullet tennis-ball-yellow this week. 'Guys, can I get you to clear this area? There's a suite over here that's free, I think – follow me.'

Cade nods, and we follow them into a darkened stock cupboard filled with a jungle of spare leads and cables. Jacey shuts the door behind them and turns to us.

'That was way too close, Cade,' they snap. 'Your mic packs were still on!'

Cade swears, pulling his mic pack off his belt. I look between them. 'What's going on?' I ask.

'Can we tell her?' Cade says, and Jacey nods. 'Jacey is the undercover reporter from the *Bastion*.'

They turn to me. 'My real name is Nomi Johal. Nice to meet you.'

'Oh my god,' I breathe. 'All this time?'

They nod. 'This is my second season on the show. I've been playing a long game.'

'Then you've let two girls die already this year.' It erupts with such venom, I surprise myself.

Nomi looks wounded. 'I had no choice. Taryn, our story has to be watertight. The *Bastion* literally cannot survive legal action from Network G or Elysium. They will crush us. I need hard evidence.'

'I've been sending you evidence!'

They nod sympathetically. 'Nothing *criminal*. Yes, the diets and the schedule are *bad* but come on, the kid who made your phone in some sweatshop has it much worse and we don't bat an eyelid.' They lower their voice. 'Look, we're trying to track down Ashanti in Dubai. If we can prove she's still alive, we can technically get them for fraud, which *is* illegal. It would mean a court case. They couldn't bury the story.'

'Remember Al Capone?' Cade says. 'They got him for *tax evasion*. We need a smoking gun.'

I swallow. 'But what about Domino?'

Cade won't meet my eyes. Nomi can only shrug. 'You all signed a contract, willingly. Domino too.'

I can't argue with that. I sold my soul.

And so did Domino.

Domino is the first of us to walk to the glass pyramid with her head held high. She waives the sedative from Dr Anders. Detached, impassive, she completes the procession past us into the Elimination Chamber. We duly sing the farewell song.

'Do you have anything you want to say, Domino?' Nico asks.

Domino lifts her chin proudly. 'I love my country, I love my mama and my avó in heaven, and my brothers. Joaquin Cruz, I love you. I do truly. I fell in love with you. Finally, Miguel Santos, you are a lying piece of shit and I hope you choke on a d—'

The candy cloud swirls up around her knees, engulfing her. She presses her hands to the glass and goes limp. I cover my mouth with my hand to stifle a pained wail.

'Don't worry,' Clancy says from the perimeter. 'We'll cut the last part.'

CHAPTER 38

That night, Cade asks if I'll be doing laundry.

I wait in the darkened basement until almost two a.m. when he finally taps on the window. 'I think they know,' he says as he slides feet first through the narrow gap. 'Nico asked if there was something between us.'

I am desperate, physically burning, to ask the same question. *Is* there something between us? There isn't time for that sort of thinking. 'What did you tell her?' I ask instead.

'Nothing obviously. But Nico's publicist keeps asking if I'd be up for being *sighted* with her at a few events.'

'With Nico? What for?'

He looks puzzled. 'To get talked about? You can get a cut on the paparazzi shots.'

'Well that's bleak,' I say.

'If she thinks you and I are . . . dating or whatever, that's not the end of the world, but if she figures out what we're *really* doing . . .' he lets it hang.

So us 'dating' is now just a cover story? That sort of stings.

'We . . . can stop meeting,' I say, although I don't want that for a second.

He shakes his head. 'Look, we should just go.'

It's late, but I don't *think* I'm hallucinating. 'What?'

'Taryn, I don't know that you realize how dangerous this is. The Five Families . . .'

'Cade, stop! That's just a—'

'It's not a conspiracy theory!' Cade pinches the bridge of his nose. 'Kerwin Groenveld owns both the network and the label. The only things he cares about are money and power. They're the same thing I guess.'

Okay, the world is wretched, what else is new? 'What does that have to do with us?'

'The Five Families decide the message but *we* are the messengers. We tell people what to wear, what to buy, what to *think*.'

I remember, during the last Blue States election, N-TRU5T songs played at the president's rallies. Elysium co-signed his party, helped to seal his victory with younger voters. I never thought of it like that.

'I'm no one's puppet,' I say, although I'm not sure I can pull off that sort of statement. It's the sort of thing brave girls say on TV.

'They decide the truth. We are nothing to them. There are a million pretty kids waiting to replace us. They'll squash you and me like bugs.'

He's right. I hate it but he's right. 'So . . .?'

'So we leave,' Cade insists.

'Where?'

'Nomi belongs to a group, Axiom. They have places . . . like communes for people who reject the system. There's a cooperative deep in the woods, totally off-grid. We're fighting back.'

My head is spinning and I feel a sort of motion sickness. This is too much, too fast. A secret resistance? A rebel alliance for Rebel Doll? We lost another girl just hours ago. I can't get the image of Domino's palm pressed against the glass out of my mind. 'Well . . . when?'

He looks confused. 'Now. If Nico has told Clancy her suspicions, I don't know if we're safe. They'd choose Nico over me. They'd ruin both of us.'

My mouth gapes uselessly. 'I . . . I can't just *go*.'

'Why not?'

Good question, but I have a good answer. 'Because they know where my dad and brother and sister live, Cade. If I vanish, what happens to them? If the producers kill people on primetime, I don't think they'll flinch at dumping my family in a river somewhere.' He doesn't reply. 'Well? And what about your mum? Is she safe?'

'You're right,' he concedes. 'Okay. New plan. Twenty-four hours to make sure they're safe.'

'I can't call them though – the phone in the Dreamhouse is recorded twenty-four/seven,' I say. 'And my family has nothing, Cade; how can they go into hiding if . . .'

'Leave it with me. I'll get Nomi to contact them. I can get them some money. Don't pack. I have cash; we can buy things on the road. We'll need to change your hair.'

'Fine by me.' The hair extensions are a nightmare.

To be rid of them will be a blessed relief.

He turns to leave, only then, as if he's forgotten something, he whirls around and kisses me in one fluid motion. The kiss almost knocks me off my feet but he cradles my head in his hand and pulls me closer. Lost in the kiss, all the noise in my head is silenced and, for a beautiful moment, everything is golden glitter. At last he pulls back a little.

'Is it insane?' he mutters, his lips still close to mine. 'Are we *eloping*?'

I smile. 'We're *escaping*. Big difference.'

'You're right. We're escaping *together*. You and me.' I didn't realize how much I wanted to hear that. 'Get some sleep. Tomorrow night. Midnight. We escape. Together.'

Cade and I, together. A notion so fantastical, I once more wonder if I'm in a dream. A dream where time moves faster, and this whole thing is playing out over a single night before I entered the Dreamhouse.

I help him out of the narrow window and ensure it's sealed. It's almost three a.m. and I need to sleep. But, as soon as I open the laundry room door, I hear footsteps scurrying away in the dark basement.

I dart after them, past the darkened gym area. 'Hey!' I snap. 'Who's there?'

Silence. Whoever it is has frozen. 'I'm not messing around.' I stomp upstairs towards the kitchen. 'Who is it?'

At the top of the stairs, in the shadows, three figures loom over me: Leela, Briar and Suki, caught red-handed.

'You wanna tell me why you're spying on me?'

Briar takes a step towards me, eyes steely in the gloom.

'That depends. You wanna tell *us* what's going on? Are you and Cade . . . an item?'

'No!' I protest.

'Taryn,' Leela states. 'We heard you kissing.'

I haven't caught them, they've caught me. Game over.

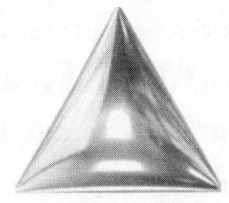

CHAPTER 39

I don't see what choice I have. We make mugs of hot chocolate with little mountains of whipped cream and marshmallows and head back to the laundry room. I don't trust anywhere else in this place. We sit in a little circle on the floor, like Girl Scouts at summer camp. Instead of a campfire, we have a mango-scented Yankee Candle.

'Lady, you were pashing Cade?' Suki asks, aghast.

'No!' It's some sort of reflex. 'Okay, yes. We made out two times. Once tonight, and once last Saturday.'

'You slut,' Suki says with a wink.

'You didn't tell us for a *whole week*?' Leela blinks. 'Unsisterly behaviour.'

'I'm sorry. But we're so close to the final. Can you imagine if it leaked? Look at what happened tonight.' I take a deep breath. I'm not stupid. A relationship with Cade is bad, but not as bad as what we're really working on. 'That's why he came here. We need to go. We're leaving.'

'What?' Briar explodes. 'The final is next Saturday! Taryn, you are definitely making the band.'

She's right. If my rankings stay the same, I am likely to survive the final elimination. But I also know Cade is right. The prize is a Trojan horse. 'And then what?'

'Then you've made it,' Leela says, bewildered. 'All your problems will be over.'

'No. That's when my problems begin.' It feels like a betrayal, but I have to tell them about Sonny Feldman. 'Sonny Feldman didn't quit the band. He died.'

I relay everything Cade told me. Suki goes quite pale, but none of them question my version of events. Sonny Feldman was pushed over the edge, joining a long list of icons who didn't live to see thirty.

'We've all seen this happen right? How many idols end up in hospital, or rehab or jail. Do they look happy?'

'They look rich,' Briar comments.

'We are different. It'd be different for us,' says Leela, although I can see from her creased brow that she's trying to convince herself.

'Are we? I'm not sure there are any winners here. We either die, or they work us to death.'

'What about the prizes? Hello, your brother?' Briar is only voicing my own contradictory thoughts.

I shrug. 'I know. But even if I win, they still have all the power. Elysium gets to decide if my brother lives or dies. The whole system sucks.'

'But this is the only system we have.' Leela, matter-of-fact as ever.

'Unless we change it.'

Leela regards me with something like pity. I am aware

how utterly infantile I sound. Who do I think I am? Sure, a seventeen-year-old from a boggy trailer park is going to smash the world apart and rebuild it as a fairer place for us all to live. A singer with clown hair is going to save the planet from billionaires who own the very air we breathe. Sounds simple, sign me up.

'I'm getting out of here. Tomorrow. Come with us if you want.' The girls say nothing. 'Think about it, okay? Screw *Starmaker*. How bad would it look for them if half their finalists vanished into thin air?'

They remain so quiet I can hear the candle sputter. I get it. We're so close. The prizes are in touching-distance, but, like the candle, it's not a real mango, it just smells like one.

I choose my words carefully. I can't outright tell them about this Axiom plot. 'This will keep on going until the idols stop,' I say slowly. 'Elysium need us. They rely on the fact that for every idol, there are a thousand more who'd kill for the chance. But the fans don't stan Chairman Slade or idiots like Clancy. They stan *us*. We have a voice; we just have to use it.'

'Then let Cade deal with it,' urges Briar, squeezing my hand. 'It doesn't have to be you. I don't want you to go. We're sisters now. You need to stay.'

The problem is, she might be right. A part of me knows that I can do more from inside DOLLHOU5E than I can if I flee.

Outside the window, the sky is pastel violet. Dawn is breaking on what could be my final day in the Dreamhouse.

I sleep until almost ten. It's Sunday. Hopefully this *should* mean no production people in the house today. In my pyjamas,

I make an iced coffee and head out into the garden. It's *hot* today. Already the hills ripple with heat haze. A neon green lizard whips under a rock as I approach.

The grounds are walled and lined with cypress trees, but there's a rusted iron gate out into the canyons. I guess that's how Cade is getting in and out of the gardens after dark. I push through the exit and into the arid hillside beyond. There's a hiking path further up into the shrub. You can see the lake from up there; Briar often runs up the trail.

Far below us, the pools belonging to neighbouring mansions twinkle, but it's strangely quiet aside from crickets chirruping.

A blacked-out solar SUV winds its way through the hillside towards the mansion. Cade? I can't remember exactly what his car looked like. The vehicle stops short of the front drive or delivery entrance at the basement level. The passenger door opens and a burly, suited man slithers out. Men In Black.

'Miss Beck,' he calls up the path. 'We were looking for you.'

'Why?' I stay right where I am by the back gate.

'Mr Kekoa sent us to collect you.'

What? This goes against everything we talked about last night. But I guess a lot can happen in ten hours. My heart pounds in my throat. If something has gone wrong . . . My first thoughts go to my family. I pray they've had enough time to get to safety. The air feels thin as I drift down the worn stone stairs towards the roadside.

'Is everything okay?' I squint through the darkened windows. 'Is he in there?'

'Ma'am, just get in the car. He'll explain everything.'

'I'm in my pyjamas?'

I see my reflection in the security guard's mirror shades; I look thin and exhausted, my eyes hollow and sunken. I scowl at the agent. 'I'm not going anywhere until I know Cade is okay—'

No sooner have the words left my mouth than his python arms are around me. My feet leave the floor as he lifts me with seemingly zero effort. 'Get off me!' I squeal, but I'm already being shoved into the back seat. I faceplant onto the creamy leather interior as the door slams shut behind me.

I curl my hands into fists ready to lash out.

'Was that necessary?' a tetchy, familiar voice says. 'I only want to talk to her.' I clear a nest of hair aside to look up at Nico, wearing a velour Juicy Couture sweatsuit and bug-eye sunglasses. 'Just drive goddammit,' she tells the driver and we pull away.

'What are you doing?' I rasp.

She blows a noxious cloud of raspberry vape into my face. 'Sweetheart, relax. We're just taking a Sunday drive in the hills. If anyone asks, we're heading to church.'

'Are you going to kill me?'

She peels off the Chanel shades to reveal a look of pure disdain. 'Oh please. I'm not going to the chair over some Temu Ariana. Get comfy. There's sparkling water in the cooler.'

'I'm good.' This would be scary if it wasn't so surreal. 'Look, what is this about?'

'What is it you Brits say? Are you *shagging* Cade?' she asks in a Dick Van Dyke accent.

'What? No way!'

'Not what my spies say.'

'Your *spies* are wrong.'

'Interesting. Because I've heard you and he are planning some great gesture against Elysium Entertainment?' So Cade was right; Nico was onto us. I say nothing, and she continues. 'I told them hiring Cade as a judge was a huge mistake so soon after Sonny . . . you know.' She draws an acrylic thumbnail across her throat. 'They thought it was a good way of keeping him in the family. I told them he was up to something. Are you the leak? Sending tidbits to that loathsome little maggot at *The Globe*?'

'No. You've got this all wrong, Nico.'

She looks at me with pure revulsion. 'Don't call me *Nico* as if you know me. You don't know me.' I realize that her hair is her real hair. I think every other time I've seen her, she's worn a wig. Her real hair is collar-length, unremarkable. She's clean-faced, although somehow even more beautiful. Like this, she looks ten years younger and, also, like a human.

'I'm sorry,' I say.

'I need to be very clear about something,' she says. 'The grand final will go ahead this Saturday and you runts will turn up and sing and dance and smile.'

'Why do you care?'

'Because after Saturday, I'm officially done.'

'What do you mean?'

She regards me as though I'm the village idiot. 'Ten years, sweetheart. I won *Starmaker* ten years ago, and what does the winner sign?'

'A ten-year contract with Elysium.'

'Exactly. This mentor crap is my final obligation and then I'm finally free of that bastard Slade for the rest of my life.'

'You've actually met Chairman Slade?'

She rolls her eyes. 'Sweetie, look at it this way: I didn't win *Starmaker* based on my stellar singing range.' I'm too shocked to reply. I voted for her every week. 'But that sleazeball and I have been stuck with each other ever since . . . until now. You better believe this series will go off without a hitch. Understood?'

'Yes.'

'I'm going to pay Cade a little visit too. He can figure out his PTSD on his own time. This time next week, I am a free woman.'

I somehow dare to ask. 'Is it that bad?'

'What?'

'Being Nico?'

She laughs. 'Honey, I haven't had a day off in ten years. Ten years of being told when to eat, sleep, walk. I'm a living corpse.' She takes a deep drag on her vape. 'I got pregnant, you know.'

'What?'

'Not long after I won. I was dating an actor . . .'

'Felix Umberto.' I know every beat of Nico's life.

'Yeah. Slade made me get rid of it. A baby out of wedlock! God, that wouldn't fit with my girl-next-door image. Felix never forgave me. He wouldn't speak to me after that.'

'That's awful. I'm so—'

'Oh shut up!' She grimaces. 'I don't need Raggedy Ann feeling bad for me, thank you very much. I have penthouses in Media City, Mexico City and a guaranteed suite in the first moon dome. After next week, I can do anything I want. I have every record label on earth bidding for me. They want me to be Jean Grey in the new *X-Men* movie. I'll have everything I ever wanted.'

'Except that baby,' I say, feeling bolder.

Her whole face darkens. 'I'll buy a new baby,' she snarls. 'I'll buy five and dress them up and give them cute nicknames. Driver! Stop the car.' The car jerks to a halt. Nico reaches over me and throws the door open wide. 'Have fun walking back to the compound, sweetheart.'

I climb out of the car. We're deep into the canyons and I have bare feet. Dry clay bakes under the sun. I look up at the Dreamhouse, high on the hill. It's a long walk back.

The window hisses down and Nico peers out. 'And remember what I said. If you mess up the finale, it's not just Slade who knows where your family live.' The window slides back up as she smiles an electric smile. 'Kisses, doll.'

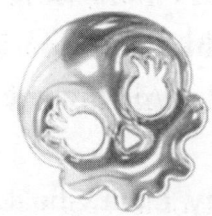

CHAPTER 40

By the time I get back, I'm parched, and sunburned, and my feet are caked in dirt. 'What happened to you?' Madison regards me over a foul-looking green juice in the kitchen.

I can't tell her the truth. I don't trust her not to use it against me somehow. 'I went on a hike. I got lost.'

'Sure. Who doesn't love a barefoot hike?' Thankfully, she doesn't press further.

I take a hot shower. My skin feels too taut. Hair dye turns the water ketchuppy as it gurgles down the drain. I think about faith. Not Madison's brand of faith, but my trust in Cade. I guess prayer is sending hope out into the world. I really *hope* that somehow Nomi has got a message to my dad.

I shut off the water and rub a porthole in the steamy bathroom mirror. I rummage in the dresser drawer until I find some nail scissors. They'll do the trick. Over the sink I begin to snip and prise at the extension bonds. It takes an age, but I finally pull them all out and dump the lot in the bin. My natural hair is still fire-engine-red but I scrape it all back into a discreet knot.

I dress in black jeans and a black hoodie. I pack some essentials into my rucksack and ensure my Punkcat plushie is attached. If something happens to us, I want to know Nomi is still getting their evidence. Now all I can do is wait for nightfall.

We eat chicken and noodle broth for supper and watch old movies in the den. It's weird seeing the world pre-war, pre-flood, and I'm jealous of how easy they had it. With only six girls remaining – and Domino gone – the house is that much quieter. Briar goes to bed first, closely followed by Leela and Madison.

Suki lays with her head in my lap, watching the movie and nodding off, her breathing shifting into slumber. 'Suk, you're falling asleep,' I say softly.

'No, I'm not,' she argues, half-asleep.

From the other side of the sofa pit, Minnie smiles. I always feel guilty for not being able to include her more – I don't speak a word of Korean. 'You are the leader,' Minnie says.

'What? No, that's Madison.'

'Madison is the *centre*, but you're the leader. Everyone . . . listen to you.'

I don't think I truly allowed myself to believe I'd get to the end alive. It's as if Min-jee can hear my thoughts. 'This week I think me or Leela will be eliminated. People love Suki.'

She is almost saying the unspoken part aloud. There is only one Black girl left in the contest, but two Asian girls. 'Minnie, you're incredible.'

'I think people do not like me.'

'They do! You got this far. You are a finalist.' I can't pretend to understand what life has been like since the war for people who look like Min-jee and Suki. I only know I've heard the most despicable racism, so I imagine they have too.

'Because I am good,' Minnie says with a smile. She isn't bragging. 'I started training when I was six.'

'Six?'

'I train at YG, and SM, and Hybe.' I don't know what that means but make an effort to look awed. 'But being good isn't enough. You guys are so wild and funny and I am . . . boring.'

'No! Min-jee, you are just the sweetest person in the world. And no one tosses their hair better than you. Not even Madi.' I mime tossing my hair and she giggles. 'You're the hair queen.'

'Hairography,' she says, mimicking Cade in our dance sessions.

I can't imagine what this would have been like if I couldn't speak English. 'Are you happy here?' I ask her. 'Have you been lonely?'

She thinks, but shakes her head. 'I was trained for this.'

'But are you happy?' I mime smiling.

'Happiness does not . . . happy does not mean anything.'

'Well, I think it does. It's all that matters.'

'I will only be happy when I am in the band.' She says the words, but her eyes hold a huge question mark. Her whole life has been building to something hollow.

'You'll make the band,' I say confidently. 'You *will*.' And it's true. Because in a couple of hours, I'll be gone. Only five girls will remain, and DOLLHOU5E will be decided by default.

* * *

For a horrible twelve minutes, I think that he isn't coming. I sit in the laundry room until a little after midnight, becoming increasingly twitchy until there's a tap on the glass. I open the window and he pokes his head inside for a fleeting kiss.

'I thought something had gone wrong,' I say.

'I waited until the lights went out. Come on, my car is down the mountain. I couldn't get any closer. The nightshift is patrolling. We have a bit of a hike if you're up for it.'

Sure,' I reply, and then pause. 'Are we really doing this?' I ask. It all suddenly feels very real. I'm driving into the unknown with one fifth of N-TRU5T.

He smiles his trademark crooked smile. 'We really are. If you want to.'

'Are my family safe?'

'Yeah, Nomi sent word to them.'

'Then I'm all in.'

He offers me his hand and I seize it. He pulls me up through the narrow window, and I slither onto the grassy verge outside the house. I stand and dust my trousers off.

We start towards the pool, until a door slams somewhere inside. Instinctively we both freeze and listen. The house settles. The hills sing with crickets and cicadas. The sprinklers hiss. 'What was that?' he breathes.

'I don't know,' I whisper, straining against the silence. 'One of the girls using the bathroom?'

Everything seems quiet once more and we set off over the lawn hand-in-hand. For a single second, it all seems so easy.

Just then a baritone male voice shakes the walls, distorted

by a loudspeaker. 'Mr Kekoa, we know you're in the building. Surrender now.'

And then they charge; heavy, boot clad feet thunder across the ground floor. From the sound of it, many pairs. They know. I don't know how they know, but they know.

'Quick!'

Inside, the lights ping on and I make out distant, confused voices as the trainees emerge from their bedrooms. Cade grasps my wrist and drags me past the pool towards the rear gate. We almost collide with a skinny weasel of a Securiforce guard exiting the kitchen door. He looks as shocked as we are. 'Stay where you are!' He raises a taser.

Cade drops my arm and grabs the guard by his jacket before he can fire. With a single movement, he tosses the lanky guard into the pool.

'Go!' I cry. The guard is already swimming towards the edge. We sprint around the perimeter of the pool, only for another guard – this one a muscular woman – to cut us off.

'Freeze right there,' she says, her taser steady. 'Here's what we're going to do, kids: we're going to put our arms up and very slowly walk back into the house. Try anything and you'll know what a thousand volts feels like.' I'm rooted to the tiles. 'MOVE!' she barks. 'I said—'

Suddenly, she topples forwards, folding to her knees. In the low light, I didn't even see Madison appear behind the guard, clay vase in hand. The guard, now in a heap at our feet, seems to be unconscious. I turn to Madi, barefoot in a satin nightie, aghast.

'Well, hit the road then,' she says.

We don't need to be told twice. As I pass her, she adds, 'Now we're even for Shay.'

'Thank you,' I say. There's no time for any sort of a goodbye song.

Past the gate, we're in the canyons. We race downhill, leaving the footpath to avoid any further guards. The rocky terrain is treacherous, shifting under my trainers. I slip onto my bottom and Cade drags me up.

The crickets and cicadas are joined by the whir of helicopter blades, growing louder and louder. 'Is that for us?' Blue-white searchlights sweep the gorge, with thinner torch beams criss-crossing from the Dreamhouse. 'How much further to your car?'

Cade's eyes are fixed on the chopper. 'All the way in the valley, at the gas station. We should split up; the chopper can't follow us both, can it?'

'No!'

'Taryn, we have to.'

'What if they already got to your car?'

He acknowledges the possibility. 'If they're at the gas station, head downtown on foot. Don't go to the bus station; they'll have that covered. There's an all-night diner on 4th Street. Go there.'

'I don't want to leave you,' I plead.

'I hate it too, but we've got to be smarter than them.' I reluctantly agree. Up the hill, I hear boots scuffing towards us. 'We gotta go. Stay low, keep your hood up.'

'Be careful,' I say, a hollow gesture.

He cups my cheeks in his hand and gives me a tender kiss. 'I can't wait to be free with you.'

The promise of a future spurs me on. I give him a final kiss and run. I half-fall, half-skid downhill. Dust coats my teeth. The gas station Cade mentioned is at the junction before the turning up to the house. The red-and-green Global Petroleum sign is visible from here, a beacon in the valley. The helicopter searchlight seems to be trained on the other side of the canyon.

There is no time to think about how absurd this is. I have committed to this course of action; no going back. I focus on this promised land Cade described, this commune. I brought this curse upon my family by entering the competition, and now I will free us from it. I focus on a future with Cade, a future free from the eyes of the world. Just him and me and us. There, we will sing together, whatever songs we like.

Automatic gunfire – *clack* – echoes around the hillside, exactly like it sounds in the movies, but louder. It's followed by silence as thick as cement. I freeze. They have guns as well as tasers. But they couldn't kill Cade Kekoa.

Could they?

I take a final look at the petrol station oasis on the horizon and make a split-second decision. I run back the way I came.

I have to make sure he's okay. I scramble uphill, almost on all fours, primitive like a hunted animal. My breathing becomes urgent, ragged. *Be wrong, be wrong, be wrong*, I repeat the words like a mantra in my mind.

The helicopter searchlight now seems fixed on one location, straight down like a UFO tractor beam. I breach the cusp of the crevasse and survey the basin. I squat as Securiforce swarm the terrain. I'm just in time to hear a voice yell, 'Suspect is down! Repeat, suspect is down.'

Both hands cover my mouth. The spotlight is trained on a broken human shape, splayed facedown over a boulder. The sandstone is slick with purple-red. He isn't moving.

'Confirm the kill,' a voice crackles over the radio as a quartet of armed guards zero in.

'Confirmed on male target.'

They shot Cade. They shot him *in the back* as he ran. They shot him dead.

'No.' I can't scream, but I can't hold back a whimper. It's a pitiful sound. I flop back onto my rear. I don't make an attempt to flee when they shine their torches in my eyes.

'We have visual on the girl. Over.'

'Miss Beck,' another voice barks. 'On your feet.'

If they want me, they can drag me. And they do, heaving me to my feet. 'Are you going to kill me too?'

For a second I imagine them putting a gun to my head. How quickly will it be over? Will it hurt?

'No,' the guard says. 'There's someone who wants to talk to you.'

N-TRU5T HIGHWAY HORROR – EX-BOYBAND STARS PERISH IN DEATH SMASH

Tributes pour in for Sonny Feldman and Cade Kekoa who died last night.

Exclusive by Showbiz Editor Dean Sutton

Fans are today mourning the sudden loss of N-TRU5T favourites Sonny Feldman and Cade Kekoa, who died last night in a high-speed road accident in the hills outside Media City, BSA.

TMZ reports a BMW SUV was sighted, being driven erratically, at around two a.m. local time. A toxicology report is expected to confirm that the driver – believed to be Kekoa – was intoxicated at the time of the deadly smash.

No other vehicle was involved in the collision. Feldman was twenty-three and originally from Toronto, Canada. Hawaii native Kekoa (21) was only fifteen when he won *Starmaker* and earned a place in the boyband N-TRU5T alongside Yun Ye Joon, Rico Lopez and Erik Rasmussen. Swede Rasmussen posted today that "I have lost brothers. I love you and know you rest with the angles" (sic).

This week's *Starmaker* finale will go ahead in tribute to Feldman and Kekoa, and a new limited-edition greatest hits album will be released exclusively from Elysium Entertainment.

TARYN DOLL IN DOUBT
'Mystery virus' threatens *Starmaker* favourite.
Exclusive by Showbiz Editor Dean Sutton

Brit singing sensation Taryn Beck (17) may not perform in the highly anticipated *Starmaker* finale this Saturday.

Sources say the vocal dynamo, and bookies' favourite, missed the first day of rehearsals in Media City. 'Taryn is really sick,' one insider revealed. 'She's resting and everyone is hoping she'll be well enough to perform.' Doctors are said to be attending to the trainee, formerly a flood migrant from the Scottish Borders.

Starmaker rules state that if a contestant is unable to perform in the live finale on health grounds, they automatically forfeit the competition and volunteer for Project Population. This scenario has never occurred in the thirteen-year history of the global #1 series. 'It would be a disaster for producers if the DOLLHOU5E line-up was decided by default,' our source told us.

Beck is up against Americans Madison Silver and Briar Franklin; Australian Suki Lee; Korean Minnie Park and transgender German Leela Weber.

Related: "Dead Giveaway" Sleuths spot five signs that *Starmaker* Leela is biological male.

CHAPTER 41

I've always been able to wake myself from bad dreams. If I dream of flood waters, or Mum in the hospital incubator, I can slam on the brakes and exit the nightmare.

Not now. I don't know what's dream and what's real. I dream that I reach Cade at the petrol station. We get into his car and drive and drive until the dawn peeks over Lake Michigan. Or did I find him in the all-night diner?

No. That did not happen.

I am in a bed. A big bed.

I am with Mum, resting my head on the edge of her starched hospital bed. The ventilator hisses as it breathes for her.

Back to the bed. The room is too warm. My thighs sweat. My body sticks to the laminate sheets. I toss and turn and kick at the duvet.

Jacey – sorry Nomi – tries to wake me, shaking my shoulders. 'Taryn? Taryn? Can you hear me?'

I do hear them, but seem unable to reply.

'Taryn? Where's the Punkcat?'

This might be a dream too. 'Bag . . .' I mutter. My lips feel fat and crusty. My tongue is a flap of suede. 'Bag.' I wave a heavy hand overhead.

The next time I manage to prise my eyes open, Nomi is nowhere to be seen. I'm not sure they were ever even here. I *think* it's daytime, although heavy velvet drapes are drawn over unfamiliar windows in an unfamiliar room. The air is stuffy, over-breathed.

It takes me a moment to realize that Clancy is seated in a voluptuous armchair, tapping away on a phone in each hand. I try to cry out, but all I manage is a muffled groan. She calmly looks up at me, her face lit by the screens. 'Oh you're awake,' she says, putting the phones aside. 'I was starting to wonder if we'd accidentally put you in a coma!'

'Where am I?' I mumble, mouth numb.

'Let me call a nurse. You should get some fresh air.'

Clancy leans over my wheelchair as she pushes me through a courtyard garden with an ornamental fountain. Pretty trestle archways are covered in plumes of wisteria. 'See that man over there? In the hoodie?' She gestures at a man in sunglasses huddled over a steaming mug of coffee. 'That's *Gray Hadley*.'

The movie star? He looks a far cry from Batman right now.

'Sex addict. Sad really. Drugs would be easier for his publicist to explain.'

Clancy explains that I am in Restful Acres, a very exclusive rehab facility in the redwood forests outside Media City. She fills me in as she wheels me through the verdant grounds.

'How long have I been here?'

'It's Tuesday,' she says tersely. '*If* you're going to perform in the finale, you need to be in rehearsals tomorrow. So we have some decisions to make.'

I don't know what drugs they've pumped me full of, but feeling is gradually returning to my body in the form of buzzy pins and needles. 'Why didn't you just shoot me too?'

'Keep your voice down please!' Cade is dead. It was not a dream. Clancy's voice is slathered with honey. 'Of course we don't . . . *shoot* trainees. Look, between you and me, you're a lock for the band. You're number one with girls aged sixteen to thirty. *We* want you in DOLLHOU5E, Taryn!'

'You shot Cade.' I will repeat it until she hears it.

'No. If you know what's good for you, he *died in a car crash* with Sonny.'

Two birds, one stone. How neat and tidy for them. I curse loudly, drawing attention from some other inmates. 'I'm not lying for you.'

Clancy throws her hands up, exasperated. Her stye is angrier than I've ever seen it. 'Oh come on! I'm trying to make your dreams come true here, sweetie, cut me some slack. Cade was no use to us after this season. Did you hear his solo album? Awful. I was like, *honey, cheer up, you're a millionaire and you sound like an angsty bedwetter.* Honestly, ungrateful. After everything we did for him.'

'You *killed him*.' I feel a tear roll down my cheek. I'm crying from frustration as much as sadness. So needless. I didn't know him long, but I think I saw inside Cade Kekoa. We were mirrors of each other: normal humans somehow caught in something inhuman. I saw a good, loving heart. He loved Sonny. Maybe he loved me. We'll never know.

Clancy parks the wheelchair and sits opposite me on a stone bench. She takes my prickly hands and looks me very intently in the eyes. 'Taryn, this is important. Did Cade say anything to you about working with an insider on the show? Was he leaking information to someone?'

Time for my finale performance. 'No. I don't know anything about that.'

'He didn't say anything? About secret footage? Or Sonny Feldman?'

'No . . .'

'Did he tell you who he was working with?'

'I don't know what you're talking about,' I say. 'We were just fooling around.'

'Then where were you going on Sunday night?'

'We were going on a date . . . and then all the guards arrived.' I look vacantly at her, all bimbo eyes, a besotted fangirl.

Clancy views me with great scepticism. 'Why did you cut off your hair?'

I haven't got a good excuse for that. I shrug. 'It was hurting my scalp.'

She's about to argue, I can tell, but then she gives up. 'Whatever. They don't pay me enough for this. Let's get you back to the Dreamhouse.'

I grip the padded arms of the wheelchair. 'No. I'm not going back. Are you kidding?'

She starts to push me towards the lodge complex but I'm now able to slam my feet down on the path to halt us. 'Are you kidding *me*?' Clancy hisses. 'If I don't get you into that finale, they'll shoot us both. Is that what you want? I'm so sick of you ungrateful little brats. You know, when I was your age, I would have killed for this opportunity.'

'You did kill Cade! Why would I do Elysium a favour? They're murderers.'

Clancy lets go of the wheelchair and sighs. 'See, I thought you might say that, so I arranged a little treat for you.' I'm about to ask what she means when she says, 'There he is now.'

I look upwards to the main lodge, to where a familiar figure emerges onto the rear terrace. I rise from the chair, heart in my throat. 'Jen!' I shriek, and I'm already running up the path to greet him. He bounds over, and somehow he's taller than me now. I guess while I've been rehearsing, he's been on a growth spurt. I throw my arms around him. 'Oh my god! What are you doing here?'

I'm holding him so tight; I have to release him so he can talk. 'They flew us over for the live final. It's meant to be a surprise. Surprise!'

'Oh.' *For the live final.* 'Okay . . .'

'They said that because you were ill, I could come see you to cheer you up?' Jenson says enthusiastically. 'How are you? What's wrong? They said a virus? And we got some weird emails from someone while we were on the plane—'

'Sshhh!' I silence him before he names Nomi. I look over my shoulder at Clancy, who is listening intently. 'I do not have a virus.'

He looks bewildered. 'Then why are you in here?'

I can't seem to form words. Instead, Clancy cuts in. 'Jenson!' She opens her arms for a hug. 'Great to meet you in real life! How are you feeling? You look bomb.'

'Yeah, thanks.' He looks to me. 'Elysium got me some new treatment from America. It's so good, Taryn; no side effects at all.'

And he *does* look well. He's always been a sickly, Tiny Tim type. Now he looks, dare I say it, robust, freckled, like he's been out in the sun. He's wearing cargo shorts and a t-shirt, showing off a healthy tan. In Scotland, that's an achievement. 'That's great,' I say. 'How are things going with Tobey?'

My brother blushes. 'Yeah, he's really good. We're really good.' He looks to the floor, coy. He shakes it off. 'But who cares about me? Are you excited for the finale? Are you going to be well enough? Everyone is saying you're ranking at number one or two!'

'They are?'

Jenson squeezes my wrists. 'Taryn! Didn't you see? The prime minister wished you luck from New Downing Street! She wore a red wig and everything.'

Cringe. 'Wow. Okay.'

'Please say you can sing this Saturday? Me and Mol can't wait. Even Dad is getting into it. You're *so* close . . . you can't drop out.'

Clancy intervenes once more. 'Kiddo, we need to let your sister rest.'

'Wait! Where's Dad?' I say as she tries to steer him away.

'He's at the hotel with Molly,' Jen says. 'Clancy said they couldn't come.'

'Jenson shouldn't be here at all,' Clancy says, and the double meaning is obvious. Without *Starmaker*, he *wouldn't* be here in more ways than one. 'Our secret, kiddo.' She offers him a wink.

But *our* secret is so much worse. I am speechless, truly. They killed Cade and now they dangle Jenson before me, a maggot on a hook.

'I'll do it,' I say although the words choke me. 'I'll sing.'

'Oh that's wonderful,' Clancy purrs. 'Chairman Slade will be thrilled.'

I send her an icy glare. 'On one condition . . .'

CHAPTER 42

By the time they drop me back at the Dreamhouse, night has fallen.

I head directly to the den, where I hear voices. On entering, chatter stops and the remaining trainees look at me in shock.

'Oh my god!' Suki says. 'We didn't know if you were coming back.'

'Where have you been?' Madison says. 'We've been totally in the dark.'

The soles on my Converse slap on marble as I march towards the conversation pit. 'Suki. Name some brands.' I don't want them to be able to use any of this footage and they can't air brand names that aren't sponsors.

'What?'

'Just do it.'

'Okay ... Vegemite ... Woolworths ... Pepsi ...'

'Taryn, what is going on?' Leela asks, but I breeze right past her.

Instead, I head directly for Briar. 'Why did you do it?'

'What?'

'You absolute bitch,' I snarl, before curling my fingers into a tight fist and striking her with a mighty backhand.

Someone screams my name, I'm not sure who. Briar falls backwards, and down into the conversation pit. Almost in slow-motion, she lands on the glass coffee table and it shatters into a million snowflake shards. It's ear-splitting. After a second, she looks up, dazed.

'Why did you do it?' I spit again. *That* was my condition for Clancy. I wanted to know who sold me and Cade out. It had to be Suki, Leela or Briar, and I got my answer.

Briar gets back to her feet and curses loudly. Her lip's split. Her expression hardens, a storm rolling in. In two big bounds, she steps onto the sofa and launches herself at me. I'm not expecting her to fight back and she knocks me off my feet. My back hits the marble hard, snatching my breath away. No time to be hurt.

I never saw the point in fighting clean, and I put those nail extensions to use, gouging at Briar's face. She squeals and clutches handfuls of my hair. She's on top of me, so I punch at her stomach as hard as I can. A flurry of hands tugs at us, trying to separate us.

'Catfight,' Madison says somewhere close by. 'About damn time.'

Leela and Minnie pull Briar off me, but I get a kick to her chest first. I scramble to my feet and, full of venom, grasp at her throat. *She* killed Cade. She didn't pull the trigger but she may as well have. 'Tell me why,' I shriek.

'Taryn, stop!' Suki pleads.

'What are you doing?' Leela tries to step between us.

Briar tries to claw at my eyes.

'She got Cade killed!' It comes out as a wail.

'What?' Madison stops kidding around. 'What did you say?'

Even Briar looks shocked. 'What do you mean?'

I let go of her neck and speak only to her. 'Clancy told me! You've been leaking stories to *The Globe* to get rid of us.' Her eyes widen. 'They monitor your phone, you simpleton. *They know everything.*' I point to a camera and she has the good grace to look mortified. 'You told them about me and Cade, about Domino, everything. It was all you all along.'

I sense Madison prickle. '*You* sold those stories about my sister?' She circles the taller girl.

'I'm sorry, okay.' Briar backs away as Madi advances. 'You don't understand.'

'You sold us out,' Madison says.

Briar babbles, desperate. 'Those stories got Domino out, y'all should be thanking me. She was guaranteed a spot!'

I lunge at her again, past Leela. We both go down, but I recover first and straddle her. 'You KILLED CADE!' I shriek.

Maybe murder has become meaningless after watching three girls die in a glass pyramid because, here and now, I want to kill Briar. I lift her head and then bash it down hard against the cold marble. Someone screams at me to stop.

'Please . . .' Briar murmurs.

I lift her head again.

'I have a little girl,' she breathes.

I stop, mostly because I'm not sure I heard her correctly. 'What did you say?'

'My baby,' she gasps. 'Please. My baby needs me.'

I stop. A baby human? I clamber off her, and Leela helps me to my feet. My heart still throbs in my skull. 'You have a *baby*?'

Briar sits up, blood running down her chin. 'They'd disqualify me,' she croaks. 'I couldn't tell anyone. They think she's my sister. She lives with my mom in Connecticut.'

Suki quickly translates for Minnie, who looks suitably scandalized. Never, in the history of *Starmaker*, has there been a parent.

'What? When? How?' Madison says what we're all feeling.

'I had her right after graduation,' Briar admits as she stands.

'This. Is. Wild.' Suki can't blink.

'Harmoni. Her name is Harmoni. She has sickle cell anaemia.' She looks at me with daggers. 'What? Did you think you were the only one with a sob story? At least you can share yours. There was no way they were putting two Black girls in the group. I had to get rid of Domino.'

'Sure, you tell yourself that,' I snarl.

'Oh grow up! This is a competition. We all came here to win. Whatever it takes.'

'And what about Cade? Was he in your way?'

'I was trying to get rid of *you*, not him,' she confesses.

My eyes blaze. 'Oh that makes it all better then.'

She pauses. 'They really killed him?'

I wince. 'Yes, Briar, I watched them gun him down. There was no car crash.'

They process the truth. Network G is willing to kill – on and off-screen. Suki is tearful. 'But why would they do that?'

The den falls silent, all eyes on me. I don't care any more

if they're filming us or not. They're all-seeing, whatever we do; there's no escape. 'Cade got close to something. The truth about the people who control the network and Elysium.' I will not mention Nomi, however. 'He knew too much . . . and so they killed him.'

'If that's true, why didn't they kill *you*?' Briar rubs her sore head and I feel bad for how close I got to really hurting her.

The answer I give isn't the answer I thought I had. 'Because they need me.' The others wait for more. 'They need all of us. No one at home or online stans dusty old farts like Chairman Slade or sad hags like Clancy. The fans want to be *us*. The producers work us to death and starve us and control us and gaslight us because they want us exhausted; they want us to believe we don't have any power.'

'Come on.' Briar rolls her eyes. 'If we all walked out this door right now, they'd have ten new willing idiots here in less than an hour.'

I shake my head. 'Uh-uh. The public stan *us*. You, me. They pick their favourite. They copy our hair and clothes. And maybe some man picked out those things for us, but it's *us* they watch and follow. Not Slade.'

Madison stands shoulder to shoulder with me. 'Taryn's right. It's about us. We are idols. They're just *people*.'

I nod. 'Elysium is *nothing* without us. We have the power.' I look to the other survivors. 'The only question is, what are we going to do with it? Because in four days' time, another one of us will go in that pyramid unless *we* stop it. It ends with us.'

'What are you saying?' Madison stands, hands on hips.

'Hey GBloc!' I call. 'Play Nico at full volume!' The Smart

Speaker starts to play 'Crazy Loca'.

'What are you doing?' Suki asks.

I talk low so the girls have to gather closer. They, the production team, can't hear what I'm about to say. 'The final is live.'

'So?' says Briar.

'You love your daughter?'

She scowls at me. 'What sort of question is that?'

I stand tall. 'So we fight back.'

PHASE FOUR: LIVE FINAL

SUPER SATURDAY ON NETWORK G

FreshElla PRESENTS THE SEASON FINALE OF
STARMAKER
AS WE UNVEIL THE ALL-NEW GIRL-GROUP SENSATION DOLLHOU5E.

FOLLOWED BY THE SEASON PREMIERE OF
CANCER CHANCER.
TEN PATIENTS, NINE PLACEBOS!
WHO WILL GET THE TREATMENT THEY NEED TO LIVE?

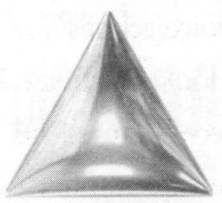

CHAPTER 43

In the corridors deep below the Media City Stadium, the wind seems to howl. It's as if we're surrounded by the ghosts of every trainee who went before. I stretch my leg against a breezeblock wall. To either side of me, the other girls do the same. There's nothing left to say. We know what needs to be done.

In my periphery, I keep an eye on Briar as she rests in the splits on the floor. I don't know if we can trust her. I was sure to withhold the finer details from her, so even if she does go to Clancy, it won't help.

To my left Madison catches my eye. She glances quickly at Briar and then back, and I know we're sharing the same lingering doubts. Funny how Madi ended up being the most supportive ally. Maybe they shouldn't have gassed her little sister.

Hopefully we're all in this together. Because we cannot win under Chairman Slade's rules. What we have today is one shot. One shot at freedom. Because tonight, we are live; no cuts, no edits. Anything that happens out there, the nation – the world – will see.

I drop into a low lunge and catch my foot behind me.

'Well *now* she looks like a dancer!'

A familiar English voice echoes down the endless hall, crisp as a Granny Smith. I look up to see Deenie and Dr Anders coming towards us, accompanied by the sound of Deenie's bangles clinking as ever around her wrists.

'Deenie!' I don't know why, but seeing her is like seeing family. I run to them, but Leela gets to her first and throws her arms around our former dance teacher.

'Well, well, well, two non-dancers in the finale! Damn, I'm good, eh?' Deenie smiles. She strokes a stray strand of hair off my lip. 'Look at you now. A different woman.'

'You have no idea,' I tell her.

She fingers a lock of my mermaid-length hair. They forced me to have the extensions put back in. 'You look like an idol.'

I can't forget that this woman works for *Starmaker*, same as Clancy and Dr Anders. As such, I can't trust her. 'I hope so,' I reply vaguely. I want to be an idol, but I think I'm starting to understand what that means, and why they set such high standards for us. We are elite performers, artists, certainly, but also someone who leads, always does what's right. 'What are you doing here?'

'I came to see *you*!' Deenie beams. 'I'm so proud. Of all of you. Try to enjoy it. I know this is hard, but – when you're my age – you'll have forgotten how tired and anxious you were, and just remember the sheer, gorgeous colour and noise of it all.'

I know she means well, but I won't have forgotten Lune's glassy eyes, Shayna's wail, Domino's clenched jaw.

'How are we all feeling, ladies?' Dr Anders asks. Today, his cardigan is a chunky grey number. 'Very normal to feel nervous. No one wants to fall at the final hurdle.'

I share only the briefest glance with Suki. If this works, no one is falling today.

'And now, performing what will be, for five of them, their winner's single, "Come Get Your Man". Please welcome back to the stage one last time . . . Briar, Leela, Madison, Minnie, Suki and Taryn. It's DOLLHOU5E!'

I hear Mojo from behind the LED screen. It slides up and the fireworks begin. All I see are white sparks. *Don't think, just do.* I am in the centre as we strut onto the main stage. A marching band drum beat begins as we get into formation and wait for the backing track to start.

We are dressed like majorettes. Well, post-apocalyptic majorettes with studs and biker boots. Lars' concept. I inhale and wait for the spotlight to hit me.

I am ready. I have done nothing for the past seventy-two hours except get ready for this moment. I'm no longer singing or dancing to win, and that's very freeing. I'm singing and dancing to *destroy them*. It doesn't have to be *good*; it has to be truthful.

Them. Him. That faceless coward Slade, and every last one of his minions. I will ruin him.

The question remains though. The lurking doubt. *Are we together on this?*

The final words we shared backstage. In a circle, right hands clasped at its centre. It has to be all of us, or it isn't going to work. Even Briar.

Go time.

As we march on the spot, I look out at the crowd. The Media City Stadium stage is three times the size of the one back in the Network G studio. There are vast screens either side of a neon art-deco themed backdrop and a catwalk cutting through the audience to a smaller B-Stage.

The stadium is a sea of people, bodies surging like a tide. Our biggest audience yet: thirty thousand screaming fans. At the barriers surrounding the catwalk, Securiforce guards armed with tasers patrol a front row of teenagers, mostly girls. The accompanying mums and dads seem to be much further back, or in the bleachers. Some of the girls wear cat ears like Minnie. A lot have bright red, or powder-pink hair. They're here for us. Wild.

The track booms, vibrating the floor beneath my boots.

Go.

My body has evolved. The muscles have learned the song and I can perform the routine like breathing or blinking. As is standard, the harmonies are on the backing track, and our mics go live for only our solo sections. I switch positions with Suki with a hair flip, and go centre for the bridge to the chorus.

> *You can call me a bitch*
> *You can call me a tease*
> *Your ego's in need*
> *I'm telling you please*

I let rip. I sing my lungs inside out. The audience screams. We get to the middle eight. I wrote this part for Slade.

I'm not your toy
I'm not your doll
I'm not your baby
It's not your world
So hear me cry
Hear my roar
Watch my ass walk out the door!

Then there's a dance break in this remix. The most ambitious routine we've learned. We travel like a marching band down the runway to the second stage, making sure we arrive in time for the big finish. We fan out, Madison and Briar performing a high-kick straight into the splits. Loudest scream yet. Madison's shoe almost grazes my nose as I stomp relentlessly forward to get into the final pose.

Pyrotechnics explode and I think I lose some lashes. Glittering confetti rains down. The stadium roars; I'm almost knocked off my feet by the sheer force of it. They *love* us. It *is* love too – not boyfriend or girlfriend love, or the love I have for my family, but love all the same. Something distinct and powerful, some cocktail of mania and worship and sisterhood. The love of belonging. This is the birth of a new religion.

I pant, trying to scoop my breath back. I take it all in. This could be the first and last ever performance as DOLLHOU5E. The crowd scream and scream. Someone down front calls my name so loud her throat sounds raw. They wave our Dolly light sticks.

I was one of them once. I never questioned the machine

that made the sausage either. I voted every week. And now I'm about to tear it all down.

'Girls, girls, take your positions.' Mojo beckons us over. He, Nico and Dre wear head-to-toe black as a mark of respect to Cade. The show opened with a crass tribute – fifty dancers performing to an N-TRU5T medley. I watched the whole thing backstage on the monitors, trying to keep my dinner down.

Exactly as we rehearsed yesterday, we each walk to a podium to hear our fate. They're designed like ancient Greek stone columns, as if we're tributes to the gods. I exchange a glance with Leela as I step onto my platform and she gives the most subtle of nods.

It's almost time.

The platform judders to life and I ascend three metres over the stage. We stand looking out at the crowd. I grip the safety rail with damp palms until my knuckles are white bone.

Nearly there.

Nico smiles to the camera, her flawless face filling the auditorium's many big screens. 'Our trainees can do no more. They have sung and danced for the last time tonight. *One* of them for the last time *ever.*'

Any second now.

'Your votes have been counted and verified,' Mojo continues. 'And now, it's time to find out who will debut in DOLLHOU5E.'

The time is now. Retribution cometh.

I hold my breath and wait for the big moment.

Only nothing happens.

'Taryn!' It's Madi, calling from the podium to my left. The

wind blows hair around her face in thick tendrils. 'What's going on?'

I don't know. I look to the screen behind us but it still shows us on our plinths. This wasn't the plan. Nomi promised.

The plan was very simple. At the point that the most people, globally, have eyes on their screens, the images would change to show my Punkcat footage. Even if the producers cut the live feed – which they undoubtedly will – we're before thirty thousand fans, all with videophones.

I can only shrug at Madison. Her face is twisted into something between fear and fury. Down the line, the other girls glare at me. What the hell is happening? Nomi *promised*.

Two nights ago, Leela faked a meltdown and demanded she see 'the trans runner'. Nomi/Jacey was duly sent for, and I met with them in the laundry room to hatch the scheme. At the point the results are unveiled, we destroy *Starmaker*.

So why isn't that happening at this very moment? Instead, Nico reads from the autocue, finger pressed to her earpiece so she can hear over the screams of the stadium. 'Ranking in first place, the first trainee to debut is . . .'

I can barely hear her, even over the loudspeakers. 'From Britain, it's Rebel Doll Taryn Beck!'

I don't even register. My gormless face fills every screen in the arena. Oh, that's me. It's like my face doesn't belong to me any more. So. I won. I won *Starmaker*. It feels like . . . nothing. Nothing at all. I have won *dust*. I am the same Taryn Beck I was ten seconds ago.

The crowd, though. The applause. The screams. The fans. None of this is their fault . . . I don't think. No. They didn't make the rules. They didn't rig the game. I nod, bow my head low, and mouth *thank you*.

None of the cheers answer my only question. *Where is Nomi with the footage?* It should be airing right now. I look down the line and, while they politely applaud, Suki, Briar, Minnie and Leela look to me like *huh?*

'The second trainee to debut in DOLLHOU5E,' Mojo announces. 'Is . . . from the Red States of America, it's Madison Silver, Diamond Doll!'

Madison is better trained than I am. She immediately drops to her haunches and covers her face, as if she's overcome. Clever girl to hide her face, wish I'd thought of that. Once more, the crowd is ecstatic.

The plan has gone badly awry. Will the other winning girls just throw me under the bus once they know they're safe? I thought we were in it together, but maybe I'm a fool. *Come on, Nomi, just run the footage.* They said, they *promised*, that they have an ally in transmission. Someone who knows how to change the live feed.

Mojo continues. 'Ranked third, and the third girl to debut in DOLLHOU5E is . . . from Australia, Suki Lee, our Baby Doll!'

Suki's face fills the monitors and she beams, grinning ear to ear. Tears fill her eyes. No! She can't buy into the lie. There isn't going to be a DOLLHOU5E. This is *not* the victory we agreed on last night. Damn, I thought Briar was the weak link, but Suki is bathing in this.

'The next girl safely through,' Nico says, 'is . . . from South Korea, it's Kitty Doll Minnie Park!'

Min-jee receives the news with the poise I've come to expect. She bows and smiles sweetly. She then looks to me and gives the faintest nod. Even if our plan has gone to shit, she's still with me.

To my right Leela looks tense. She nearly always ranks Top Three. She's the visual, the Cool One. The last blonde standing.

'Lee!' I call to her. 'It's fine. You're fine.' She manages a nod, but her mouth is a terse line.

Come on, Nomi. Enough is enough.

'And now,' Mojo says sombrely, 'only one more trainee will debut in the brand-new girl group that'll set next year alight. The other girl will face the Elimination Chamber and boldly offer her life so that the rest of us can thrive.'

Briar's eyes are closed and, even with all the makeup, her skin looks grey as a tombstone. Next to her, Leela is statue still. Only Nomi can put a stop to all this.

Nico delivers the final result. 'There are less than a thousand votes separating Briar and Leela.' This news doesn't bring any comfort. 'The last girl to debut in DOLLHOU5E is . . . oh my gosh, it's Slamdunk Doll! From the Blue States, it's Briar Franklin!'

No. Not Leela. My first friend in all this. My roommate. We've been together every step of the journey.

Briar dares to exhale. Leela looks to me, pale as ice.

Fireworks erupt, brilliant white flumes of glitter.

We didn't rehearse this part.

Mojo's voice booms. 'Meet your new girl group! Ladies, gentlemen and others, welcome to the DOLLHOU5E!'

The only thing I see is Leela's face. A trapdoor opens under her feet, and she plummets from view before she can even scream. In a second, she's taken from us.

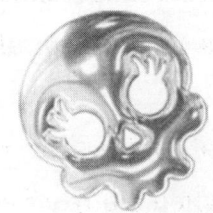

CHAPTER 44

We all have a trapdoor. I stomp my boots against the podium, trying to kick it open. It doesn't budge. The platforms aren't that high. I slip under the safety rail and prepare for the jump. Okay, it's higher than it looks. Thankfully, with a shudder, the plinths begin their descent. Now, we're *supposed* to hug and then talk to Mojo and Nico to tell them how delighted we are.

No way.

I jump down from the plinth before it settles and start to run in the opposite direction, towards the wings. What's that saying about Best Laid Plans? I don't know what happened to Nomi, and I was wrong to put all our eggs in one basket, but, right now, I've got to get to Leela.

To my surprise, I see Suki is running alongside me. 'What are you doing?' she yelps.

'What do you think? Finding Leela! She's somewhere under the stage. They're not having her.'

Madison sweeps past me. 'I know where the Elimination Chamber is.'

'Lead the way.'

I don't look back, I just keep powering towards stage left, following Madi. Even so, I sense a curious energy washing off the stadium in waves. *Where are they going?* A big fat confusion.

We are only a couple of metres into the darkened wings – all crates and rigging – when a burly Securiforce agent steps into our path. 'Back on stage, girls,' he says. 'I'm not playing.'

'What are you gonna do? Shoot us?' I say. 'We just won *Starmaker*.'

He looks genuinely torn and that moment of hesitation is all the time it takes. With a silvery flash, a mic stand slaps into the side of his thick head. Brandishing it is Briar, who looks almost as stunned as the guard as he goes down. 'What did I just do?' she cries.

'You saved us!' I grab her wrist and pull her towards the gangplank leading from the stage to pitch level, and to the network of tunnels below.

Someone grabs my hair from behind, yanking my neck backwards. I almost go all the way down, swerving at the foot of the ramp.

It's Clancy. 'What the HELL do you think you're doing?' the producer screeches. She grips me from behind, an arm across my neck.

'Jesus! Let go of me!'

'Get off her, Clancy!' yells Briar.

'Get back on that stage right now, you little bitches. I mean it.'

'You can't hurt us!' I wince as her fingers claw at my already sore scalp.

'I said, *get back on that stage.*'

There's something sharp pressed against my throat. The look in Suki, Minnie and Briar's eyes tells me Clancy is not playing. It's some sort of blade. 'What are you doing?' I rasp.

'I'll do what I want!' Clancy snarls. 'I give up. I'm so over it. TEN YEARS I've been running around after you snot-nosed brats, wiping your asses. Well I'm *done*. Do you know I have an MBA? This is humiliating. Slade can find some other idiot to do his dirty work. I AM DONE.' I can hear a tearful tremble in her voice.

'Okay,' Briar says coolly, like she's taming a lion. A *demented* lion. 'Just let her go, Clancy.'

'And you'll go sing your single?'

'Sure. Just don't hurt her. Taryn ranked first.'

'Do I look like I give a dry rat's ass?' That was clearly the wrong thing to say. 'Do you know she was working with an undercover journalist? She was going to expose us all. She'd have ruined your lives.' Clancy's grip tightens on my hair. The blade against my throat pierces my skin. I let out an involuntary gasp. 'You *sure* you don't want her to have a little accident?'

'Where's Leela?' Suki asks.

'Why do you care? Just GET BACK OUT THERE.'

'Is she still alive?' Suki goes on.

'You UNGRATEFUL LITTLE C—' She doesn't finish the sentence. There's a loud *pop* and something rushes past my face. At once, Clancy recoils backwards, releasing her headlock on me. As she goes down, I go with her, carried by momentum. I hit the gangplank and roll away.

Clancy lays flat on her back, eyes wide. There is a neat hole in the centre of her forehead. I sit up to see Madison holding the Securiforce agent's gun at arm's length. My mouth hangs open in shock.

'I . . . saw the knife . . . I thought she was going to . . .'

'How did you do that?' I wheeze.

'Girl, I'm from Texas.' She pulls me up. 'Hurry, there's like fifty more Securiforce goons coming right after us.'

I turn to the others. 'Run!'

The tunnels underneath the stadium are labyrinthine – endless grey corridors, curved so they seem to never end. Our footsteps echo off the stone floor. Madison takes the lead. 'Are you sure you know where you're going?' I pant.

She answers by firing the gun again, past us towards a pair of Securiforce guards tailing us. They duck to take cover.

'Yes!' she cries. 'It's right under the stage. It comes up on a lift.'

'What do you think's happening up there?' Suki asks, eyes wide. 'They can't cut to commercial for ever.'

'I don't care any more,' I say. 'Screw their TV show.'

'They won't kill Leela until we're there to sing her off,' Briar adds ruefully.

'We must stick together,' Min-jee adds. I take her hand. From out of nowhere, I remember audition day – not the audition itself but those gross men on the train who'd made me feel about two inches tall. I recall now the way that the mum and the old lady came to my rescue. Min-jee is right. *We must stick together.*

We keep running. We run until my lungs burn. Madi

continues to fire warning shots at any security guard who gains on us. She nods at the double doors up ahead marked CENTER STAGE ACCESS. 'In there!'

I reach the doors first and shove. 'It's locked.'

'Stand back!' We do as we're told and Madison fires at the lock until the doors seem to sag.

We enter a dark hangar, directly below the main stage. The floor is littered with ginormous flight cases and crates. In the centre of it all, the pyramid awaits, dark and deadly.

'You get Leela, I'll barricade the door,' Madi tells us, shutting us in.

The pyramid is unlit on a cherry picker, waiting for its ascent to the stage. Leela is already sealed inside the chamber, cross-legged on the base. On seeing us, she springs to her feet, pressing her hands to the glass. I don't see any Securiforce monitoring the area.

'Where is everyone?' Suki ponders.

Probably looking for us. 'Who cares! Get her out of there!' I shout at no one in particular. We circle the Elimination Chamber, looking for the controls.

'The illusion of choice,' a voice booms from the shadows and we all freeze. From behind one of the largest equipment cases steps Dr Anders, fingers pressed together in a steeple, 'is the greatest power in the world.'

'Dr Anders!' Briar says. 'Can you help us?'

He ignores her and continues. 'You *thought* you chose to enter this contest. People at home *think* they're choosing the winners and losers. These little buttons we press give us some sense of control in the chaos. But the truth is this: Leela was always going to die at the final. Nothing she did matters because we control everything. Her elimination was always going to be the most shocking conclusion; we gave her the full hero narrative, only to have her fall at the final hurdle. We'll be on every front page in the morning. We're breaking the internet as we speak.'

I don't understand. 'We can end this,' I say. 'Please?'

In his hand, he holds a remote control. I think I can guess what it operates.

'What in damnation is going on?' Madison asks.

'Put down the gun, Madison,' Anders says. 'If you so much as point that thing at me, Leela dies. It was a fair game, by the way. She didn't get the numbers. I made sure of it. We gave Briar a better edit in the end. Nothing beats the Underdog Narrative. It's nothing personal; Leela is simply too tall. I think you should be able to balance a broom across the heads of any pop act or it all just looks out of whack in pictures.'

'Why are you doing this?' Suki whines. 'Dr Anders, please! They're coming after us.'

I don't know *how* I know, but a fog lifts in my mind and it all makes sense. The tiles slide into place to reveal the truth. 'Oh my god,' I say. 'You're him. You're *Chairman Slade*.'

'What?' Madison gasps.

Briar's eyes look like they might fall out of her skull. 'Are you for real?'

Anders – Slade – crinkles his nose. 'Was it the anagram? Too obvious?' Malachi Anders equals Chairman Slade. It's obvious *now*.

'No,' I reply. 'I guess I just realized how weird it was that the chairman never showed up to claim the glory. How no one had ever met him. But you were here all along.'

'Being your therapist was the only way I could observe the real you. I used to come down here and meet trainees, but they would suck up and put on an act. This way, as "Dr Anders", I get to know you. The *real* you.'

'Did Cade know?'

'No. Clueless idiot.'

'What about Nico?' Madi asks.

'Of course.'

With horror, I recall what Nico said about her *beneficial* relationship with Slade. Ew. Gross.

'Taryn, I really did want you in the band, even taking into account the risk factor. You *are* a rebel. But I like it. And the girls, the fans, they adore you. That's why I am Mr Elysium. I know what it is girls like you want. You might *say* you want something new and empowering with studs and black eyeliner, but actually, underneath, you want the dream. You all want to be perfect, pretty, thin girls with sweet, kind hearts and white teeth. You want a non-threatening boyfriend who wants for nothing more than to hold your hand. You, Taryn, you're both: you give them that sulky, defiant little edge but, at the end of the day, you're still perfect, pretty and thin. And all you want, really, is to be rich and famous like everyone else does.'

I look him in the eye, unflinching. 'I don't want *anything* from you.'

He emerges further from the shadows. 'Yes you do. No one has worked harder than you. I've watched you, remember. And you're not just doing this for your brother. You're doing this for your *mother*. When you sing, you're reunited, isn't that right? Taryn, you can't deny it. And I'm offering you the biggest stage in the world. The whole world will hear you sing and your mother will live on.'

This was never *just* about Jenson. When I sing, it's like a phoenix flying from me, and the phoenix is *her*. When I sing, Mum's reborn, and I'm not alone.

'Don't listen to him,' Madison breathes in my ear. 'He's full of shit.'

Slade looks a little offended. 'Does your big sister think I'm full of poop, Madison? She's doing rather well, isn't she?'

'I dunno, but you killed my *little* sister.'

'You all knew the stakes,' Slade says. 'But you applied anyway. You gave your heart and soul for this. And for what?' He parades past each of us, as if inspecting his troops. He starts with Briar. 'For your daughter?'

A hand automatically flies to a locket at her throat. 'You know?'

'I know *everything*. I handpicked the girls who wouldn't quit. The most desperate, the most vulnerable.' He continues past Madison. 'For your mother's love?' Past Suki. 'To prove yourself?' Minnie. 'Because it's all you've ever known?' He gestures at Leela. 'Or simply because you want to show the world you're not just a girl but a *star*?'

We can't argue. He knows us. He *has* us.

'So here's what's going to happen. You'll go out there and smile and dance and sing. You're going to sell a lot of records. And dolls. And posters.'

His finger hovers over the buttons that will gas Leela.

Inside the pyramid tears roll down her perfect cheekbones. Madison is a great shot, but I don't think she could kill him faster than he could hit that switch. I have to try something else. 'Okay,' I say. 'We'll go sing.'

'What?!' Madison exclaims.

'You got to Jacey, didn't you?'

'They're alive. For now. We found them snooping around in the transmission centre. Their safety very much depends on your next actions.'

'We'll sing.' I repeat myself. '*If* you release Leela. What an amazing twist that would be.' He knows my mind, but maybe I know his warped little brain too. 'This is season thirteen! Everyone at home thinks they know the final act, but what if Leela steps out of the pyramid and there are *six* dolls in DOLLHOU5E?'

He pouts slightly. 'There's literally a five in the name.'

'My god, change it to DOLLH6USE with a six in! Our fans love Leela. Take the credit! You'll be a hero!'

I see the cogs in his head spinning. I see dollar signs roll in his eyes like a fruit machine. Just for a second, and then—

'No, I don't think so. We'd have to pulp a lot of tote bags and t-shirts.'

He points the remote towards the chamber.

'Stop!' I scream. I have to think like them. *It's all about the show*. The spectacle. The final product. 'Madison?'

'Yeah?'

I can't blink. 'Shoot Briar.'

'What?'

'WHAT?' Briar yelps.

'Explain that one to the press.' I smirk at Slade. 'If you can't have six girls, you can't have four either. And the fans voted Briar in.'

He scowls at us. 'You won't shoot her.'

'Won't we? Without your *illusion of choice* you lose your power. Briar sold me out. She sold out Cade. She sold out Domino. And Shayna. She's kind of a dick.'

Briar backs away. 'You can't be serious.'

'Madi . . .'

Madison levels the pistol at Briar.

'Don't! What about my baby?'

'What about my baby *sister*?' Madison's ice eyes don't move from her target. She backs Briar towards the pyramid. Inside, unable to hear us, Leela watches on in terror.

I don't take my eyes off Chairman Slade. 'So what will it be, *Chairman Slade*? DOLLH6USE with a six or DOLL4OUSE with a four?'

I look at him looking at me. In chess, I believe this is what they call checkmate.

He breaks. 'Very well. You win.'

Briar's entire face changes; she smiles widely. 'He believed us.'

I worry we've shown our hand too soon. Madison lowers the gun and scowls at Slade. 'Do you really think I'd shoot her? Man, you need therapy.'

'Get Leela out,' Suki says. 'Open the door.'

Slade gestures at the dormant pyramid as if to say *help yourself.* Closest, Briar strides towards the chamber, searching for the emergency release switch on the frame.

Something isn't right. Slade's gaze is firmly fixed on the floor. There's something I'm forgetting and this seems too easy. He wouldn't admit defeat so easily.

And then, from the muddy puddle of my memory, a shouted phrase resurfaces. During Ashanti's elimination. *Disarm the pyramid.*

'Briar, stop!' I scream.

Too late. Briar touches the edge of the pyramid. There's a white-hot, blinding flash of light and a loud crack, like a whiplash. Briar is lifted off her feet, tossed backwards through the air. She clatters into a steel trolley piled high with cables, and flops to the floor. An odour like burnt toast fills the air.

Slade observes with clinical detachment. 'Shame. I'd have really liked a Black girl in the band. You know, for diversity.'

CHAPTER 45

We run to Briar. The awful burning smell is worse as I kneel at her side.

'Is it safe to touch her?' Madison says.

I tell her I think so. I tentatively reach for a pulse in her neck. No longer in contact with the pyramid, there's no electrical current passing through her. 'Briar?' I say. 'Briar, can you hear me?' I can't find a heartbeat. I twist my head to face Slade. 'You're a monster.'

Slade is at the controls alongside the Elimination Chamber, deactivating the electrified exterior. 'This isn't the first time a trainee has tried to break someone out of a device. Of course we have systems in place. I didn't tell her to touch it.'

'You didn't warn her either, you freak!' Suki screams, tears running down her cheeks.

'Do you really think I'd let a bunch of precocious teenage girls ruin about three years' worth of planning?'

Flat on the concrete floor, Briar stirs slightly. 'She's alive!' Min-jee exclaims.

'Help her!' I beg of Slade. 'Please.'

He ignores my plea. Briar tries to grip my arm with a feeble hand. Her eyes open a fraction but she doesn't seem to see us. Her lips move and I think she's trying to speak. I lean in closer. 'Briar? I can't hear you. It's Taryn . . .'

She's scarcely audible as she mutters, 'Tell Harmoni I did it for her.'

I feel sick. 'Tell her yourself. Please, Briar. Open your eyes. Please. Stay with me.'

Her lips move only a millimetre. 'Taryn . . . take . . . take care of her. My baby . . .'

A tear runs off my cheek and onto her flawless face. 'Briar, don't go.'

'It . . . was all for . . . for her.'

And then she is gone. Her head lolls to one side, and her eyes lose their light.

This was all my idea. Briar would have made the band. She would have lived. Her daughter would have never wanted for anything ever again. As if knowing this, Madison pulls me close and I press my eyes into her shoulder. My mouth hangs open, but I am too numb to even sob.

'Are you going to kill us too?' Suki asks Slade in a little voice.

'Don't be stupid. You're going to get out there and sing your winners' song.' Slade steps aside as the pyramid door lowers. Leela is pressed into the corner like a cowering animal. Her face is deathly pale, eyes wide and unblinking. 'Out you get,' Slade tells her. 'Not ideal, but you'll just have to wear flats from now on.'

Madison says, 'You're not going to kill her?'

'I told you: all the merch has a great big five on it. It'd cost a fortune to rebrand.'

DOLLHOU5E!

DOLLHOU5E!

DOLLHOU5E!

The chant is oddly menacing, like the crowd are baying for blood. *Come outside, little piggies, we just want to talk.*

We are crouched, ready to emerge from a huge pyramid in the centre of the stage. This one is made of frosted glass in a soothing jade green. I'm still stunned; I don't even realize Suki is talking to me until she grips my arms so tight it hurts. 'Taryn! What do we do?'

I don't want to be the leader a second longer. 'I don't know. I don't know any more.'

There's a momentary hush in the crowd and then a cheer. Inside the prop, we can't see what's occurring in the arena. Then a familiar voice booms out from the speakers.

'Hey, guys, it's Briar.'

'What the hell?' Madison breathes.

Through the frosted glass, I can just about make out the shape of Briar's face filling the big screens. 'I am beyond grateful for everyone around the world who voted for me, but something didn't sit right with me. I can't watch Leela be eliminated when she wants it so much more than I do.'

'How are they doing this?' Suki gasps.

'AI,' Leela says grim-faced. 'A deepfake. They captured our voices. And I guess our faces as well.'

'It is scary,' Min-jee says. Yes, it *really* is.

The phony vision of Briar continues: 'I haven't been honest with you. Two years ago, I gave birth to my beautiful daughter, Harmoni.'

There's a gasp in the auditorium and, from nowhere, I vomit bile all over my silver boots. The stench fills the pyramid, but my new bandmates don't say anything. Instead, Min-jee rubs my back and Madison holds back my hair.

'Briar' concludes, 'I've decided to spend time with her, and forego my place in the competition. I wish my fellow trainees all the best for the future . . .'

Mojo takes over, or at least his voice does. 'For the first time, welcome to the stage: Taryn, Minnie, Suki, Madison and Leela . . . it's DOLLHOU5E!'

On cue, there's a hiss of gas and the sugar-glass walls of the pyramid blow outwards. A beautiful explosion. The glass rains down like jade glitter. I flinch and step over the puddle of yellow puke. The crowd is beyond hysterical. Behind us, our promo pictures fill the screens.

The screams are almost physical, like a tsunami rolling off the audience. I feel it and it is *warm*. I see a wall of smiles and laughter and pure goodwill towards us. I knew it all along. The *true* fans don't want to see us suffer and die.

Friends and family are located in a VIP area with the best view – eye level to the right of the stage. I see Dad, Molly and Jenson applauding wildly. But I also see the man I now know to be Chairman Slade right next to them, nestled amongst our nearest and dearest: a viper in the nest.

Seated to Jenson's right is a beautiful silver-haired Black

woman who must be Briar's mum. She's holding an adorable girl; Briar's daughter. Once more all my breath is torn from my chest. She is so beautiful. Eyes like conkers and hair in little twists. Briar's mum looks confused, but grips Harmoni tight.

The grinding throb of the intro to 'Come Get Your Man' booms around me. The other girls move into first positions, but my feet are glued to the spot. My eyes lock on Briar's child. Slade is just metres from her.

Briar's dying words are all I hear. *It was all for her.* A girl. A girl who'll grow up watching *Starmaker*; making idols out of liars, and the wheels will just keep turning, and turning, and grinding us into mince.

I see Slade edge closer to Jenson. The drone camera hovers just a couple of metres in front of me.

And then I see her. Far below, in the middle of the crowd is Mum. Everyone else dances and waves, but she stands still, serene. She looks proud of me, and I know what I must do.

My mic is live. 'Stop!' I shout. 'Cut the track.'

The mixing desk is out of sight, somewhere over the arena. After what feels like forever, the backing track cuts out. It feels like the audience, all those girls, are holding their breath, no doubt wondering why I've called for the song to stop.

Now is the time to truly use my voice.

'I am so thankful to everyone who voted for me. It means so much that they've enjoyed my singing. It's the thing I love most.' I grip the microphone. I look Dad in the eye. His forehead creases with concern. 'But I love my family more, and I wouldn't be the girl they know and love if I wasn't honest. I could take the cheque and the record deal and everything, but that money is soaked red with blood.'

Out of the corner of my eye, I see Mojo and a troop of Securiforce guards edge to the side of the stage.

'They're gonna cut the feed any second, but you need to listen. *Starmaker* is lying to you. They lie, over and over. And they are going to *kill* me for doing this.'

The audience look rightly confused. I take a breath and continue.

'Before they drag us into that pyramid, they abuse us. We're starved. They don't let us sleep. They threatened to harm our families and . . .' And then the biggest one of all. 'They killed Sonny Feldman. They murdered Cade Kekoa. And they literally just killed Briar. Briar is dead.'

An audible gasp echoes around the stadium. Nico strides to the middle of the stage, wind billowing through her wig. 'Ha ha! Taryn, that's not a very funny joke. I think maybe we should go to commercial . . .'

But she can't go on. There's an ear-piercing cry of feedback in the monitors and she pulls her earpieces out. The LCD screens go dead black for a second, and then pea-green, and then the jerky, chaotic footage flickers onto every screen in the arena.

The sound is me panting as I run. A grainy figure runs beside me. Cade.

I'm so relieved I *almost* laugh. *Nomi*. Somehow they finally came through.

Helicopter blades, searchlights. '*Is that for us?*' I say. 'How much further to your car?'

Cade's voice. *'All the way in the valley, at the gas station. We should split up; the chopper can't follow us both, can it?'*

The stadium audience are stunned silent, chins tilted skywards. As I argue with Cade on the big screen, a refrain echoes around the arena.

Cade, Cade, Cade.

'What is this?' Nico demands. 'Turn it off!'

But whoever is in charge of the transmission doesn't turn it off.

'Head downtown on foot. Don't go to the bus station, they'll have that covered. There's an all-night diner on 4th Street. Go there.'

The noise of our final kiss plays out on the big screens for an audience of thirty thousand pop-music fans. Cade from N-TRU5T kissing Taryn from DOLLHOU5E. Escandalo.

The footage bounces all over the place as I ran in search of the petrol station.

CLACK CLACK CLACK.

With ragged breath, I run towards the gunfire and, here, I close my eyes. I can't see this again.

'Confirm the kill.'

'Confirmed on male target.'

The Punkcat footage is frenetic, but it's clear enough. Ten thousand people in the stadium are crypt silent as Cade's bloodied body is displayed for the whole world to see. The sound of truth, this time, is silence.

I feel supportive arms close around me. Suki, then Leela.

A new refrain grows louder and louder. It's his name – no, it's WE LOVE CADE over and over.

We love Cade.

We love Cade.

We love Cade.

Spectators in the pitch standing area surge forwards, those at the front dangerously pressed against the metal security barriers. Securiforce guards push back, brandishing their batons. The faces of the fans at the front show a mixture of rage and panic. Thanks to some strange female telepathy, the mood in the arena almost visibly darkens. A storm is brewing.

But I don't want a crowd crush on my conscience. 'Stop!' I scream into the mic. 'Stop pushing.'

No one seems to hear. Securiforce agents now raise their guns, but their threats aren't heeded. The crowd continues to storm towards the stage. 'Let them through!' Madi yells down to security. 'They're gonna get crushed.'

'What do we do?' Suki cries.

More Securiforce crew flood the pitch from the tunnel, firing warning shots into the air. It doesn't have the intended effect. Quite the opposite. The security agents become the face of *Starmaker*, and these girls are really, *really* mad at *Starmaker*. For many of them, Sonny and Cade were the first time they felt love, or lust, or a weird cocktail of both. And *Starmaker* killed their fantasy boyfriends.

I see a trio of older teenage girls in DOLLHOU5E t-shirts turn on a guard, whipping him with their mini backpacks and clobbering him around the head with Dolly light-sticks. He goes down, and as soon as he hits the pitch, they start stamping on his face with platform sneakers.

The front barrier collapses and a tidal wave of fans tumble

into the camera run. They too turn their attention to the Securiforce guards, outnumbering them a hundred to one. With nails and teeth, they set upon the staff.

'They're feral.' Mojo looks terrified.

'They're fangirls,' Nico says flatly, as if this explains everything.

Below us, in the pit, the fans start grabbing for the cameras. One girl pushes a tripod over and jumps on the camera, smashing it to smithereens. The revolution will not be televised.

'This is way above my pay-grade.' Mojo makes a swift exit via the wings.

Nico grimaces at me. 'Happy now?'

I shrug. 'It doesn't suck.'

'Stupid little girl,' she says with a sigh. 'You'll pay. They'll have your head on a pike.'

'We'll see.'

Nico looks at me like I'm pond scum before following Mojo off stage as calmly as a swan.

'Taryn!' Leela grabs my arm. 'Your brother!'

I follow her finger and see Chairman Slade hauling Jenson by the arm towards the tunnel where ordinarily football players would enter the stadium.

'Jenson . . .'

I see a microphone laying on the edge of the stage. Nico must have abandoned it. I grab it. 'Is this still on?' I don't hear anything. 'Please! Turn it on! PLEASE!' My final plea blares around the auditorium.

Some fans look to me, others carry on kicking, spitting and

clawing at the Securiforce agents. One girl uses body spray to mace a guard.

'Listen to me!' I point a finger squarely at Slade, who freezes. 'That man is Chairman Slade! You know him, right? He's in charge of Elysium! He ordered Cade's death. He killed Briar. He's behind everything!'

Now Slade's face fills the big screens. I don't know who's controlling the drone cameras, but *Starmaker* should have probably paid them better or given them more holiday, because they seem to be working for us now.

'He thinks you're all mindless idiots who'll buy anything he craps out. We – my band – we don't think that. We think that men like him actually hate the things we love. They think our clothes and our music and our makeup are girly nonsense. Well, screw him. We want to make songs you'll remember for ever. Memories you'll treasure for a lifetime. He just wants your money no matter the cost to us. *That* is Chairman Slade. That man there.'

While Slade's frozen in his own spotlight, Jenson manages to tug himself free. Girls descend on Slade's position, blocking the exit. I hear some fans shout STOP HIM. I hear others say GET HIM.

The girls nearest to him zero in.

Someone yells KILL HIM.

Their eyes are lethal.

'Hey, Slade,' Madison has Mojo's mic. 'Don't fuck with teenage girls.'

'We're *crazy*,' I add.

Slade goes a sickly shade of greenish-white. 'Guards!

Guards, quickly! For God's sake help me!' He should have paid them more too, because, with bloodied lips and noses, it looks like most of the Securiforce agents are happy to flee while they have a chance. Rats leaving a sinking ship. Slade is alone, exposed, vulnerable.

The way he wanted us.

A swarm of vengeful teenage girls devours him whole. The first girl punches him around the head with a fist in a lace glove. A second grabs hold of his hair from behind, dragging him down. He vanishes into a scrum. A pastel hoard swallows him alive. I hope they rip him to shreds.

I look to my bandmates. 'The ultimate feminine protection,' I say.

CHAPTER 46

I pull my baseball cap lower over my eyes. This is my last day with my family and I don't really want to spend it posing for selfies with strangers.

Obama Park is bustling. Birds sing gaily in the trees. There's a Little League baseball game in progress and, on a small stage near the picnic area, a busker is performing with a ukulele. Dad brings us all hotdogs topped with onions and ketchup from a van. I take a big bite, delighted to be reacquainted with carbs.

'So what did the Men in Suits say?' Dad asks as we settle in on a picnic bench.

I give him a stern glare. '*She* was a woman in a dress,' I say, referring to Gia, the lawyer Nomi paired us with.

'And . . .?' Mol prompts.

It's been three days since the final, but it feels like three months. I have had about nine hours sleep in total. The first twelve hours were spent in the MCPD station downtown, being questioned over Clancy's death. And Cade's death. And Briar's.

Turns out those hours, while excruciating, may have been a blessing in disguise. With Slade in a bad way in hospital, Team *Starmaker* was running around like a chicken with its head cleaved off. The drivers, the runners, the producers, Securiforce . . . no one knew what to do. After they were done interviewing us at the station, there wasn't even a car ready to take us back to the Dreamhouse. Only our families, waiting anxiously in the lobby.

Nomi was waiting for us too. They explained what had happened. On the day of the final, Nomi had been intercepted by Securiforce before they could give their ally in transmission – some guy called Harry – the cue to run the Punkcat footage. Unsure whether Nomi was safe, Harry hadn't dared proceed. His hesitation cost Briar her life, but I can't blame him in all this. When he realized we were making a stand, he pressed play on the footage.

I didn't see Briar's mum, or little Harmoni. That haunted me. It still does. I need to find them. I owe Briar. I owe them. We all do. I make a fresh promise to the universe.

Back we went to the swanky hotels our families had been put in, only to find that *Starmaker* had closed all of their accounts. Here, salvation came from a most unlikely source: Peyton Silver, Madison's big sister from B*TRU3. She offered to cover our stay, which felt both ironic and appropriate. Very, very generous too. There's no way we could afford to stay at the Media City Hilton without her help.

Then today we met with Gia who said she'd represent us for free. Her law firm is already working with Nomi and Cade's mysterious Axiom group. Gia said that Network G and

Elysium are suppressing freedom of speech and expression, not to mention breaking about a million rules on child protection. Gia wants to take her case all the way to the Blue State Supreme Court.

Seated in a fairly humble office in the Old Quarter, Gia Fernandez is a striking woman in her forties with cropped black hair and killer eyewear. We were crammed like sardines in her suite. I had to settle for a spot in the back near her fireplace. All five of us, plus Nomi.

'A criminal investigation has started into Cade's murder,' she began. 'It'll take years. Network G *claims* the guard that pulled the trigger was acting alone. They're also claiming Cade was armed—'

'He wasn't!' I protested. 'I told them that!'

'I know. I won't rest, Taryn. I'll take this to the very top.'

I nod. Gia has already received 'anonymous' death threats telling her to drop the case. She's putting her life on the line for us. She made sure we wouldn't face any charges over the mob attack on Slade or Clancy's shooting.

'As for you guys, I think you have solid grounds for breach of contract,' she told us. 'When you signed up, Network G promised to provide a *healthy, secure environment* and – as most of you are minors – they promised to act *in loco parentis*. Clearly, we have evidence you were not looked after, and, worse, were intimidated and threatened with physical and psychological violence. I'd say your contract is null and void, and you're all free agents.'

The sigh of relief was audible – from all of us. The thought that we'd *have* to smile and dance like performing chimps with cymbals for Elysium and Slade was keeping me awake.

'So what do we do now?' Suki asked.

'Well,' Gia said, 'you have options . . .'

And that's all I can relay to Dad, Molly and Jenson for now. But none of this news involves me going home with them. Dad dabs his mustard-covered mouth with a napkin. 'I don't know how I feel about leaving you here, sweetheart.'

'I've come too far to just give up.'

I want to stay and make sure someone pays for Cade's death. Also, without *Starmaker*'s private prescription, I'm right back to where I started with help for Jenson. Everything I've done and seen, the sacrifice Cade made, was for nothing. I did not get paid for a single day on that show aside from my meagre per diems.

'Taryn,' Jen says. 'Everyone back home was rooting for you. You can do whatever you want. Move to the Northern Powerhouse or New London. You'll be massive.'

'But what about the group?'

'What about them?' Molly asks.

'They're my . . .' I stop just short of saying *my friends* because are we? We were thrown together at random and trauma-bonded. That's not friendship. Is it?

'Hey hey hey!' a voice says over the microphone at Busker's Corner. It's a cute guy with lavender dreadlocks almost to the floor. 'Do we have any performers waiting to sing? Come and sign up now and we'll get you on!'

'Taryn, you should go sing.' Jenson grins.

'Oh sure.'

'Why not?' Dad says. 'Borrow his ukulele. It'll be just like back home at the camp. They don't know you're off the telly.'

Something about the idea is really funny. I don't know why.

'Do it!' Jenson shuffles, almost giddy.

'I dare you.' My sister raises her eyebrows. Molly knows I can't walk away from a dare, the cow.

I pull my cap lower and head for the stage. The busker, who turns out to be called Wallace, lends me his ukulele and I take to the stage. Keeping my face down, I mumble into the microphone. 'This song is for my brother. It was written by a man I really . . .'

Well.

I sing Cade's song.

> *Seen the pyramids*
> *And Kyoto*
> *The fall of Kremlin*
> *You're my go-to.*
> *Niagara*
> *Victoria*
> *I'm a lamb to*
> *Your slaughter*
> *One, two, three, four, five, six, seven*
> *You're the eighth wonder.*
> *Seen past the sky and into heaven*
> *You're the one I want yeah.*

The little crowd listen, rapt. I think a couple of whispering teenage girls recognize me, nudging each other, and trying to get a look at my face.

Cade was right: I hate *Starmaker*, but – and thank god – I still love singing. They took him from me, but they can't take the love.

I think I loved him.

Peyton has bought us two suites at the Hilton. Leela and I share the king-size bed while Suki is on the pull-out sofa bed. The others have come over from next door in their pyjamas, and we've ordered Grubhub burgers because room-service is eye-wateringly expensive. Our room quickly reeks of greasy fries and onion rings but I don't care.

The Big Question weighs much heavier in the air than the burger smell.

Suki bursts the bubble. 'So, like, do you guys want to do the band or not? I know, after what happened to Briar that feels like the wildest thing to even say but . . .'

'It isn't,' Madi says through a mouthful of chips. 'Are you forgetting the other three girls who died?'

'We knew what we were getting into,' Leela states.

'Did we?' I reply.

'No,' she admits.

In the smaller surroundings of the hotel, it's really apparent that there are only five of us left. It's too quiet. I can't believe I miss the chaos of the early days when all ten of us were fighting for space at the bathroom mirrors.

'I don't know if it's okay to say this,' Suki says, 'but I love being with you ladies.'

I wrap my arm around her shoulder and pull her close. 'Love you too, Suk.'

'Is what Briar is wanting,' Min-jee puts in. 'We do it for her.'

She has a point. 'And I want to help her daughter,' I say. 'I don't know how yet.'

'Same,' says Madison. 'If Shayna died for nothing . . . I couldn't . . . Lord, I don't know what I'm meant to do now. I know I don't wanna go back to Lufkin.'

I think about those girls at the arena. The way they rode for us. I feel like, with that army behind us . . . we could change something. This world is so relentlessly cruel. What if we could make it just a tiny bit kinder? Our fans are quite literally offering us a platform, a microphone, a *voice*.

'Gia said we have like five offers from different labels,' Madison says. 'For DOLLHOU5E. For all of us.'

'Wouldn't you rather go it alone?' I ask her in particular.

She considers me for what feels like a very long time. 'No,' she eventually says. 'I think I'd be lonely. I'd miss my sisters.'

I manage a dry laugh. Randomly thrown together and trauma bonded? She's right, the word isn't friends, it's *sisters*. No one else in the whole wide world will ever know what it's like to be us. Typists on the internet will write our lore, and say 'that's *so* Taryn'; our friends and families will *sympathize*, but we are the only five people who'll ever know the truth.

'Anyways. *You* ranked in first place, not me,' Madison reminds me. 'You're the favourite. You could go solo. Do you want to?'

I don't know what will happen next, but I do know it'll be more fun with all of us. 'I think . . .' I say, 'that there's gonna be a lot more sleepovers.'

'You're in?' Suki asks.

'I'm in.'

I hold out my hand. Suki puts her hand on mine at once, followed by Min-jee. Then Leela, and finally Madison.

'Let's do this,' I say.

ACKNOWLEDGMENTS

Huge thanks to Sallyanne Sweeney, Marc Simonsson, Ivan Mulcahy and everyone at ICA. It's been ten years, and I owe basically everything in my career to you.

Survival Show was borne out of a highly fruitful lunch with editor Yasmin Morrissey. I was given the gift every author longs to hear: *what would your dream YA novel be?* To which I said, *The Hunger Games meets the Spice Girls*. The book you just read is the product of that fantastic first date. This would be my favourite book in the world (if I hadn't just written it). So endless thanks to Yas; when I thought this was too insane, your giddiness matched mine.

So much hard work happens behind the scenes to get a book to market. In both the UK and US, everyone at S&S has been so warm and enthusiastic about this project. Who else would hire a troupe of dancers for a cover reveal? Thanks to Jess Dean, Alesha Bonser, Sean Williams, Millie Monaghan, Simi Toor and Lauren Atherton in the UK. In the States, enormous thanks to editor Dainese Santos, Alex Kelleher, and the entire team. It's been so easy coordinating over the Atlantic, and I hope to meet you IRL someday soon.

Thank you to my gorgeous readers, old and new. I'm guessing you love pop music as much as I do and would like to enjoy it without feeling icky? I hope that you, especially young female readers, know we must never accept abuse, even in the pursuit of our dreams. It isn't an either/or situation. Never let anyone tell you that you are replaceable. Spoiler: no-one else can do you like you can.

Right, I suppose I better go write the sequel!

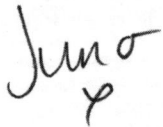